To: Steven & Diane
From: Dad & Pa

SWEET LOVE REMEMBERED

by

HELEN CORTEZ STAFFORD

DESERET BOOK COMPANY
Publishers
SALT LAKE CITY, UTAH

Second printing of the second edition 2007

The historical characters in this book will be readily recognized.
All others are fictional, and any resemblance to real characters is a matter of coincidence.

Cover art, *Parting of the Ways, Actual Mormon Trail,* by Diana Pitcher
Cover design by Catharine Verhaaren

Printed by the Edward I. Rich Family Association
156 Braewick Rd.
Salt Lake City, Utah 84103

To contact this organization visit www.ccrich.org.

ISBN 978-0-8425-2695-1

DEDICATED

TO THE MEMORY OF MY MOTHER

EVELYN CLARK CORTEZ

Contents

When, in disgrace with fortune and men's eyes,
I all alone beweep my outcast state,
And trouble deaf heaven with my bootless cries,
And look upon myself, and curse my fate,
Wishing me like to one more rich in hope,
Featur'd like him, like him with friends possess'd,
Desiring this man's art, and that man's scope,
With what I most enjoy contented least;
Yet in these thoughts myself almost despising,
Haply I think on these, and then my state,
Like to the lark at break of day arising
From sullen earth, sings hymns at heaven's gate;
For thy sweet love remember'd such wealth brings
That then I scorn to change my state with kings.

—William Shakespeare

FOREWORD

The characters in this story, except for a few minor ones, are real people designated by their actual names. I have written the story as I found it in the autobiographical sketches and memoirs of the principal characters, and as it was told to me by Minerva ("Nanie") Rich Woolley (deceased 1939), Doctor Ashbel Pomeroy (deceased 1938) and Doctors Ezra and Edward Rich of Ogden, Utah.

I wish to express my appreciation to the following people: Doctors Ezra and Edward Rich and many other members of the Rich family whose names cannot appear here; Gertrude Zahniser of Los Angeles, California; Zula Cole of Logan, Utah; Hinda Teague Hill of Los Angeles, California; the Committee representing the Relief Society Board of Utah; Mr. and Mrs. George Beattie of East Highlands, California; Alvin F. Smith, Librarian of the Latter-day Saints Library of Salt Lake City; Edna Martin, reference librarian of the Bancroft Library of the University of California at Berkeley; Mary Isabelle Fry, reference librarian of the Huntington Memorial Library in San Marino, California.

If this book, now finished, justifies in some measure all that they have done for me, I shall be satisfied.

HELEN CORTEZ STAFFORD

Los Angeles, California.

BOOK ONE

THE PATTERN

The old order changeth,
yielding place to new.

—TENNYSON.

I

1.

Laura Phelps, a small, rigid figure in her low chair beside the open fire, stared fixedly at the rough log wall where leaping flames wove eerie patterns in the deepening shadows. Already, early October darkness had enveloped the Missouri countryside. Her precious hour was almost gone, with the older children at a neighboring farm and her husband on the other side of the hearth, she could have unburdened her mind of all that troubled her. Yet she had scarcely spoken.

She moved restlessly and drew her shoulders, broad for her height, into a straighter line. Why hadn't she been able to talk to Morris? She looked at him, his big body fitted neatly into a large pine-wood armchair. The Book of Mormon lay open across his knees. It was too dark to read. His head rested against the tall, straight back of the chair and his eyes were closed. Laura wondered almost angrily how he could appear so relaxed when all that they cherished was at stake. At once, she was ashamed. Morris was worried just as she was, but his thoughts could not be in such wild disorder as hers. Never before had she wavered in a muddle of indecision—not in all the twelve years of her wifehood. Even at eighteen, when she and Morris were married, she had known exactly what she wanted to do, but now . . .

The dread and uncertainty that had tormented her ever since that night a week ago when Morris had been called to Crooked River swept over her afresh. He had wanted to go. Feeling against the Mormons ran high in some districts and there had been many outrages. When word came of a mob gathering at Crooked River, preparing to march on the near-by settlement of Far West and give it "fire and thunder," there were plenty of Mormon volunteers. They had dispersed the mob only to learn that the men they had attacked were a body of Missouri State militia. Anything might happen now.

Laura's thoughts trailed off as her eyes roamed over the big low-ceilinged kitchen. The bright rugs she herself had woven, the small cherry chest that had come all the way from Connecticut, the pine dining table, the stove, the spinning wheel in the corner, all seemed to cry out to her, "Not this home. The others didn't matter—but this home has roots." Pain clouded her brown eyes. A little moan, scarcely audible, escaped her lips.

Morris stirred in his chair. "Did you speak, Laura?" His voice was warm and reassuring.

Laura's head with its crown of heavy brown braids turned slowly as her husband rose and stood with his back to the fire, tall and straight, looking down at her. She was glad that he did not press her for an answer. How weary he looked. The firelight touched deep lines about his eyes and mouth—flickered upon the light-brown hair thinning at his temples. He looked more than his thirty-five years. She could feel his intent gaze searching her face. She looked up and met his quiet gray eyes squarely. The tension eased within her. Rigid shoulders slackened and her body relaxed to the curve of her chair. She even managed a brief smile.

"Now, that's better, my dear," was Morris' only comment.

2.

Thick tallow candles glowed softly from the shelf above the fireplace and the table beside the armchair. Morris had gone for their three small daughters. The boundary of the Thompson farm lay just across the road, but Laura had been reluctant to let them go. These days, she was uneasy whenever they were out of her sight. But the Thompson children were wholesome company and the girls had begged so hard. "Please, Mother! It's Hallowe'en and there'll be fried cakes and apple cider." So they had eaten an early supper and departed just before dusk. She had watched them from the doorstep—Paulina, the oldest, her light-brown hair in soft ringlets, Mary Ann, next younger, corn-yellow braids bobbing, and between them small Harriet, her hands clinging to theirs, her chubby legs flying to keep pace with their swifter gait. How precious they were—they and little toddling Joseph, asleep in an adjoining room.

A smile curved Laura's lips as she seated herself near the light and adjusted the rug she was hooking on the frame Morris had made for her. Each child represented a definite period in their married life. Morris always laughed when she said that—accused her of cataloguing their children—but it was true.

Paulina's birth in the second year of their marriage had for a time calmed Morris' restlessness. Laura had felt his discontent with their life in the small pioneer community of Willow Springs, Illinois. It had been a disappointment to Morris' people when they had chosen Willow Springs for their first home. A place had been waiting for Morris in his father's business at Kirtland, Ohio, but they would have none of it. They had stood at the window on their wedding night with the vast sweep of prairie stretching out into mysterious darkness, and Morris had held her close. "Together, my dear," he said, "we shall seek the new." And she had repeated the words like a vow.

There had been much talk of "the new" that first year. It all came back to her now—the young people of Willow Springs gathering in the Phelps' home excitedly discussing new movements — Jacksonism, anti-slavery, the liberal ideas of Emerson. Morris had been a leader in these groups, always. Reaching out. Seeking satisfaction for some inner urge that pushed him on to untried things.

It had flared up again when Mary Ann was a baby. But in 1831, her second year, Morris had found an outlet. That was the year when they had begun their trek. Harriet's birth, the following year, marked their arrival in Independence, Missouri.

Laura bent over her work and traced the rug's pattern with a slender finger. It was fascinating to watch it take form beneath her hands, dim background and glowing colors blending into something beautiful, something substantial and worth while that she could bring into being. Life was a pattern, too.

"Together we shall seek the new." She smiled. There had been no more talk of that after they reached Missouri. They were too busy living it. She had been skeptical at first when missionaries came to their home preaching a new religion, Mormonism. So many new creeds were springing up, all revolts against the old order of things. But Morris had been deeply interested and soon she found herself as enthusiastic as he. It had strengthened the bond between them.

How happy they had been since they had come to Far West and established their home here on the farm where Joseph had been born. "He symbolizes our contentment in this home," she thought; and again that wave of sick foreboding swept over her. She should have talked to Morris. With enemies closing in around them, was it fair to the children? . . .

From outside came a dog's sharp bark and the sound of young laughter. Candle flames bent and sputtered as the kitchen door burst open and three small girls came tumbling into the room. A large shaggy dog slipped in behind them, his tail barely escaping the door as a sudden gust of wind sucked it shut with a bang. There was a commotion of wriggling out of coats and of high childish voices. The dog leaped about wildly.

"Down, Jack!" said Laura sharply. "Girls!" she cautioned. "Remember the baby. And hang up your things."

The din subsided. "Father stopped at the barn," Paulina explained, "to see if everything is all right." She drew closer to the fireplace and held out her hands to the blaze. "We had such fun, Mother!"

"I'm cold, too," Mary Ann said. She dropped to the floor before the fire and smiled up at Laura while chubby little Harriet firmly pushed aside the rug frame and climbed into her mother's lap.

The door opened and closed and Morris joined the group. He stood with an arm around Paulina, quietly listening with Laura to their daughters' excited account of the evening. His eyes sought hers and together they smiled in deep content and understanding.

3.

Laura helped the girls to undress and tucked all three into the wide bed which they shared. They were asleep almost instantly. For a moment she lingered near their bed, then turned to the cot of her son. He was so well bundled in blankets that there was not much of him visible except a fringe of bright red hair and the tip of his pink nose. Laura smiled as she regarded him. That hair always startled her, yet it was so characteristic of him. He was a handful to manage, especially now that he was walking alone.

Her throat tightened suddenly. Three precious daughters and a son. Surely they deserved the security of a permanent home. Neither she nor Morris had the right to deny them that. Weren't they worth the wrench of leaving this dear place? Should their future be weighed against loyalty to anything—even religion? Let others stay and fight for Mormonism. Men and women who had no children.

"Laura?" Morris called softly from the doorway.

"Sh-sh!" Laura placed a finger on her lips. "Just a minute."

"Wait," he whispered. "Let me look at them, too." He tiptoed into the room and stood beside her, looking first at his son, then at his girls.

Laura took the lighted candle from a stand near the window and lifted it high. The light falling upon Morris' face showed his heavy brows contracted in a worried frown. Were his thoughts the same as hers? If only she could ask him!

"Come," Laura urged very low. "We may wake them."

Morris put his arm about her slim waist and drew her out of the room. Her head just reached his shoulder. She had to tilt it back to look up at him. He closed the door behind them.

"My dear," he said, "we have each other and we have them.—And we have our faith," he added slowly. "We ought to feel rich and secure with all that."

"Yes, Morris," Laura repeated. "We ought to feel rich with all that."

If he noticed her omission of security, Morris made no comment.

Morris replenished the fire and settled himself in his chair. Jack, stretched full length and completely relaxed, dozed on the hearth. Laura's head bent low over her rug. The steady tick of the clock on the kitchen shelf seemed unbearably loud in the stillness.

Suddenly Jack scrambled to his feet and dashed across to

the door, his nostrils quivering. Hoof beats pounded on the road and slowed at the Phelps' gate. Laura and Morris exchanged swift, apprehensive glances. Rapid footsteps rushed up the path. There was an agitated knocking.

Morris was already at the door. In the brief moment before he flung it wide, Laura knew. Fists clenched, she braced herself to receive the news, then, strangely, a great calm enveloped her.

Hyrum Stone, a close friend and fellow church-member stood in the doorway.

"Phelps!" his voice was high and strained. "Missouri State militia is on its way to Far West. You know what that means. Harness your team and get over there."

So it had come, thought Laura, this thing she had been dreading. "Hurry, Phelps!" Stone's cry echoed behind him. "Hurry!"

Morris closed the door. "My dear," he said, "how can I leave you here alone? You and the children?"

Agonized indecision was in his tone. His eyes appealed to her. And suddenly everything was clear.

"Go at once, Morris," she said. She knew just as Morris knew that his place was in Far West with his Mormon brethren, doing his share to defend the town against the invasion of the Missouri State troops.

5.

Laura, a shawl thrown about her shoulders, waited at the gate in the split rail fence for Morris to come from the barn. The wind that had come up earlier in the evening had died down. Everything was quiet. The full moon rode high and the landscape was white in its light.

Morris pulled up the horses as he reached the gate, laced the reins around the whip socket and jumped down from the wagon. He strode to Laura, put one arm around her shoulders and with his free hand tilted her chin back so that he could look into her face. His eyes held hers steadily for a moment. She was white and grave but her lips were drawn into a determined line. There were no tears in her eyes.

"Don't worry, Laura," he said. "Everything will be all right."

She did not answer, only clutched his arm convulsively. He released the firm, round chin and lightly touched the thick braids bound about her head. Somehow he always .hought of those braids as a badge of her personal dignity.

"Oh, Morris," Laura whispered.

He knew that she dared not speak further. He drew her close, bent his head and kissed her on the lips. In an instant he was back on the wagon-seat, untying the reins while Laura opened the gate. Then the wheels of the wagon were grinding an accompaniment to the clump, clump of horses' hoofs as Morris Phelps drove through the gate and turned his team in the direction of Far West.

Carefully, Laura closed the gate and started up the path toward the cottage. The creaking of wagon wheels grew fainter. Soon Morris would reach the bend in the road. But she did not turn to watch him out of sight.

2

Far West, Caldwell County, Missouri, lay in a practically unsettled area. A low range of hills, thickly forested, bordered the town on the east. To the north, south and west, open prairie, dotted with farms—some large, some small—rolled to the distant horizon. And Far West, in 1838, was the recognized headquarters of the Mormon Church—designated by the Prophet Joseph Smith as the "center of Zion," when forced to abandon the former "center" at Independence, Jackson County, Missouri.

Since its foundation by Joseph Smith, Junior, April 6, 1830, the Church of Jesus Christ of Latter-day Saints had grown to proportions that alarmed civil authorities in sections where Mormon "stakes" were established. The Mormon belief, resting upon the Holy Bible, the Book of Mormon, and the Book of Doctrine and Covenants (containing the "revelations given to Joseph Smith, Junior, the Prophet, for the building up of the Kingdom of God in the last days") was being rapidly spread by zealous missionaries; and once converted, each new Mormon burned with the same holy zeal.

The Saints were a perfectly fused and unified force; a force to be reckoned with, under the direction of a complex organization, whose ideals involved temporal as well as spiritual well-being. God, the supreme temporal and spiritual Ruler—His commands the law—His will and authority made known and exercised upon the earth through the medium of a Priesthood—the officers of the Mormon Church.

The central governing authority was vested in the First Presidency—the First President, two Counselors (or aids), the Twelve Apostles, the Seventies, the Presiding Bishop and High Patriarch of the Church; and radiating from this center was a far-flung network of "stakes" and "wards"—territorial units—each with its own administrative officers, all operating under the supreme authority of Joseph Smith, the First President—the Prophet of God—the seer and revelator—the executive, the lawgiver and the judge in all matters of Church interest. Through unbroken channels straight from the Prophet to each individual Saint, God's will was made known.

Small wonder, then, that elaborate plans had been made for the upbuilding of Far West. Ninety per cent of its inhabitants and of the entire county were Mormons. Caldwell County had been set aside for them by the State of Missouri, and the Saints, driven out of Jackson County, had flocked to the new "abiding place."

Morris Phelps, like others, had visioned great things for Far West. A large slice of his slender inherited capital had gone to purchase an interest in the town's general merchandise store. The Phelps' farm, a scant two miles out, was small and easily managed. By hiring the oldest Thompson boy to help with the chores, Morris was free to spend several hours each day in the store. With the Prophet and his Council in their midst and a friendly understanding between the Saints and their non-Mormon neighbors, prospects had seemed very bright.

And yet, Morris realized now, that very zeal and optimism had proved the Saints' undoing. The rapid growth of Far West and the Mormon expansion into Carroll and Daviess counties had aroused the Missourian's jealousy. Everywhere there were rumors that the State authorities were going to demand complete expulsion of the Mormons from Missouri.

Missouri, Morris thought. *Revealed in a vision to the Prophet as the permanent abiding place of the Saints!* The way things looked now it would be anything but permanent.

Mechanically, Morris held his team to a swift gait. Frost was in the air. His breath hovered about him in a white mist. The wagon rattled over the familiar road—unfamiliar in the moonlight's magic. A silver ribbon flung across the black prairie. Moonlight played queer tricks. He could see Laura's face, upturned in farewell. He shouldn't have left her alone with the children. Perhaps he'd better go back for them. They would be better off on the Clark farm with her father and her brothers.

The Clarks, too, were Mormons—all but John, the oldest boy. John was younger than Laura, but he had been old enough to know his own mind when Morris had converted the family. He had refused to accept the faith. Morris had been somewhat surprised that John had accompanied the family, when they had come to Caldwell County to live. But Mrs. Clark's health had failed. She had gone back to Quincy, Illinois, with her daughter Rhoda to care for her.

The Clark farm lay well beyond the opposite boundary of Far West. *They'd be safe there,* Morris thought. *Church or no Church, I shouldn't have left them alone.* He reined in abruptly. The horses reared and shied. But Morris did not turn them. For a moment he sat, the reins loose in his hands; then, with sudden determination, he urged the team forward at a gallop. "Go at once," Laura had said. Laura was courageous. Laura would expect him to be there, fighting shoulder to shoulder with his brethren. Everything hung in the balance—the security of their homes, the safety of their families—perhaps, even, the future of the Mormon Church.

He scowled and his jaw hardened. It was the injustice that enraged him. By what right did the Missourians persecute the Saints—driving them out like cattle? Morris lashed his whip across the horses' backs and stood erect, shouting at them. The frosty air stung his nostrils and whistled past his ears. With the help of the Almighty, he and his brethren would teach these Missourians something. The wagon lurched crazily around a turn in the road. Morris reined in sharply.

Faint lights were visible just ahead. He was approaching Far West.

3

The click of the latch behind her as she entered the cottage and closed the door, seemed like a given signal to set Laura's paralyzed thoughts in motion. For a moment she stood, eyes closed, icy hands clasped tightly at her breast. In a surge of pure spiritual exaltation she had sent her husband forth to face danger—possible death. Yes, she had sent him. Morris was easily influenced. Deeply as she loved him, Laura realized that hers was the stronger nature. She had never blinded herself to his faults. His outbreaks of rebellion against monotony, his volatile joy and somber gloom, the occasional bursts of violent anger—so unbecoming in a professed Saint—sometimes she felt that she loved him more because of them, because of the protective instinct aroused by his dependence upon her. Suppose she had given way to her weakness and told him of her fears? Thank God, who had sealed her lips and opened her eyes in time!

With quick, firm steps she crossed the room and began, with practiced efficiency, to assemble necessities. Now, she could make preparations with a clear conscience. If they must take flight it would be in the line of duty—not because of selfishness or cowardice.

Methodically, she folded pieced quilts and warm garments,

piling them neatly in the center of a blanket spread upon the floor. On the table near the fireplace the Book of Mormon lay where Morris had left it, beside a well-thumbed copy of the Holy Bible. Laura's finger tips caressed the dark leather as she slipped the volumes between folds of clothing. These were Morris' most treasured possessions, her gift to him four years ago when he had been sent into the mission field, preaching the gospel of the Mormon Church. She had been brave then, left alone with three small children to support on her slender earnings as a teacher and a midwife. And God in His mercy had rewarded her; for among Morris' converts in Chicago were her own family, the Clarks. All but brother John. If only John were with her now! Although he was eight years younger, in time of trouble Laura instinctively turned to John. He would come if he knew she was alone, but unless she could get word to him, he might as well be still in Illinois as on the Clark farm, so short a distance from her.

She tightened the straps around the compact bundle and placed it alongside the wall near the door. She could hear Jack whining on the doorstep. She had forgotten to let him in. He might help to dispel this dreadful loneliness. She opened the door and Jack nuzzled close to her side, worshiping her with soft brown eyes. She stooped to pat his head and suddenly was conscious of wagon wheels faintly creaking. She stepped out into the yard, straining her eyes toward the road. In the Thompson's yard the dim bulk of a wagon took shape, moving slowly toward the gate. Brother Thompson, Laura thought, departing to Far West. But why had he delayed so long? She had wondered why he hadn't left with Morris, but had dismissed it from her mind, supposing that he had gone on ahead.

The wagon was now close to the gate and in full view. Brother Thompson was not alone! His entire family was with him, clearly visible in the bright moonlight. Strange, thought

Laura, that he should be taking his family to Far West to danger. She ran across the yard to the fence by the main road, calling out to the Thompsons, but if they heard her they paid no heed. Then she stood, rooted in her tracks, too stunned to move. Brother Thompson had not turned his team toward Far West. He was taking the road north. Brother Thompson was deserting his Mormon brethren.

Laura was appalled. Then shame surged through her. How short the time since she had entertained the same idea! She whistled to Jack and together they crossed the yard and entered the cottage. She did not realize until after she had closed and bolted the door that there were no other farmhouses in this section of the county. Except for her children, she was entirely alone.

4

1.

Every window in Far West showed a light. The business street, usually deserted at this hour, was thronged with grim-faced men. Solemn groups scattered to make a path for the wagon as Morris threaded his way toward Church Headquarters at the far end of the street. There were brief, abstracted greetings from the brethren but Morris did not pause to ask questions. Better report at Headquarters promptly. He would learn all about it there. Other wagons crowded his in the narrow street. Tension was in the air. Even the horses seemed to feel it—tossing their heads, rearing, champing at their bits.

As he came abreast of his store, Morris noticed considerable activity. Customers lined the counters and bunched in the doorway. He could see his partners scurrying back and forth to the stock-room at the back of the building. For a moment Morris wondered if he could not go in and help. Waiting on the customers was his special duty and in this emergency he must be sorely needed. Then the memory of Brother Stone's frantic message sent him resolutely forward. This was no time for personal problems.

From the dim windows of homes on straggling side streets, shadowy women peered, with children clinging to their skirts. Thank God, Laura and the children were not here. Fighting was man's work. His excitement mounted. That skirmish at Crooked River! What a good feeling it was to meet enemies face to face, to strike smashing blows in defense of home—of faith! His breath came faster and the blood pounded in his temples.

A man detached himself from the crowd and approached the wagon, waving his arms. It was Hyrum Stone.

"Turn around, Brother Phelps," he directed. "I'll show you where to go." He braced a foot against the front axle and pulled himself up beside Morris on the wagon-box. "It's bad," he said. "The State troops are advancing from Richmond, and we figure they'll try to enter Far West at the southern boundary."

"And the brethren?" Morris asked as he turned his team. "Are we to resist this invasion?"

"With God's help, yes," Stone said. "We have about five hundred volunteers, with Colonel Hinkle in command. Our leaders have determined to barricade the southern border. They have divided us into groups and assigned certain tasks to each group. You, and others with teams are to snake logs and timber from the west border of town to the danger point."

"A fitting symbol," Morris remarked bitterly. "Logs and timber intended for Far West's new buildings must be used for a barricade to protect it."

2.

More and more, as he plied his team throughout the night, Morris brooded on the cruel irony of the situation. He had seen this coming for months—ever since that afternoon last spring. It had been almost closing time when two men entered the store. He had recognized them as non-Mormons, local farmers. They had made their purchases in a businesslike and friendly fashion and had leaned against the counter talking, while Morris wrapped the packages.

At first he had paid no attention to their conversation, but the word "Mormon" and some reference to Joseph Smith aroused his interest. He had purposely fumbled with the wrappings.

The men were discussing the Mormon towns being established in Carroll and Daviess counties.

"I can't say it's wise," one drawled. "The legislature sort of set aside Caldwell County for the Mormons. They ought to be satisfied with that. Personally," he went on, "I've nothing against the Mormons — they're sober and industrious. But they're growing mighty fast and I don't like all this talk about the 'chosen people' and Missouri being 'the center of Zion' and the land 'destined by God' to be theirs."

Morris had found it difficult to hold his tongue but the other man spoke just then.

"Wasn't it that kind of thing that got them into trouble in Jackson County?"

"Yes," the first man answered. "That and other things. The main trouble was that there were too many of them—what with new converts and all. Maybe the people of Daviess and Carroll counties feel the same way."

They had gone then, leaving Morris greatly disturbed. But he had forced himself to dismiss his fears. Surely the Mormons would be welcome in these new centers. There would be no more persecutions.

"I should have known better," Morris thought, as he unloosed another log from the chain. . . .

3.

Back and forth, back and forth, from the west border to the south—Morris worked mechanically, wrapping the chain around a log, hooking the chain to the doubletree—over and over, like his weary thoughts.

The night was wearing on and the Mormons were working feverishly to complete the barricade before dawn; but Morris was scarcely conscious of rapid hammer-blows on stakes driven into the ground—of the resounding thuds of logs deposited on the rapidly growing pile.

All summer he had watched the breach widen. The Mormons had not been welcomed in Carroll and Daviess counties. The people had openly resented the founding of Mormon towns; they had even protested to the State authorities. By late summer news had spread that both sides were armed and ready to fight, and the Governor had ordered part of the State militia to the disturbed areas. Even then Morris had hoped for a compromise, but the fall days marched relentlessly on, bringing rumors of outrages by mobs that roamed about, disregarding law and private property rights. When the Mormons, despairing of peace in the adjoining counties, began to abandon their homes and come to Far West, Morris had given up hope.

And how brave the Saints had been, maintaining imperturbable calm in the face of all this—the men going about their business as usual, the women carrying on the routine of their homes, yet all the while gripped by dread just as he himself had been.

Anger welled up in him and he kicked viciously at a log. Always before, the Mormon had submitted; but this time, by the Heavenly Father, he hoped they'd fight it out to a finish!

4.

Slim taupe clouds changed to pink, to rose red, then suddenly, to shimmering pearl as the sun burst into full splendor over the eastern hills. *The night passes,* Morris thought, *and the sun comes up as usual, no matter what strange or terrible scenes men spread before it.* With heavy, bloodshot eyes he viewed the results of the night's work. The crude barricade was completed, sprawling in an uneven line close to the town's southern boundary. A long line of wagons, placed end to end, was drawn in immediately behind it. The volunteers, gathered in small groups behind the wagons, rested and waited for further instructions from their commander, Colonel Hinkle.

Morris leaned against a wheel and surveyed the barricade. "Well," he said, "it's finished. Pray God it will serve its purpose."

"Amen, Brother Phelps." One of the group placed a friendly hand on Morris' arm. "God will not forsake us. We are His chosen people. The Prophet—" he broke off suddenly. There was a clatter of hoofs at the west end of the barricade. A man, leaping from his horse, tossed the reins to a bystander and pushed his way through the crowd to where Colonel Hinkle was standing. Like a breeze rippling a wheat field the news ran through the groups. General Lucas and his troops were within one mile of the town.

Morris felt himself stiffen. His eyes, now alert, saw heads lift and shoulders straighten. Alive, vibrant, as he was, the Mormon volunteers were tense, ready to spring to the defense of Far West.

5

1.

It was two o'clock in the morning. Laura, a small blanket around her shoulders, dozed fitfully in the armchair by the fire.

She had not gone to bed. To lie quietly, even fully clothed, would have been torture. Sick at heart from the shock of the Thompsons' flight, she had sought comfort in the children's bedroom. Paulina was smiling, deep in dreams. Laura bent and kissed the soft mouth. No danger of waking Paulina; she slept through everything. All three were warmly covered. Baby Joseph stirred, and Laura had slipped from the room and settled herself before the fire, to wait.

Now, the logs were crimson embers slowly crumbling to gray ashes. Jack, curled on a rug close beside Laura, his head pillowed on one great shaggy paw, barked sharply and leaped to his feet.

Laura sat bolt upright. For a moment the room swam dizzily before her—then her vision cleared. Jack faced the door, his teeth bared in a snarl, the hair on his neck erect and bristling. Suddenly there was a loud knocking.

Laura's heart leaped. It must be a messenger from Far

West. She threw off her blanket and started for the door, but something about the dog—his threatening growl, the way he crouched by the door, trembling and alert, slowed her progress.

The knock was repeated, this time more insistent. A man's thick voice called, "Open up. I know someone's there."

Fear seized Laura. This wasn't a messenger. A messenger wouldn't approach her home in this manner. She stood perfectly still, her eyes fixed upon the wooden panels, but her voice was steady when she spoke. "Who are you and what do you want?"

"Never mind that," the man growled, "open up."

The mob! Laura thought. She had heard rumors of mobs in other counties, attacking homes, looting, preying on defenseless women. *But,* she thought, *this can't be the mob. No commotion outside—only one voice speaking.*

The pounding was deafening now, and the long wooden bar that bolted the door jiggled wildly. Jack hurled himself forward, barking furiously.

"Down, Jack! Be quiet." Faced by an emergency, Laura's self-possession was returning. "Tell me what you want," she commanded in a clear, strong voice.

"I want Phelps—Morris Phelps," the voice rasped. "I know you're there, Phelps—you damned Mormon!"

Laura's heart contracted. Morris! Why should this man want Morris? The nauseating wave of terror receded, leaving her cold and wary. She could hear other voices now. "Heavenly Father, give me strength," she whispered. Then aloud, with a calm intensity that surprised herself, she called out, "Morris Phelps isn't here. He's gone to Far West."

"Bah! he's there, all right — hiding behind a woman's skirts. Open this damned door or I'll break it down." The hammering started again, and Laura heard the voice shout, "Get an axe, Jim."

It was no use. The bolt wouldn't hold. Already the hinges

were working loose from the wood. Laura glanced at the insecure windows. She had better open the door. If she allowed them to search the house, they might go away quietly. Her heart seemed to be marching across her chest and dropping into bottomless space, but her hand did not tremble as she slid back the wooden bar and opened the door.

A tall, rawboned middle-aged man stood on the doorstep. His legs were spread wide apart. There was a gun in the holster on his hip. In his right hand he held an evil-looking whip.

Jack lunged at the man. "Jack!" Laura screamed. "Jack!" But it was too late. The man was slashing out unmercifully, the whip whistling through the air—each blow marking Jack's rough coat with streaks of red. Even in his pain the dog's eyes turned to Laura, a plea for forgiveness as he slunk away, whimpering, into the yard.

The man laughed and slouched into the room. "I don't like Mormons nor their dogs," he said. His black eyes, under heavy brows, appraised Laura sharply.

Laura shrank backward a step, then, drawing herself to full stature, she stared back at him unwaveringly. *You beast!* she thought. *You cowardly beast.* She wanted to scream, "Get out of my house!" Instead, she addressed him calmly. "Good evening, sir. What can I do for you?"

"Where's Phelps?" he demanded.

"If you mean my husband, Morris Phelps, he's in Far West. What is it you want of him?" Laura asked. "Perhaps I can help you."

He ignored her question. "I don't want your help—I want Phelps," he growled.

"I'm sorry, he isn't here. He went to Far West early in the evening."

The man took a step toward Laura. She could see his eyes flashing angrily.

"I am speaking the truth," she said quietly.

The man regarded her closely. She held her breath. Could it be that she was convincing him? But no—for suddenly he turned to the door which still stood open behind him. "Jim!" he called. "Hank! Come here. We're going to search the place."

Laura braced her back against the pine dining table, her hands clutching its edge. Two men came out of the shadows in the yard and lumbered into the cottage. "What's the orders, Johnson?" one asked. Laura judged him to be in his middle thirties. He was of medium height—surly—with a thin, nervous face.

The tall man motioned with his head toward the trap door near the west wall. "Search the cellar, Hank."

The third man was short and stockily built. His face was florid and good-natured. Laura noticed him cringe when Johnson spoke.

"You, Jim," he commanded, "search that room over yonder."

"No!" Laura cried. "No!" She darted to the door of the children's room and stood with her back against it—arms flung out protectingly. "Please," she pleaded. "My children are asleep in here."

"Better get out of the way, ma'am," Jim advised. "I don't crave to hurt ye." He picked up a candle and advanced to the door, pushing Laura aside.

There was no use protesting further. It would only arouse their suspicions. She stood rigidly in the doorway while Jim made his search. It was brief. There was no place to conceal anyone—four bare log walls—no closets or alcoves.

Laura watched Jim place the candle on a stand and lie flat on his stomach, to peer under the girls' bed. Paulina's head was barely visible, and Harriet, cuddled close to her, was completely submerged, but Mary Ann lay straight and rigid, close to the edge of the bed. As Laura watched, she saw the child's blue eyes fly open, then quickly close so tightly that her face presented an almost comical expression. But she did not stir. Laura knew that her daughter would not cry out.

Jim's head came out from under the bed, and he stood up. He moved closer to the bed, and Laura's heart sank; but he did not touch the children. He picked up the candle and tiptoed out of the room. There was a flicker of shame on his face. *He's young,* Laura thought. *He's only behaving this way because he's afraid of that man.*

Laura closed the door of the children's room. She could feel Johnson watching her. "Get over by the fireplace," he ordered, "and stay there."

She stood with her back to the dead fire and watched Hank emerge from the cellar. He was carrying a side of bacon, and his pockets were bulging with apples. Her precious winter stores!

"There's nobody down there," Hank said, "but there's some mighty good food."

"It's not food we're after," Johnson grunted. "It's that blasted Mormon."

Hank dumped the bacon near the door and went into the bedroom where she and Morris slept. She could hear his voice and Jim's—talking as they searched. It made no difference what they did, Laura thought, or what they took—so long as they didn't harm the children or her.

Johnson, left alone, ambled across the room to a small trunk. Earlier in the evening Laura had packed that trunk, hopeful that even though a call to flight should come, they might be able to take it, as well as the roll of blankets and clothing. She clenched her fists as Johnson lifted the lid. His long, hairy hand dived down and began tossing the trunk's contents out upon the floor. Her Sunday best alpaca—a suit of Morris', that his people had sent from Kirtland—a sampler that her grandmother had embroidered—the few books she and Morris had brought with them from Illinois.

Laura knew that the man was torturing her—because of some obscure hatred he had for Morris—or perhaps merely because of his scorn for the Mormons.

Jim and Hank returned from the bedroom, and Johnson lost interest in the trunk. Her face expressionless, Laura listened to his profane directions for their search of the barn. When they had gone out, he strode over to Laura but she did not flinch. She hoped he would not notice her shaking knees. If only she could keep her strength and courage a little longer. A derisive smile played about Johnson's lips. "So," he said. "Your husband went to Far West, eh?"

"Yes," she replied. Her face was hot, her mouth dry. Anger choked her, but she kept her voice level. "You'd find more excitement there, I think. Things are happening in Far West."

"What do you mean?" he questioned. Laura could see a gleam of interest in his eyes.

"I know only what the messenger said when he came here early this evening—that the State militia was on its way to Far West." She paused and looked at him defiantly. "Why don't you go and see for yourself? They may be giving the town 'fire and thunder.' "

"Well, now, maybe I will," he replied. He was already moving toward the door. On the threshold he turned and faced Laura, his eyes narrowed to black slits. "I'm going, but listen—you Mormon—if you've lied to me, I'll be back, and the next time it won't be so pleasant." He stepped out into the darkness and slammed the door behind him.

Laura flew to the door and bolted it. She could hear the screaming cackle of the hens in their coop and the bawling of the cow in her stall. Hank and Jim were still searching the premises and helping themselves, she thought dully. She leaned weakly against the door, not daring to move. Her hands and face were wet, and she was panting as though she had run for miles. At last the gruff voices faded, and the heavy footsteps crunched down the path toward the gate where the men's horses were tethered.

2.

Laura thought, *I must go to the children.* Her feet were numb; would they carry her across the room? But even as she wondered, the bedroom door opened. Mary Ann peered out cautiously, then closed the door softly behind her.

Laura felt her strength returning. She opened her arms and started toward the child pattering across the floor, her long white nightgown trailing behind her. Then Laura was drawing Mary Ann into her arms. "Oh, Mother, oh, Mother!" The childish voice broke—the blue eyes were swimming in tears.

Laura held her daughter close. "Hush, darling," she said. "Everything is all right, now."

6

1.

General Lucas, with two thousand men, was encamped just outside of Far West.

Inside the barricade five hundred Mormons waited, grimly braced for action. The return of Colonel Hinkle's scout had warned them of the enemy's advance, and in the clear morning light they had watched for the Missourians, but they had not been prepared for such overwhelming numbers. As troop after troop of militiamen broke ranks and swarmed in an orderly horde over the prairie, eagerness and excitement in the Mormon ranks gave way to apprehension and doubt.

At eight o'clock, a messenger had come from General Lucas, and the leaders of the Church had gone into solemn conference.

Morris, gazing moodily at the mockery of morning sunshine flooding the deserted streets of Far West, wondered about that message. Did it dictate terms of surrender? Would the Church leaders accept such terms, or would orders be to resist? Whatever the decision might be, the volunteers would abide by it; but as minutes dragged into hours, the men were losing heart.

Young David Knowles, son of Far West's blacksmith, cleared his throat nervously. "What do you think, Brother Phelps? Have we any chance at all?" He jerked his brown tousled head toward the Missourian's camp, spread like a panorama just beyond the barricade. Men were moving about, calm and unhurried, intent upon their tasks. *Killing is their business,* Morris thought.

He shook his head, gravely. "I'm afraid not, lad. We are hopelessly outclassed both in man power and arms. No matter how staunch and courageous we may be, a battle would mean a massacre."

It was mid-morning when the word came. The demands of the Governor of Missouri would be met. The leaders of the Church were to be given up as hostages; arms of every description were to be relinquished, and all Mormons were to leave the State. The Church leaders had accepted these terms. Far West was to surrender at once to General Lucas.

To surrender without resistance! The barricade would not be needed. Morris' first reaction was bitter disappointment. There was to be no fight. Then, relief swept over him. Thank God, that the Mormons had been spared bloodshed and violence. It was something that they were to be allowed to return to their homes until they could make arrangements to leave the State.

2.

Morris' hands shook as he coupled his team to the wagon and skillfully maneuvered it out of the line behind the barricade. His one thought now was to get to Laura, much as he dreaded to break the news. The Mormons, he thought, were paying a high price as a guarantee against violence. The surrender of Joseph Smith and other Church officials—the promise to leave the State—the Missourians could not have demanded greater sacrifices. And how could the Mormons face their ordeal without the guidance of their beloved Prophet? The thought filled Morris with misgivings, but he put them aside. The Mormons possessed a unity of spirit that could not be broken. Persecution drew them more closely together. They would carry on as a unit even though they were temporarily deprived of their leader.

Morris drove into the main street of Far West. How much had happened since he had last come this way! The Missourians were in full possession of the town. General Lucas had established his headquarters in the public square, and the firearms surrendered by the Mormons were being stacked in a pile near-by. Guards patrolled the square and the streets.

Morris' progress was slow, for there were many teams and wagons ahead of him, all homeward bound. He was nearing his store now, but the familiar glow of pride was short-lived. He would have to give up the store just as he would have to give up his farm. He averted his eyes as he drove past. Would the State, he wondered, offer him any compensation? Not likely. He remembered bitterly the expulsion from Jackson County. The State had refused to reimburse the Mormons then, why should they expect fair treatment now?

Morris had left the business section and was on the open road that led out of town. Where would the Saints go now, he wondered dully. How long would it take them to achieve what they had accomplished here? Yet, beneath his despair, something stirred within him. A new home to be established—a new center to be found for his Church—a thrill ran through him as he approached the spot where the road forked to the east and to the west.

3.

Two guards stood at the fork in the road. Already, Morris realized, the military routine was functioning. According to the terms of surrender, guards were to be posted at every road leading out of the town. He pulled up instantly at the order to halt and both guards approached the wagon.

"Name?" one questioned.

"Phelps. Morris Phelps."

The guards exchanged swift glances. The one nearest the wagon nodded and jumped aboard, seating himself beside Morris. Morris felt the muzzle of a pistol pressed against his side.

"Turn around, Phelps," said the guard. "The General wants to see you."

"But I don't—" Morris started to protest.

"You'll do as you're told," the guard growled. "You're wanted at headquarters. Turn around, now, and no shilly-shallying."

The weapon was digging into Morris' ribs. He turned his team and started back toward Far West.

7

1.

Faint gray light was beginning to show through the kitchen windows. Laura moved about quietly. The children must sleep as long as they would. She must find courage to face them naturally. Mornings were always so happy. Perhaps if she kept them busy and let them chatter, they wouldn't miss her laughter. Her head felt dull and heavy, and every separate, throbbing nerve seemed to center in her aching back. But her small, capable hands busied themselves with accustomed tasks—kindling a fire in the cook-stove, measuring water, salt, and corn meal into the big iron kettle, raking cold ashes from the fireplace, and nursing the new fire into a cheerful blaze.

The room looked quite as usual, Laura thought, tugging at a heavy log. There was no need to alarm Paulina and Harriet. What a blessing that they had slept through the night—and the baby, too! It was truly a miracle. Mary Ann wouldn't talk. It was almost uncanny, the perfect understanding between Laura and this small daughter. Words were not necessary. With a rush of tenderness Laura remembered the tear-stained face, the sweet warmth of the relaxed little body as she had carried Mary Ann back to bed. Around Paulina and Harriet the covers were tucked in snugly. Frightened as she was, Mary Ann had paused to do that before seeking the comfort of her mother's arms! Yes, Laura thought, Mary Ann would understand.

Understand—what? She, herself, did not know. Even now she had no idea of who those men were or why they had wanted Morris. She drew a long, shuddering breath. This uncertainty—not knowing—waiting. How could she bear it? What had happened in Far West? Where was Morris?

2.

It was quite light now. She must go to the barn, find out what damage had been done. As she unbarred the door, Jack dragged himself from behind the stove and limped toward her, stiffly. "No, boy," Laura said, "you needn't come. I'll be quite safe." She had found him last night, crouching in the shadows near the house, and had dressed his wounds, her heart bursting with indignation. "Good dog," she told him now. "Go back to bed and take care of the children." His tail waved feebly, but he did not return to his pallet; as Laura stepped outside, he was stretching himself out painfully, before the children's door.

Frost coated everything with a glistening film. Close beside the door a single stalk of purple asters reared its head defiantly. Laura felt a strange kinship with the flower. She had been like that, last night. Far West was like that, too, standing brave and alone against the onslaught of the Missourians.

There was a rosy glow in the east; ribbons of soft pink, gold, and violet streaked the cold gray of the sky. Laura loved the sunrise. Even this morning, despite her anxiety, she could feel her spirits lift. The hen-house door was unlatched, but the hens had recovered from their fright and were clucking and pecking busily. Laura did not stop to count them. She closed her eyes instinctively, as she stepped into the shadowy barn. Suppose they had taken Dove, her saddle-pony? But Dove whinnied from her stall, and Betsy mooed plaintively, near-by. Laura gave thanks that the animals had been spared. Somehow, their placidity reassured her.

But as morning wore on to midday with still no word from Far West, the sunrise mood of optimism dissolved. Laura dared not let the children see her alarm. They were all so dear—helping with the chores at the barn—curious, though, about Billy Thompson's failure to appear. But they had accepted Laura's explanation of this and of their father's absence, with only a few questions. None from Mary Ann.

Laura could hear them now—gales of laughter and excited cries. She had sent them to the hen-house to gather eggs. Bread, milk, scrambled eggs—that would do for dinner. She skimmed thick cream from a pan of milk and poured the milk into an earthen pitcher. She thought, *If news doesn't come soon, I'll go to Far West.* Ridiculous! There was no one to leave with the children. Four children — one riding pony. Joseph, sitting on the floor, contentedly banged a tin pan with his spoon. Again Laura's eyes strayed wistfully across the road, but the Thompson cottage, already wrapped in the indescribable aloofness of a deserted house, only stared back, bleakly.

She arranged bowls and pewter spoons on the table and set a plate of bread beside the pitcher of milk. She wondered about her father. He was getting along in years. He had broken visibly, since her mother had been so ill. But the boys were young and strong. Perhaps she and the children should have gone with Morris and tried to reach her people. *No,* she thought. *That would have delayed Morris. This is where I belong. I must stay and protect our home until Morris returns.*

3.

Laura, her nerves stretched to the breaking point, sat in a low rocker with Joseph in her arms.

The afternoon was typical of Indian summer, and the girls were outside in the sunshine. Joseph had become fretful and a bit feverish after dinner, and any indulgence was justified if it would soothe him. Now he was succumbing to the slow, even rocking. His head burrowed against Laura's breast, and his eyelids were drooping.

Laura, herself, was grateful for the lull—a momentary peace, cradled in the swaying of her chair, frightening thoughts held at bay. Suddenly Mary Ann stood in the doorway. "Mother," she said, "someone's coming."

Laura was on her feet. "Mary Ann," she said sharply, "come here and sit down." The child, wide-eyed, sat down in the rocker, and Laura thrust the protesting Joseph into her arms. "Sit perfectly still," she commanded, "until I come back. And whatever happens," she called back as she stepped into the yard, "don't try to carry the baby."

A man on horseback had passed the bend in the road. She would have to hurry to reach the gate before he did. Laura started to run, Paulina and Harriet at her heels. She stopped short, almost upsetting them. "Go back to the cottage, girls, and help Mary Ann with the baby." She paused to catch her breath. "Hurry, now. And don't come out of the house until I call you." She ran on toward the gate. She'd been harsh with them, but she couldn't have them with her now.

The horseman was Albern Allen, whose farm was about three miles north. Laura did not wait for him to greet her. "Brother Allen!" she called. "Oh, I'm so glad to see you! Tell me what has happened. Where is Morris?" The words tumbled out in a breathless rush.

Allen jumped down from his horse and approached the

gate. He looked puzzled. "Isn't Brother Phelps here?" he questioned.

"No, no," Laura answered impatiently. "He went to Far West last night. He hasn't come home."

Allen shifted his weight from one foot to the other. "I don't understand it," he said. "I saw him leaving Far West around noontime. He was headed this way. He should be here by now."

"You mean—you saw him start for home?" Laura asked haltingly. Her mind was racing. Those men! They had waylayed Morris. They had harmed him. And it was she who had sent them to Far West. She clung with both hands to the top rail of the gate, trying to still her trembling.

"It's strange." Allen rubbed his chin thoughtfully. "He left right after we heard the terms of surrender."

But Laura scarcely heard him. "Oh!" she gasped. "You must help me to get to Far West. I must get help—find Morris—" her voice trailed off into a sob.

Albern Allen stared. "In God's name, Sister Phelps!" he exclaimed. "What are you saying?" He unloosed her rigid, clutching fingers and pushed open the gate. "You must calm yourself," he said sternly. "All this doesn't make sense."

His tone steadied Laura. "Oh, yes, it does," she retorted. "Now, you listen to me." Rapidly and clearly she related the events of the night.

Albern Allen scowled. "It's outrageous," he muttered. "They might spare our womenfolk." He shook his head. "Going to Far West wouldn't help, Sister Phelps."

"But I must do something!" Laura cried. "Don't you see? I must!"

"I know how you feel, but here's the situation," Brother Allen reasoned. "Your husband left Far West about an hour before I did, and I've traveled over the same stretch of road. If those men had attacked him, I should have seen some signs of a struggle. That's all open country for miles around."

Laura made no answer, but her eyes, dark with fear, searched his troubled face.

"The more I think about it," he went on, "the more I'm convinced that Brother Phelps did not leave Far West. He probably remembered an errand, something he'd forgotten to do at the store. I'm sure he'll be along presently."

It was possible, Laura thought. As her panic subsided, she realized that Brother Allen was anxious to be on his way. "I'd like to stay and help you, Sister Phelps," he apologized, "but I must be getting on. My wife and children are waiting for me. Little Clarissa is ailing, you know."

"Of course," Laura replied, contrition in her voice. "I forgot everyone else in my anxiety for Morris. I'm so sorry."

Allen was already mounting his horse. "Try not to worry," he advised. "Keep your faith. Everything will come out all right."

Laura, watching him ride away, suddenly realized that she had learned nothing of what had happened in Far West. Brother Allen had said something about a "surrender," but it was all so vague. How could she have been so stupid?

8

1.

John Clark was bound on an unhappy errand. His young shoulders drooped, and his keen dark eyes were veiled and somber. He was going to tell his sister Laura that her husband was under arrest.

It was early evening as he drove Morris' team out of Far West and turned the horses toward the farm. His eyebrows were drawn into a thick, black V. It wasn't likely that Laura, isolated on the farm, had heard about today's events. Much as he dreaded telling her, John would prefer that to having her hear the news from some stranger.

John was very fond of Laura. She was older, of course, but now that he was twenty-two and a man, the gap of years had narrowed. Thinking of her now, in trouble, John felt tender and protective. They had been separated for a while after she had married Morris and gone away, but when the Clarks had followed her to Missouri five years ago, the childhood bond had been renewed. Even the fact that he alone, of the whole Clark family, had not become a Mormon, caused no barrier between them.

It was growing dark. A pale golden moon floated over

blue-black hills to the east. John urged the horses on. Poor Laura. She must be frantic with worry. Morris had been called to defend Far West. She could not know why he had failed to return.

These Mormons, John thought. *What is it about their religion that fills them with such fervor?* Sometimes he wondered if it had been boyish resentment over Morris' zeal that had turned him away from Mormonism. He had been only seventeen when Morris converted the rest of the family, and the idea of Morris going off on a "mission"—leaving Laura and the girls unprovided for, while he traveled around converting people, was just too much. But Morris thought he was doing right, and Laura had been fierce in her defense. John smiled. She was always ready to fight for her ideals. He wondered if this whole-hearted devotion to the Mormon faith was bringing her true happiness. She had changed in some respects. Living in a continuous state of religious fervor must be hard on a sense of humor.

One thing he'd have to admit, though. Neither she nor Morris ever preached to him. Laura always said, "It has to come from within, John." Yet, he knew they wondered why—living among the Mormons—sympathizing with them—he had never become one of them. Sometimes he wondered why, himself.

Many times, during these past five years, he had been tempted to go away—back to Chicago, maybe, or farther west. He had heard of the Oregon country. It stirred his imagination. That feeling of unrest—perhaps it came because he was out of place among the Mormon people, not being a member of their Church. Or maybe it was a secret desire to strike out on his own. Whatever it was he was glad now that he had ignored it. Laura was going to need him these next few weeks.

The road swerved sharply to the right. John recognized

the knoll ahead. Beyond it was another sharp turn and the Phelps' farm lay just beyond. He slowed the horses as they started over the knoll. Strange, that two groups, each composed of intelligent people, could not settle their differences without violence. Of course, the Missourians would never willingly be put in the minority—especially by a close-knit unit like the Mormons. Where would the Mormons go now—and would he go with them or strike out alone? Time enough to think about that. He would not leave Laura as long as she needed him. There was the cottage. God, how he hated to tell Laura!

2.

Laura was already on the doorstep. She came running out as John drove toward the barn and reached him just as he jumped to the ground.

"John!" she exclaimed. "Oh, John, I thought you were Morris." She peered into his face in the gloom. "Where is he, John? Where is Morris?"

John clasped her small, cold hands between his big palms. "Morris is safe, Laura," he said. "He—"

"Then why hasn't he come home?"

John tightened his hold on Laura's hands. He could feel her shaking. "Steady, now," he said. He paused for a moment, then put his arm around her. "Morris has been arrested, along with some other Mormons."

"Arrested?" Laura echoed incredulously. "But—that—that can't be." Then, in the same breath—"Where is he? Can I go to him?"

"No, my dear," John said gently. "I'm afraid not—at least, not now. You see, they are taking him to Richmond, the county seat of Ray County. They are going to hold him for trial."

9

1.

Evening shadows, black and threatening in the unlighted streets of Far West, added to the pervading sense of gloom and desolation.

The Mormon prisoners were on their way to Richmond. Marching two abreast, the long procession plodded slowly along the main street, headed for the open road to the south. Ahead, rode officers of the Missouri State militia. Mounted troopers guarded both sides of the line, and a band of State militia brought up the rear.

To Morris Phelps, marching well toward the end of the line, the slow pound of feet on the hard-surfaced ground was like the measured beat of a drum. He kept his cap pulled down and his eyes straight ahead in the hope that his marching companion would not attempt conversation. He wanted time to collect his thoughts; to discover, if possible, some reason why he had been arrested—why he was being taken thirty miles away, to Richmond, to await trial.

This afternoon when he had stopped at the border of town, he had been sure that it was a mistake, but at headquarters, after waiting under guard for two hours, he had been informed that he, along with sixty other Mormons, was under arrest; that the State had plenty of evidence to warrant his arrest, but that the evidence would not be disclosed to him until after he reached Richmond. He knew no more than that, nor did any of the other Mormons who were under arrest.

The whole thing, Morris thought, *was unbelievable.* He had done nothing to warrant arrest. His mind went back over the events of last night, over the events of the past week, back to the night when he, with seventy-five Mormon volunteers, had gone to Crooked River. *Could it be?* he thought. *That's it.* He kicked at a clod in his path, and his companion looked at him curiously. *Yes, that was it, all right,* Morris thought again. Most of these men who were under arrest had been members of that volunteer company. The affair at Crooked River had been interpreted as an uprising against the State! Could it be that he and his companions would be charged with treason when they reached Richmond? "No," he said vehemently. "No."

His companion, startled, turned. "Did you speak to me, Brother?" he asked.

"No," said Morris again, "but I shall. Talk to me, please—about anything at all. I cannot bear to think."

2.

Four days later, Morris Phelps, crouched on the floor of a filthy room in the Ray County jail, lived over that grueling march from Far West. Two nights and a day of it—of hell, he had thought then. But now he remembered it wistfully. At least there had been air. Air you could breathe without retching. Cattle. That's what they were treated like. Cattle. Herded about by the Missouri State authorities with never a word of explanation. But no self-respecting farmer would herd his cattle in such a pen as this.

His sick glance wandered about the room where sixty Mormon prisoners were confined. It was a fair-sized room, but much too small for sixty men. It was in an unfinished part of a wing being added to the Ray County Court House. Bars covered the windows, but there was no other protection from the chill November winds that whirled smoke from the logs burning in a fireplace at one end of the room, and mixed its smarting tang with the foul body odors of sixty unwashed men.

There were no chairs—no beds. The prisoners, still dressed in the clothes they had been wearing when arrested, sprawled on the floor in the midst of unspeakable filth from which there was no escape.

Morris closed his eyes and held his breath for momentary relief. Yet in the midst of his revulsion he thought, *I can endure this. I could endure anything, if only I knew what was happening to Laura.* Laura faced this emergency alone. Alone at the farm—alone in Far West—alone—alone—. Over and over it revolved in his mind. The thought was driving him crazy.

10

1.

In a dingy room of the Ray County Court House, Laura Phelps, a small, taut figure in her black alpaca dress and neat bonnet, leaned forward in her chair, her eyes, hollow from lack of sleep, fixed upon the inscrutable face of Lawyer Donephon.

Donephon was not a Mormon, but he was reputed to be a fair man. In retaining him to defend Morris, Laura had followed the example of many other Mormons who feared that a lawyer of their own faith would fare ill in the courtroom.

Ten days after their arrest, Morris and the other Mormon military prisoners had been turned over to the civil authorities of Ray County. A Court of Inquiry was now determining whether the evidence warranted holding the prisoners for Grand Jury investigation.

Laura had come to Richmond to attend the concluding sessions of the Court. Never before had she left the children even for a night, but there had been no question in her mind. Ellen Stevenson, a comfortable middle-aged woman—"Aunt Ellen" to every child in Far West—had been glad to stay at the farm, and Laura had closed the door of her mind to everything but Morris. She must be with him now to comfort him; to strengthen him; to protect him, by sheer force of her will, from any further threat of disaster.

Gusts of cold wind rattled the grimy window, and snowflakes whirled in a mad dance against the gray November sky. With his back to the dim light, the lawyer's expression was hard to read.

Laura clasped her hands tightly together. "Mr. Donephon," she demanded, "are you sure that nothing more can be done?"

"I'm sorry, Mrs. Phelps." His fingers drummed nervously on the table's edge. "I have done everything within my power —for the time being, at least."

"But you realize," Laura protested, "that the prisoners haven't a chance of release, with only the prosecution's evidence being presented to the Court of Inquiry."

"Yes," he said. "I know. The defense is greatly handicapped by not being able to present evidence."

"A travesty of justice!" Laura retorted bitterly. "Judge King, of the Circuit Court of Ray County, instructs the Mormons to secure witnesses. When the witnesses appear to testify, the honorable judge orders their arrest!"

The lawyer nodded gravely. "I agree with you, Mrs. Phelps. Such procedure is unjustifiable and disgraceful. Another vent for the hatred and persecution of your people, but—" he spread his hands—"what can I do? I was hopeful at first that we could present our witnesses, but after three attempts failed, I realized that it was no use. We were only making things worse by subjecting more Mormons to arrest." He sighed. "But you mustn't lose heart. Mr. Phelps and the others may be released. Even if your husband should be held for Grand Jury investigation, that would not mean that he was accused of any specific crime."

"I know," Laura said, "but I want to make sure that he

won't be held. How can that affair at Crooked River be construed as an act of treason?" she asked indignantly. "The Mormons went to disperse what they thought was a mob—to protect their homes and their families. The moment they learned that they were opposing the militia, our men turned over to the State all prisoners and firearms they had taken. That should prove their good faith."

"That is true, Mrs. Phelps, but it will take witnesses to prove it to the State, and—"

"And," Laura cut in sharply, "those witnesses, too, are now in prison charged with treason! Oh, Mr. Donephon, we must do something. Can't we appeal to a higher court—or perhaps to some other department of the government?"

"There can be no appeal—not at this stage," Donephon said. "But we are drafting a petition setting forth the Mormons' grievances. It will be sent to the State Legislature. Perhaps some action will be taken. At least we can hope."

"Yes," Laura said wearily. "At least we can hope."

2.

Laura shivered and drew her shawl more closely about her as she passed through the doorway between the main building and the unfinished wing of the Court House. Gaunt beams and ragged ends of timber loomed weird and fantastic in the gloom of late afternoon. Icy blasts swept the corridor that ran alongside of the prison quarters. Laura, gripped by the numbness of despair, remembered her first sight of those quarters and fought off the nausea that engulfed her whenever she thought of that horrible room.

Several guards were patrolling the hall. Laura could feel them staring at her. With head high and quickened pace she hurried along, close to the rough board partition which walled in the prisoners. At intervals small apertures had been cut in the partition so that the men inside might stand and talk to visitors; but no face was visible at any of the openings. Apparently Morris had given her up. He knew that she was stopping with friends of Mr. Donephon—no doubt he thought that she had gone on with the lawyer.

A small group of guards was gathered near the outside door at the far end of the corridor. Laura summoned her courage and approached them. "Will you please tell my husband I am here? I'm Mrs. Phelps. I—"

A guard laughed boisterously. "Mrs. Phelps! Well, by God! The wife of that damned Mormon murderer!"

Laura shrank back instinctively, then started toward the street door—cheeks flaming, lips tightly compressed to hold back words she dared not utter.

"Tell him to burn his Mormon Bible," sneered one. "Maybe that might get him out of jail."

"Bible—hell," another drawled. "That ain't no bible—it's just a book."

There was a burst of raucous laughter and an obscene oath as Laura stepped into the street. Her strong, slender fingers curled convulsively. "Foul-mouthed beasts!" she whispered. "If I were a man I'd strangle every one of you."

But hastening along through the wintry twilight, her rage subsided and cold fear closed in around her heart. Those guards had called Morris a murderer!

II

1.

"Tell him to burn his Mormon Bible!" The mocking words echoing through the bare corridor aroused Morris from a lethargy of wretchedness. Laura! It was Laura those guards were insulting. So strong was the conviction, that he was across the room, peering out into the dim hallway before the thought took form. He saw her then—the erect shoulders, the small, proud head that he loved. Her step did not falter as she passed the jeering guards and disappeared through the door into the street.

"Laura, my dear!" The words escaped his lips in an agonized whisper. He huddled against the partition, moving his long-fingered hands in helpless gestures, heedless of the confusion as his fellow-prisoners surged angrily about the apertures shouting protests and defiance at the guards.

Anger, shame, self-reproach. Long after the uproar had ceased, Morris, bundled in his blankets, stared at the smoldering fire and battled with himself. "Burn his Mormon Bible." Never! And yet, the unforgettable picture of Laura going through that door. In that moment, in one blinding flash, it came to Morris that he alone was responsible for Laura's situation. His imprisonment was a circumstance beyond his control; but if at the beginning of their married life he had not been so intent upon "seeking the new"—if he had realized his responsibilities—Laura would have had security and peace. Did he have any right to ask further sacrifice from her?

How loyal she had been. How generous and understanding. And that wonderful faculty she had of making every crisis seem a normal circumstance of living. He remembered the September afternoon when he had been summoned to go out into the mission field. They were living in Liberty. Life had just begun to settle down, following their enforced flight from Independence. He had come into the big kitchen, exhilarated by the honor conferred upon him, yet troubled by the thought of what it would mean to Laura.

So clear was the memory that for a moment, instead of the fetid, stagnant air of the prison, Morris breathed the spicy fragrance of cookies baking and the appetizing odor of vegetable soup, bubbling in a big iron kettle.

Laura had been kneading bread.

"My dear," he had burst out, "the Church has called me on a mission!"

For the space of a breath her hands had hovered motionless above the loaf she was shaping; then she had brushed the flour from her fingers and faced him with dancing eyes. "Oh, Morris, how splendid! When do you leave?"

He remembered laughing at her excitement, then sobering as he asked, "You understand what this means, dear? I shall be away two years. You may have to help earn the living."

"At last!" she cried gaily. "At last I shall have a chance to make use of my training."

"So you will, 'school-marm,' " he retorted. Before their marriage he had teased her continually about her ambition to become a teacher, but as the years passed, he had almost forgotten about her training for the profession.

And so she had made his going away a happy occasion. Never once, during the two years, had he found anything but encouragement and inspiration in her letters.

A mournful wind wailed through the rafters of the unfinished prison room. Morris shifted his position and hunched deeper into his blankets. He tried to picture Laura in the home of Mr. Donephon's friends. Probably she had gone directly to her room, to regain her composure after that humiliating experience. But whatever heartaches she might have tonight, she would not discuss them with him tomorrow. Early in their marriage she had warned him in her funny, solemn little way, "Never let me take my heartaches out and examine them."

"Why not?" he had demanded.

"Because," she said, "the moment I do, I shall begin feeling sorry for myself."

It had amused him at the time, but the practice had tided them over some trying situations. And yet, Morris wondered, had it always been wise? He had known during these past weeks that Laura wanted to talk, yet he had avoided it, just as he had done on that last night spent in their home.

How blind and selfish he had been! All these years he had taken Laura for granted, confident that she would never fail him. Yes, she must be spared further suffering. There was a way. He would tell her in the morning.

3.

Laura awoke to a day as gray and bleak as her mood. The moment Mr. Donephon saw her, he knew that something had happened. Her face was pale and drawn, and there was fear in her eyes. He listened quietly while she told of her experience with the guards.

"Their insults were of no importance." For a moment her

eyes were scornful, then the fear returned. "But, Mr. Donephon, they called my husband a murderer. It wasn't just idle talk—they referred directly to Mr. Phelps. Called him by name."

The lawyer fingered his watch-chain. "Those rascals are likely to say anything," he remarked.

Laura's hands twisted in her shawl. "Are you keeping something from me? After all, I have a right to know the truth. I don't want to be spared."

"To be perfectly honest with you, Mrs. Phelps, I do know that some of the prisoners will be held on a charge of murder."

"Not—not Mr. Phelps?"

"No one has been named. That is," Donephon amended, "no one that I know of. You see, Mrs. Phelps, I'm almost as much in the dark as you are, but I understand that anyone who took part in the Crooked River fight is likely to be held. Whether the charge will be treason or murder remains to be seen."

"You didn't mention murder yesterday."

"No. I knew so little, I didn't want to alarm you unnecessarily."

Laura's blood had begun to flow again. "There was only one Missourian killed at Crooked River," she said, "and he lost his life in the skirmish."

"The State," Donephon said, "now claims that other lives were lost that night and that those men were murdered."

"It's preposterous." Laura's voice rose. Her eyes were flashing with anger, now. A slow, red flush crept upward to her cheeks. She rose suddenly and brought a clenched fist down on the table before her. "My husband is guilty neither of treason nor murder." She paused. "If he is held on either charge, I shall never stop until I secure justice." She turned and left the room, closing the door sharply behind her.

The lawyer sat for a moment staring at the door. *That*

woman, he thought, *has courage and spirit. She will never accept defeat.*

3.

"Morris," Laura was ashamed of the impatience in her voice, but she was at a loss to understand her husband this morning. She had come to him straight from Mr. Donephon's office. Twice, now, she had spoken his name, but he had seemed not to hear—only searched her face with somber gray eyes. "Morris," she said again, "listen to me. Do you recall everything you did that night at Crooked River?"

She had succeeded in arousing his interest.

"Of course," he said wonderingly. "Everything. But why—"

"And you were not alone?" Laura persisted. "Not even for a moment, during the entire night?"

"Positively not," Morris answered. "There are plenty of witnesses to that. But why do you ask?"

Laura hesitated. Apparently Morris had not heard about the threatened murder charge. Better wait until he had talked with Mr. Donephon. "It's just that so much depends upon the statements you may make," she said. "I wanted to make sure that everything about Crooked River is clear in your mind."

"Laura," Morris said slowly, "right now there's something more important than Crooked River."

"More important?" she looked her surprise.

"Yes, my dear. You. Your situation."

"I don't understand."

"You must go away. Now—at once."

"Go away?" she echoed, in bewilderment.

"Yes, Laura. I want you to return to Far West, get the children and go to my people in Kirtland. We've saved more than enough to see you through. When this trouble is over, I'll join you there."

"Morris!" Laura cried. "Have you taken leave of your senses?"

"No." His eyes fell before hers, and he gazed at the floor as he spoke. "I've thought it all through, Laura. I have no right to ask you to go on this way—you and the children. You must have security."

Security, Laura thought. Two weeks ago it had seemed vital. But that was because she had allowed herself to become bogged down in contentment, had lost sight of real values. It was this moment that was vital. She had to make Morris understand how she felt. She regarded him intently. "Morris," she said, "I am not the only woman who is in trouble. There are other wives—mothers—sisters." She gestured toward his fellow-prisoners.

"But that isn't the point, Laura. I have been unfair to you. I want you to have happiness."

"And you think I'll find it in Kirtland?" A moment's anger made her voice faintly scornful. "Security I might find, but not happiness. My happiness lies with you and with the Mormon people."

He looked at her sadly. "You don't know, my dear. Life holds so much that I have cut off from you."

She was desperately sorry for him. He was trying to convince her of something he, himself, did not believe. "Morris," she asked, "if a State official should ask you to give up your religion in exchange for freedom, would you do it?"

He ceased staring beyond her, and his eyes came suddenly alive. "No," he said. "Never."

"But don't you see that you are asking me to do almost the same thing?"

"Well—perhaps. I hadn't thought of it in that way."

"You know it's true, Morris. We are part of a movement that is bigger than either of us."

For a long moment he looked at her strangely, then he smiled. "You are right, my dear. We are part of a great movement, and we can never be separated from it." There was pride in his eyes. Quiet understanding flowed between them once more.

In the rush of joy Laura forgot her fears. For a moment she was completely happy. "It's our life, Morris," she said softly.

"Our life," he repeated.

4.

Morris Phelps had been indicted for murder. Joseph Smith, the Prophet, had been committed on a charge of treason to the Clay County jail in Liberty. Most of the other Mormons had been released, but Morris, with King Follet and the Apostle Parley P. Pratt, was being held in the Richmond jail. Follet was charged with robbery; Parley Pratt with treason; but Morris had been indicted for murder.

John Clark, guiding his team along the road to Far West, covertly observed Laura, seated beside him. The wintry sunshine showed her face drained of all strength, but at last she was beginning to relax. The rigid line was gone from around her mouth, and her hands, that had been moving constantly in wild, nervous gestures, lay lightly clasped in her lap.

They had left Richmond that morning. It was noonday now, and they were well along on their journey. John opened his lips and closed them again. Something in Laura's face warned him not to intrude upon her thoughts—not just yet.

Again, John was grateful for the impulse that had sent him to Richmond to bring her home. He remembered her face, yesterday, when she had heard the news of Morris' indictment. But whatever her thoughts had been, she had kept them to herself. Not until this morning, on the open road, had she let her defenses down. Then angry and bitter words had rushed from her lips in an incoherent jumble. Most of the things she said had not made sense, but that wasn't important. It was the necessity of release that was important. That John knew. And gradually the frenzy had spent itself, and she had begun putting her thoughts into an ordered pattern.

The horses' hoofs clattered over frozen ground. Patches of snow were melting here and there, and small rivulets of water trickled across the road. John leaned forward and tucked a blanket more securely about Laura's knees. She gave him a grateful look, then her eyes turned again to the bare rolling hills wrapped in gray November haze.

Another hour passed. From time to time John glanced at Laura. Her color was more natural, and her eyes, dull after the angry glare had faded, now sparkled faintly.

"I'm all right, now," she murmured, as if to reassure herself.

John gazed at the horses' ears. "We'll soon be home," he said.

Laura turned to him. "Home. That's where I belong—with the children. There is nothing more I can do in Richmond, at least not now."

It was good to hear her say that. "You are right, Laura," John answered.

"But I shall not lose faith," she said to herself, almost as if it were a vow. Then to John, "I do believe—I must believe that when public sentiment against the Mormons dies down, Morris will be released."

"Undoubtedly," John agreed.

"One thing I am sure of," Laura's lips drew into a determined line. "I shall never leave Missouri without Morris. I promise that to myself."

John made no comment. If the recent court procedure, he thought, was a specimen of what the Mormons could expect, Laura might not be able to keep that promise.

12

1.

Morris' trial was set for the first week in April. The news reached Laura one December morning when a white world glittered beneath a turquoise sky. The pure, cold air sparkled, too. Every breath was a heady draught, and Laura found herself singing at her work.

But the message left her silent and dispirited. Four months. Thinking of Morris in that loathesome jail, it seemed an eternity to wait. Household tasks, care of the children, lessons for Paulina and Mary Ann (since school was impossible), preparations for their coming exodus from Missouri—none of these things was enough to fill the days stretching blankly ahead.

Yet the first weeks passed quickly enough. Mormon families, driven from their homes in the outlying regions of Caldwell County, had begun drifting into Far West. To Laura, it was a heaven-sent emergency. Gratitude filled her heart and poured out in her prayers. Gratitude that she had a home to share and that, absorbed in ministering to these unfortunates, she had no time to brood over Morris—Morris, awaiting trial for a crime he had not committed.

Well into January the countryside lay under a blanket of

snow, but gradually the days lengthened and grew warmer, with finally a definite thaw. In early February the first wagon trains departed for Quincy, Illinois, the Saints' temporary haven. The people of Illinois were sympathetic. They had intimated that any or all Mormons would be welcomed in their State.

One by one, Laura bade her friends Godspeed. She had known that her own family would be among the first to leave. Her father had scarcely been able to restrain his impatience until the thaw set in, for her mother was no better.

All through January John had urged her to accompany them. "Laura, you know you can't stay here alone." "Laura, be sensible. You must come with us." But when she remained firm, he had seized her hands impetuously. "If you stay, I stay." Then, in the next breath, "No, I can't. Father needs me. Still, if it weren't for Mother—"

Laura's father had added his entreaties. "Your mother wants you, my dear." For her mother's sake Laura longed to go, but her first loyalty was to Morris. She could not leave Missouri, no matter what the emergency—not until after his trial. And in her heart she knew that her mother would understand, would want her to stay.

On the day of departure Laura and the children went to Far West to say goodbye. Laura had thought herself reconciled, but as they rode away, John waving, her father's eyes dimmed with tears, she felt suddenly and hopelessly tired, unable to face the weeks that still must pass before Morris would be tried.

She awoke next morning in vague surprise at the stillness. The children were still asleep, but not for weeks had the cottage been so disturbingly quiet. It made her acutely aware of her situation. Now, she was indeed alone. And there were two long months before the trial.

She wondered about their food supply. Her unexpected

guests had made alarming inroads on her reserves. Laura had no regrets, but since the store had been abandoned, she could no longer count upon that. She must conserve what was left.

After breakfast she descended the steep cellar stairs. She wore no wrap, and the damp, penetrating chill made her teeth chatter as she checked her meager resources. A bushel of potatoes, a half-barrel of apples, some crocks of preserves, a side of salt pork. In the corn-crib, she knew, were a few sacks of dried corn, and she still had some hens and the cow. Yes, with careful planning she could manage until April. What cash there was must be saved for emergencies. It might be needed to help Morris win his freedom.

Alone in the dim cellar, Laura's eyes filled with tears. How much had happened since November! Morris in prison. Their security almost gone. The store abandoned — property and stock a total loss. And soon this home must be sacrificed, too. Again hopelessness engulfed her in a bitter wave. Everything —life itself, seemed suddenly and utterly futile.

Quickly, she turned and mounted the stairs. The kitchen was bright and cheerful after the gloom of the cellar. The sight of Paulina and Mary Ann squabbling amicably over the breakfast dishes started tiny threads of warmth flowing through her. She walked toward the fireplace where Joseph played on the hearth rug under Harriet's watchful eye. The baby crowed delightedly and held out his arms.

Abruptly, Laura laughed. For her it was a laugh of relief, yet it held a note that halted Paulina and Mary Ann at their work to stare curiously. "Mother," Mary Ann hesitated, "is— is anything the matter?"

"The baby," Laura said. "He's so funny." She could not explain how suddenly she had realized that life could never be futile. Not so long as she had her children, Morris, and her faith.

2.

March blustered in with snow flurries and cold winds. Far West had become practically a deserted town but the last wagon train was not to leave until mid-April, and a number of Mormons were still there. The Church officials who had escaped imprisonment would remain until after the Richmond trial. It was a comfort to Laura to feel that there would always be someone in Far West to whom she could turn for help.

Hyrum Stone was faithful. He often brought news of the Mormons in Quincy. One afternoon in early March he came with clippings from the *Quincy Argus.* The Mormons, it seemed, were considering the purchase of a twenty thousand acre tract in northwestern Illinois. Laura thrilled to the news. A new home for the Saints! But a little later John wrote that the idea had been given up. "Apparently," his letter read, "the Church leaders are afraid to attempt the establishment of another distinct community. How do you feel about this? Of course, I'm still 'outside the fold,' but Father is greatly disappointed."

For a moment Laura sat staring at the letter, completely shaken. The Mormons not to establish a new abiding place? That meant that they would scatter and be absorbed by other communities. The pattern would become faint and blurred. Whatever were the Church leaders thinking of? If the Prophet had been in Quincy, this wouldn't have happened; but he was in Liberty, in prison, awaiting trial. Pray God he would be released—would get to Quincy before the pattern had completely disappeared!

3.

Paulina and Mary Ann made a game of counting the days until "Father would come home." "Mother," Paulina would call gaily, "this is the sixth. One more day gone." And the next morning Mary Ann's sweet treble, with a thoughtful note—"Mother, today's the seventh." But to Laura each day seemed a year, and each night brought with it a nameless fear she could not shake off. Impatient with her own doubts, she plunged feverishly into the work of sorting and assembling belongings for their departure in early April.

Mid-March. The pussywillows were in bud. The air throbbed with a surge of new life.

A letter from her father told Laura of their safe arrival. "Everything went fine," he wrote, "till we hit the Mississippi. It was full of ice, and we had to wait till that began to move before we could cross. Lucky you made us take those extra blankets. We used them for tents—only shelter we had while we waited for the ice to move. Food got low, too. Some had no food at all. Your mother, I'm sorry to say, is no better, although she was greatly cheered to see us. We think of you and the children constantly—"

4.

"Mother, this is the very last day of March," Paulina announced triumphantly.

"Yes, dear." For a moment Laura gazed unseeingly at the pile of neatly mended garments on the table before her. She was putting the children's clothes in order before leaving for Richmond tomorrow. How fortunate, she thought, that the children were so fond of Ellen Stevenson and that Ellen was still in Far West and able to stay with them. Fortunate, too, that Hyrum Stone, who was to be a defense witness, had volunteered to take her with him to Richmond. Laura had dreaded the long trip on horseback, alone. And, she admitted to herself, she still dreaded going. She sighed as she threaded her needle. In spite of her longing to see Morris, now that the time was at hand, she was afraid. Yet, Mr. Donephon's message yesterday had been encouraging. Everything was proceeding normally—defense witnesses had been served with subpoenas requiring their appearance for the trial—no occasion to worry. Laura felt her confidence returning. Surely, once that testimony was given, Morris would be freed. Nothing could go wrong this time.

By evening all of her preparations were complete. Ellen would arrive in the morning, and Laura would be ready to go.

The girls were preparing for bed. Mary Ann, lingering near Laura's chair, looked up with serious blue eyes. "Mother," she questioned, "what will we do if Father doesn't come home?"

Blankly, Laura regarded the child. Mary Ann had put into words the fear that she, herself, had pushed aside. "Darling," she said, "Father *is* coming home. You must believe that." She hoped that her voice was steady. She gathered Mary Ann close to hide her own wet eyes. "Father is coming home," she had assured Mary Ann; but she had not ventured to say when.

5.

But Laura Phelps did not go to Richmond. Three days had passed since the morning when Hyrum Stone had driven away without her. Laura bent over baby Joseph, laid a cool hand on his forehead and pushed back the tangle of ruddy hair. His crib stood close to the hearth where a slow fire burned. He was sleeping soundly, and his breathing was almost normal. Now that Joseph was out of danger, she dared pause to think. She remembered the queer, rasping sound of his gasps that had awakened her long before daylight on the morning of her intended journey. She had found him burning with fever. She had aroused the girls and somehow, with their help, had managed to build fires, rummage through half-packed boxes for flannel cloths and the bottle of chicken-oil, prepare a mixture for mustard plasters, drag the crib out near the fireplace. There was no time to waste.

Five minutes for the mustard plaster—the little chest an angry red; then flannel, saturated in hot chicken-oil. Cold cloths on the hot forehead. Another mustard plaster. More chicken-oil. Over and over, with swift, desperate regularity, Laura held to the routine, giving thanks that if this had to happen it had come before she left for Richmond.

By eight in the morning, when Hyrum Stone arrived with Ellen, the baby had been far too ill for Laura to be concerned with anything else. She had greeted Stone abstractedly, with a brief explanation, and he had gone on alone, promising to keep her informed. Ellen had remained to help.

All that first day, while Joseph tossed and muttered, Laura had rebuked herself bitterly. Had she neglected him, in her eagerness to go to Richmond? But he had seemed quite as usual—and she knew how suddenly a child could fall ill. "Please, God, don't let anything happen to him. Please, God!" she had repeated again and again.

Today the fever had abated, and the congestion in his lungs was gone. He had slept fitfully until late afternoon, had taken some warm milk, and was asleep again.

Her son! Gratitude welled up in Laura's heart and her eyes filled. *I must get hold of myself,* she thought. *I cry too easily these days.* She must always be brave for Morris. If only she could be with him—could know what was happening in Richmond. The trial was set for Wednesday, and this was only Thursday. It might be Monday before she would have news.

6.

By Saturday, Joseph was almost well, and Ellen had returned to town.

It was late afternoon. Laura had fed the chickens and was returning to the house when she noticed the man approaching her gate. She increased her pace. Hyrum Stone? No—it couldn't be—not so soon. He was one of the witnesses. He should be in Richmond. Already, she was running toward him.

Hyrum Stone's shoulders slumped and his face was set. Laura's heart was hammering. "What is it?" she cried. "What has happened now?" Her voice sounded shrill and strange in her own ears.

"Be calm, Sister Phelps," Stone spoke quietly. "It isn't as serious as you think—but serious enough. The case—has been continued."

"Continued? You mean—"

"I mean set over to a later date. When court convened, the prosecution, it seems, was not ready to present their witnesses; so the judge ruled that the case should be continued and a new date set for the trial."

"And the date—has it been set?" Laura asked dully.

"No, not yet. Mr. Donephon was able to secure a change of venue for Morris and Pratt and Follett. They are to be sent to Columbia next week. That's in Boone County and the trial will be held there, but a date can't be set until the prisoners reach Columbia."

Columbia, Laura thought, *in Boone County.* She didn't know the exact location. What did this mean? She pushed her hair back from her brow and shook her head slowly. Everything was confused.

Hyrum Stone took her arm and they walked toward the cottage. "I am sure this is all for the best," he declared. "In another county—a new community where there isn't so much anti-Mormon feeling, the chances for a fair trial will be much better."

But what he said did not reassure Laura. Her head was

whirling. Morris was still in prison. She would have to leave Missouri without him. And what of those long dreary months ahead of him. What would they do to his morale? For the first time she deliberately faced the stark truth, stripped of all pretense. Morris, much as she loved him, was weak. And this time she would be far away. Not able to see him. Not able to bolster up his courage.

They had reached the doorstep and stood for a moment, silent, gazing out across the rolling prairie bathed in the soft rose haze of before twilight. The tranquil beauty of the scene steadied Laura. Things might be worse. Suppose Brother Stone had brought word of Morris' conviction? Icy prickles ran along her spine. She became conscious that Hyrum Stone was talking.

"—and before I left Richmond word came from Liberty. Joseph Smith's case has been continued. He, also, is being taken to Columbia to await trial."

So the Prophet's case had been continued, too! Strange, first, the defense witnesses were imprisoned. Next, they were allowed to appear in court, but the prosecution wasn't ready. Something was very strange. Still, the law must take its normal course. Once more she would wait for that. But if Morris did not receive a fair trial in Columbia . . . Laura refused to think beyond that point.

7.

Hyrum Stone took Laura and the children to Richmond to tell Morris goodbye. It was not a happy episode. The April morning was mild. Laura carried Joseph, his small hands clutched in the folds of her Paisley shawl; the three girls, wide-eyed, hands linked, walked gingerly ahead along the corridor. They shrank back as the jailer unlocked the heavy oak door and motioned them inside the prison room. But the instant they saw their father, Paulina and Mary Ann flew to him. "Father!" they screamed joyously, "Father!" Harriet, suddenly shy, clung to her mother's skirts.

Morris dropped to his knees and gathered Paulina and Mary Ann into his arms, but across their heads he was smiling at Laura. "My dear," he said. Then gently extricating himself from the girls' embrace, he rose and came to Laura. He leaned down, pinched Harriet's cheek and kissed her swiftly, but she hid her face in the folds of Laura's dress. Morris straightened and held out his arms for Joseph. "My baby," he said, his voice trembling.

But Joseph wailed and clung to Laura, his small arms tight around her neck, his face buried against her shoulder. "Joseph, baby," Morris coaxed, "don't you know me?" Laura saw the hurt look in his eyes. She felt Harriet tugging at her skirts and looked down to see tears on the child's lashes.

Paulina and Mary Ann were clamoring for his attention. "Talk to the girls, Morris," Laura said. "I'll try to soothe the baby." She was sick with disappointment. How foolish to have brought the children. She comforted Joseph, walking up and down the prison room with Harriet trailing behind her. Paulina and Mary Ann were both chattering at once. Morris answered them, but his bewildered eyes followed Laura. Joseph raised his head, looked at his father, and began to sob again. Harriet tugged harder at her mother's skirts.

It was no use. To Joseph, Morris was a complete stranger. Harriet, herself little more than a baby, was frightened. The jailer was coming. Their time was almost up. Laura was so confused that she scarcely knew what she was saying. Then, suddenly, they were all out in the hall and the oak door was closing behind them.

"Mother," Paulina was saying, "Oh, Mother, won't we see Father any more?"

8.

The last wagon train left Far West in mid-April, and Laura and her children joined it. But before they began the long trek to Quincy, Laura received heartening news. The Prophet had escaped while his jailers were taking him to Columbia. He was now on his way to Quincy. Things would be different, now.

13

1.

To Laura, the weeks that followed were a monotonous procession of journeys—a blurred panoramic background for scattered incidents vivid enough to etch themselves upon her memory.

Far West to Quincy. Long days on the wagon-seat with strange, wild country slipping behind them. An occasional farm, its split rail fence holding the prairie at bay—its puny buildings sprawled like a child's toys against the never-ending sweep to the horizon. The girls were enchanted, but to Laura it was just so much ground to be covered. Whatever the scene before her, she was still seeing her home on that spring-scented April morning when she had left it forever. A casual closing of the cottage door, and she had climbed aboard the wagon, desperately closing her mind to everything but the momentary business of settling the children in comfort. A light slap of reins across the horses' backs, and the wagon was creaking through the gate. As simple as that. And another chapter in her life was finished.

It was amazing how quickly they settled into the routine

of the wagon train. Weary hours of driving. Camping at nightfall. A few hours of blessed oblivion—then rising, still drugged with sleep, arms and shoulders aching, every muscle protesting, to set forth at dawn.

Early in the morning with you by my side,
Jump in the wagon and we'll take a ride.

Laura often wished that she might never hear that song again, but the children loved it. Over and over she must sing it, each time with a different name—

Early in the morning with Paulina by my side—

the children's voices picking up the refrain,

Wait for the wagon—Oh, wait for the wagon.
Wait for the wagon and we'll all take a ride.

"Me, now, Mother," Mary Ann would demand, and Harriet would wriggle ecstatically as her turn approached. Even Joseph must be included. Paulina, proudly holding him, insisted upon that. Laughing eyes, eager faces. This was their great adventure, and Laura knew that she must keep it so.

But when small shoulders drooped and eyelids fluttered drowsily, the inevitable question came, "Mother, when will we come to the Big River?"

The Big River. Laura was as eager as the children to reach it, for once across the Mississippi it would be only a matter of hours until they would be in Quincy.

Visioning the river as she had last seen it, a wide, placid stream, flowing calmly and majestically between high, green banks, Laura recoiled in almost physical shock when a turn in the road revealed a broad, dark stream, swollen by spring rains, churning itself angrily into yellow-brown foam that boiled over obstacles and lashed at its banks. Suddenly, her emotions, too, became dark and turbulent. To see her parents. That was the only thing of importance. She was terribly in need of their love and reassurance. Even the girls' excitement over "driving the wagon right onto the flatboat" did not dispel Laura's gloom.

Later that night she wondered if it had been foreboding, for when at twilight they halted the wagon at the Clark home, her father, the light gone out of his eyes, had met them with the news of her mother's death. It had happened the week before—too late to send a message to the wagon train.

Always, Laura thought numbly, God provided duties as an antidote to sorrow. The children, tired, hungry, and bewildered, had to be put to bed. Necessities must be unpacked. She must consult with John about the disposal of the goods in the wagon. There was Rhoda, too. Reunion with Laura after their long separation had added poignancy to Rhoda's heartache. Held in Laura's comforting arms, she sobbed out bits of their mother's days. Her patience. Her unwavering faith. Her intense love for Laura and her family.

Faced with new sorrow, Laura realized in wondering gratitude that her faith had become an actual part of her. The loss of her mother was a crushing blow, yet she found herself burning with pure fervor. Faith was all important. It had sustained her thus far. It gave her high courage to go on.

When the first shock and bewilderment of grief were pushed aside, Laura's father gave her news of the Mormons. One of Joseph Smith's first acts after his arrival in Quincy had been to revive the plans for a new abiding-place in northwestern Illinois. He had arranged the purchase of a large tract of land and had already departed for that region. Commerce, a tiny settlement on the Mississippi, had been designated by the Prophet as the new "center of Zion," and he was appealing to the Saints to come to that spot.

Laura's father looked at her searchingly. "Do you think we should answer the Prophet's call?"

"I know we should, Father," Laura's voice was clear and

calm. "We are the Chosen People. It is our privilege to aid the Prophet in working out the pattern."

He was silent for a long time. He looked tired and old, Laura thought. Tears were in his eyes. "You are right, daughter, we must go on. If—" his voice broke, "if your mother were here, she'd want it that way."

2.

Within the week they were on their way to Commerce. All but Rhoda. Someone, she had pointed out, with a sudden blush and downcast eyes, someone ought to stay and dispose of the house and of the furnishings that could not be taken. She could come later, Rhoda said, with Ellen Stevenson and others of their friends. Laura, her own heart yearning to be with Morris, thought she understood. Even in the midst of her devotion to their mother, Rhoda had found another interest. She was not willing to leave Quincy just yet.

Up to the moment of departure, Laura had wondered whether John would come. Nothing had been said. The subject of John's plans had been carefully avoided; but twice, when Laura had surprised her brother's gaze fixed speculatively upon her face, he had flushed and looked away. She had watched him wistfully as he helped their father load the wagons—hat pushed back—shirt open at the throat—his tall body and long arms moving with easy grace and precision. When all was ready and he had helped Laura climb to the driver's seat, he stood looking up at her.

"Father's not strong," he said. "If you think you can manage, I believe I'd better drive for him."

"Oh, John!" was all she could say.

"Of course," John's eyes were twinkling, "you've done pretty well so far, but I'll relieve you now and then when you're tired." He grinned a bit sheepishly. "Good practice for my trip to Oregon."

Laura smiled with unsteady lips. Dear John. What it would mean to have him with them! She lifted her chin with a brave attempt at gaiety. "I'll consider your offer, young man. We'll see how you get on."

Her heart lifted. It was a glorious morning. Everywhere there was a feeling of things coming alive. The new center of Zion. She would be one of the first to arrive there. If Morris could only be with her. The longing for him, always in the background of her thoughts, welled up within her. Just one brief message from him since she had left Far West. He had been transferred from Richmond in late April. He should be in Columbia now.

3.

A curious exhilaration possessed Laura as they neared Commerce. The day was hot for early June and the noonday sun was dazzling. She shaded her eyes and tried to see the town, but could distinguish nothing in the white-hot glare. But as she turned into the single street, driving close behind her father's wagon, sick disappointment seized her. Commerce. Not a town. Scarcely a settlement. Laura's eyes appraised the buildings. A blockhouse, a store, a few frame dwellings. Barren and desolate, the prairie swept eastward.

"Mother," Paulina questioned, "where are the houses?"

Before Laura could reply, Mary Ann was calling out excitedly, "Mother, Mother! A flatboat! Will we ride on it?" She was gesturing toward the Mississippi, glittering in the sunlight.

"Perhaps, dear," Laura answered absently. She wasn't thinking of the flatboat or the river. Her eyes were fixed on the land that sloped from the water's edge to the scattered settlement above. Swampland covered with almost impenetrable underbrush! She turned her eyes back toward the street, staring straight ahead.

Her father had halted his team before one of the frame buildings. *The Church Office,* Laura thought, as she watched him jump from his wagon. She brought her team alongside and pulled rein. "Wait here, Laura," her father called, "I must tell the Prophet we have come."

John leaped to the ground and strolled over to Laura's wagon. "Well—what do you think of it?" His sweeping gesture took in the street and the surrounding country.

His tone piqued Laura. She drew herself up. "I think it's quite all right." She hesitated, seeing John's skeptical smile. "After all, you can't expect too much. Remember the Prophet and his associates have been here only one short month."

John made no answer. He was still smiling as he turned and gave his attention to the children.

4.

Afterward, Laura wondered how she would have stood the test; for Clark and his family did not locate in Commerce. It was Joseph Smith's own suggestion that they settle in the village of Montrose just across the river. In addition to Commerce, the Mormons had purchased land on the Iowa side, which included a part of Montrose, a part of Keokuk, and several thousand acres of what was known as the "half-breed" tract—the name a holdover from Indian days—a wild region with an unsavory reputation as a hiding place for outlaws. The small tracts of land were paid for in cash. The larger tracts were purchased on two notes signed by Joseph Smith, one payable in ten, the other in twenty years. Cash from the sale of lots to immigrants was to be used to pay the interest.

A number of Mormon families, the Prophet said, had already settled in Montrose. Living there would not be quite so primitive.

Within two days Laura's father had purchased a small farm on the outskirts of Montrose. Rhoda would soon arrive. The work would not be heavy and the boys would help. "Withour your mother," he told Laura, "I'd be lost in a town. I need to keep busy."

But Laura and the children remained in the village. Another chapter was beginning.

14

1.

On an afternoon in late June Laura hurried out from the village store of Montrose, adjusted her sunbonnet to shade her eyes, and stepped lightly along the main street in the direction of her home. Her cheeks were flushed and her eyes sparkled. A letter from Morris! The first she had received since leaving Quincy. It was postmarked "Columbia"—at least he had reached there safely. She fingered the letter hesitantly. No. She would not break the seal now. Better wait until she reached home where she could savor every word in privacy. She slipped the letter into the deep pocket of her blue and white calico dress and quickened her pace.

She turned into a side street and walked on briskly, entering the gate in a picket fence that enclosed a half-acre lot. Set back in the yard, a new frame and log house faced the street, but Laura passed it and hurried along a lane toward a single-room log cabin on the rear of the lot. She smiled ruefully as she approached it. This was home now. How different from the cottage at Far West! And what a time she'd had making it livable. The owner, who lived in the house in front, had warned her. The place had once been a stable. But

John had helped—whitewashing walls, scrubbing the slabbed floors, filling chinks between the logs. At least it was a shelter and her own. Her father, she knew, had been surprised and a little hurt by her refusal to live on the farm. But she wanted a home. A home of their own—for Morris to come to when he was released.

The room Laura entered looked almost cozy with the sun streaming through its single window picking out highlights of color in the bright rag rugs. She tossed her sunbonnet on top of the cherry chest and sank into her low rocker. Dear, familiar possessions that had traveled so many miles. They were what made a home.

It was pleasant to be alone when her letter came. She was glad, now, that she had not gone to the farm today. John had chuckled as he drove off with the children. "Make the most of your solitude, Laura," he called. "I'll have them back before dark."

She took the letter from her pocket and for a moment pressed it to her cheek; then, breaking the seal, she drew the closely written sheets from the envelope. "Laura, my dear," it began. . . .

2.

The twilight was closing in around Laura, motionless in the little chair, the letter lying in her lap. Lost in the black void where Morris' letter had plunged her, the sound of Mary Ann's excited voice brought her back to reality.

"Mother, Mother, Mother!" Mary Ann was rushing down the lane. The door burst open and the child rushed to Laura, flinging both arms around her mother's neck. "Oh, you'll never guess! Uncle John said I might come ahead and tell you—he had to stop at the blacksmith's." She broke off, stooped, and began gathering up pages which had fluttered to the floor. "What's this, Mother?"

"A letter from Father, dear."

"Oo—oo! Is he coming home?" Mary Ann began to jump up and down, her blonde braids quivering with excitement.

"Hush, child." Laura spoke gently, but the little girl's instant response was startling. Again Laura was conscious of the strong, mysterious bond between them. This dear child—so sensitive, so closely attuned to herself that she instinctively felt emotions when she could not understand!

Mary Ann stood quietly regarding her mother with troubled blue eyes. "Father isn't coming," she said slowly. "Are we going to see him?"

"I don't know, dear. I—I wish I did." Laura smoothed back the bright hair and kissed Mary Ann's smooth forehead. *Columbia,* she thought. *A hundred and fifty miles away—and no one to leave with the children.*

It was quite dark in the cabin now. Laura arose from her chair, lighted the candles and set about preparing supper.

"Mother," said Mary Ann, "I 'most forgot the surprise. A wagon train came and brought Aunt Rhoda and Aunt Ellen."

A stove-lid clattered. "Mary Ann!" Laura exclaimed, "are you sure?"

"Oh, yes." The child, delighted at her mother's evident interest, chattered on. "You can ask Uncle John. We saw Aunt Ellen in the village, and we took Aunt Rhoda out to Grandpa's. Here comes Uncle John, now. Ask him, Mother."

But Joseph, astride John's shoulders, was crying loudly. He was tired and hungry.

"Come here, precious," Laura coaxed. The little fellow

threw himself into her arms, howling lustily. "Paulina," Laura directed, "you and Mary Ann put supper on the table. Don't wait for me, John," she added. "I'll join you as soon as this young man is settled for the night."

Later, when supper was over and the other children in bed, Laura sat with John on the doorstep of the cabin. The air was warm and fragrant. Crickets chirped drowsily. To the east, dark gleams of silver marked the Mississippi's path in the moonlight.

"John," Laura said, "I've heard from Morris."

"Yes, I know. Mary Ann told me. What's the news?"

"The trial is to be held the first week in July. John, I must get to Columbia for that trial." She would not tell him what she had read between the lines—that Morris was despondent. That he needed her so terribly.

John moved suddenly. In the bright moonlight, his face, the clean line of his out-thrust jaw, the lift of his shoulders, were eager. "I'll go with you," he said.

"John—would you?" Laura clasped her hands and bent forward to peer into his eyes. "But Father—the farm—"

"Father will be all right. Rhoda's here now and the boys are big enough to help him. You can leave the children at the farm."

"I could—but," Laura hesitated, "Rhoda will have enough to do, getting settled and looking after Father and the boys. Besides, I want to keep our little home here, ready for Morris to come to after—" She paused. "John, Mary Ann says you saw Ellen Stevenson today?"

"Oh, yes. I forgot to mention it. The children fairly swarmed over her. You've a rival there."

Laura laughed. "I know. Do you suppose," she asked, "that I could get her to stay here and look after the children?"

"I shouldn't wonder. She said her family weren't here yet.

She came on with Rhoda and the Murdocks. She's coming to see you tomorrow."

"Then it must be right," Laura murmured, half to herself. "The way is being opened for me to go." She turned to John and laid her hand on his arm. "Do you think I should consult the Prophet, John?"

"Well, now, that is for you to decide."

"Then I shall. I'll feel better about it."

John rose to his feet. "Go to bed and get a good night's rest. I must get along home, but I'll come over early and we'll make plans."

"Be sure you do come early," Laura cautioned. "Seeing the Prophet means a trip across the river; but I must see him. With his blessing upon me I can conquer anything."

"Then I hope he'll bless you," John said. "Good night, Laura."

15

1.

Night was falling and the rising wind whipped Laura's skirts about her ankles. She twined her fingers in Dove's mane and bent low to shield her face from the driving rain. John, a blurred shape in the streaming darkness, guided his horse to her side.

"Luck!" he exclaimed. "Rydersville's just ahead. That's a regular stop for the post. We're sure of a hot supper and a good bed, my girl."

Laura did not attempt to answer. Somehow she must manage to stay in the saddle a little longer, to grip the reins, to brace her aching body against each wrenching jolt, as the little mare struggled for footing in the slippery mud.

Three days, from dawn till dusk or later, Laura and John had been riding south, holding a steady pace over low, rolling plains, following the course of turbulent creeks, brimming with the rains of early summer.

It had begun to drizzle shortly after they left Montrose, and a sudden heavy downpour had drenched them to the skin, but Laura refused to pause. Only at nightfall, when the horses must be cared for, would she consent to seek shelter.

Their first night had been spent at a farmhouse and the second at a crude inn, but with the earliest streak of dawn they were up and away again.

And now they had reached Rydersville. Rydersville, only two days' journey from Columbia—and Morris. *I can really sleep tonight,* Laura thought.

The horses cantered to the door of the inn and John lifted Laura from her saddle. Her feet were numb and she clutched his arm to keep from falling. The door opened and two figures were outlined against the oblong of yellow light; a small, round man and a lank, shock-headed boy, who stepped forward, grinning, to the horses' heads.

"Just a moment, lad," John said, "we'll need those saddlebags."

Then they were inside, with the door closed against the wild, dark night.

For what seemed an interminable time, Laura drooped against the stair railing. Small rivulets trickled from her mud-spattered home-spun habit and formed brown pools upon the floor. She closed her eyes and waited, too exhausted to think, conscious of John's voice and the innkeeper's. Then John's arm was around her, half-carrying her up the stairs where the little man led the way with candles.

"There you are, Laura." John deposited her dripping saddlebags on the floor inside of her room. "Get into some dry clothing and come back downstairs. The landlord will have a meal for us."

Laura stood staring at the pine-wood bed. Oh, to creep under that neat blue and white quilt and sink into a void of sleep! But, of course, she needed food. She removed the bedraggled habit and hung it carefully upon a peg in the wall. The leather saddlebags were wet and slippery, but their contents seemed scarcely damp. She had brought only the barest necessities—a dress or two, some fresh under-garments.

When she had washed, changed and smoothed her hair, she descended the stairs stiffly. The room looked cozy and inviting in the candlelight. Evidently they had the place to themselves. There was an appetizing odor of stewed meat and corn bread. John was waiting, and the little landlord settled them at a deal table drawn close to the fireplace. A cheerful blaze crackled on the hearth but outside, thunder rumbled and rain pounded at the windows.

The innkeeper shook his head. He had a straggly beard and a fringe of pale hair. The slant of his eyebrows gave his mild blue eyes a perpetually surprised expression. "A wicked night," he said, "to be sure. River's rising mighty fast."

Laura looked up in alarm. "But we'll be able to cross? We must reach Columbia without delay."

The little man looked worried. "Well, now, ma'am, you've got two likely-lookin' horses. Will they swim, if need be?"

"Yes," John broke in. "They're good swimmers, both of them. But let's not borrow trouble. Maybe the rain will let up soon."

"John!" Laura twisted her fingers nervously, "perhaps we should have gone on."

"Now, see here," John's voice was stern. "No nonsense. It's pitch black except for the lightning. All we can do tonight is try to get some sleep."

But back in her room once more Laura lay, wide-eyed, staring into the darkness. The rain was coming down in torrents, beating furiously against the window pane, drumming ominously on the roof over her head. How would this storm affect their journey? It would make traveling difficult. It might delay them many hours. It might even prevent—No! She closed her teeth grimly.

At last, from pure exhaustion, she fell asleep.

2.

Laura's first waking thought was that the rain had stopped. Her room was dark, but through the uncurtained window she could see a faint trace of gray. She arose without delay, lighted the candle and dressed. Her riding habit was thoroughly dry, but the bottom was caked with mud. She eyed it with distaste as she put it on. She would step into the yard and have the boy brush her skirt thoroughly. Today, no doubt, would bring its own mud. She sighed. These strange, harried days, so different from the old-time happy mornings with Morris and the children on the farm at Far West. She sank on her knees beside the bed. Fervently, she placed her dear ones in God's keeping. She was doing what she had to do. The Prophet had given her his blessing—she could not fail.

Downstairs, she found John and the landlord in worried discussion.

"According to the post boy," the innkeeper was saying, "the river's fair on a rampage. He came in from the south last night. Said he never knew it worse. Now, if you folks will just be patient for a spell, it'll calm down. I'd admire to serve you and make you comfortable here."

"Oh, but we couldn't!" Laura exclaimed. "What I mean is, we must go on at once."

The innkeeper rumpled his thin hair. "If you'll excuse me being so bold, ma'am, it'd be like committing suicide to try crossing that stream on horseback."

"Suppose we have breakfast," John suggested, "before we decide."

The little man rolled away muttering, and Laura's eyes sought John's.

"You won't listen to him, will you?" she demanded. "Dove and Ned are fine horses. They can swim. They've done it before."

"I know, Laura." John averted his eyes and spoke slowly. "I don't quite know how to say this, my dear, but you must think of the children. You would be risking your life. Your responsibility to them—"

"And how about my responsibility to Morris?" Laura faced him with blazing eyes. "The children need him and so do I. Do you think my life would mean anything without Morris? Do you call my existence these past months living? No! There is no one else to help him and I'm going to him." She was almost regal in her defiance. Her head thrown back, small fists clenched at her sides, her breast quivering with the tumult of her breathing.

John watched her in silence, his dark eyes unfathomable. With a sudden change of mood, Laura pointed to the window. "Look, the sun is breaking through the clouds. It's like a benediction. Surely we can't fail."

John shrugged and laughed shortly. "You haven't changed much, have you, Laura? You always did manage to get your own way. Here comes our breakfast," he added.

3.

The landlord bade them a sad farewell, his eyebrows at an alarming angle.

"He's a kind little fellow," John said. "He thinks we're riding to our death—and I'm not sure he's wrong."

"I shan't listen to you," Laura declared. She was almost gay. The cool, washed air was like an elixir. The landscape spread before them a fresh, tender green and the road was surprisingly good. Ned and Dove trotted along at a smart pace as if they, too, were filled with enthusiasm.

"You're very good to me, John," Laura said softly.

John smiled. "Stubborn as you are, I'm fond of you."

But for the most part they rode in silence. The road

became steadily worse. Long stretches had been completely washed away, and at times the horses were knee-deep in mire. The sun had disappeared and the morning mood was gone. They pushed doggedly onward, but the going was slow. It was late afternoon before they drew rein at the river's bank.

Laura's heart sank. The landlord's warnings had been justified. The river was a roaring torrent, swollen to twice its size. She was grateful for John's silence. Not a word of reproach for having forced him into this against his better judgment. The horses stamped and snorted uneasily. Angry clouds were gathering with menacing swiftness; within an hour, perhaps sooner, a heavy storm would be upon them.

Slowly Laura turned her head and met John's eyes. What she saw in them confirmed her own fears. A storm would prevent retracing their way to Rydersville, yet to go ahead seemed utterly impossible. It was appalling, too, that wide sweep of countryside with no visible sign of habitation, not even an abandoned cabin in which they might find shelter.

Laura sighed deeply. In all honesty she must admit her folly. "Well, John," she began, but John was not listening. He was gazing thoughtfully at the angry stream.

"Stay right where you are, Laura," he directed. "I'm going to look around in that direction." He gestured sweepingly toward the east, wheeled his horse swiftly, and rode away along the near bank of the river.

Left alone, Laura dismounted and walked slowly back and forth, her eyes following John. How competent he was. How dependable. A faint hope stirred in her heart. He might even find a way.

John, riding upstream, felt the old familiar thrill of adventure. The dangerous trail behind, the wilderness all about, the rapidly approaching storm—these things filled him with exultation, with a desire to pit his strength against them. Yet he must think first of Laura. He must find a place where it would be less hazardous for the horses to enter the current.

He rode cautiously, scrutinizing the river as Ned picked his way through scrubby growth along the bank. Three hundred yards, more or less, he had covered, when he paused for a moment to reconnoiter. Was it his imagination or was the depth of the water really less at this point? He rode on. Yes, beyond a doubt, the water here was shallower than at the spot where he had left Laura.

Thoughtfully, John turned his horse and started back downstream, pausing to ponder depths, estimating the force of the current—the distance from this point downstream to the regular ford crossing. He must make ample allowance for normal downstream drift.

Dangerous though it was, here seemed to be the safest place for the horses to enter the river. From this point they might be able to ford two-thirds of the four-hundred-yard width, swim forty yards through the strong current, and ford the remaining shallows opposite the normal ford crossing.

Laura was waiting where he had left her. He shouted her name and waved his arms, pointing toward the possible crossing. In a flash, she had mounted and was riding to join him.

5.

John reined in at the spot he had chosen and turned to Laura. "There's no time to go into details, but this place seems to be our one hope. Shall we risk it?"

"Need you ask?"

The trust in her eyes stirred John deeply. *She is brave,* he thought. *Not many women could face this.* He leaned toward her and laid his hand over hers. "We understand each other, my girl. No need to talk about it." For a moment their eyes held, then swiftly John dismounted and seized Dove's halter rope.

"This is just a precaution," he explained, "in case either of them should weaken or try to bolt." He fastened Dove's halter rope securely to Ned's tail, then loosened both girths, patted the animals reassuringly, and swung into his saddle. "Are you ready, Laura?" he asked.

"All ready, John."

"Then tuck up your feet and say your prayers. We're likely to need them."

Knee-deep in the stream, the horses felt their way, snorting, tossing their heads, giving no sign of fear; but John and Laura were taut and vigilant—now giving a little on the reins, now drawing in a bit. Suddenly, without warning, the animals were in over their depth, but after an instant's confusion both started to swim. Laura closed her eyes for a moment and offered silent thanks, but only for a moment. She must be watchful, alert to every new danger, ready to follow John's lead.

And John was in difficulty. Ned, usually so tractable, had determined to turn back. Frantically, he threshed about, churning the water to boiling foam; but John, with short, sharp jerks on the bit and a stinging blow on the horse's rump, was regaining control. Ned was swimming again, unevenly, while John talked to him in a soothing murmur. "Steady, now, old boy. It's all right. Steady now." Gradually, Ned ceased struggling and began swimming strongly, but John knew that they had lost ground.

He also knew that with the animals tied together, Ned's first plunge would have given Laura's mount a violent forward jerk, but in the fight to subdue his terrified horse, John had not dared risk a backward glance. Now, vast relief filled him to see that the little mare was swimming sturdily, calmly, and that Laura, although quite pale, was smiling. John smiled in return, encouragingly he hoped. The current was much stronger than he had believed it to be. Although they had crossed less than half of the deep, fast-flowing stream, they had already been swept almost opposite to the point where he had hoped to land. John was thankful that Laura did not realize the danger. If they were carried much farther downstream, it would mean disaster, for the current there swung sharply in toward a high, precipitous bank. And he was helpless! Perhaps, after all, he should warn Laura. She had courage to face death and there might be something special she would like to do—something about her religion. . . .

Again John turned to look at her. There was an appearance not quite natural. Her exaggerated erectness in the saddle, the rigid line of her jaw, her extreme pallor—He might have known! He recognized that firm set of her mouth. Not only did Laura realize their danger, but she was doing something about it. Firmly and expertly, she was guiding Dove against Ned's downstream flank. And Ned was responding to the thrust of Dove's shoulder against his rump. With a sudden, valiant lunge against the current, Ned began swimming toward the shallow water!

6.

Safe, unbelievably, on the opposite bank, John and Laura looked at each other. It was a moment too intense for words. The horses, heads drooping, breathing in great gasps, stood dripping, quivering spasmodically.

"Laura," John began, then slipping from his saddle, he freed Ned from the halter rope. "Good boy," he said, fondling the animal's soft nose. "Good old Ned."

It was almost dusk. The wind had risen and the sky was completely overcast. John frowned. "It seems cruel to expect more from these poor beasts, but we must push on before the storm breaks."

"Is there a village anywhere near?" Laura questioned.

"I'm afraid not. But the landlord said there were scattered farmhouses eight or ten miles beyond the river. We must hurry. It will soon be dark."

"John," Laura said, "you are not a Mormon, you profess no faith, but you are a fine, good man."

John saw that her eyes were brimming.

"Come, come," he muttered in gruff embarrassment, "no time now for pretty speeches." He bent over his saddle.

Laura's eyes were wet, but she was smiling as she followed him into the unknown dark.

16

"John." Laura rode closer so that she might observe her brother's face. "John, after what we have experienced these last few days, can you doubt the power of prayer?"

"Have I ever said that I doubted it?" John's eyes were fixed on the road ahead, rising and dipping with the gentle contours of the land, bordered with plumy thicket and clumps of cottonwood, washed and glistening in the morning sunlight.

"No," Laura persisted, "you've never said so, but I can't help wondering how you feel about it. Oh, please!" she added hastily as she saw his mouth tighten, "I'm not trying to convert you, dear. It's just that I feel so strongly our Heavenly Father's care and my heart is so full of gratitude to Him—and to you."

John, his bronzed young face impassive, carefully led the way around a bad spot in the road.

Laura sighed and dropped back a pace. If John could only share this feeling—this almost physical sense of God's enfolding love and guidance! From the moment that she had glimpsed that faint light, shining like a tiny beacon in the darkness, Laura had been uplifted. It was only a tallow candle in the window of a crude little cabin, but to Laura and John, soaking wet, weak from hunger and exhausted from three hours of hard riding after their escape from the river, any shelter would have been welcome. It had stopped raining, but a chill wind penetrated their sodden clothing and lashed the shivering horses plodding wearily along strange roads in the night.

For a moment, Laura had forgotten her wretchedness in amazement at the young couple who opened the cabin door. So evidently of gentle breeding, so simple and gracious in their warm hospitality, they seemed the most unlikely people in the world to be living there in the wilderness.

In spite of her eagerness to reach Morris, Laura's own common sense told her that John was right—the horses, at least, needed rest. And the delight of Robert and Susan Spaulding when they learned of her decision was heartening. Guests in this new home in the wilds of Missouri seemed the one thing needed to complete their happiness. In the two nights and a day spent with them, Laura and John had learned of a Boston home—its comforts abandoned for the adventure of life in the West; of blunders made, of hardships endured, all welcomed gaily as priceless new experiences.

What a miracle, Laura thought, *to have been led to such people in our need.* It had seemed like bidding farewell to old friends, when she and John had ridden away this morning, turning in their saddles to wave at Susan and Robert where they stood, arms entwined, framed in their doorway.

Laura stole another glance at John and with a little shock of surprise, found his dark, intent gaze fixed upon her face.

"Laura," he said, "I'd like to get some things straightened out. I know you're grateful to me for coming, but I—" he paused, seeming to grope for words. "The truth is, I came as much for my own sake as for yours. I was restless. Wanted to get away from the farm. Wanted adventure." His mouth twisted in a wry smile. "Don't give me credit for being noble. I'm not like you and Morris. I haven't any desire to reform the world. All I want is to see it. To explore new country—overcome new obstacles."

"The new and the untried." Laura's eyes were shining. "Don't you see, John? That's what all of us are seeking—you, Morris and I, those young Spauldings—pioneers, hewing logs with their own hands to build their home at the outpost of civilization! Yet that little cabin may be the beginning of a great city."

"Maybe so," John admitted, "but do you suppose the Spauldings thought of all that? Wasn't it just a sort of restlessness? The kind of feeling that keeps tormenting me to start for Oregon?"

"Restlessness, perhaps, but the kind that has real purpose as its goal."

John laughed. "Say it, Laura. I know you think I should take life more seriously, but I'm afraid I'm not built that way."

The horses had slackened their pace. Through the clear morning air a meadow lark called sweetly.

"Why should I reproach you?" Laura asked gently. "Morris, too, has a restless temperament, but he found an outlet in Mormonism. I embraced the faith for his sake, but now it has become my life, too. We have found what we wanted, John, but you haven't. You have given up your plans again and again because some of us needed you. You are generous and unselfish."

"That's a woman for you." John grinned and shook his dark head. "I explain how selfish I am and you try to argue me out of it. But there's one more thing." His face hardened. "While we're on the subject, Laura, don't worry because I'm not a Mormon. I respect your faith and your right to uphold it, but somehow I can't accept it." He rode on for a moment in silence, then chuckled suddenly. "Anyhow, I'll find plenty of adventure as long as I stay around you. Come, now, we'd better hurry if we expect to make Columbia by nightfall."

17

1.

"Well, Laura, here we are." John shot a keen glance at his sister and understood her silence. Her lips were trembling and her eyes were wet. "Let's see, now," he went on hastily. "Columbia's the county seat. The jail should be near the Court House and the Court House is sure to be located in the public square."

Laura nodded. Slowly they rode in the deepening twilight. Rows of one-story frame buildings lined the main thoroughfare. A number of teams were hitched outside of the general store, and the dusty street was still crowded with farmers, evidently in town for their Saturday trading.

At the south end of the street was a tree-lined square, centered by a vine-covered frame structure. "There you are," said John. "The Boone County Court House. And over there," he gestured toward the extreme south end of the square where an ugly two-story frame and log building stood well apart from the Court House, "that, I'll wager, is the jail."

"I'm sure you're right, John," Laura agreed, "but perhaps you'd better inquire."

John rode to the opposite side of the street where a man

lounged against a horse trough. "Please, sir, can you direct me to the jail?"

"Why, yes, stranger," the man eyed John curiously. "That's it, over yonder." He motioned toward the building John had marked. "But if you aim to get lodging there, I reckon they're full up."

"Lodging?" John repeated. "Do you mean other people—live there? Just people—not prisoners?"

"Sure. The sheriff and his wife don't need all them rooms. They rent some of 'em out."

"It's the sheriff I'm looking for," John said.

"Well, you'll find him at home," the man drawled, shifting his position and yawning. "Go 'round to the back door. The one on the west side," he called as John thanked him and rode away.

The front of the jail was forbidding, grim and blank, with heavily barred upper windows. John and Laura dismounted, tethered their horses to a hitching-post and made their way around to the west side of the building. Laura's heart lifted a little. There were bright calico curtains and rows of potted plants in the ground floor windows. As John thumped the heavy wooden door, she could feel her heart pounding like an echo. With shaking fingers she straightened her bonnet and smoothed her hair, then, taking a kerchief from her pocket, she scrubbed her face, vigorously. She must try to make herself a little more presentable before she saw Morris.

John rapped again, sharply. "Sheriff!" he called. "Is the sheriff here?"

There was the sound of a chair scraping on the floor, a shuffle of feet, and the door was flung open. The man who faced them was thick-set and middle-aged. His jaw was heavy and under his straggling iron-gray hair small, beady eyes regarded them. "Wha'dya want?" he demanded sourly.

Laura shrank back and John placed a protecting arm

around her. "Is this the Boone County jail?" he asked. "Are you the sheriff?"

"Yes. This is the Boone County jail and I'm Jonathan Scott, the sheriff." The sharp eyes were appraising them shrewdly.

"I understand you have some prisoners here," John's manner was casual. "Some Mormons—Morris Phelps, Parley P. Pratt and King Follet. My sister, here—"

"I'm Mrs. Phelps, Sheriff Scott," Laura broke in, "the wife of one of your prisoners."

"That so?" the man's tone was indifferent, faintly contemptuous.

"Yes," Laura hurried on, "and we've ridden a hundred and fifty miles to see my husband. It was a hard journey," she added after a momentary silence.

Scott spat a stream of tobacco juice and wiped his mouth with the back of his hairy hand. "Guess you made the trip of your own free will, ma'am."

"Oh, I did." Laura was doing her best to control her agitation. "I knew it would be dangerous and wearying but I had to come—to see my husband—to be near him during his trial. Please, may I go to him now?"

" 'Fraid not, Mrs. Phelps. We don't take kindly to visitors in this jail. Leastwise not womenfolks."

Laura swayed a little and John's arm tightened around her. "See here, sheriff," he protested, "my sister has gone through five days of hell and risked her life crossing the river. You have no right to keep her from her husband. It's inhuman!"

"Better change your tone, young man." Another volley of tobacco juice cleared John's boot-tips by a narrow margin. There was an ugly glitter in Scott's eyes.

"John," Laura laid a restraining hand on her brother's arm. "Please." She took a step forward. Her eyes, shadowed by bluish circles of fatigue, were dark and anguished. "Mr. Scott," she pleaded, "in the name of God I entreat you—don't send me away without seeing my husband."

"Jonathan, Jonathan!" A woman's voice called from within the house. The sheriff's head jerked toward the sound and he stepped aside nimbly. A woman of huge bulk filled the doorway. Her eyes, pale blue and twinkling in a chubby face, were brightly alert. "What's all this?" she demanded. "What's the trouble, Jonathan?"

"This here woman," the sheriff explained, "is the wife of that Mormon, Phelps. She wants to see him."

"And why shouldn't she?" the woman retorted. She faced Scott, arms akimbo, withering his faint protests with a look; then, turning to Laura and John she smiled, her cheeks rippling into soft folds. "I'm Mrs. Scott," she said. "Won't you come in and sit?"

"Oh, thank you." Laura's gratitude was in her voice.

Mrs. Scott led the way into a large room. It seemed to cover half of the entire ground floor and obviously served as a combination sitting room, dining room and kitchen. Laura and John followed the woman, and the sheriff, muttering, trailed behind them.

Mrs. Scott indicated chairs and seated herself upon a sturdy bench. "So," she said, "it's Morris Phelps you've come to see?"

"You don't know what it means to me, Mrs. Scott," Laura's eyes clung to the round, good-natured face. "My brother and I have come a very long distance. I've left four young children at home." Her eyes filled.

"Don't you worry none, Miz Phelps." There was grim finality in the woman's voice. "My husband ain't got the least objection to your visiting your husband. Have you, Jonathan?" She shot out the question with explosive force.

"No, I 'spose not," the sheriff grumbled, "but don't go blamin' me if anything happens."

Mrs. Scott sniffed audibly and heaved herself up from the bench. "Come along with me, Miz Phelps. Your brother can stay here with the sheriff." She started toward a flight of stairs in the corner of the room. "We keep the prisoners up yonder."

"Your husband's a right pleasant fellow," Mrs. Scott volunteered, as she preceded Laura up the stairway, "a real gentleman. You wouldn't believe," she puffed, holding to the stair rail while she paused for breath, "what I have to put up with sometimes."

Laura murmured sympathetically and the ascent continued with frequent pauses for rest and a running fire of comment by the sheriff's wife. Mr. Phelps' anxiety about his wife. His frequent references to the children—wasn't one of them named Mary Ann? *The woman is kind,* Laura thought. *I have waited this long. I must be patient a little longer.*

Like an echo of her thoughts, Laura heard Mrs. Scott's question. "How long since you last saw your husband?"

"Early in April—almost three months ago."

Mrs. Scott paused on the step above, panting. "You'll find him changed," she warned. "He don't complain, but he's been right poorly." She wagged her head. "That Richmond jail! I wouldn't treat a cur dog like them prisoners was treated."

Laura drew a sharp breath. "I'm sure you wouldn't," she agreed after a moment. "If you're rested, could we go on, now?"

"Why, yes," Mrs. Scott conceded, "I expect we could." And once again, with Laura following, she began to climb the stairs. Another step—another . . .

"Sam!" At Mrs. Scott's summons a tall, loose-jointed youth in blue jeans uncoiled himself from a chair in the corner and came toward them. "This here's Miz Phelps," the sheriff's wife announced. "You let her talk to her husband for half an hour. And don't eavesdrop! She might have something private to tell him."

Laura braced herself at the threshold. The key was grating in the lock. At last she was to see Morris.

2.

In a small, bare room on the second floor of the jail Laura was preparing for bed. Conflicting emotions, shifting with bewildering rapidity, had left her confused and weary, but through it all ran the deep, underlying consciousness of protection—the feeling she had tried that morning to express to John. In the face of all obstacles she was actually here, under the same roof with Morris. Separated from him by only the width of the corridor! And the surprising suggestion had come from Mrs. Scott herself. Blinded by tears after taking leave of Morris, Laura had been met at the foot of the stairs by the sheriff's wife. "I've just been tellin' Jonathan," she announced, "I don't ca'late no harm could come of our giving you board and lodging. Your brother can go to the tavern, but you can stay here if you're a mind to. Providin' you can pay in advance, of course."

"Well, I don't like it." The sheriff scowled. "We ain't never boarded relations of prisoners. Don't reckon the County'd like it, neither."

"You and the County make me tired," Mrs. Scott had remarked placidly.

Laura found herself smiling at the recollection.

The room was little more than a stall; one of three, directly opposite the prison quarters. It was scarcely large enough to hold the narrow cot and crude pine washstand. Wide cracks in the board partition afforded little privacy when the adjoining room was occupied. But what did these things matter? She was near Morris. Every day, she could see him and talk with him, even though bars did separate them. Laura sighed. Those bars. What a disappointment they had been. Sam, the guard, had unbolted a heavy oaken door and she had followed him eagerly inside, only to be confronted by an inner door, its upper half of bars.

Midway in the weaving of a smooth brown braid, Laura's fingers paused for a moment. Morris. How pale and thin he was. It had wrung her heart to see it and the dullness of his deep, sunken eyes. To hide her shock she had chattered volubly—of the children—of the new little home in Montrose—of the Spauldings—anything, everything. And almost imperceptibly, faint color had crept into Morris' cheeks; the set look had disappeared from his smile.

All too soon the guard had come for her. But there would be tomorrow's visit and other visits in the coming week. . . .

Laura blew out the candle and parted the calico curtains. The town was dark and still. She could hear distant hoof beats and the faint creak of wagon wheels. Some farmer, delayed in the village, starting for home. Home! If she and Morris could be driving home through the night—but it would not be much longer. The trial would soon be over.

Abruptly, Laura left the window and crossed the room to her cot. That despairing look in Morris' eyes when she had mentioned the trial! She had arrived none too soon to check the slow ebb of his courage. She must think of new ways to cheer him, to renew his hope, to restore his confidence and faith in God's unfailing mercy. Far away in the night a whippoorwill cried plaintively and Laura drifted into slumber.

18

1.

The last juror was being sworn in. Laura moved her head slowly from left to right to relax the strained, taut feeling in the muscles of her neck. It seemed a long, long time since court had convened.

The courtroom was crowded with spectators. Laura could feel their eyes appraising her avidly. "What did they expect to see?" she asked John bitterly. "After all, Mormons are human beings." John, seated beside her, made no reply, but laid his big hand over hers and squeezed it. Orson Pratt was on her other side. It was comforting to have them there although there was nothing they could do. Many in the crowd were women. *How would they feel,* Laura thought, *if their husbands were in Morris' place?* But their husbands weren't Mormons. She lifted her head proudly. Her eyes were calm as she surveyed the room.

Morris was sitting beside Lawyer Donephon, his big body rigid, his eyes fixed on a point straight ahead. Deep wrinkles furrowed his pale, drawn face and his lips were set in a hard line. Laura's heart ached for him. If only she could reach out to him—touch him—perhaps catch his eye. She wondered if she could force herself to smile. Those hours she'd spent with him. She knew she had left him stronger, more confident, better able to face this ordeal. But now she wasn't sure of her own confidence.

A ripple of anticipation ran through the courtroom. The bailiff had finished with the jurors. The judge leaned forward. He had a broad, flat face, unhealthy-looking yellow; his hands were square with thick, stubby fingers. Laura stared at those hands stabbing at his papers. She dreaded to shift her eyes. Then the judge was speaking, in a rasping drawl. He was hunched forward, peering down at the prosecuting attorney—instructing the prosecution to proceed.

Laura tried to swallow. Her throat was dry. Her heart seemed to shudder with every beat. She looked at Morris. He was leaning forward, his eyes riveted on the prosecuting attorney.

The prosecuting attorney rose. "Your Honor," his voice was cool and deliberate. Laura could hear every word, but for the first shocked moment her brain refused to grasp his purpose. He was offering a motion for continuance. The prosecution regretted that it had been "unable to produce certain important and material witnesses, therefore . . ."

Donephon was on his feet, moving toward the bench. "Your Honor!" His voice shook with anger. "The defense protests!"

Even in the midst of her despair Laura felt a dull surprise. She would not have supposed Lawyer Donephon capable of such fire. She leaned forward in her seat, clinging to John's hand, her eyes fastened on the judge's face, as he listened to Donephon's vehement appeal that the trial might proceed. The judge's eyes were narrowed—he seemed to be listening intently. Laura closed her eyes. The judge *must* understand. She *willed* him to understand . . .

"Your Honor," the prosecuting attorney's cold voice cut in sharply, "the prosecution objects."

"Objection sustained," the judge drawled. There was an excited buzz of voices. The judge rapped for order. Lawyer Donephon was resuming his seat. Quiet settled over the courtroom.

Orson Pratt was whispering something, but Laura did not hear what he said. She nodded automatically without taking her eyes from the judge's mask-like face. She laced her fingers in a tight grip and waited. The judge deliberated for a long moment. His stubby fingers poked among his papers. He cleared his throat . . .

Laura drooped in her chair. All the strength had drained out of her body. John and Orson, their heads almost touching, bent toward her — indignant, sympathetic, comforting — she wished she had energy enough to speak to them, to ask them to move their heads. She could not see Morris. He was being led from the courtroom. She tried desperately to get hold of herself, to face this situation. The motion of the prosecution had been granted. The case would be continued until the next regular session of the District Court. And the prisoner would be held without bail.

2.

Twilight was falling over Columbia. Laura sat on a secluded bench in a corner of the public square. She stirred and sighed. She had been here since late afternoon, alone, thinking things through. John had understood. *There are times,* she thought, *when no human being can help.* She looked down at the square toe of her shoe.

The State of Missouri had no intention of giving the Mormon prisoners a fair trial. That she knew. It was not a conviction that had come suddenly. It had been growing all through these months of anxiety and suspense, and the outcome of today's court session had made it perfectly clear to her. She'd accepted everything—Morris' arrest, his indictment, the continuance of the case in April—had made herself believe each time that eventually justice would triumph.

Morris was innocent. There must be no more weeks of waiting. Now was the time to do something. She drew a long, deep breath and arose from the bench. She must find John and Orson at once.

19

1.

On the morning of July Fourth Laura awoke at dawn. This was the day! All was quiet. It would be some time before the Scotts were up and about.

Lying motionless in her narrow cot, Laura reviewed the plan of escape. She had worked it out carefully with Orson Pratt and John, and bit by bit, during the past two days, she had explained it to Morris. Nothing must go wrong. Every detail must be so clear in her mind that no upset could confuse her.

Orson and John were supposedly leaving town. She was to go to their hotel and publicly bid them goodbye, but they would circle back through the fields and be waiting in the thicket with the horses. Orson's horse was for his brother, the Apostle, but both Morris and King Follet needed mounts, so John would ride Ned and lead Dove. Dear little Dove. It would be hard to part with her. It was frightening, too, to think of being left here alone with no horses, no means of escape. Laura pushed the thought away.

Her mouth set grimly. It was her part to make sure that the prisoners had their supper at sundown as usual. John had made the reason clear. At sundown, in the shadowy twilight, it would be much easier to elude pursuers; especially in the midst of crowds and holiday confusion.

Laura frowned. She must be sure that Morris understood everything. He and King Follet would have to protect Parley Pratt. Pratt was an Apostle. Nothing must prevent his escape. "And no matter what happens, Laura," John had warned her, "keep your hands off. If you take any active part, it will be a penitentiary offense." She must remember that. There was so much to remember.

The three prisoners would be lying in wait, ready to overpower the jailer when he brought their supper. Then they would run downstairs, out through the kitchen, and make for the thicket half a mile away. Laura's heart was thumping. Morris to be free at last! How was she ever to go through this day—live the endless hours until sunset?

She flung off the bedclothes, arose and walked to the window. A fresh breeze fluttered the calico curtains and the sun, fully risen, beamed from a cloudless sky. Perfect weather to bring crowds to the day's celebration.

Laura dressed rapidly. A smell of coffee and the clatter of dishes told her that Mrs. Scott was already downstairs. As she entered the corridor, Sam was unlocking the prison quarters across the hall, the breakfast tray on a small table beside the door. Laura could feel a guilty flush creeping upward from her throat. Hastily, she averted her eyes from the tray and returned the deputy's "Good morning." Sam was quite obviously dressed for the festivities, self-conscious and awkward in tight-fitting gray trousers and short blue coat.

"Are you having the day off, Sam?" Laura asked.

"Part time, just. Me and the sheriff's goin' to spell each other."

Laura hugged the thought as she descended the stairs.

There would be only one man to fight—not two. Her cheeks burned.

"Morning, Miz Phelps." The sheriff's wife gestured toward the table. "Set right down. Scott's had his breakfast. Left early. Lots of folks in town today—likely to be some fights."

She, too, was dressed for the occasion. A basque of vivid green outlined her massive bosom, and a red and black striped skirt billowed around her thick ankles. "My sakes," she complained, "holidays just mean more work, and I'm all wore out as it is." She slapped a plate of steaming fried mush before Laura and sloshed coffee into a heavy cup. "You look sort of puny yourself, Miz Phelps. Are you feverish or somethin'?"

"Oh, no. I'm quite well, thanks." Laura fixed her eyes on her plate. The telltale flush deepened. But the return of the sheriff claimed his wife's attention. He stood, twirling his hat, just inside the doorway.

"I been thinkin'," he began cautiously, "you might cook up an early supper for them prisoners. Goin' to be a band concert and speech-makin'," he added hopefully. "We could get away by five o'clock."

Laura choked and set down her cup with a clatter. It was still broad daylight at five o'clock. John and Orson—could they do anything? She must see them at once. She must . . .

"Now, ain't that just like a man, Miz Phelps?" Mrs. Scott had poured herself a cup of coffee; she waddled to the table and eased herself down opposite Laura. "If you think, Jonathan Scott, that I'm a'going to spend Independence Day bendin' over a hot stove—"

"I never," the sheriff protested. "I just thought—"

"Well, you just thought wrong." Mrs. Scott eyed her husband coldly. "I don't suppose you remember," she said, "that the Public Dinner Committee promised to send over our evenin' meal? The prisoners will eat at their regular time."

"Oh, all right," said the sheriff, resentfully, "have it your own way." He clapped on his hat and closed the door behind him with a terrific bang.

Laura's fingers loosened their grip on the table's edge.

"That man!" Mrs. Scott shook her head. "If I listened to him we'd never make a cent. Why should I waste food when we're promised a free meal? Anyhow, I've got enough to do."

"Oh, please," Laura rose eagerly, "let me help you." *I can't sit and wait,* she thought. *I must keep busy.*

As they worked through the morning, washing dishes, making beds, putting rooms in order, Laura was dimly conscious of Mrs. Scott's voice rising and falling endlessly. There was no occasion to answer. She needn't even listen. In terrifying detail Laura was picturing a scene. Sam, or the sheriff, entering from the corridor, unlocking the inner door—opening it barely wide enough to admit the tray. King Follet and Morris crouched just inside, ready to spring upon the jailer, to fling the door wide, to open the way for the Apostle Pratt and follow him to freedom.

A sudden, echoing silence aroused Laura. Mrs. Scott's twinkling eyes were regarding her curiously. "I'm sorry," Laura said, "I didn't quite hear—"

"I said, 'How long are you planning to stay on here?' "

"Oh!" Laura swallowed hard. "Probably for several days. Orson Pratt is eager to get back to Quincy. My brother and he are leaving today. Some—some friends are coming through here on their way to Iowa. I shall wait for them." It sounded convincing. Laura was surprised and a little disturbed to find that she could lie so glibly. But surely it was justified.

The sheriff did not come home at noon.

"Sulkin', most likely," his wife surmised. "It's right cozy

just the two of us, and no man around," she chuckled. The mere sight of her plate, heaped with meat and vegetables, swimming in a sea of gravy, made Laura's stomach contract into a hard ball; but she forced herself to eat. Mrs. Scott was shrewd, and must not be made suspicious.

When the meal was finished and the kitchen had been put to rights, Laura looked at the clock. "I must hurry," she said, "my brother will be leaving soon and I want to say goodbye." A wave of nausea swept up and receded, leaving her cold and shaking, but Mrs. Scott had not noticed. She was rocking noisily and fanning herself with her apron.

"Go right ahead, Miz Phelps," she said. "I'm going to rest a spell before I go out."

2.

Along the crowded streets, Laura hurriedly made her way back toward the jail. She would be late for her regular visit with Morris. She had not meant to be away so long, but John and Orson had insisted. She must wait until they were ready to depart and bid them goodbye, before plenty of witnesses. It had been hard to smile as they rode away. Dove had whinnied reproachfully and balked a little. If they had dared to procure an extra horse in the village—but, of course, they couldn't. Perhaps Morris would ride Dove. Oh, what did it matter which horse he rode, as long as he escaped!

She was troubled at the number of soldiers mingling with the crowd. Could it be that they suspected something? *Nonsense,* she reassured herself. *This is Independence Day.* From a pole in a near-by window a flag was suspended, a crude banner of white with the word "Liberty" in large red letters. *Liberty,* Laura thought. *How little these people realize what that word can mean.* From the public square guns boomed in salute, followed by a blare of trumpets. The band concert was about to begin.

The Scott's kitchen was stuffy and quiet, with the strange stillness of an empty house. Laura removed her bonnet and pushed the damp hair back from her forehead. She turned her head to listen, then tiptoed to the foot of the stairway. She must see Morris once more. Resolutely, she started up the stairs, the old boards creaking beneath her light tread.

Chair legs banged down and Sam's long shape appeared at the head of the stairs.

"Oh, it's you, Mrs. Phelps," he said.

"Yes." Laura paused a moment. "I know it's late, but I've been telling my brother goodbye. May I see Mr. Phelps —just for a few minutes?"

Sam hesitated. "Well, now, maybe it ain't quite regular, but I reckon it's all right. Come on up."

Laura ran up the remaining steps and followed Sam down the corridor. "Here's your wife, Phelps," he called, as he opened the outer door. But after admitting Laura, Sam returned to his post in the corridor. It was evident that he was taking no chances. He was in charge during the sheriff's absence. He would not leave them alone today.

Laura spoke with forced gaiety. "Well, Morris, the boys have gone. Bidding them goodbye is what delayed me." Her face was pressed to the bars. Her dark eyes clung to his. Love, longing, desperate courage—all that she dared not say was in that look. Morris' lips trembled.

"Judging from the sounds," he said, "there must be quite a celebration."

"Oh, yes." Laura spoke distinctly, loud enough for Pratt and Follet to hear. "Even you are to take part. You are to have some of the holiday food. But your supper will be served at the usual time—you won't have much longer to wait."

Morris nodded, his eyes intent. "Did the boys send any message?"

"Yes," Laura answered. "They said to tell all of you to

stop worrying about lawyers and trials, that everything will come out right. I hated to see them go," she added slowly. "I watched them ride away toward the forest and—for a moment I was desperate. But that was foolish, I know. Our Heavenly Father will watch over us."

A door slammed below. Laura clutched the bars. "God keep you, dear," she whispered. "Faith will protect you." And then, aloud, "I must go now. Goodbye." She was conscious of Sam in the doorway and faced him, smiling with stiff lips. "Thank you," she said, and started down the stairs.

3.

"This waitin' around is a lot of blamed foolishness." The sheriff glowered. "I'm hungry and I want my supper."

Mrs. Scott rocked placidly. "No hurry, Jonathan. Supper'll be along 'most any minute, now."

Laura stole another glance at the clock. Almost seven. Only a short time now. . . .

Sam came clattering down the stairway whistling between his teeth.

"Where are you goin'?" the sheriff demanded.

"Oh, just out and around. Ain't this my time off?"

"Well, you stay where I can find you. Liquor's flowing and I look for trouble."

"Better go look for our supper, first," Mrs. Scott suggested. "I'm gettin' a mite hungry myself. You know, Miz Phelps," she confided when the sheriff had gone, "Jonathan's all right if you know how to handle him."

Laura felt vaguely remorseful. Mrs. Scott was mercenary but she had been kind. It was a poor return—planning to trick these people. But the sheriff's entrance with the food broke off the thought like a snapped thread. Stiff and wooden, she stood near the window, conscious of sound and movement;

shouts and laughter, music—loud and strident—from the nearby bandstand; and then, from within the room, the sheriff's shuffling, heavy tread, as burdened with the tray, he made his way laboriously up the stairway. All of Laura's sense perceptions seemed centered in her ears. Every sound had a meaning now. The slow steps along the corridor. The grate of a key. The rattle of dishes. The creaking of a hinge. In a moment, now . . .

"Whatever ails you, Miz Phelps? You're actin' mighty queer." Mrs. Scott's tone was querulous, her pale eyes bright with suspicion.

Laura tried to answer but her throat contracted. She stared at the woman in fascinated dread. A fly buzzed loudly in the stillness. And then it came—a rending crash, a thud, the sheriff's bellow, "Help! Help! Help!"

"Jonathan!"

It was incredible, Laura thought, that the woman could move so swiftly. Already she was across the room, her unwieldly bulk charging up the stairway, her screams of rage mingling with the frightful tumult of blows and stamping feet.

Morris and the sheriff were fighting their way down. Laura could see them clearly. The sheriff was a big man, but Morris was fighting with the fury of desperation. Back and forth they writhed, panting, grunting, slammed to the wall—crashing against the stair rail.

Someone was sobbing in soft, shuddering gasps. Herself? Laura was mildly surprised. But she could not move. Mind and body alike were numb.

Mrs. Scott had reached the landing and was grappling with Morris, pulling at his arms, dragging her weight upon him, but he wrenched himself free of her and leaped, plunging downward several steps and carrying the sheriff with him. The woman's face was purple and contorted. She shrieked and flung herself down upon Morris, kicking and clawing.

She tore at his hair. Her finger-nails raked his cheek, leaving thin, red streaks.

Something snapped within Laura and a wild rage seized her. She caught up a chair and, holding it high above her head, rushed to the foot of the stairway. In a moment the struggling trio would be close enough. She could crash the chair down upon that fat, venomous woman. She could. . . .

"Laura!" The horror and despair in Morris' cry brought her to her senses. The chair slipped from her grasp and crashed to the floor. John's warning! She had completely forgotten it. She shrank back, trembling. God be thanked that Morris had seen her and had strength left to call out.

On the landing above, Pratt and Follet were waiting, ready to dash for freedom. Another lunge brought Morris rolling to the bottom of the stairs. In a moment he was on his feet and the Scotts swarmed over him again. The way was clear. Pratt and Follet were racing down the stairs. Laura wrung her hands. Surely they would help! Surely this dreary struggle would not go on and on . . .

But Pratt and Follet were unable to dislodge the Scotts, clinging to Morris like limpets—doggedly persistent—blind to the escape of the other two, who ran into the night. But Morris had seen them go. His face, Laura thought, showed that. To have borne the brunt of combat and now be left alone—alone with no one to help him!

Then, suddenly, Laura remembered. They were not alone. Not helpless. "Oh, Thou God of Abraham, Isaac and Jacob!" she prayed. "Deliver Thy servant!" She thought she had whispered it, but her voice rang out, firm and clear and strong. And Morris heard. With a sudden, tremendous effort he wrenched himself free and was gone.

The sheriff scrambled to his feet and raced in pursuit, but Mrs. Scott turned for a moment, in the doorway. "You snake!"

she screamed. "You ungrateful Mormon hussy! You'll pay for this."

Laura got to the door somehow. She clutched the casing and pulled herself up on tiptoe, her eyes straining toward the massed blackness of the thicket.

"Stop that Mormon! Stop that Mormon!" Mrs. Scott's raucous cries were echoed by the gathering crowd. Laura saw the woman stumble and sprawl on the ground, but in a moment she was up again, still running, still screaming. The band had stopped playing. Men armed with clubs and fence stakes were racing toward the thicket. Armed riflemen vaulted into their saddles and galloped toward the main road. What possible chance was there for Morris—for John—for any of them?

I must get away, Laura thought. But she was very tired. She had been standing in that doorway forever. She closed her eyes. Dogs barked. Cows bawled. If the noise would only stop perhaps she could move. *But what does it matter?* she thought. *What does anything matter?*

Above the din came the piercing blast of a bugle. As it died away Laura heard a shout, "We've caught one of those damned Mormons!" Then another, "We'll roast him alive—over a slow fire!" The crowd took up the cry, "We'll roast him alive—alive!" a dreadful rhythmic chant.

Laura found herself in the open. Mrs. Scott and the sheriff were coming. Close behind them King Follet marched between two soldiers. Hot prickles circled Laura's throat and ran down her spine. King Follet—not Morris. Oh, thank God! Sam followed behind the soldiers. He was leading Dove. Her horse—that would mean . . .

"There she is. She helped them!" The sheriff was pointing to Laura. He was far away, then suddenly very close; so close that Laura recoiled from the red, furious face, the bulging, beady eyes. "You damned dirty Mormon!" he roared. His hairy hands doubled into huge fists.

Curiously, Laura felt no terror; but for that matter, she felt nothing at all. The sheriff towered over her. "Get out of my sight," he said hoarsely. "Get out of my sight before I—" His fist came up like a hammer.

"Jonathan!" Mrs. Scott struck down the arm. "You dumb fool," she hissed, "ain't you got no sense? Get this crowd away before they start askin' her questions." She gripped Laura's arm and jerked her into the shadows. "Damn you," she said softly, "get away from here and stay away. You can send for your clothes." She released Laura's arm with a vicious shove that sent her staggering into the midst of the throng now surging back toward the bandstand. The music had started again. The crowd closed in on Laura and carried her along, jostling, pulling — someone was pulling her away from the crowd. Someone was talking to her—a tall, slender lad. "This way," he kept urging. "This way." She obeyed without question, too exhausted to resist. It was quite dark now. Before a thick clump of shrubbery the boy halted. "Here," he said, thrusting Laura into the shadows. "Stay here. And don't move till I come back."

20

1.

Morris, his breath coming in painful gasps, had reached the welcome concealment of the thicket. The shouts of the mob were fainter here, the clamor not so deafening. For a moment he stood, head inclined, listening intently. Then leaves rustled, a twig snapped and John was beside him, leading Ned.

Morris tried to speak but no sound came. He wavered toward the horse. John seized his arm. "Steady, man. I'll help you mount." He crouched beside the horse. "Up you go, now."

Morris braced a foot on John's hand and lurched into the saddle. He gripped the reins and the whip that John thrust into his hands. Ned reared and snorted.

"That road runs through the timber," John said, pointing to the north. "Follow it to the sawmill, then take the left fork to the North road. Good luck, Morris," He slapped Ned across the rump and the horse leaped forward.

Morris turned in the saddle. "Take care of Laura," he called.

The Mill road was twisted and uneven. Ned wove in and

out of the timber, never slackening speed. Morris had scarcely adjusted himself to the saddle when the mill loomed in sight. He reined in and wheeled the horse into the left fork, up a short, steep slope and onto the North road.

Morris gave his horse free rein. Ned raced along, his hoofs clattering in rhythmical beats over the hard-packed dirt road. The evening air felt cool and soothing to Morris' scratched face. He glanced backward. There was no one in pursuit. A surge of exhilaration filled him. He was free—free.

Blood from the scratches on his face trickled into his mouth. He spat vigorously. The road was rising gently through rolling hills to a ridge about a mile straight north. Ned was slackening speed. Morris reined him to a trot.

At the ridge the road dipped sharply to a hollow. Morris pulled Ned to a walk as they started downhill. He strained his ears, alert for sounds of pursuers. In the shelter of the hollow, he halted. Clumps of willows, dark and forbidding, were massed along a creek on the east side of the road. Frogs croaked hoarsely from within. Morris flicked Ned lightly with the whip and sent him forward to the ridge beyond, then drew rein and sat motionless, listening. He had not been mistaken. He had heard hoof beats—could hear them now quite distinctly.

Morris glanced at the road beyond, then back toward the willows. The hoof beats were growing louder. Morris whirled his horse and crashed downward toward the willow clump.

Twilight was fading. Stars were beginning to twinkle in a moonless sky. Morris slid from the saddle and dropped Ned's reins to the ground. He was concealed from the road, yet he could see the crest of the ridge to the north. The hoof beats were very close now. Then suddenly they ceased. In the sudden silence a cricket droned in the gloom. The riders had paused at the top of the ridge. Could they be Pratt and Follet? He dared not attempt to find out.

There was a sound of horses descending the hill—stopping in the hollow. Ned stirred and the willows crackled. Morris' heart contracted. He nuzzled Ned's head close to his shoulder and soothed him with gentle pats. Laura's words came to him — "Faith will protect you" — he believed that. Yet it seemed a long time before those horses began moving uphill.

Morris peered around the willows, straining his eyes toward the road. Two horsemen, their dark forms hunched forward in their saddles, were nearing the crest of the north ridge. They halted and turned their horses to face the east. They were gesturing toward the willows and the faint sound of their voices came to Morris in the stillness. Then one began shaking his head and pointing to the north. Their voices, raised in argument, trailed bits of talk in the night breeze. "Willows," Morris heard. Then, "Hell!—road ahead." The frogs croaked lustily.

Suddenly one of the men whirled his horse and rode forward. He paused, turned in his saddle and motioned urgently to his companion. Morris held his breath, but at last, after a lingering look toward the willows, the second horseman followed. There was only a pad of hoofs, fading in the distance.

2.

The big dipper hung in the north. Morris judged that it was nearing midnight when he came out from the willows. Even now, he was probably taking a desperate chance in going forward. But there was no other choice for him. He must be out of the vicinity before daybreak. He couldn't go back to Columbia. If he tried skirting back through the hills, he'd never find the main road again. He must get ahead. He wouldn't be really safe until he reached the Mississippi.

He mounted and walked Ned slowly up the hill, scanning both sides of the road warily. At the top of the hill he laid the whip lightly across Ned's back. The horse needed no urging—he shot ahead at full speed. Morris held him to a steady gallop, slowed only for short intervals, that Ned might regain his wind. The road dipped—curved through rolling hills. Morris had lost his hat. The night breeze ruffled his hair. The dreary months in prison seemed to be dropping behind with the miles. Freedom was a tonic. He was alive again. He had some ninety miles ahead of him—miles that must be covered at night. . . . He squared his shoulders. He would get to Quincy. Nothing could stop him.

On and on and on . . . drumming of hoofs, road slipping backward—always backward. A little before daybreak Ned slowed down. Morris could see that the horse was spent. His own spirits ebbed. Blood had dried on his face and the skin felt tight and stiff. A spot between his shoulders ached abominably. Questions stabbed at his mind. Had John got back to Laura? Was she safe? What had happened to Pratt and Follet? They were men—could shift for themselves. But Laura . . . How could he have felt so excited and almost happy? It was an empty victory, with Laura left behind; yet it was the only way. He had to believe that.

Faint gray light was beginning to streak the sky. The road had dropped into bottom lands, dotted with thick shrubbery.

Ned's pace was very slow, now; his head hung low. Morris leaned forward in the saddle and stroked the quivering neck. "Good old boy. Hard going, you've had." Ned lifted his head and dropped it again, wearily. All at once Morris realized that he was weak and hungry and utterly miserable. It was quite light now. No longer safe to be on the road. He turned Ned into a thicket.

21

1.

Left alone in the darkness Laura sank down, a small, inert heap concealed by overhanging branches. She could not think —she could only feel. There was a leaden weight inside of her; a leaden weight filled with sharp pain that reached out and gripped and twisted her. The pain eased. She fought nausea. She mustn't be sick. There was something she must do . . . something . . . She sat up and pushed her hair back from her hot forehead. That boy. Who was he and why had he hidden her here? She must get away before he returned.

She got to her knees and stood up, shakily. The band was playing a rollicking march, but the yelling and confusion had subsided. Perhaps now, she could slip away without being noticed. Somewhere, a safe distance from the Scotts. Somewhere that she could watch for John. . . .

Someone was coming. She drew back into the shadows and held her breath, but the footsteps and voices came closer.

"There she is, Father. See?"

Laura recognized the young, excited voice. The lad stepped forward eagerly and seized her arm, pulling her toward a man and a woman who stood close by.

"Randolph," the man spoke in mild reproof and the boy dropped Laura's arm.

"My name is Richardson," the man said, "and this is my wife."

Laura mutely inclined her head. In the darkness she could not see their faces, but the man's voice was kind. "I'm—Mrs. Phelps," she said, unsteadily.

"My son tells me that the sheriff has been abusing you." Mr. Richardson's pleasant drawl invited confidence, but dared she trust him?

"You are very kind," she began, "but—"

The woman took a swift step forward and laid her hand on Laura's arm. "I don't blame you for hesitating. You've been badly frightened and I'm afraid Randolph was a little abrupt."

Laura's eyes stung with sudden tears. The woman seemed so kind.

"You're right, Martha," Mr. Richardson said approvingly. "Mrs. Phelps," he went on, "all I know about you is that you are a woman and in trouble. My wife and I want to help you; what can we do for you?"

"If you could take me to the village inn," Laura said, "I should be greatly obliged."

"Are you alone, Mrs. Phelps?" Mr. Richardson seemed hesitant.

"Yes." *Better not mention John,* Laura thought. They had planned to meet at the inn. If she were only there now—alone. The pain was beginning to clutch her again.

"Well," Mrs. Richardson said emphatically, "the inn is no place for a woman alone; at least, not now. You must come to our home."

"Oh, no," Laura protested. "I couldn't—"

"My wife is right, Mrs. Phelps." Mr. Richardson spoke as if the matter were settled. "Now, then," he added briskly,

"I must be getting back to my livery stable. You go along with my wife and Randolph. I'll be home before long."

"But I must go to the inn." Despairingly, Laura realized that she would have to tell them about John. "My brother—" she broke off with a sharp cry and bent over, her arms laced across her middle. She felt Mrs. Richardson's arm around her. The pain ceased, then stabbed at her again. What would these people think of her? She no longer cared. Her pride was gone. She could fight no longer. She was going to be very sick.

2.

Lingering in the pleasant borderland of sleep, Laura became dreamily aware of sunlight streaming through crisp, white curtains and across a gay patchwork quilt. She was blissfully content. She did not want to wake up. Something was crouching, waiting to pounce upon her. Something grim and ugly that she must face.

Her eyes flew wide open and she sat bolt upright in the high four-poster bed. Unfamiliar objects reeled crazily and she lay down again, quickly; but in a little while the dizziness passed. She was remembering now. The jail break—the sheriff's abuse—the Richardsons. That was why she was in this wide, soft bed.

She lay very quiet, a shamed flush staining her cheeks. The humiliation of knowing that strangers had seen her and ministered to her in her abject misery!

Laura pushed back the coverlet and slowly swung her feet to the bright braided rug beside the bed. She sat on the edge of the bed for a moment. Her head was quite clear, now. Muffled by distance, she could hear voices and morning sounds. Her clothes were spread neatly on a chair near the bed. She rose and walked unsteadily to the chair. She must dress at once, go to the Richardsons and tell them everything.

3.

Laura hesitated in the doorway of a big cheerful kitchen. Mr. and Mrs. Richardson were having breakfast at a table near the window. A stripe of sunlight lay across the bright red checkered table cloth.

"Good morning," Mr. Richardson said. He rose and came toward Laura. "I was afraid we would disturb you. We had to get up early to get Randolph off to the country."

"You should have stayed in bed," Mrs. Richardson protested before Laura could say anything. "How do you feel?"

"Very much better, thank you," Laura said. Mrs. Richardson was plump and rosy, with brown hair that crinkled and soft hazel eyes, filled now with concern. Mr. Richardson drew out a chair and Laura sank into it, with a smile. "I'm so ashamed about last night. You—your husband—I shall never forget your kindness."

"Don't think about last night. I'm going to fix you some toast and tea." Mrs. Richardson was already at the stove, putting the kettle to boil.

Mr. Richardson seated himself across from Laura. "Mrs. Phelps, I wish you would tell me everything. I am quite sure I can help you." His eyes were warm, gray, and friendly. There was something very likable about the big, square-shouldered man.

"I want to tell you everything," Laura said.

"Good," Mr. Richardson nodded. "Of course, I know that you are a Mormon and the wife of one of the prisoners who escaped. The whole town was talking about you last night. But don't let that disturb you."

Laura flushed, but her head went up proudly. "They accused my husband of murder," she said, "but he is innocent." Her brown eyes flashed fire. "If he'd had a trial, he would have been released."

"I believe you," Mr. Richardson said. "I—"

"You are even kinder than I thought," Laura broke in, "to have taken me in even after you knew about me."

"You would have done the same for a woman. I'm sure my wife and I will never regret it."

Mrs. Richardson stepped to the table with a cup of steaming tea and a plate of golden brown toast. "Here, Mrs. Phelps; this will be good for you."

"Thank you," Laura said. Her voice broke, and she sipped hot tea and nibbled a bit of toast, struggling to regain composure. "Please forgive me," she begged. "I'm not quite myself. I have been under a fearful strain. I think I'd better begin at the beginning."

It was a harrowing tale. Recounting the events of the past eight months, Laura found herself wondering how she had borne them. The Richardsons listened, spellbound. Mrs. Richardson had begun quietly to clear the table, but within a moment or two she was seated, leaning forward, following every word with amazed, wide eyes. Mr. Richardson, with a long forefinger, traced intricate paths between the checks of the tablecloth, nodding now and then over some detail—Morris' arrest and indictment—the little new home and the children—the hazardous journey to Columbia—the jail break—and, finally, Laura's plan to meet John.

"About your brother," Mr. Richardson asked, "you say you were to meet him at the inn?"

"Yes." Laura started to rise from her chair. "I must go there at once."

"Sit down, Mrs. Phelps." Mr. Richardson was on his feet, moving to the door. "I'll handle this for you. I know your brother."

"You know John?"

"Yes. He and young Pratt stabled their horses with me. I've had several chats with them." He snatched his hat from a hook on the wall. "I'll find your brother if he's in this town," he called back as he dashed out of the door.

4.

"John! Oh, John!" Laura dropped the potato she was peeling and flew to her brother. John's arms went around her and for a moment she stood there, her face hidden against his hard, young chest.

"Oh, Frank, I'm so glad." Mrs. Richardson's face was beaming. "How did you find him? Sit down and tell us all about it." She hitched her chair forward eagerly.

"There's not much to tell." Mr. Richardson was looking complacent. "I stopped Clark on his way to the inn and told him that his sister was safe with us." He paused to chuckle. "This young man didn't trust me. Said he'd believe his sister was safe when he saw her. So I brought him along."

"I'm sorry." John grinned engagingly. "I can see that my sister is in excellent hands. I'll do anything you say."

Laura had gone back to her chair and John stood beside her, his hand resting on her shoulder. Mr. Richardson shook his head.

"I'm glad I found you when I did, Clark. You must get out of town at once. Mr. Follet is back in jail and I understand the innkeeper had orders to turn you over to the sheriff if you turned up." He paused. "Where did you spend the night?"

"In the forest. Pratt and I were trapped. I was frantic about you, Laura, but the forest was carefully watched. The guard was removed this morning, so I came into town. Pratt started for Quincy on the North road."

Mr. Richardson nodded. "That's fine. Then we can go through the forest. My plan is to go to my stable, get horses, and then follow the trail through the forest to the North road.

We'd better be getting along. No time to lose."

"But my sister?"

"She must stay here. I haven't located her horse yet and anyhow she is in no condition to travel. We like having her. Our son has gone to the country for a visit and she is fine company for my wife."

John looked at Laura. She smiled. "You must go, John. Perhaps you will be able to help Morris."

"Then promise me that you'll stay here until I send you word. I will try and come back for you."

"I promise," Laura said. "Goodbye, dear." She rose and stood on tiptoe, winding her arms about his neck. John bent his dark head and kissed her cheek, gently.

Mr. Richardson was already at the door. "He'll be all right, Mrs. Phelps. I'll take him out about five miles. Look for me sometime this afternoon, Martha," he called, and the door closed behind them.

5.

Mr. Richardson returned in the late afternoon. John had found Orson and they were safely on their way. "You needn't worry about those two," Mr. Richardson assured Laura. "They know how to take care of themselves. At the rate they are walking, they should be in Quincy by the end of the week."

Laura knew he was right. And John was enjoying this experience. She had seen his eyes sparkle with that strange light. This was adventure.

That evening there was more good news. Sam, the sheriff's helper, had brought Dove to the Richardson stable shortly after dusk. Laura was greatly relieved. But she was worried when she learned that Mr. Richardson had gone to the Scott's and demanded her clothes. "Now you will be involved," she protested.

Mr. Richardson smiled quizzically. "Don't let that trouble

you," he said. "You see, the Scotts had no business to take you in. They are allowed to keep lodgers, but not members of a prisoner's family. I think the sheriff will be glad to forget about you."

6.

Ten days passed before Laura heard from John. *If Morris had been captured,* Laura thought, *word would have come.* But there were other dangers. After eight months of prison confinement, his fierce struggle with the Scotts must have left him utterly spent. Laura could picture him, riding desperately through the darkness, lurking by day in some shadowy copse—weak—hungry—never daring to approach a house. . . . She would turn on her pillow to confront other specters. What was happening to the children? She could see Joseph's little rusty head twisting in delirium. How suddenly that illness had swooped upon him. And there were accidents, too. Harriet was venturesome. Ellen Stevenson would have her hands full, but Paulina and Mary Ann would help. Somehow, young as Mary Ann was, Laura relied on her.

It was difficult, after such a night, to appear cheerful at the breakfast table. Mrs. Richardson, Laura suspected, saw beneath the surface of her determined gaiety. The clear, hazel eyes were often troubled, but no word was ever spoken that might undermine Laura's self-control.

There was much to talk about. Laura was grieved that she dared not visit King Follet in jail, but she, as well as the Richardsons, realized that it was not to be thought of. Follet had narrowly escaped death at the hands of a drunken mob, and the less attention Laura herself attracted the better for all concerned.

When John's message came from Quincy, Laura was radiant. Morris was there, safe at King Follet's home, and the Apostle Pratt had also reached Quincy. Laura was to leave at once, for by the time she received the message John would be on his way to meet her. He would wait for her at Robville, a town about thirty-five miles from Columbia.

"I can scarcely believe it," Laura told the Richardsons. "Everything seemed so hopeless. But our faith has brought us through."

Early the next morning Laura left Columbia. Mr. Richardson had arranged for her to ride with the post boy as far as Robville. "You have been through enough," he said. "We must make sure that you will be safe until you reach your brother."

Laura and Martha Richardson embraced when they said goodbye. There were frank tears in Mrs. Richardson's eyes, and Laura's lips quivered. "I wonder if you realize what you have meant to me?" she asked. "I was a stranger and you took me in. Friends like you and your husband are gifts from God. If I only knew how to repay you!"

Mrs. Richardson's serene face was thoughtful and her eyes shone. "You have already repaid us, dear Mrs. Phelps," she said softly. "You have taught us the meaning of faith."

22

1.

"O give thanks unto the Lord; for *he is* good" . . . "Thou hast loosed my bonds" . . . "Make a joyful noise unto the Lord, all ye lands." . . . Riding with the post boy along firm, white roads dappled with shade, it seemed to Laura that all things were rejoicing with her. The leaves, rustling in a gentle breeze, the haunting sweetness of birdcalls, a rainbow, prisoned in a dewdrop. The sun was brilliant and the pure, deep blue of the sky caught up her heart and lifted it to heights where the psalmists's words sang themselves within her.

How different from that nightmare journey to Columbia! But physical hardships did not matter. Today, Laura thought, she could plunge into that same roaring torrent, joyous and confident. *Although,* she admitted, smiling to herself, *I should feel much safer with John along.*

The post boy was young and ill at ease in her company. All through the day he managed to keep a few paces ahead, and the back of his neck and ears crimsoned whenever Laura addressed him. But by sundown they were riding through a thickly wooded section. The road narrowed. Dark branches arched overhead and shut out the faint light that remained.

Laura urged Dove forward, barely clearing the heels of the post boy's mount. Mr. Richardson had been right. It was dismal and lonely. She was thankful for company—even this silent youth.

Emerging from the dark forest into the gold and rose of the afterglow seemed to Laura symbolic of her life these past months. *Out of darkness into light,* she thought, *and beauty.* The drumming of hoof beats aroused her from her reverie. Silhouetted against the still glowing sky a horseman was rapidly approaching. There was no mistaking those straight, young shoulders—that eager up-thrust chin. John was riding to meet her. Soon, now, she would be with Morris.

2.

Mrs. Follet turned the knob softly and motioned Laura into the dim, quiet room. Laura did not hear the door close nor the sound of footsteps receding down the hall. She stood, transfixed with horror, staring at the ghastly, greenish pallor of Morris' face. Then a half-hysterical sob caught in her throat. It was the curtains! They were of thin, pale green, drawn against the afternoon sun. But the effect of the light filtering through upon the sharpened angles of Morris' face was terrifying.

Laura tiptoed over to the bedside. How ill he must have been. Half-starved, Mrs. Follet said, and burning with fever. But he was better now. With rest, and nursing and proper food, he should be able to travel in two or three weeks. Laura yearned over him. But she must not wake him—she would sit in that low chair where he would see her face when he opened his eyes. "Oh, Morris," she whispered, bending over him.

He could not have heard, but his eyes opened. Incredulity, doubt, joy—in quick succession Laura saw them flit across his face. Then his arms opened and she was kneeling beside him. She kissed him lingeringly and laid her slim finger upon his lips. "Don't try to talk, dear," she cautioned. "There will be plenty of time for that."

Morris clasped her hand in both of his and drew it down upon his breast. "Plenty of time," he murmured. "All of our life." His eyes closed and he was asleep.

4.

It was late July before Laura and Morris left Quincy. With Morris too ill to travel, Laura had been more than ever concerned about the children. So John had gone on at once. It was a great relief to know that he was with them. *John is always ready when I need him,* she mused.

And now, on a blazing August day, Laura and Morris were approaching Commerce. They had traveled on horseback by easy stages with frequent pauses for rest, as Morris was still far from strong. His mount was a fine young chestnut that one of the brethren wished taken to Commerce. Laura was riding her faithful Dove.

When they reached the outskirts, they drew rein for a moment. Laura waved her hand toward the little settlement. "There it is," she said. "The center of Zion—and our new home. I warned you not to expect too much. The Saints have not had much time."

Morris leaned from his saddle and took her hand in his. "I dreamed of this—those black nights, riding the roads."

As they rode on into the town, Morris' eyes darted here and there, observing everything. "Laura," he declared, "this is a magnificent site." He flung out his arm in a sweeping gesture, from the wide expanse of the Mississippi, with the town fronting it on three sides, to the prairie stretching away limitlessly. His eyes were dreamy, yet singularly alive. "Some day," he said, "there'll be a fine city here."

Laura smiled. *How like Morris,* she thought, *always dreaming of the future.*

5.

It was late afternoon when Morris and Laura rode through the quiet streets of Montrose. They turned a corner into a side street. "That's our gate — oh, Morris, look!" Laura pointed. Perched on the gate post and almost hidden by the big cottonwood, was Mary Ann. In an instant she had spied them and was on the ground, flying toward them, yellow braids bobbing. "Mother—Father!" she screamed. "Paulina! Aunt Ellen!"

Morris and Laura dismounted just as she reached them. Laura dropped to her knees and took her daughter in her arms. Then Morris, too, was on his knees, with his long arms around them both. Paulina was racing down the street, plump little Harriet at her heels, and at the gate Aunt Ellen stood waiting, with drowsy little Joseph in her arms.

"Morris," Laura said. "Morris, dear, this is home."

23

Morris was at work among his flowers. From the steps of the cottage, Laura could see his expression of absorbed contentment as he bent to examine a bud, or probed for a weed with his long, strong fingers. It was good for him, she thought, and he had done wonders in the year since they had come to this new home.

Morris had not been satisfied to remain in Montrose. That first view of Commerce had aroused his enthusiasm. "We must live there," he said, his eyes alight. "We must do our part in building a beautiful city." And his words now seemed prophetic; for the town's name was changed soon afterwards. "Nauvoo" it had become. Nauvoo—the ancient Hebrew word for "beautiful." A charter, incorporating the settlement into the city of Nauvoo, had been granted to the Mormons by the Illinois state legislature.

The sun had set and a fresh breeze from the river made the September twilight pleasantly cool. Laura was glad they had located on the outskirts of town. A two-acre plot was not much of a farm—still, it was enough for Morris to manage, with his carpentry work in Nauvoo. And they were close enough for the children to attend school.

There was a peal of laughter from the house. Laura

smiled. The girls were clearing up after supper. They were always happy together. It reminded her of the days in Far West. This home was very like that cottage. She had remarked it the day they moved in. She remembered her singing happiness on that day. A home of their own—a reunited family—she could not ask for more. . . .

She sighed. *If I just weren't so tired,* she thought. It was frightening, this weariness that she could not shake off. A dull, cold heaviness—creeping around her heart. She couldn't analyze it. She only knew that it set her apart, lost and lonely—remote. Always, it filled her with a frantic need for Morris or one of the children. She rose hastily and crossed the yard to the garden.

It was a hodgepodge riot of color. The fall flowers were in full bloom. Blood-red dahlias shouldered purple asters and crowded out the lacy cosmos of more delicate tints. Morris' garden, Laura reflected, was like a patchwork quilt, pieced without thought of design. The effect was pleasing. Still, she liked a design.

Morris had been putting away his tools. "Well, how do you like it?" he demanded, gesturing toward the flower-bed.

"It's coming along beautifully," Laura assured him.

"This is only a beginning," he boasted. "In another year—"

"Oh, don't!" Laura cried. She hadn't meant to say it. There was hurt bewilderment in Morris' eyes, but she couldn't explain to him — couldn't justify this strange certainty that there would never be another year for her. "It's Joseph," she said. "I must make him stop circling around that tree. It makes me dizzy to watch him."

She turned away quickly and walked toward her small son. Around and around the willow he was slinking, his eyes half closed, intent and vigilant. At Laura's approach he looked up with a warning gesture. "Go 'way, muvver. You'll scare the fox."

Laura laid a finger on her lips and retreated cautiously. It would be a pity to spoil his game. She lingered near the gate. The girls had finished their work and were on the porch.

My darlings, Laura thought. Another year and she would not be with them. How could Morris carry on alone? His health was better, but he always had depended on her so. Paulina would be all right. Paulina was practical—she would never war within herself. And Harriet and Joseph were young. Someone would look after them. But Mary Ann—sensitive—independent — intuitive — life would hold problems for her. *I know,* Laura thought. *I understand her because she is so like me.* And suddenly the weight lifted from her heart. She was serene again and warm and happy. She would never really leave them. In Mary Ann her spirit would go on and on. . . . With quick, firm steps she walked back to the house.

"Mother, dear," Mary Ann called, "we're waiting for you. We want you to sing."

"We'll all sing," Laura said. "That will be much better." She sat down on the step beside Morris and slipped her arm through his. She must make him forget his hurt. "You choose the song, dear," she urged.

His quick smile showed his pleasure. "How about 'Lead, Kindly Light'?" he suggested. "That's a beautiful song."

Laura hesitated for a moment, then her sweet soprano floated out into the shadows—

Lead, kindly Light, amid the encircling gloom,
Lead Thou me on.
The night is dark. . . .

Her voice broke, but the girls and Morris sang on. . . .

Keep Thou my feet,
I do not ask to see—

Laura's shoulders straightened and her voice rang out, happy and triumphant. . . .

The distant scene; one step enough for me.

BOOK TWO

THREADS IN THE WARP

When any great design thou dost intend,
Think on the means, the manner and the end.

—DENHAM.

I

1.

On a bright May morning of the year 1844 the small ferry-boat *Good Luck* slowly churned its way across the Mississippi River, bound from Montrose, Iowa, to Nauvoo, Illinois. Foam-capped ripples danced and sparkled in the sunlight as the paddle-wheel cut deeply into the stream. It was only half after seven o'clock, but even at this early hour the *Good Luck*'s small decks were crowded to capacity; for today the Mormon city of Nauvoo was celebrating its fifth anniversary. Practically every Mormon inhabitant of the outlying settlements on the Iowa side of the river was on his way to take part in the festivities.

In a far corner of the rear deck John Clark, his long, angular body braced against the rail, was gazing at his niece, his dark bright eyes intent under the shadow of his hat brim. Mary Ann stood calm and erect a few paces from him, quite evidently absorbed in her own thoughts. She was small-boned and slender with the delicate roundness of sixteen years. Her blue and white pin-checked dress billowed to the floor from a tight basque. A tuscan straw bonnet revealed corn-yellow braids bound tightly about her ears.

She's a woman, John thought. *A lovely woman, with poise and dignity beyond her years.* It was not surprising. These last three years had been full of heartbreak and adjustments for Mary Ann; her mother's sudden death, her father's remarriage, her responsibilities. . . . *It's not right,* John thought rebelliously. *She's been cheated of her girlhood.* He stretched forth a muscular sun-browned hand and drew her gently close to him. Her head barely reached his shoulder. "Happy?" he questioned.

"Oh, *yes!*" Mary Ann lifted her face, a smile crinkling around her blue eyes. "Isn't it wonderful—this celebration? And I'm going to see my family—Paulina, Harriet, Joseph—" The smile flickered and was gone; "and Father," she added, her tone oddly deflated. She turned her head abruptly and stared out across the water.

John regarded her thoughtfully but made no comment. He was troubled. Mary Ann had been excited and happy at the thought of seeing her sisters and her brother. Her change of tone and manner when she mentioned her father—that, John knew, was because of her stepmother. The hurt was still there, deep down inside of her. The stunned surprise and shock of Morris' marrying again only a year after Laura's death. Mary Ann hadn't been able to fight down the feeling, hard as she had been trying, these past two years while she had been living at the Clark farm.

John frowned and fixed his eyes on the shifting crowd, only half conscious of what he saw. Men in neat homespun or broadcloth suits and stiff, high collars, moved about the decks greeting friends and neighbors. Women, their bonnet strings tied primly beneath their chins, gathered in gay chattering groups, their full-skirted dresses of bright printed ginghams, pastel cashmeres and shining alpaca, making vivid splashes of color against the drab, weather-beaten boat.

John twisted his shoulders uneasily. Sometimes he wished

that he could forget his concern for this niece of his. Eleven years was a wide gulf to bridge. If she were not so much younger, maybe he could understand her better. But there was something—a bond he himself could not explain. He was fond of her sisters, but it was to Mary Ann that he had always been drawn. Perhaps it was because, as a little girl, she had confided in him so completely. Probably it was because she was so like her mother. Laura had been his favorite sister. There was a wrench of pain at his heart as he thought of her now. Pain and bitter self-reproach. Death had come so quickly, so unexpectedly. Just a cold . . . no one had thought it serious until it was too late. They had all taken Laura for granted. Her strength, her good health. *But I should have known,* John thought. *I knew what she had been through*—those long months of Morris' imprisonment, the fear and anguish and physical strain—of course, they had sapped her resistance. If only. . . . But wishing would not bring her back. He'd failed Laura but he would not fail Mary Ann.

He looked at her now. She was leaning lightly against the rail, her eyes turned toward Montrose as it receded from the ferry's stern. *Something is troubling her,* John thought. But he wouldn't ask questions, he'd wait for her confidence. Since her mother's death there had been a new quality in the feeling between Mary Ann and him.

A vague longing came over him as he, too, looked across the river toward the west. He sighed. If Mary Ann hadn't come to the farm to live, he'd be in the Oregon country now. He had been ready to leave then, but he couldn't go when Mary Ann needed him. It had made him secretly proud to realize that with her world shaken to its foundations, she had turned to him rather than to her grandfather or her Aunt Rhoda. And he had been better prepared to help her because of something Laura had once told him. "Mary Ann is deeply hurt by things she doesn't understand," Laura explained. "She needs someone with patience, someone she can turn to until understanding comes." And Mary Ann had not understood her father's marrying again.

Poor Morris. John felt genuinely sorry for Mary Ann's father. He had married because of the children, to give them a mother. But it hadn't worked out that way. Mary Ann had withdrawn herself completely. Paulina, older and of a different disposition, had resigned herself; but now she was going out nursing—becoming independent. Harriet was younger, had adjusted herself more easily. But John noticed that she was always reluctant to leave the farm after a visit with Mary Ann. The boy, Joseph, was all right. He'd get along, the little rascal. But Morris—John shook his head. Still bewildered. Still groping for a solution to the problem that he, himself, had created.

"Uncle John." Mary Ann was pulling at John's sleeve. "Do you mind if I go over and talk to Clarissa?" She motioned to a dark-eyed girl about her own age, who stood across the deck, her black curls flying in the breeze.

"Your old uncle isn't very entertaining this morning." John grinned.

"Oh, it isn't that," Mary Ann said quickly. "Clarissa is going home today and I have something to tell her."

"Don't take me so seriously," John chuckled. "You run along." He watched Mary Ann walk away. Her head had the same proud tilt that Laura's had always had. Her face lighted up as she greeted Clarissa. Too bad Clarissa was going home. She had been good company for Mary Ann and they seemed to have become fast friends while she was visiting a neighboring farm. Mary Ann would miss her. It was lonely for her with no other woman about but Rhoda. And now Rhoda was planning to be married; she would have little time for the girl. John grinned briefly. He was glad he had no inclination toward matrimony.

John shifted his position a little. He was content to remain in his corner. Most of the men kept milling about the decks as if some restless urge made them impatient. Why? Did their Sunday suits make them ill at ease, or was it because they were unaccustomed to leisure? Perhaps some indefinable fear was beginning to prick at the contentment they had known these past five years. There were rumors—especially now that Joseph Smith had announced his intention to run for the Presidency of the United States—that all was not well between the Saints and their non-Mormon neighbors. His father had mentioned dissension within the Church. *That might be pretty serious,* John thought. Of course, not being a Mormon himself, he wouldn't know—but he'd heard enough to indicate that the Church officials were worried.

Deep within him John felt a familiar stir, a quickening of his pulse at the prospect of excitement. Things were going to be lively these next few weeks. Of course, he'd hate to see the Mormons in real trouble like they'd had in Missouri—still, a little opposition made things interesting. And it was fun to be looking on from the outside.

2.

A shrill whistle pierced the morning calm. The *Good Luck* would dock in five minutes.

John looked over at Mary Ann. She and Clarissa were talking earnestly—a pretty picture—Clarissa so dark and vivid and Mary Ann fair and blonde. He straightened up and moved away from the rail, his thick dark eyebrows drawn in a frown. Perhaps taking Mary Ann to Nauvoo was a mistake? It was bound to reopen an unpleasant situation. Yet she had seemed so eager to come. Would Morris want her to remain in Nauvoo? Lately, he'd seemed more reconciled to her being at the farm.

The crowd pressing forward, surged between John and the girls, but he kept them in view. He would join Mary Ann on the forward deck.

The *Good Luck* swept toward the landing at the southeast curve of the bend. John never viewed Nauvoo from the river without being newly impressed by its location. The city looked down upon the stream from the curve in a sharp horseshoe bend; it might better be described, John thought, as lying at the apex of a triangle. It faced the river on three sides, and the gentle incline from the water to level ground above seemed to lift and hold it up to the sky. The wide streets, crossing at right angles, were clearly outlined in the bright morning sunlight and it seemed to John that this morning the city wore an air of conscious pride.

John felt a light touch on his arm and found Mary Ann at his side. She was not smiling; there was an odd gleam in her eyes and a determined set to her firm, slightly pointed chin. "Uncle John," she hesitated a moment, "I am not going back to the farm tonight." She sighed as if relieved to have said the words. She had reached some sort of decision, John knew, but he made no comment as they followed the crowd ashore.

2

1.

John cupped his hand beneath Mary Ann's round elbow as they started up the climbing street that led from the ferry landing to the business section of Nauvoo. People brushed against them, gay laughter and chatter eddied all about them, but between them hung a constrained silence.

Mary Ann kept her head averted and John studied her profile. Bright color stained the soft curve of her cheek. Her lips were drawn in a straight line. He sighed. He knew that look. She had made up her mind. John smiled wryly. He might as well be honest with himself. He'd known that sooner or later she would want to leave the farm and return to her father's home—that was only natural; but secretly he had been hoping that the time would never come.

Midway up the hill Mary Ann halted abruptly. "Uncle John," she demanded, "aren't you interested in what I said on the boat? Don't you want to know everything?" There was a strained note in her voice and her eyes were too bright.

John released her elbow and slid his big hand down her arm in a reassuring caress. "That's a downright foolish question. You know I'm interested. But hadn't we better get out of this crowd first?"

Mary Ann nodded and started on again, walking a little ahead. Her back was very straight. Her head high. She had been withholding her confidence, John realized, and now she was impatient to tell him everything. That was like Mary Ann. She had to think things out for herself—make her own decisions, before she was ready to talk; but once ready, it was difficult for her to keep the bottled-up thoughts safely corked.

The crowd was thinning out. John swung alongside Mary Ann and linked his arm through hers. "Not so fast, young lady. Remember my age."

She laughed, as he had hoped she might, but the laughter was high-pitched and unnatural. They had reached the top of the hill and the crowd was moving northward, but John guided Mary Ann in the opposite direction.

2.

"Now, then," John said, "tell me all about it."

The rustic bench where they sat was in a secluded spot. Far below them the Mississippi crept between its curving banks. In the branches over their heads birds twittered busily. John cleared his throat. "Have you told your father?" he prompted gently. "Does he know that you are coming home?"

"I am not going home," Mary Ann said with careful distinctness. "I am not going back to my father."

"But, I don't understand!" John leaned forward to scan her face, pushing back his tall crowned hat with a bewildered gesture. "What *are* you planning to do?"

"I'm going to visit Clarissa for a while." Mary Ann's long fingers plucked nervously at the collar of her dress.

John laughed a little in relief. "That's nothing to make

a fuss about. But you should have told your Aunt Rhoda and me before you left the farm."

"I know, Uncle John. I'm sorry—but I couldn't talk about it until I was sure. This isn't just a visit. I'm going to stay with Clarissa until I find work."

"Work?" John echoed the word incredulously.

"Yes. I'm going to live in Nauvoo." The words were coming in a rush. "I've been thinking about this for a long time, Uncle John, and I have made up my mind."

"But—"

"Let me explain." She laid an appealing hand on his arm and met his eyes squarely, her own grave and troubled. "I want to live near my family. I've missed the girls so much and—I love Father, too. But you know how I feel about Sera." She hesitated, then went on slowly as if thinking aloud. "I don't resent Sera as I did when Father married her—and I've stopped being angry with Father. I—I understand things better now. Still, I can't bear to see anyone in Mother's place."

John patted the hand on his arm, but she drew it away suddenly.

"I'll never understand why he chose someone so different from Mother." She shook her head, her eyes fixed on the grass at their feet. "But that isn't Sera's fault. And Father needs her." She spread her palms in a small hopeless gesture. "I've tried not to show it, but both of them know how I feel. It isn't right for me to live with them. I'm miserable and I keep them from being happy." Her voice broke a little. "Mother would understand. Mother always wanted Father to be happy." She sighed.

John was silent for a moment, deeply moved. She was so young. He longed to comfort her in his arms with her bright head nestled against his shoulder. But she was no longer a child. He respected her new-found dignity and was impressed by her keen insight into the situation at her father's home.

She was so right about her mother, too. No sacrifice had been too great for Laura, where Morris' happiness was concerned. The thought was tinged with bitterness, but he must not let that influence him now.

"I understand, dear," he said, "and I know you are in earnest about all this." He could see the relief in Mary Ann's eyes. "But I'm not sure it's practical," he added. "It won't be easy to find work in Nauvoo. What are your plans?"

"Nothing definite," she admitted, "but I've done sewing and weaving in Montrose. And," she went on eagerly, "I heard Aunt Rhoda say that Miss Ellis needs an assistant in her Nauvoo dressmaking and millinery shop. I thought I'd see her today."

John shook his head. "You mustn't be too optimistic," he warned. "I know you've had experience like that and earned some money in Montrose; but Montrose isn't Nauvoo. Living on your grandfather's farm and working for your friends is quite different from having to earn your board and lodging." He hated himself for discouraging her, but she must realize what she faced.

She stiffened indignantly and color flamed in her cheeks. "I've thought of all that." She lifted her head, proudly. "I'll help in someone's home, if I must, to pay for my lodging." Anger had deepened her eyes to violet. "I've got to be independent," she said, softly vehement. "I'm through being a burden to you or anyone else." She turned from him quickly. He could see the pulse beating in her throat, the rise and fall of her round young breast with each rapid breath.

Her words echoed in John's ears with strange unreality. For an uncanny moment it was Laura beside him. Laura in the little inn, blazing her defiance of danger—ready to dare anything in order to reach her goal. And this was Laura's daughter.

"Mary Ann," he spoke her name softly. "Mary Ann," he

repeated. He took hold of her shoulders and turned her to face him. "You're not a burden to me. You must never think that. All I want is for you to be happy. This thing is too important to risk making mistakes."

For a moment she did not answer, but when she spoke her voice was low. "I'm sorry, Uncle John. I do want your help. I couldn't get along without it."

John smiled. "Then will you promise me something? Don't do anything more about this until we've talked it over again. And I wouldn't mention it yet to your father or the girls."

Mary Ann lifted her eyes. "I promise," she said solemnly.

"That's fine." John closed his fingers around hers and rose from the bench, drawing her to her feet. "The morning's half over. We'll be missing all the fun." But as he hurried her along in the direction of the city, he had no thought of the festivities. A plan was forming in his mind and he wanted to carry it out, without delay.

3

1.

The Mansion House, Nauvoo's leading hotel, stood at the north end of Main Street on the crest of a hill overlooking the river's edge; and it was here that Joseph Smith—President of the Mormon Church, Commander of the Nauvoo Military Legion, and Mayor of the city—made his home.

John slackened his pace at the gate in the white picket fence. Mary Ann knew nothing of his intention. He had left her with her sisters and had come directly here. There was no question in his mind. Smith was the only one who could advise him.

The Mansion House, a two-story rambling white frame building, was set well back from the street in its rolling, green velvet lawn. John entered the grounds, strode along a path bordered by neatly clipped evergreens, and hurried up the front steps. Men were gathered in groups on the wide veranda, some standing, some seated with chairs tipped back and feet braced against the railing. Several of them spoke to John and he returned their greetings absently as he entered the door leading into the lobby. He hoped that Smith might still be in his office, but on a day like this it was not likely.

There was a steady hum of conversation in the crowded lobby. John made his way to the desk. He had stayed at the

Mansion House several times, but the clerk on duty was strange to him. "Good morning," John offered pleasantly.

The clerk acknowledged the greeting without enthusiasm. He had pale, expressionless eyes and a drooping mouth.

"May I see General Smith? My name is John Clark."

It was evident that the name meant nothing. The clerk was eyeing him with suspicion. "Is your business important?" he questioned sharply. "General Smith is a very busy man." His tone and manner conveyed a nice mixture of aloof condescension and dignified reproof.

John inclined his head gravely, concealing his amusement. "I understand your position," he said, "but I am not a stranger here. I live in Montrose and don't get across often. It is quite important that I should see the General now."

The clerk reddened and smoothed the air with apologetic palms. "I'm sorry. I've been greatly annoyed this morning—so many seeking interviews out of mere curiosity—" his scornful glance swept the crowd. "But I'll have to ask you for a reference, Mr. Clark."

John thought for a moment. "Tell General Smith that Laura Phelps' brother wishes to see him. I think that will do."

"Please wait here. General and Mrs. Smith have a suite upstairs." He left the desk and hurried across the lobby.

John's feelings were curiously mixed as he watched the man disappear up the stairs. For the first time he felt a little uncertain. Smith was a man of wide and varied interests. Mary Ann's problem might not seem important to him. Perhaps this interview was a foolish idea. But the clerk was beckoning from the stairway. John squared his shoulders. He had set this thing in motion—he'd see where it led.

2.

Joseph Smith, seated in a large armchair at his desk, did not raise his head when John entered the study. "Sit down,

Clark," he directed pleasantly. "I'll be with you in a moment." His voice was soft but authoritative. Long, incredibly thick light brown lashes veiled his eyes.

John seated himself in a chair opposite the desk. He was glad for this interlude. He could be marshaling his facts while, for the first time, he observed Smith at close range. The Prophet was oddly lacking in physical symmetry. His head was oval in shape, his luxuriant light brown hair fine and soft. John was particularly struck by the small white hands, pawing among a litter of papers, and the long, thin arms—so completely out of proportion to the thickness of chest and the broad, muscular shoulders displayed to advantage in a smartly tailored uniform of the Nauvoo Legion.

John shifted uneasily in his chair. He could feel Smith looking at him from behind that screen of lashes, and in some embarrassment, transferred his attention to the array of pamphlets on a near-by table. Abolitionist literature mostly, he saw.

"So." Smith spokc suddenly. "You are Laura Phelps' brother." He was signing a letter. He laid down the quill pen and pushed the letter aside. His lashes swept upward, revealing his eyes, light hazel in color.

"Yes," John said. He thought, almost with disappointment, *why, his eyes are quite ordinary.*

"Laura Phelps," Smith repeated thoughtfully. "A truly sainted woman." He paused. "Really a martyr to our cause."

Anger flared briefly in John, then died. Laura had done as she wished. She had been happy doing it. That was all that mattered.

"I've come to see you about Laura's daughter Mary Ann," John said.

"Mary Ann. The one with yellow hair." Smith leaned back in his chair. Sunlight streaming through the east window burnished the gold epaulets on his shoulders. "I remember her very well. I blessed her when she was a little tot. But I haven't seen her for some time."

"Since her father married again, she's been with us on the farm at Montrose," John said. "Now, she wants to leave."

"Oh." Smith's large foot in the shining black military boot beat a light tattoo on the floor.

"You're probably wondering why I've come to you, rather than to her father. It's a long story, but I'll try to be brief." John leaned forward and plunged into Mary Ann's problem, talking swiftly. But he omitted none of the important details. How close to each other he and Laura had always felt. The tenderness and depth of understanding between Laura and Mary Ann, and the child's natural turning to him at her mother's death. "She is so like her mother," John explained, "that she knows I understand her. At least, I thought I did," he added with a rueful grin, "but I'll confess she took me by surprise this morning. I've had a feeling that she wasn't happy, but I had no idea that she was making plans." Clearly and simply he went on to outline the situation in the Phelps' home and Mary Ann's earnest desire to do the right thing. "She loves her father and she doesn't blame him. None of us blame him," John said. "But something has to be done."

Smith, his eyes veiled again, had listened intently, his elbows resting on the arms of his chair, the fingers of his well-kept hands forming a graceful pyramid. He nodded at intervals but did not interrupt. When John paused, he looked up. "I must be sure about her father's attitude. Was he satisfied to have her living with your family?"

"Not at first," John admitted, "but he soon realized that it was best. Things haven't been easy for Morris. Having Mary Ann in good hands made one less worry for him."

"Do you think he will be willing for her to take this step?"

"I'm sure he will, when he understands. I'll talk to him. Seems to me the main difficulty is getting her located."

Smith leaned forward. "I believe you are heaven sent, Clark."

Surprise for the moment rendered John speechless, but Smith seemed to expect no comment.

"You tell me," he went on, "that your niece would serve as companion in a home. I think I have just the place for her." He paused impressively. "Charles Rich—General Rich, of the Legion, is looking for a young woman to stay with Mrs. Rich and the children while he goes East on Church business. From what you say, Mary Ann is the right person for the place. You know Rich?"

"I knew him in Far West, but I've seen very little of him these past five years. He's a fine man, though, and Laura always spoke highly of Mrs. Rich."

While John talked, Smith had been writing rapidly. He reached across the desk and held out a sheet of paper. "Here is General Rich's address. I suggest that you and Mary Ann call at his home. I shall see him this afternoon when I review the Legion and I'll tell him to expect you this evening."

"This is very kind of you, General Smith, I—"

"Not at all, Clark," Smith broke in. "Glad to help you. By the way," he opened a desk drawer and took out a long envelope. "I'd appreciate it if you would stop in at the *Nauvoo Neighbor* office and give these notes to John Taylor. I'd like them to catch the next edition." He rose to his feet and handed John the envelope. The interview was over.

3.

There was a spring in John's step as he left the Mansion House grounds and swung into the wide, elm-shaded street leading toward Nauvoo's business section. A weight had been lifted from his shoulders. He had gone to Smith for advice and had come away with a practical solution of Mary Ann's problem. Smith was a remarkable man. No getting around that. His searching questions and swift grasp of the situation—his intimate knowledge of Mormon family affairs—the way he made decisions—yes, going to him had been the right thing to do. *"Heaven sent!"* John smiled broadly. *"Well, maybe I was,* he admitted to himself. Laura would have said so. And Mary Ann, too, had always admired and looked up to Joseph Smith. She would be delighted to know that the Prophet had given personal thought to her troubles. And she would be eager to carry out his suggestion.

John thrust his hands into his trouser pockets and strode along, whistling softly, his heels clicking on the hard-packed dirt sidewalk. Of course, there were still some details to be settled, but he was confident that everything would work out right. Only one thing really troubled him. His thick brows knitted thoughtfully. Morris must be told. This morning, when Mary Ann's idea had seemed so impractical, he had advised her not to tell her father about it; but things were different now. Now, she must tell him—and she must tell him today, before she presented herself at the Rich home. John sighed. If only he could do this for her. But that wouldn't mean anything. This was a matter that Mary Ann, herself, must face.

In the business district, Main Street was dressed up for the celebration. John realized, faintly surprised, that it had made no impression upon him before. Mary Ann had been too much on his mind. Flags fluttered from every window. Flung wide across the street, a banner announcing in bold, challenging letters, JOSEPH SMITH—NEXT PRESIDENT OF THE UNITED STATES. John frowned. Maybe Smith knew what he was doing, but he might find that he'd stirred up a hornet's nest.

It was almost noonday and the streets were thronged. Streams of people who had attended the early morning pageant in the public square, were now pouring back to the center of town. John wove in and out among them, stimulated by the holiday atmosphere, admiring the gaily decorated stores. He paused before a low frame building with a sign, WHIG HEADQUARTERS, above its door. A large placard in the window caught his eye. "Fifty-four Forty or Fight" it read. A pang of disappointment stabbed him. Oregon would be a territory of the United States before he had even seen it. Maybe, now that Mary Ann was going to be all right. . . . He shrugged, threw back his head and moved on.

At the corner of Main and Parley a peddler was chanting his wares. John, vaguely remorseful over his momentary disloyalty, selected a string of bright blue beads for Mary Ann. As an afterthought, he also bought a red string for Paulina and a green one for Harriet. He felt better, somehow, as he stowed the package in his pocket.

In the window of the corner eating-house a row of apple pies and a mound of sugared fried cakes tempted him, but he fingered the envelope in his breast pocket and quickened his pace, walking east on Parley toward Bain Avenue, where the office of the *Nauvoo Neighbor* was located.

The *Neighbor,* Nauvoo's only newspaper, was owned and edited by John Taylor. It was three years ago that Taylor had come to John for an unbiased version of the jail break at Columbia, and they had been good friends ever since. John had formed a habit of dropping in at the *Neighbor* office whenever he was in Nauvoo. Mr. Taylor always made him feel welcome and at ease, and living as he did on the Iowa side of the river, John was able to supply firsthand information about the Mormon settlements around Montrose and an occasional sensational happening in the half-breed tract. He was pleased, now, at the prospect of a chat with Taylor. He chuckled to himself, picturing Taylor's astonishment. *He'll think I've turned Mormon,* John thought, *playing errand-boy for Smith.* One of the things he liked about Taylor was that he respected a man's convictions. Although he was an Apostle of the Church and a deeply religious man, he had never attempted to convert John. "Clark," he had once remarked, "you've never been baptized in our faith, but you're one of us at heart." *Maybe I am,* John mused, as he entered the *Neighbor* office.

4

1.

Roger Parker was discovering Nauvoo.

John Taylor, his uncle, busy with an editorial for the next issue of the *Neighbor,* was at work in his small private office, and Roger's brief newspaper experience at the *Boston Herald* during vacations had taught him that an editor at work is best left alone.

The *Neighbor* office, fronting on Bain Avenue, was directly opposite the public square and Roger soon found himself utterly absorbed in study of the crowds surging past the windows. People interested him, and these people were so different from what he had expected to find in what he had been thinking of as a frontier town. Women dressed in the latest fashions and men in broadcloth suits as well cut as his own, rubbed elbows companionably with others, plainly garbed—farmers, perhaps, or laborers with their families. All hurrying to and from the square. All with that same keen expectancy so evident in their faces. Even the children shared it.

Roger's Irish blue eyes kindled beneath his straight black brows. What luck that he should have arrived yesterday—just in time for this celebration! He'd like to be out there joining in the fun, but he wouldn't stir out of the office. If Uncle Taylor should want him to do anything, he wasn't going to miss the chance. He smiled and a deep crease etched itself beside his mouth, giving him a look of quizzical wisdom far beyond his twenty-one years. He wished he knew more about what was going on. His eyes grew thoughtful. He had been in Nauvoo less than twenty-four hours, but already this amazing city hovering on the fringe of civilization had taken hold on his imagination. His mother's letters had told him very little about Nauvoo. "I want you to form your own impressions," she had written, "and I want you to come out here, dear son, the moment you are free." She was living in the Taylor home, and Roger, anxious to see how she was situated, had started West as soon as he finished college.

Her conversion to the Mormon faith soon after his father's death the preceding fall, had come as a complete surprise and something of a shock to Roger. Like most conservative Bostonians, they had always been dutiful churchgoers and Roger had been baptized and brought up a Methodist. Mormonism seemed so foreign to their life that at first he had been seriously alarmed for his mother. Grief, he thought, might have unhinged her mind. But he knew that it was John Taylor, his father's foster brother, who was responsible for her action, and there was no doubt as to Uncle Taylor's sanity. For that matter, John Taylor, himself, had once been a Methodist preacher.

Roger had seen nothing of his uncle these last few years, but he realized the depth of affection between his father and this foster brother with whom he had grown up in England. Roger had heard the story often. Little Loren Parker—orphaned at six — taken into the home where two-year-old Johnny Taylor had lost his older brother, and welcomed a new one with open arms. And the bond had never broken. Loren Parker's small inheritance had been sufficient to educate him. He had become a teacher, had married Ruth O'Neil, and in 1823 she had borne him a son. John Taylor, meantime, had started preaching. In 1830, when Taylor left England, Loren Parker and his family also sailed for the New World. Taylor had gone to Canada and married soon afterward, but Roger's father had secured a teaching post in a small Massachusetts academy, so the Parkers settled there.

Roger could still remember his parents' grave concern when Uncle Taylor and Aunt Leonora had become Mormons, and later, when they had gone to Far West. It seemed incredible that his mother could have changed so completely—yet she seemed perfectly sure of herself, and she was happy and at peace.

Roger, as was his habit when deep in thought, rumpled the unruly black hair, which he wore cut short to discourage its crisp curl. Right or wrong, Mormonism had filled a void in his mother's life. And he could well understand some phases of her enthusiasm. Every moment of his journey West had been a revelation. Two weeks of travel, by rail, stagecoach and boat. Strange scenes, unfamiliar places, new people—everything so different from what he'd always known. And that last lap of the trip—on the river steamer *Amaranth*—churning along the mighty Mississippi from St. Louis to Nauvoo. He would never forget his first glimpse of this city, so beautifully laid out, so neatly fitted into the triangle of land that jutted out into the river. He had at once been struck with the feeling that Nauvoo had been made to order for this spot and placed in it like a jewel in its setting. It had been nearing five o'clock when the *Amaranth* drew in toward the dock. Rays of late afternoon sunlight slanted across the city and were caught and reflected by the countless windows of spacious, stately homes. And high on a hill, apart from the rest, stood an uncompleted building, its white walls glistening in the mellow light. Even in its unfinished state it was imposing. "That building," Roger questioned a fellow traveler, "what is it?"

"That," said the man reverently, "is the Temple. The House of the Lord."

Roger understood now what his mother had meant about first impressions. He had felt that Nauvoo was a city born of a dream. He still felt that way. Yet he had learned, even in the few short hours since his arrival, that hard-headed planning and heart-breaking sacrifice had made the dream a reality. What lay behind all this? What was the force that drew together and unified these people—people like his mother, like Uncle Taylor, like these crowds in the street outside?

The crowds were thinning out now. Only a few stragglers were drifting past. The door of the private office stood ajar and from his chair near the window, Roger could see his uncle bent over his desk, still hard at work. The *Nauvoo Neighbor* was published bi-weekly and as Roger well knew, there was plenty to be done before the next issue came out; but, eager as he was to help, he felt somewhat diffident about offering his services. After all, he had not had much actual experience, and Uncle Taylor didn't realize how determined he was to be a newspaperman. His studies, his reading—everything he'd done the past few years had been aimed at that goal.

There was nothing more to see in the street. Roger got up from his chair and entered the large front office through a gate in the long wooden counter that fenced it off from the public. The entire south wall was lined with shelves, divided into sections, each section neatly labeled to describe the stacks of papers and magazines. Among the "Local Publications" were files of the *Times and Seasons Magazine,* a monthly periodical published in this very office. Roger was more or less familiar with this, as his mother had sent him several copies. He paused before the shelves labeled *Millennial Star.* This, he knew, was published by the Liverpool, England, branch of the Mormon Church. He'd seen a copy of it last summer, in the office of the *Boston Herald.* He'd like to know more about the *Star*. He selected several copies. And here was a section devoted to "Non-Mormon Publications of Hancock County." He thumbed through the stacks, rapidly appraising each paper, and pulled out several recent issues of *The Warsaw Signal* and *The Hancock Eagle*. His face was intent and his eyes bright with interest as he sat down at a low table and began pouring over the printed pages.

2.

John Taylor straightened up in his chair, drew a deep breath, and gathered the sheets he had been checking into a neat pile. The article was for the *Millennial Star* in Liverpool, and he must get it to the Church office in time to catch the next mail for New York. He became suddenly aware of the silence around him. Could Roger have left? He hadn't meant to neglect the boy. He leaned forward, concern in his pleasant brown eyes. Ah, there he was—amusing himself very well, evidently.

Taylor regarded his nephew thoughtfully. Roger was a lot like his father, but much more alive and forceful. Loren had been a scholar and a dreamer, but Roger had always possessed this quality of aliveness. Taylor remembered having mentioned it to Loren once, when Roger was about ten. Loren had laughed. "The boy gets that from his mother," he said. "It's the Irish cropping out." Until yesterday, John Taylor had not seen Roger again, but the memory of that ten-year-old lad had stayed with him. It had prompted him to urge that Ruth insist upon Roger's coming West. She had told him of her son's newspaper ambitions, and to Taylor it seemed providential. He needed an assistant since he had bought out his partner, Wilford Woodruff. But Ruth had not mentioned this to Roger. "Wait," she advised Taylor, "until you see him again. See if you still feel the same after you are better acquainted with him."

John Taylor ran the fingers of one hand over his smooth, square chin and smiled. He had no doubts about Roger. His training had been sound, he had the fine character traits of his parents, and he had something more. Imagination and insatiable curiosity. Taylor chuckled a little. He'd discovered that in the first hour after Roger's arrival. The boy was a born newspaperman. . . . Of course, he wasn't a Mormon—but he would be. There wasn't much doubt of that. "Roger," he called, "come in, please. I want to talk to you."

Taylor observed his nephew approvingly as he approached the door; the ease of motion, the slim, well-knit body, the fine head. Roger's blue eyes had lost none of their boyish sparkle, but there were deeper lights, too, that had come with maturity.

"Sit down, lad." Taylor waved his hand toward a chair opposite. For a moment or two he gazed searchingly into the young man's face. "You are very much like your father," he said.

"I'm glad to hear you say that, sir."

"Your father was a fine man. I couldn't have loved him more if we had been blood brothers. We had some fine times together when we were boys in England. I regret that I didn't see more of him after we came to this country."

"Father felt the same way. He and Mother talked of you so much." Roger paused a moment. "I want to thank you, Uncle Taylor, for all you've done for Mother. It has been a godsend for her to be with you and Aunt Leonora while I finished school."

"We enjoy having her, Roger. Boston was no place for her, after your father's death."

"I know." Roger hesitated. "I want to say, too, that I feel better about her being a Mormon. It seems to have made her happy. The only thing is," he added, his forehead puckered in a worried frown, "I'm afraid she won't want to go back with me. She feels that she belongs with the Mormon people, now."

"But why should you go back, my boy?" Taylor seized upon the opening. "You can stay on here with me. I need an assistant."

"Please, Uncle Taylor," Roger protested. "You're very kind, but I couldn't think of letting you make a place for me." He flushed a little and stiffened with youthful dignity. "I have some very good prospects in the East."

John Taylor's eyes twinkled. "Look here, young man, this is no spur-of-the-moment offer. I don't do things that way. Your mother has told me about you but I wanted to judge for myself." He smiled, and smoothed back the thick brown hair, graying slightly at his temples. "I don't often go wrong in my opinions of people and I'd like to have you with me, Roger."

"Thank you, sir." Roger spoke gravely. "I value your good opinion. If you don't mind, though, I'd like time to think a little before I decide. My plans were all made to go East—and there are some other things to consider."

"Of course. Of course." Taylor agreed heartily. "I don't want to rush you into anything. But I do need you and I hope you'll stay."

"Thanks, Uncle Taylor; I have a feeling that I shall." Roger's face lighted up and his eyes glowed. "I'm tremendously interested in Nauvoo."

"That's fine." Taylor pushed back his chair and stood for a moment by the desk, an impressive figure of a man, tall and muscular, yet carrying himself with easy grace. "Would you mind waiting here, Roger, while I go over to the Church office? We are not officially open today, but I am expecting a messenger with some important papers from President Smith."

"Of course, I'll stay, Uncle. I'll be glad to."

Taylor put on his hat. "Make yourself at home," he urged. "Look things over. It will be safe to go back into the press-room now. Brother Robinson is out." He laughed. "Henry resents visitors. He's quite a character. Eccentric, stubborn—exasperating at times. But he's an excellent typesetter and a fine, loyal man. I couldn't get on without him."

Roger grinned. "If he comes back, I'll try to convince him that I'm all right."

Taylor paused on the threshold, smiling. "That shouldn't be difficult. Convince him of your real interest in the *Neighbor,* and he'll accept you without reservations. I'll be back soon," he promised. "Have Joseph Smith's man wait. I want to see him."

3.

Roger stood leaning against the counter. His eyes followed Taylor's tall figure swinging down the street, but his thoughts were intent upon his own problem. If he remained in Nauvoo, it would make his mother happy. She had not so much as mentioned their future plans, but he knew what she wanted him to do. And yet, if he did not follow up those eastern offers, he might never again have the opportunity. But this city! Teeming with news. Just the thought of delving into it filled him with mounting excitement. Surely the eastern papers would welcome authentic information such as he could give them. That might be the solution. But—could he be happy here? He ran his strong, long fingers through his hair and it came alive at his touch, crinkling into a black crest above his forehead. After all, he needn't decide now. Something might happen during the next few days that would help him make up his mind. In the meantime, he'd keep his eyes open.

The presses stood in a large back room to the left of Taylor's office. Roger paused before them. Presses always seemed alive to him, even when they were at rest. His imagination played with the idea. They were feigning sleep, secretly watching him. How quickly they could awaken, their greedy jaws ready to gobble bits of type and spew forth printed pages whose message would spread to thousands. He smiled at the conceit, but deep within him was respect, touched with awe, at the power of good or evil confined within those walls.

The smell of printer's ink, the familiar-looking supplies—everything about the well-equipped plant filled Roger with a longing to strip off his coat and go to work. There was a door leading from the pressroom into his uncle's office. Roger entered the room, but lingered only a moment. This was a private sanctuary; he was ill at ease here. As he returned to the big front room, a movement in the street caught his eye. A young man was approaching the office, a tall young man with an unhurried yet purposeful walk, his face, lean and healthily brown. The face of an outdoor man. He stepped into the office and his eyes, dark and bright, swept the room and returned to Roger. "I'm looking for Mr. Taylor," he said questioningly. "My name is Clark. I have some papers from Joseph Smith."

5

1.

At two o'clock, the infantry cohort of the Nauvoo Legion was to pass in review before its commander, Lieutenant General Joseph Smith. This would be the high point of the day.

It was half after one when Mr. Taylor, John and Roger reached the parade grounds on the outskirts of the city. On his return to the office Taylor had been surprised and pleased to find Roger in animated discussion with John Clark. Clark would be a fine influence on Roger. When the lad understood that Clark wasn't a Mormon, he would talk with him freely. And John Clark was fair. His sympathies were with the Saints. He might well bridge the gap that separated Roger from the Church. Taylor had insisted that they all have dinner and go to the review together.

Early as it was, the grandstand was two-thirds filled. John Taylor led the way to seats in the center section. Near the front, a few rows were roped off. "Those seats," he explained, "are for the Church officers. I'll be expected to sit there with the other Apostles, but I needn't go down yet." Across the parade ground the troops were lined up by squads, ready to go into formation. A trumpet sounded, loud and clear. The

Legion band, pride of the city of Nauvoo, was assembling at the west end of the field.

Roger's eyes, alert and keen, took in every detail. "This Legion," he asked, "how many members does it have?"

"Five thousand, in the entire Company." There was pride in Taylor's voice. He paused. "You see, it's an independent military force, provided for in the Nauvoo Charter. Every man between eighteen and forty-five must belong to the Legion if he lives in Nauvoo. Of course, the City Council exempts a few from service, but they must have good reasons for being excused."

"You, Uncle?" Roger questioned.

Taylor's eyes twinkled. "I'm an Apostle—one of those exempt. But in an emergency I'd be pressed into service."

Roger looked at John. "And you," he asked, "do you—"

"No." John shook his head. "I'm not a member. I live in Montrose, on the Iowa side of the river." His dark eyes, under their heavy brows, regarded Roger with a calm, direct gaze, then shifted to the parade grounds.

Roger was thoughtful for a moment, watching John. He had liked this big, quiet man from the first. His handclasp was firm, his smile warm and friendly; and the occasional pithy remarks he had contributed during dinner indicated clear insight and tolerance. But he puzzled Roger. He seemed to be so much a part of everything, yet at the same time so aloof—so completely detached. Roger addressed his uncle again. "These five thousand men—do they drill regularly?"

"Yes, indeed," Taylor answered. "Right here."

"But who is responsible for the Legion?" Roger persisted. "Does the State control it?"

"It was authorized by the State legislature, if that's what you mean," Taylor paused. "And it is at the governor's disposal for public defense, just like the regular militia."

John had seemingly been completely absorbed in the band's

maneuvers, but now he hitched himself around to face Roger, his head inclined a little to one side, so that he could see Mr. Taylor's face. It was apparent to Roger that John was waiting for Taylor to go on. He did not go on.

John looked at Roger. "The Legion is completely independent of State control," he said. His words were measured, unhurried. "It's governed by a court martial composed of its own officers." He paused. "And that, too, is authorized by law." His eyes sought Taylor's face. "That's right, isn't it, sir? You see, Parker, I'm not a Mormon but I know a lot about them."

Roger's surprise at these words did not blind him to the quick, penetrating glance that his uncle shot at John; but when Taylor spoke, his tone was even. "Clark's right, Roger. But don't forget that membership in the Legion is not confined to Mormons. Any man of military age who is a resident of Hancock County may volunteer for service, regardless of his religion—or of his political creed," he added, smiling. "The Legion exists for the good of all," he went on earnestly. "Here in Nauvoo, the mayor may call on it to see that city ordinances are carried out, or to preserve law and order, if necessary."

"But, I don't understand." Roger was frowning in intense concentration. "All this elaborate military organization—does your mayor need a military force to carry out city ordinances? Does this city need special defense?"

For a moment, Taylor's eyes blazed. Then the fire died out and quite suddenly he looked tired, almost old. "Roger," he said gravely, "our city does need special defense—and our people need special protection. If you had been with us in Missouri, you would understand. Clark knows. He was there even before I was. But I went through the Far West affair." He laid a friendly hand on Roger's knee. "You'll understand after you have been here for a while."

Roger wondered about that. There was something beneath the surface here. Some strong emotion that he could not analyze. Would he ever feel it, too? Of course, he could investigate—inform himself—but wouldn't he still be an outsider? That flash in his uncle's eyes—the deep feeling behind his words just now. Uncle Taylor was in this heart and soul. And Roger wanted to remain in Nauvoo. He knew that now. But ought he to accept his uncle's offer? He could give him loyalty and cooperation, but would that be enough here?

The band was in parade formation now, and the troops, a solid mass, spread across the field. Officers, resplendent in blue coats, white trousers and shining black boots, were riding back and forth, busy with last minute instructions. Their gold epaulets glittered. The bright ostrich feathers, in varied colors to denote rank, gave a jaunty air to their triangular hats. The grandstand was almost completely filled, but Roger noticed that there were still a few vacant seats in their section.

Mr. Taylor pulled out his heavy gold watch. "It's almost two o'clock," he said. "I must go down front. Wait for me at the entrance when it's over, Roger." He rose to depart and John and Roger stood with him.

"Uncle John—Uncle John!" A girl's voice floated up from below. Mr. Taylor turned, surprised. Roger looked first at him and then at John. John laughed and waved a welcome to three girls who stood below, their faces upturned expectantly. "My nieces," he explained. "Paulina and Mary Ann Phelps, and their friend, Clarissa Allen."

"Well, why not have them come up here? There's plenty of room, especially now that I'm leaving." Mr. Taylor motioned to the vacant seats beside John.

"But, sir—"

"It's quite all right," Taylor broke into John's embarrassed protest. "Come along with me and bring them up."

Roger's eyes followed John and his uncle as they went down the steps. These nieces were a surprise. Somehow he hadn't thought of Clark as being involved with a family. But then, he had been wrong about his being a Mormon, too. Evidently, though, he was not married or his wife would surely be with him today.

The band, now in position at the northwest end of the field, broke into a lively tune. The martial music set Roger tingling. He was enjoying all this. Mentally, he recreated the scene on paper. The excitement, the color, the motion. The troops massed in the field, the crowds still pouring into the grandstand—all this would be easy to picture. But the people, themselves? He looked about him, his eyes intent on the faces that surrounded him. Serious, even stern in repose, with eyes that held a quiet kind of courage. What were they thinking, these people? What were they feeling? That was the important thing. He must know them. He would know them.

John and the girls were coming up the steps. Roger straightened up and adjusted his stock. These girls were extremely pretty. Two of them led the way; one, dark-eyed and vivacious, her black curls caught in a cluster at the nape of her neck, her crisp white dress with its cherry-red figures, swirling around her little feet as she picked her way gingerly up the steps. There were cherry ribbons on her bonnet. Her eyes were sparkling and her face gleeful as she chattered to her companion. The other girl had merry brown eyes. Brown ringlets swept her shoulder as she inclined her head to listen. Her dress of pink-sprigged lawn was a froth of ruffles from top to toe. Suddenly she laughed—a happy, carefree laugh, her head tilted backward. *Those two are a pair,* Roger thought, smiling in sympathy. John and the other girl were talking earnestly. Roger watched her as they approached. She was yellow-haired and slender, and her face was grave and sweet. *She's different,* he thought.

There was a confused moment of introductions and getting seated. When they were settled, Roger said, "Now I want to have everything clear." He turned to his right. "Miss Clarissa?" Clarissa nodded, her dark eyes smiling under the cherry ribbons. "And Miss Pauline?" he asked, turning to his left.

"Paul*i*na," she corrected, accenting the long "i."

"Sorry," Roger said. But he was looking at Mary Ann, who sat to the left of John. Corn-yellow hair, deep blue eyes that crinkled at the corners when she smiled. For she was smiling now, a shy smile, as she looked at him. "Miss Mary Ann." Roger repeated the name softly. "Miss Mary Ann." Color flushed her cheeks and crept upward to her forehead. She turned her eyes away.

But John answered for her. "That's right," he said, cradling her hand in his big palm.

2.

There was a blare of trumpets from the band. Excitement ran through the grandstand. Mounted Legion officers were riding forward, their horses prancing to the music, arching their shining necks proudly.

Lieutenant General Smith, accompanied by his two aides-de-camp, led the group. The crowd rose to its feet. The music swelled, but the final bars were lost in a roar of applause that swept the stand in a great wave.

Mary Ann stood close to John, her arm linked through his. Tiny warm threads of excitement ran through her as she watched General Smith. John had told her that the Prophet had a plan for her, but there had been no time for details. He had asked her not to question him until the review was over. But it was good news—she could tell that from the look on his face. She sighed. This day was so full of happiness. The relief of having told John her decision, the pleasant morning with the girls, and now the review and John's news. She stole a glance at Roger. He was busy talking with Paulina and Clarissa. They were laughing. If she could only be more like Paulina and Clarissa. It seemed so easy for them to say amusing things. Suddenly, Roger's eyes met hers. She looked away quickly, biting her lip. Why should she feel so confused every time he looked at her?

Joseph Smith had mounted the reviewing stand directly opposite where they sat. An aide-de-camp stood respectfully at attention beside him. The band was playing again and one of the squads was marching and countermarching. A broad-shouldered officer mounted on a spirited black horse was riding toward the reviewing stand. Mary Ann's eyes followed him. Something about him held her attention. She had no idea who he was, yet somehow she felt that she knew him. His horse, nostrils flaring, reared and wheeled suddenly, fighting the control of the firm hand on the reins. Mary Ann drew her breath in sharply and gripped John's arms. But the horse quieted. The officer dismounted, threw the reins to an orderly, and walked briskly to the reviewing stand. He was fully six feet tall, his carriage was erect; his thick black hair, worn long, with side-burns, added to his distinguished appearance.

"Uncle John," Mary Ann questioned eagerly, "who is that man?"

John laughed a little. "I was waiting for you to ask me," he said. "That man, my dear, is Major General Charles Coulson Rich, and you are going to meet him very soon. We are going to his home this evening."

6

1.

Mary Ann and John walked slowly. They had much to discuss before reaching her father's home. The business district with its noise and confusion lay behind them. It was peaceful here in this quiet street, with the branches of tall trees forming a green arch overhead.

Mary Ann listened silently to the detailed account of John's visit to Joseph Smith, but her silence was charged with excitement that made her blue eyes brilliant. "So now," John finished, "you understand why we are to see General Rich this evening. You can see," he went on after a moment, "that you must talk this over with your father now. It wouldn't be right to go ahead without telling him. As it is, I am afraid he is going to resent my part in this."

"Oh, no, Uncle John! He mustn't," Mary Ann protested. "It was fine of you to do what you did. Even if this hadn't come up," she added slowly, "I should have had to break the news to him about leaving home. I'm glad I have something definite to tell him."

"Just one more thing, my dear," John said. "Be frank with

your father. Talk to him as you did to me this morning. He'll be much more likely to understand, if you do."

They were nearing the Phelps cottage, now. It had a forlorn, dejected look. The porch needed paint. Mary Ann sighed. She could remember so well when the house was new. It had been on the outskirts of the city, then. And—Mother had been with them. Mary Ann found herself looking back with gentle sadness at those two precious years in this home, all together. She knew, now, that they had been the happiest time in her life.

The gate sagged from a broken hinge. Mary Ann could see her father at work in the garden. She smiled. No matter what happened, Father would have his garden.

"I won't go in," John said. "You have your talk and I'll come around after supper to take you to the Riches. If it's not too late when we leave there, we'll go on to the outdoor dance at the Grove."

Mary Ann brightened. "Oh, I'd like that. But we'll have to come back here for Paulina—unless Father will bring her. I'll ask him." She hesitated. "Do you think Mr. Parker will be there?"

John shot a quick look at her. "I rather think so," he said. "He's just come to Nauvoo and won't want to miss anything. Why?"

Mary Ann's cheeks were pink. "Oh, nothing — only he seemed to like Paulina and Clarissa." She laid her hand on the latch and her heart caught. Just to be turning in at this gate brought back the old ache. Her lips trembled as she turned to bid John goodbye.

He took her by the shoulders and she tried to smile. "That's right," he said. "No tears. Remember, you are your mother's daughter—and your father loves you." Then he released her gently and turning, walked away.

Little Laura Ann came toddling down the path. Mary Ann tried to smother the resentment that always flared in her at the thought of calling this baby "Laura." She stopped and stood gazing solemnly up into Mary Ann's face. *She's a lovable little tot. After all, it isn't her fault,* Mary Ann thought. Impulsively she stooped and kissed the little face, then gathering her skirts about her, she walked on along the path to the flower-bed where her father knelt, setting out new plants. He was completely absorbed, his head bent low, his long fingers digging into the soft, dark earth.

"Father?"

Morris sat back on his heels and lifted his head. "Mary Ann!" he exclaimed. There was surprise and pleasure in his voice. "I didn't expect you so soon." He started to rise.

"Don't get up, Father," Mary Ann said. "I'll sit here and we can talk while you work." She spread her skirts carefully and sat down upon a near-by tree stump.

Morris picked up his trowel. "I'll put in the rest of this row, if you don't mind. I get so little time to work in my garden. We are very busy at the Temple, now," he explained. "The roof is nearly finished. We all agreed to work today, but I got away a little early."

"It's lovely out here." Mary Ann looked around the garden. The May air was soft and warm. Tiny buds on the lilac bushes along the fence were about to burst into bloom.

"You look very pretty today, my dear." Morris smiled at his daughter. "Isn't that a new dress?"

"Yes," she answered, in pleased surprise. "I made it myself. I'm so glad you like it."

"And the new bonnet—did you make that, too?"

Mary Ann did not answer for a moment. She removed the bonnet and held it in her lap, fingering the ribbons. "I helped trim it," she said slowly, and felt a qualm of guilt. She *had* shortened the strings and adjusted the bows. She was very proud of this bonnet, for it had come from the Ellis Bonnet Shop—a present from Aunt Rhoda. But she couldn't tell her father that. It might hurt his pride to think that he hadn't been able to give it to her. But he was absorbed again, gently patting fresh earth around a tiny plant.

Mary Ann watched him. This was the time to speak. "Father," she stopped and began again. "Father, I've something to tell you."

Morris looked up. "Very well, my dear. Just give me a minute." He laid down the trowel and hastily pushed the remaining young plants under the shade of a bush. An undefinable misgiving seized him. Judging from Mary Ann's expression, this was something important. It had been so long since they had really talked together and even then there had been restraint between them.

Near-by, stood a rough bench littered with gardening tools. Morris tipped them to the ground and dragged the bench closer to his daughter. "Now, then," he demanded, seating himself opposite, "what is this all about?"

Mary Ann leaned forward, her blue eyes looking straight into his. "I have a lot to say, Father. I don't quite know how to begin." She hesitated. "I think I'd better go back to that year before I went to Montrose to live."

Morris' heart sank leadenly. So, at last this was coming out in the open—this thing that had lain between them. He dreaded it, yet he welcomed it, too. His eyes, fixed on Mary Ann's face, grew somber as she spoke of the months when she and Paulina had kept house for him after Laura's death.

"I missed Mother terribly," she said, "but somehow I felt that I was carrying on for her. Doing what she would have wanted. And then—then you brought Sera home." Her lips quivered. "I couldn't bear it, Father. An outsider, taking Mother's place. And someone so different. I couldn't understand. It—it hurt me dreadfully. That's why I went to Grandfather's to live." Her eyes were brimming, now. She could not go on.

Morris looked away. He could not bear to see her cry. His shoulders drooped. He felt beaten and unutterably weary. Those first few months after his marriage had been hard on him, too. Mary Ann leaving, the other children slow to adjust themselves, Sera grieving because she felt that instead of easing his burden she had added to it.

"Mary Ann," he said, groping for words, "you are older now. Perhaps you can understand a little of what I felt. I—I loved your Mother," he went on painfully. "No one can ever take her place. Sera has always known how I feel about that. But I worried about you children. I had to be away so much. I was proud of you and Paulina, but it wasn't right for you to have all that responsibility. You were both at an age when you needed an older woman with you." He sighed heavily. "Sera is kind and good. She hoped that you children might learn to love her. She wanted to make us happy. But I'm afraid she made a bad bargain. Somehow, things seem to have gone all wrong for me." His glance touched the drab-looking house, the sagging gate, the baby playing in the dooryard.

Mary Ann reached out and touched his hand. "Thank you for telling me, Father. I wish things had been different. But I want you to know that I don't feel as I did at first. I like Sera now—really I do. Only—" her eyes clouded. "Mother's always between us. That's why I can't live at home."

"Can't you, dear?" Morris' voice was wistful. "I've been hoping you were going to tell me that you are ready to come back."

"I'm sorry, Father. I couldn't." In the momentary silence, Mary Ann's words echoed with chill finality. Then she spoke again. "I have some news for you, though. I think I'm going to live near you—right here in Nauvoo."

"In Nauvoo? What do you mean?" Startled from his melancholy, Morris stared at his daughter. Her cheeks were flushed, her voice breathless as she told him of her plan and what had come of it. Morris was conscious of a slow, growing anger. She had been thinking of this for months. Why hadn't she told him? He was her father. He had a right to know. So. John had gone to President Smith. John—a non-Mormon—had consulted the Prophet about Mary Ann, and the Prophet had arranged for her to see General Rich. Morris' smoldering anger flamed hotly. She should not do this. Live in Nauvoo in someone else's home? He wouldn't allow it. What would people think? He had some pride left.

"And I'm going to see General Rich tonight," she was saying, "right after supper." Her eyes sparkled as they sought his face, eagerly awaiting his reply.

Morris labored to control himself. He must move carefully—handle one thing at a time. He spoke, finally, his voice oddly muffled in his own ears. "Your Uncle John and you must have been planning this for some time. It seems strange that you haven't told me."

"That isn't fair," she answered quickly. "You must have misunderstood me, Father. Uncle John knew nothing about it until this morning. I told him then because he had to know that I wasn't going back to the farm." There was anxiety in her face and her eyes were troubled.

Remorse pulled at Morris, but anger drove him on. "Fair?" he repeated. "Was John fair to me? Ignoring me—humiliating me by going to President Smith in that high-handed way?"

Mary Ann's chin went up. "I'm afraid he didn't stop to consider your feelings. He was thinking of me. Trying to help me. Oh, Father," she pleaded, "let's not have any more misunderstandings. Uncle John didn't mean to hurt you. He was so upset by what I had told him that he acted on impulse. It must have been hard for him to go to the Prophet, but he'd do anything for me."

Morris' face burned dull red and the blood throbbed in

his temples. Every word Mary Ann said unconsciously revealed her attitude. John had supplanted him. John had robbed him of these precious years when she had been passing from girlhood to womanhood. She turned to John, now, not to her father. He had felt her slipping away from him, but it hadn't hit him with full force before. Well, there was one thing he could do. He could put a stop to this Rich affair. After that he'd think of something that would bring Mary Ann home.

He looked at her, sitting there so quietly determined, and wondered if he had ever really known her. She loved him, yes. But she had always been her mother's daughter. "I won't have it," he said abruptly. "I can't let you keep that appointment with General Rich. You don't realize what you are doing, child. Surely," he appealed to her, "you couldn't go to live with other people? Not while I have my home here."

"Oh, Father, dear," Mary Ann said wearily. "We've been over all that. Don't you see," she demanded almost fiercely, "it isn't all for me. I'm thinking of your happiness, too; and of Sera's. I must keep my appointment with General Rich. President Smith has told him to expect me."

"I'll attend to that," Morris said. "I'll go to him myself, and explain."

"But you can't!" Mary Ann stared at her father, aghast. The new bonnet fell to the ground unheeded.

Morris did not answer. Then, from the cottage, Paulina's voice broke the silence. "Mary Ann," she called. "Mary Ann! Come and help me with supper."

Mary Ann rose and stood before her father, looking down into his face. "Please," she implored. "Please don't decide anything until you've thought it over. I know how you feel. It's all come up so suddenly—but I—" Her voice broke and she stood for a moment, silent, then swiftly she bent over him and pressed her warm young lips to his cheek. "I do love you,

Father," she murmured, then turned hastily and hurried toward the house.

4.

Long shadows stretched across the garden. The tools still lay scattered on the ground at Morris' feet and the little plants under the bushes were forgotten. He could hear Sera singing in the cottage. He wished she'd stop. He got up heavily from the bench. It would be half an hour before supper was ready. He would have time to go up Temple Hill. Things always seemed different when he was up there. He went out through the back gate to the street.

It was two blocks from the house to the foot of Temple Hill, but Morris covered the distance quickly in forceful strides. And as he walked, thoughts and emotions began to sort themselves out of the turmoil. He started up the hill slowly. He had played a sorry part, just now. He shouldn't have talked that way about John. He owed a lot to John. He had been fine during all those months of imprisonment and trouble. *I'm to blame,* Morris thought. *If John means more to Mary Ann than I do, it's probably my own fault.* After all, he hadn't been much of a father to her these last three years. He realized that. But he'd been caught in a web of adverse circumstances. He'd been . . .

Morris pulled himself up in the midst of a thought and kicked savagely at a rock in his path. This was no time for excuses. It was time to look himself squarely in the face. Mary Ann wanted to be independent. She had a fine opportunity in the Rich home. If he stood in her way, wouldn't he be placing his pride above her happiness?

He paused on the brow of the hill and looked up at the Temple. The last rays of the setting sun bathed the white limestone walls in a rosy glow of almost unearthly beauty.

The House of the Lord, Morris thought. How proud and happy it made him to have a hand in its construction. He started toward the building, then stopped short. Someone was standing in the shadow of the unfinished portico. It was Joseph Smith.

Smith laughed. "Don't look so surprised, Brother Phelps," he said. "I know you are wondering how I happen to be here on such a busy day." He drew a deep breath and exhaled it slowly. "Today wouldn't have been complete," he said softly, "without these few minutes up here. You can understand, Brother Phelps, what it means to me to stand here and look down on this city—a city that was only a dream five years ago."

Morris made no reply. He knew, somehow, that the Prophet expected none. They stood, side by side, looking out over the city now wrapped in the blue haze of May twilight.

"Something is troubling you, Brother Phelps," Smith said. "I could see it in your face just now as you stood before the Temple. Is it your daughter Mary Ann?"

Morris nodded without speaking.

"I thought so. Clark came in to see me this morning—but I suppose you know that?" He paused. "I know how you feel, Brother Phelps. Yet I think you'll be wise if you let Mary Ann go into the Rich home. I think I can guarantee that she'll be happy there." He laid his hand on Morris' shoulder for a moment. "I must be getting along, now." He had started on down the hill before Morris could reply.

The blue haze deepened to purple and the evening star hung like a jewel against dark velvet. Peace descended upon Morris and enfolded him. He knew, now, what answer he would give to Mary Ann.

5.

The Phelps family was at supper. Morris sat at the head

of the table with Mary Ann at his right. He had not spoken to her since she left him in the garden. She searched his face for some indication of his mood, but it revealed nothing. Beside her, Harriet was deep in an argument with Joseph, who sat across. At the foot of the table, Sera, her dark hair in a loose knot at the nape of her neck, was laughing at one of Paulina's sallies. They were talking in undertones. Mary Ann felt a sharp stab of loneliness. It was almost as if she were not there—as if the family ties had already been severed and she was no longer one of them.

But Harriet was plucking at her sleeve and one look into the child's adoring gray eyes dispelled Mary Ann's imaginings.

"Are you coming home to live, now, Mary Ann?" Harriet asked hopefully.

Mary Ann patted her sister's hand. "No, dear," she said quietly. But the disappointment in Harriet's face made an empty feeling around her heart.

"Why don't you eat, Mary Ann?" Joseph sang out. He grinned at her, his freckled face impish under a thatch of rusty hair.

"Joseph!" Sera exclaimed in mild reproof. She looked at Mary Ann and smiled apologetically. Mary Ann tried to return the smile.

After supper the family assembled on the front porch. Mary Ann sat on the top step and wished desperately that her father would say something—anything. This prolonged suspense was becoming unbearable. She couldn't shake off her anxiety. But Paulina was in high spirits tonight and no one seemed to notice Mary Ann's silence. When at last the gate creaked and John came up the walk, her heart leaped, then fell back heavily.

John did not sit down. "I won't have time," he said. "Are you ready, Mary Ann?"

But it was Morris who answered. "She'll be ready in a moment. Get your bonnet, my dear."

Mary Ann's knees shook as she rose. She wondered if she could get across the porch. Then her father smiled at her—his old smile that she remembered from childhood. She straightened and smiled in return, her eyes misty. But her head was high as she went into the house.

When she returned, her father was standing with John at the foot of the steps. "Mary Ann and John have an appointment," he explained. "We'll see them later at the dance in the Grove. I'll walk to the gate with you, John."

He linked his arm through Mary Ann's and the three of them walked wordlessly down the path. At the gate Morris extended his hand, and John's met it in a firm clasp. Morris sighed. "There isn't anything I can say, John, but thank you." He looked at Mary Ann for a long moment. "Goodbye, my dear," he said.

Mary Ann and John walked away from the house in silence. "It's strange, Uncle John," she said after a moment's thought, "but Father must have forgotten he'll see us at the Grove. Did you hear him say 'goodbye' to me?"

"Yes," John said. "I heard him. But I don't think he had forgotten."

6.

Roger's eyes traveled the length of the Taylor's dining table. Soft candlelight fell across the snowy linen cloth and caught the delicate rose pattern on Spode cups. The pleasant murmur of voices and an occasional laugh mingled with the subdued clink of silver on porcelain plates.

Roger had looked forward to this occasion. It would serve a double purpose, Aunt Leonora said; presenting him to President and Mrs. Smith and honoring his mother, who, because of her mourning, had as yet taken no part in Nauvoo social affairs.

"You must be finding this rather dull, Mr. Parker," challenged little Mrs. Keely, seated at Roger's left. She was warm and friendly. Her smooth brown hair, silvered at the temples, was parted and drawn into a simple knot. Her dress of moss-green challis deepened the green lights in her wide-set hazel eyes. She smiled up at Roger. "All of us are so much older," she said. "I'm afraid you'll be bored."

"Quite the contrary," Roger assured her. "I'm enjoying this. But I believe Aunt Leonora has asked some of the young people to stop in after supper on their way to the Grove. I'm to be initiated into the custom of out-of-doors dancing."

"I'm sure you'll enjoy that." Mrs. Keely smiled. "And you'll like our young folks. Many of them are students at the University."

"I understand your husband is president of the University of Nauvoo," Roger said. "Won't you tell me something about it?"

"There isn't much to tell," she responded. "It was provided for in the Charter, and we have four instructors, now. Classes are held in our home here on the Knoll. The registration—" she paused and leaned forward. "James, how many students do we have registered now?"

Professor Keely's fine intelligent eyes lighted up. "Seventy, to date."

"We are very proud of our University." Emma Smith's deep, throaty voice took up the conversation. Roger watched her intently. She had interested him the moment he saw her. A handsome woman, tall and straight, with fiery dark eyes and hair as black and lustrous as her brilliantine dress. The gold chain at her throat and the white embroidered silk shawl draped around her shoulders made her olive skin seem darker.

"The instructors have had good training," she said with calm assurance. "We plan to have more teachers this fall."

"And the Academy?" Roger now directed his questions to Emma Smith. "Is the Academy conducted by Adela Cole and Eli Kelsey a part of the University?"

"No," she replied, "that's a private school. They give instruction from the lowest grades up through preparatory school."

Mr. Taylor broke in with a smile. "I think," he said, "that we'll have to persuade Roger to give a course in English at the University this fall." He looked at Emma for a moment, then down the table at Professor Keely. "He is very well fitted for that."

"Indeed?" the professor looked up with interest. "Would you consider that, Mr. Parker?"

Roger flushed, a little embarrassed and secretly annoyed. Uncle Taylor was taking a lot for granted. "I really don't know, sir," he said. "It is very kind of you, but my plans are too indefinite."

There was silence for a moment as the dessert was passed. The sweet, brittle tinkle of a music box drifted in from the hall.

Roger looked down the table to where his Aunt Leonora, gracious and smiling, pushed aside the silver cake stand as she gave her attention to Joseph Smith. Smith's face was animated as he talked. This was the second time Roger had seen him. Tonight, in his well-cut broadcloth suit, his snowy, pleated shirt, his wide black silk stock, meticulously arranged, he was every bit as impressive as he had been on the reviewing stand. He had inclined his head and was listening to Roger's mother. Roger felt a glow of pride as he watched her. She looked absurdly young in her dull rose gown, her black hair, scarcely touched with gray, in ringlets over her ears. Her blue eyes were dancing and a gay smile played over her small, piquant face as she talked. Suddenly Smith threw back his head and laughed uproariously—checking himself long enough for an explanatory word to Mrs. Taylor, then going off into another spasm of mirth. In a moment everyone at that end of the table was laughing.

Roger found himself smiling, too, but he was thoughtful. These people were cultured, intelligent, accustomed to the niceties of living; and in spite of their religious fervor, they were human and fun-loving.

Mrs. Taylor was rising. The supper was over. One of the most interesting, Roger thought, that he had ever attended. But now he was conscious of kindling excitement—expectancy. This dance. What would it be like? Would those girls he had met be there? And would he dance, perhaps, with—Mary Ann?

7

1.

The city of Nauvoo had a most unusual government. It passed its own laws, established its own courts and maintained its own militia. It was virtually an independent state within a state.

Trying to form a clear picture of Nauvoo's government, Roger thought, was like tracing down intricate family relationships. The mayor, four aldermen and nine councilors made up the City Council, authorized by the charter to pass laws that did not conflict with federal or state constitutions. The mayor and aldermen were also justices of the peace and formed the Municipal Court. The mayor had sole jurisdiction over all cases involving city ordinances, with right of appeal to the Municipal Court—and the mayor was a member of that Court.

The mayor, Roger thought, had a hand in everything. He helped make the laws, he put them into effect, he gave them legal interpretation. And in the year 1844, Joseph Smith, President of the Mormon Church and Lieutenant General of the Nauvoo Legion, was Mayor of the city of Nauvoo.

These facts and many more Roger learned in the first

week after his arrival. He was amazed, on first reading through the Nauvoo Charter, that the State of Illinois should ever have authorized such a scheme of government. As he began to dig beneath the surface, studying the history of the Mormon movement, following it through newspaper files and periodicals that dated back to the time when the Mormons came to Illinois, one fact became increasingly evident. The Mormons were a perfectly fused group; a group that thought and acted as a unit; a group that was constantly growing in membership. Politicians, Roger knew, had not lost sight of this fact.

Representatives of both leading parties, in their anxiety to win the support of the Mormons, had been responsible for the successful passage of the Nauvoo Charter.

The Mormons' attitude toward these parties was interesting. "Whigs or Democrats we care not a fig for them; they are both alike to us; but we shall go for our friends, our tried friends." In these words Joseph Smith had expressed the views of his people. And Smith had adhered to this promise—swinging the vote of his people to whichever party was most favorable to the Mormon group. Roger pondered a long time about this. Of course, it was natural that Smith should play one party against the other for the sake of his people, but such tactics aroused antagonism. Once or twice apparently, the situation had been pretty tense. Open hostility had been avoided, but Smith had made enemies all along the way. And Smith's enemies were the enemies of his people.

And now Smith, himself, was a candidate for President of the United States. Roger smiled. That must have been a shock to both parties. Now the Mormons had their own platform, formulated by Smith, their own candidate. What, Roger wondered, would be the results of this latest move of Smith's in the field of politics ?

2.

Tonight, a week after his arrival in Nauvoo, Roger sat in the office of the *Nauvoo Neighbor* waiting for John Clark. It was early evening. The street was quiet and deserted. Roger looked at his watch. Clark was due almost any moment now. He liked Clark. An evening with him was worth looking forward to. The crease deepened at the corner of Roger's mouth as he smiled, recalling John's comment when he heard the news that Roger had accepted his uncle's offer. "So," John had said, offering his hand, "you, too, are going to be an onlooker from the inside. Let me know if I can help." There was warmth in John's handclasp and friendliness in his eyes. Roger had understood. He and John had something in common. And he knew that he had found a real friend.

"I'll be needing your help," he told John. "There is so much I need to know." He was still a little embarrassed over the way he had at once started to hurl questions.

John had laughed and fended him off with a brown palm. "Wait a minute, young fellow," he said. "I could answer you now but I won't. It will be much better for you to do some investigating for yourself, first."

It was then that they had planned this evening together, when John would be in Nauvoo.

Roger rose and began to walk about the room. He thrust his hands into his pockets and threw back his dark head. He understood now, what John had meant. In this short week he had crammed so much into his head that tonight he felt as though he'd lived a lifetime with the Mormon people. Yet he knew that he'd only scratched the surface. *Well,* he thought, *at least I know now what to ask about.* He looked up. John Clark was coming across the street.

3.

"I'm staying over, tonight." John settled himself comfortably in a chair opposite Roger's desk. "We can talk as long as you like."

"Good," said Roger. "I've been following your advice and I've plenty of questions to keep you busy." His blue eyes were alight with eagerness. "In fact, I've been impatient for you to come—hoped you might get in this afternoon." He sat on the edge of his desk, swinging his long legs.

"I've had a busy day." John shifted in his chair. "Errands for my father. But my real reason for coming today was to settle my niece Mary Ann at General Rich's home. She is going to live there for the next few months." He looked at Roger. "You remember her?"

"Indeed I do," Roger replied emphatically. "She's the dignified one with the yellow hair."

John nodded, his eyes twinkling.

"I met the other two girls in General Smith's store yesterday," Roger said, "and we went for a walk—up Temple Hill. It was the first time I'd seen the Temple at close range.—Those girls," he chuckled. "They are a merry pair. I haven't laughed so much for months. They're all right. I like them."

"They like you, too, I understand." John smiled. "You see, I've already had a report on you. I talked with them this afternoon."

Roger got down from the desk and walked to the window. He stood for a moment, silent, gazing out into the shadowy street. Clark hadn't said whether Mary Ann liked him. But after all, why should she? Why should she even remember him? She'd only seen him twice. But he kept remembering her, as she had looked that night at the Grove, her golden head shining softly in the dim lantern light. The lovely ripple of her skirt as as she moved through a graceful quadrille, her feet seeming scarcely to touch the thick grass carpet. In that strange setting, encircled by tall, black trees, she had seemed like a dream figure surrounded by other dream figures dancing in the fitful light. But, when he had danced with her, she was warm and alive, her eyes brilliant as sapphires, her smile radiant. There had been something about her that night—some inner joy, something—Roger came to himself, his face flaming. What would Clark think of him?

But John was reading a paper, seemingly quite oblivious to Roger's momentary lapse. *How understanding he is,* Roger thought. Then he spoke, abruptly. "Look here, Clark, Uncle Taylor may be working here this evening. Do you think we might take a walk?"

"That's a good suggestion," John agreed. "We'll walk for a while, and then I know just the spot where we can have a good, quiet talk."

Roger already had his hat in his hand. "Then you're the guide," he said. "Lead on."

4.

Roger and John had spent fully an hour walking beside the river and talking. John had done most of the talking—answering Roger's many questions—questions about the origin of Mormonism, its spread, the trouble in Missouri and the expulsion of the Mormons. Twilight had faded and the pale disc of a full moon brightened slowly to silver as they reached the bench on the bluff, the same bench where Mary Ann had announced her decision to John. It was a mild evening; stars flickered in the sky, and lights twinkled from the windows of houses scattered over the Knoll.

"You think then," Roger questioned, "that this close-knit unity of the Mormons was the reason they were driven out of Missouri?"

"I believe that was the underlying cause." John was

thoughtful. "Of course, the Mormons claimed that the land was 'destined by Heaven' to be theirs, but the Missourians might not have taken that seriously if the Mormons hadn't been so united and so strong in numbers."

"How about slavery? What is the Mormon attitude toward that?"

"They are strongly opposed to it. That was another thing that helped to arouse the Missourians."

"Did the Mormons ever get reparation for the property they lost in Missouri?"

"No. Smith took the case to Washington, but nothing ever came of it. The Mormons' case against the State of Missouri, it seems, did not come under the jurisdiction of the federal government."

Roger frowned. "One thing bothers me. Where does the money come from? To buy all this land—to support the Church?"

"The land was bought on Joseph Smith's notes. The tithing system is the Church's main support. Every member must contribute one-tenth of his annual income; and that system, by the way, was one of Smith's 'revelations'—way back in 1838."

"Clark," Roger said earnestly, "you don't know how much you've helped me. This talk has cleared up a lot of things. I've kept Uncle busy every spare moment explaining the Mormon beliefs, and, of course, Mother has told me a great deal, but I want to get at the root of things. I needed an unbiased version of what has happened in order to understand the Mormon situation now."

"Well," John asked, "what do you think of it by now? What impresses you most?"

Roger did not reply for a moment. "That's difficult to answer," he said. "There is so much that amazes me—the strange form of government and the enormous power it gives Smith. This city—" he gestured toward the hills, "its rapid growth. Uncle says the population of Nauvoo and the outlying area is close to twenty thousand."

"That's right," John said. "Astonishing, isn't it, when you compare it with other cities. Chicago is next largest in the State, and it has only about five thousand."

"It isn't normal." Roger leaned toward John, his words coming in a rush. "Uncle says that over nine-tenths of the people here are Mormons who have come as a result of proselytism. That means that less than one-tenth have come for natural business reasons. I tell you, Clark, it isn't normal."

"No," John said, "it isn't; but Mormonism seems to fill people with a holy zeal to bring others into the fold. That's how they have run into trouble in the half-breed tract across the river."

"Trouble?"

"Yes. Haven't you heard any of the talk about counterfeiting in Nauvoo? And complaints about Mormons stealing?"

"No," Roger said, "I haven't and I don't believe it. None of the Mormons I've met would be guilty of such things."

"That's just the point," John explained. "This half-breed tract is old Indian land—wild and uncultivated. A refuge for as hard a lot as you'd care to meet—thieves, counterfeiters—any desperado in hiding from the law. But the Mormons didn't know that. The tract was part of the land they had bought, and they at once began trying to convert their new neighbors."

"Of course!" Roger exclaimed. "I see what happened. These outlaws became Mormons because they realized how the Mormons stand together and protect one another."

"It's a bad situation," John said. "Protection has made them bold. They have made Nauvoo a receptacle for stolen goods. There have been so many complaints about thefts by Mormons that the Church has been issuing public rebukes."

"Well," Roger said slowly, "I suppose a large group like this is a like a nation—made up of good and bad. All kinds of people with all sorts of motives. I've been watching the converts pour in," he went on. "Every river boat that docks brings more. There were some on the *Amaranth* with me. I talked with them. They came from everywhere—even from Europe. I wanted to question each one. To find out why each one had accepted Mormonism."

John stirred on the bench. "I believe you'd find one thing true with all of them. Mormonism satisfied some personal need."

"Maybe you're right. It was like that with Mother," Roger admitted.

They sat in silence for a moment. A light breeze from the river rustled the leaves overhead. Below them, the dark triangle of land jutting into the Mississippi was clearly outlined in the moonlight.

"Clark," Roger hesitated. "Do you mind if I ask you a personal question?"

John laughed. "I think I've already guessed the question. You are wondering why I've never become a Mormon."

"Well—yes."

"I often wonder, myself," John said musingly. "My sister Laura, Mary Ann's mother, always said that the desire must come from within. I've never felt it. But whatever it is, it's deep-rooted and all-absorbing. That's the thing that binds the Mormon people together."

Roger wondered. His uncle, his mother—they had this deep-rooted feeling. Would it ever come to him? And if it didn't, would he be able to keep on an even keel, as Clark had?

"I'm glad," John was saying, "that it has never gripped me. I suppose I'm selfish, but I don't want to be absorbed. The middle of the road has been mighty interesting all these years. Most of the time I've sympathized with the Mormons. Sometimes not. One thing I could never swallow," he said, striking his knee with a clenched fist, "is the divine 'revelations' to Joseph Smith. And that's the underlying idea—the very foundation of Mormonism."

Roger chuckled. "From what I've been able to gather, these 'revelations' are quite practical. They seem to cover everything—new 'centers of Zion,' the building of new Temples, tithing—even politics. This matter of Smith's running for President. Do you think he's serious?"

John shrugged. "Well, he has most of the high Church officials out working for him. He calls them 'missionaries,' but right now they're all talking politics."

"It's dangerous for one man to have so much power," Roger said. "I have a feeling that there's something brewing inside of the ranks."

"What gave you that idea?"

"A biting remark I heard Uncle drop about Smith's enemies within the Church. I tried to make him explain, but he shut up like a clam. And another thing, I've been hearing a lot of rumors about this 'plural marriage' matter, but Uncle ignores it and all the Mormon newspapers deny it. Do you know anything about that, Clark?"

"No more than you do. But I believe you're right about trouble brewing. I can smell trouble, too."

"What would that mean, Clark? Expulsion again? Where would the Mormons go if they were driven out of Illinois?"

"Who knows?" John returned. "Smith, I understand, has already suggested the possibility of moving his people West, beyond the Rocky Mountains."

From far out on the river came the hoarse bellow of a passing steamer. Slipping into the distance, it trailed fingers of shimmering light across the dark water. A dream ship on a dream river with a dream city on its banks. Roger was filled with aching melancholy and vague foreboding. A dream city, breath-taking in its peaceful beauty; but underneath, forces were gathering—dark forces that seethed and boiled and bubbled. What would happen when the eruption came?

8

1.

It was four in the afternoon when Mary Ann came out of the Ellis Bonnet Shop on Main Street. She felt important and businesslike. She glanced again at the paper in her hand, covered with Miss Ellis' spidery handwriting. She was to deliver it to the *Nauvoo Neighbor*. Perhaps Roger Parker would be there. Her heart skipped a beat and a tingle of excitement ran through her.

But she forgot about Roger when she turned north toward Parley Street. It was the hour when women, finished with their errands or their shopping, paused in store entrances or at street corners to chat with friends before going home. Mary Ann walked slowly, looking in at the shop windows, pleasantly aware of the activity all around her. She loved it. And now that she was to work for Miss Ellis, she would have a part in all this. It was wonderful. She had thought it enough to be in the Rich home. But Mrs. Rich had said, "Mary Ann, I think you should see Miss Ellis. I believe you are the very person she needs. Of course, I could keep you busy all the time—but I don't want to do that. I think you need other experiences." And she, herself, had taken Mary Ann to Miss Ellis and made arrangements for her to start work today.

As she reached the corner of Parley Street, someone called out a greeting. Mary Ann's face lighted up. "Good afternoon, Sister Kimball," she answered happily. How pleasant it was to be doing things she enjoyed—meeting people she liked. She wished she might share her joy with everyone on the street. She turned the corner and walked eastward. So many nice things had happened this past week. Sometimes she was afraid that she would wake up and find herself back on the farm.

Mary Ann was nearing the *Neighbor* office. She adjusted her bonnet and smoothed the skirt of her new batiste dress. She stepped inside the *Neighbor* office and closed the door behind her, standing with her back against it as she tried to overcome the flutter in her throat.

Roger was alone, bent over his desk. At the click of the latch he turned. "Miss Mary Ann!" he exclaimed, instantly on his feet. "This is an unexpected pleasure." His blue eyes were warm. "What brings you here?" he asked, advancing toward the counter.

Mary Ann had herself well in hand now. "I have a notice about the Bonnet Shop," she replied sedately.

Roger took the sheet of paper she extended and spread it out upon the counter. " 'Miss Ellis respectfully requests the Ladies of Nauvoo to call,' " he read aloud, " 'and examine her assortment of Fashionable and Approved styles of Bonnets at moderate prices.' I'll venture that's important to the ladies," he teased.

"It *is* important," Mary Ann said with dignity. "Miss Ellis wants it printed in Friday's paper. I'll explain." She leaned over the counter, underlining the concluding sentences with a slim forefinger. On Wednesday, May 29, all proceeds from the sale of Straw Bonnets will be given to the

Relief Society of Nauvoo. All kinds of produce taken in exchange.

Mary Ann's head was very close to Roger's and for a moment their eyes met. Then she straightened up, blushing. "That's why Miss Ellis wants the notice to go in on Friday," she said quickly. Then added, a little confused, "I must go now."

Roger laid a detaining hand on her sleeve. "Don't go," he begged. "Couldn't you—would you be willing to wait while I put things away? It won't take long and I'd very much like to walk home with you."

Mary Ann hesitated, then nodded. "If you'll hurry. I promised Mrs. Rich that I would be home early. I'm to fix supper tonight."

"Well, how about five minutes?" Roger's blue eyes were sparkling. "And won't you come in here to wait?" He opened the gate invitingly.

"Oh, no, thank you." She refused hurriedly. Shyness had descended upon her. "I'll sit down here." She indicated the bench outside the counter.

"Just as you say."

Mary Ann seated herself, spreading her skirts carefully. She watched Roger as he worked. She liked the quick, sure motions of his hands—the orderly way he arranged the papers on his desk. He looked up for a moment and smiled at her. She could feel her heart beat faster. *Wait until I tell Paulina and Clarissa about this,* she thought, with a little exultant thrill. Then quite suddenly she knew that she wasn't going to tell them. This was something that belonged to her alone.

2.

Mary Ann and Roger sauntered along Kimball Avenue, a

quiet street, shaded by tall elms and maples; a street of Colonial style homes with beautifully kept grounds.

"Tell me about your work at the Bonnet Shop," Roger suggested.

Mary Ann laughed. "There isn't much to tell. I'm to do odds and ends—like running errands. Of course, I'll have a chance to learn something about millinery and I'll help in the dressmaking shop when I'm needed. But sometimes Miss Ellis gets an order for weaving. That's one thing I know I can do well."

"Do you think you will like it?"

"Oh, *yes*!" she said, her tone implying that anything else was unthinkable. "And to be living right here in Nauvoo—Isn't our city wonderful?"

"It is, indeed," Roger said, "and full of surprises."

They had reached the corner of Carlin Street. "We turn here," Mary Ann said. "That is the Rich's home on the corner."

It was a white frame cottage with a clean, shining look, less pretentious than the homes on Kimball Avenue, but there was something about it that appealed to Roger. There were crisp, ruffled curtains at the windows and a wide porch with an overhanging trumpet vine. *It's a home,* thought Roger.

Mrs. Rich was in the garden. Mary Ann waved to her and turned to Roger as they paused at the gate. "Won't you come in a moment? I want you to meet Mrs. Rich."

They walked along a graveled path bordered by cobblestones. Mrs. Rich was coming toward them, her arms full of lilacs. She was a small, brown-eyed woman. *Thirty or so,* Roger thought. Her hair was parted precisely in the middle, with braids looped around the outside of her ears. She greeted Roger pleasantly when Mary Ann presented him.

"Won't you sit down, Mr. Parker?" she asked, nodding toward the porch with its comfortable looking chairs.

"Thank you," Roger said, "but I must not stay. Mother will be expecting me." He paused. "I believe you know my mother, Mrs. Rich?"

Mrs. Rich smiled. "Ruth Parker? Indeed I do. Your mother is one of the best workers we have in the Relief Society."

The side gate clicked. A tall, broad-shouldered man had entered the yard. "Charles!" Mrs. Rich called.

"It's General Rich," Mary Ann told Roger in an undertone. But Roger had recognized General Rich. Mounted and in uniform at the Legion review, he had stood out among the other officers. In civilian clothing, Roger thought, he looked equally distinguished. He removed his hat and approached them with quick, easy strides. He was very erect. The thick, black hair springing from his forehead, and his dark, brilliant eyes gave an impression of force and vitality. As he joined the group, he laid a hand on his wife's shoulder in brief caress.

"Charles," she said, "I want you to meet Mr. Parker. He is John Taylor's nephew," she explained as the two men shook hands.

"I am very happy to know you, sir," Roger said. He could feel Rich's penetrating dark eyes appraising him. He had been wanting to meet Rich, who, although only in his middle thirties, held an important place in the community. *It's not surprising,* Roger reflected. The General had a commanding presence.

"I am glad to welcome you, Parker," General Rich said. His voice was deep and vibrant. "Your Uncle tells me that you plan to stay."

"I do; and I am glad to be here, sir," Roger said. "I know my work will be interesting."

"I hope that you will come to some of the young people's meetings at the Church."

"The Relief Society is having an open air supper in the

public square next Wednesday," Mrs. Rich said quickly. "There will be plenty of young people there. I do hope you will join us."

"Thank you. Perhaps I shall. And now I really must go."

Mary Ann walked with Roger to the gate. "Are you going to this supper?" he asked her.

"Why—why, yes."

"Then I must plan to go."

They stood at the gate, Roger twirling his hat, his eyes on Mary Ann's face. She looked up at him, smiling. *She is shy and sweet,* Roger thought, *yet she has dignity.* "Goodbye," he said, extending his hand.

She laid hers in it, flushing a little at the warm pressure of his fingers. "Goodbye, Mr. Parker. I am so glad you met General Rich. He is going away soon. Isn't he a fine man?"

Roger stiffened and released her hand with a little bow. "Yes, indeed," he said, "and a very handsome one. Goodbye, Miss Mary Ann."

Mary Ann lingered at the gate, her puzzled blue eyes following Roger's erect young figure. She was troubled and a little hurt. What had happened to change him so suddenly? She sighed. Life was very complicated.

"There she is, brother! There's Mary Ann!" Little Sarah Jane Rich and the baby were hailing her with shouts of delight. Resolutely, she turned away from the gate and started up the garden path to meet them.

3.

Sarah and Charles Rich sat on the porch at twilight. The air was warm and sweet with the odor of lilacs. The sound of the children's prattle and an occasional ripple of laughter came from the kitchen where Mary Ann was preparing supper.

"I shall miss you, Charles. But I know that you must go," Sarah said.

"It is always hard to leave my home and my wife," he said. "I am glad you have Mary Ann with you. She is a fine girl, Sarah."

"Yes. I am becoming very fond of her. But I feel responsible for her while she is with us. This young man—Roger Parker. He seems to admire her. But he isn't a Mormon. Do you think she should continue to see him? I want your opinion before you go away." She paused. "I wonder if I did the right thing, inviting him to the supper?"

"I believe you did, Sarah. He is a fine young man, I can see that. Brother Taylor is very fond of him—hopes that he will become a Mormon. We must do our part." He looked at his wife gravely. "Mary Ann is firm in the faith and she has a level head. I believe she can do more toward converting Parker than any of us."

"I am glad you feel that way, Charles." There was relief in Sarah's voice. "You are so kind—so understanding."

Rich leaned forward and laid his hand over hers, loosely folded in her lap. "My dear," he said, "kindness and understanding belong to marriages like ours. You have those qualities and you look for them in me. Come," he said, smiling, "Mary Ann is calling us to supper."

9

1.

There was a bustle of activity in the Bonnet Shop on Wednesday. Mary Ann had come down early to help. It was almost noontime now. The morning had passed quickly. Mary Ann had been busy—running errands, waiting on customers, making herself generally useful. Once she had held a very new baby while his mother made her purchases. It was all very exciting. And always in the background was the thought of the evening to come. The supper in the square.

Miss Ellis' notice in the paper had brought results. There was a pleasant jingle of silver in the cash box, and in the back room sacks of potatoes, jars of preserves, a crock of butter, several dozen eggs, a side of bacon and a pound cake—all to be distributed by the Relief Society wherever they found the need.

"There, Sister Hyde, I've adjusted the bow. I think that will be right." Mary Ann held up a white chip straw with a cluster of yellow daisies underneath the brim. "Wouldn't you like to try it on again?"

As she handed the bonnet to Sister Hyde, Mary Ann glanced through the window and gasped. Clarissa and Paulina were crossing the street, coming toward the Bonnet Shop. *Oh, dear,* she thought, *I wish they wouldn't come today.* In her dismay she was only half conscious of Mrs. Hyde's thanks—of her pleased acceptance of the bonnet. It would be fun, of course, to see the girls, especially Paulina, who had been on a nursing case. But Miss Ellis might not like their coming into the shop to visit, especially if they were in one of their teasing moods. Mary Ann glanced apprehensively at Miss Ellis, slender and dainty in her dark blue alpaca with its fine lace collar. She was waiting on Sister Darrow, a tall angular spinster, with eyes like black beads, and hair tightly crimped and drawn up into a corkscrew knot on top of her head. Miss Ellis was having trouble in finding a bonnet suitable for her. Miss Ellis' patience, Mary Ann knew, was being sorely tried. It was decidedly the wrong time for Paulina and Clarissa to come, but they were already entering the shop.

The girls greeted Mary Ann with enthusiasm, both talking at once. She could see the glint of mischief in Clarissa's eyes as one swift glance took in the tableau of Miss Ellis and Sister Darrow.

"If you please, Sister Phelps," Clarissa began with mock solemnity. Mary Ann held her breath for a moment, but Clarissa went on sweetly. "I've come to see about the bonnet Mother is having remodeled, but I'll have to talk to Miss Ellis. No thanks—don't trouble." Airily she waved Mary Ann away. "I'll amuse myself while I'm waiting." She began wandering about the shop, trying on bonnets, standing back from the mirror to admire herself.

Mary Ann's anxious eyes followed her, even while she tried to listen to Paulina. Paulina loved nursing. She had been in Apostle Amasa Lyman's home. It had been so interesting she was sorry it was over. She didn't mean that, really. Of course, she was glad Sister Lyman was well again, but it was dull at home. . . . She chattered on and on. Nervously, Mary Ann glanced across the room. Sister Darrow had lost interest in bonnets. Her ear was cocked in their direction and her gimlet eyes bored into Paulina when Sera's home was mentioned. She was avidly curious. Only this morning she had been making pointed remarks about Mary Ann's leaving home and living with the Riches.

Clarissa whirled about, holding up a willow straw. "Isn't this lovely!" she exclaimed. Paulina joined her and bent over the bonnet. Their heads were close together and they were talking in low tones. Mary Ann didn't know what to expect. There were no other customers in the shop now. Miss Ellis' brow was drawn into a worried frown. Mary Ann started toward the girls. She must warn them.

Then, all at once, Sister Darrow plopped her old bonnet over the corkscrew knot. "I'll come in another day," she said, her voice high and shrill. "There's nothing here fit to wear." She swished past the girls, her head held high. As the door slammed behind her, Paulina and Clarissa broke into gales of laughter. Mary Ann shook her head in reproof. How could they! Her cheeks burned with humiliation as she turned to Miss Ellis. But Miss Ellis, too, was laughing helplessly, wiping away tears of merriment with her small, ladylike handkerchief. It was too much for Mary Ann. For a moment she stared round-eyed—then she, too, joined in the mirth that swept away all of her little worries in Sister Darrow's wake.

2.

In the public square, the women of the Relief Society and their guests lingered over dessert at the long tables set up under the elms.

Roger and John, Mary Ann and Paulina, and the two Spencer boys with Emeline Grover and Clarissa, made up a group some little distance from the official tables where President Smith, the Church officers and their wives were seated.

"Mr. Parker, you must have another piece of this pie Emeline made," urged Paulina who sat at Roger's right. She thrust a knife into the rich, brown crust. Thick apple syrup tinged with cinnamon oozed up around the blade.

Roger held up his hand in protest. "I couldn't eat another mouthful—although it is delicious." He smiled across at Emeline, a tall, gray-eyed girl, on the opposite side of the table. "You know, you Nauvoo ladies are constantly surprising me. So beautiful, so charming, so intelligent—and wonderful cooks, as well." His eyes touched each of the girls in turn, lingering on Mary Ann. "You are almost too perfect," he added. "I can't believe that you are real."

"Now, Mr. Parker," Clarissa chided from the end of the table, "aren't you being disloyal to the ladies of Boston?"

"I have completely forgotten the ladies of Boston," he retorted with a little bow to Clarissa, but this time his eyes sought Mary Ann's boldly, and her lashes fell under his steady gaze.

"Do tell us about Boston," Clarissa urged. She leaned forward, her dark eyes sparklng.

"Well, now—just what would you like to know? I could tell you about—"

Roger did not finish. A trumpet note sounded and a hush fell over the tables. President Smith was rising. All eyes were turned toward him. There wasn't a whisper now. The Prophet was going to address his brethren.

"I compliment the ladies of the Relief Society for providing this happy occasion and for the splendid work they are doing among the poor." There was a murmur among the women and a satisfied nodding of heads. "They do not confine their work to the Saints . . . " Smith went on, but Roger was only half conscious of the words. His interest had shifted to the people around him. Two weeks ago these people had been strangers to him. Now he was better acquainted with them, yet they baffled him still as they had on that first day.

He watched them—sitting quietly, their faces alight, rapt, almost worshipful as they listened to Smith. It was amazing! People from all walks of life and all parts of the world. There was Professor James Keely, President of the University of Nauvoo, educated at Trinity College, Dublin—his sensitive face aglow. At the same table sat Cobbler Stone, a man of little education, round and good-natured, his face wreathed in smiles. They were all bound by a common tie—an abiding faith in their Church and its leader.

Smith was now speaking about the founding of the Relief Society. Roger sat looking about him, trying to identify the people he had met. His attention was caught by a man seated alone at a table to the left. His eyes, too, were fixed upon Smith, but his expression showed plainly that his feeling toward the Prophet was quite different from that of the crowd. A derisive smile, almost a sneer, twisted his lips. Roger knew that he had seen this man before, and all at once remembered. The man had come into the office a week ago—something about a notice for a steam mill. He had gone into the private office and within a few moments Roger had heard angry voices. When the man came out, striding through the outer office and slamming the door after him, John Taylor had boiled over. Roger had never seen his uncle so enraged. He had said some things. . . .

A burst of applause broke into Roger's thoughts. Smith had asked the president of the Relief Society to stand. Under cover of the noise Roger turned to John, sitting beside him. "Who is that man at the next table?" he asked. "The one with his chair tipped back."

"That's Law," John said. "William Law. He and his brother have a steam mill here."

Roger nodded but made no comment. Smith was launched on the political situation. "You all know," he said, drawing himself up proudly, "why I stand here before you a candidate for the Presidency. I am doing this so that you may be spared the necessity of voting for some unworthy candidate." He breathed deeply and went on with heavy irony. "The great Whig National Convention has at last labored at Baltimore and brought forth 'Harry of the West,' for President." Roger smiled. *Harry of the West. What a name for Henry Clay!* "Clay says," Smith continued, "that he must go into office free and unfettered, with no guarantees but such as are to be drawn from his whole life, character and conduct." He paused for a moment as if gathering himself for action. He leaned forward. "Can anything be drawn from Clay's life, character or conduct that is worthy of being held up for the nation's gaze?" Smith shot out the question dramatically and answered it with force. "No! I tell you that Clay's whole life, character and conduct have been spotted with deeds that cause a blush of shame on the face of a virtuous patriot!"

There was vigorous applause. To Roger, the words had a familiar sound. He pondered a little and then realized that Smith had been quoting from a letter he had written to Clay. It was to appear in the June 1st issue of the *Times and Seasons Magazine* and Roger had read copy in the *Neighbor* office.

The applause had died down and Smith was naming the measures he proposed as remedies for "the evils that threatened the glory of American liberty." Roger was already familiar with the main features of Smith's platform—membership in Congress to be reduced one-half, with members paid two dollars a day and board; abolition of slavery by 1850; a national bank with branches in every city—the officers to be elected by the people. But it was interesting to note Smith's earnestness, his vehemence, as he voiced these principles. There was fire in his words now. "The President," he said, "must have full power to send an army to suppress mobs . . . Every lawyer should be sent, as soon as he repents and obeys the ordinances of heaven, to preach the Gospel to the destitute, without purse or scrip." There was a burst of cheers. Now that Roger knew something of the Missouri experiences, he could understand those last provisions and the enthusiasm they evoked.

Smith leaned forward, seeming to draw his audience close. "I would, as universal friend of man, open the prisons, open the eyes, open the ears, open the hearts of all people to behold and enjoy freedom." The afterglow of sunset hung over the square and shadows deepened under the trees. Smith's voice took on a deep, full note as he began his concluding remarks. "England," he said, "expects every man to do his duty. When an American is told to go and accomplish an adventure he replies, 'I'll try.' But the Latter-day Saint—" he paused, "having a more sure word of prophecy—when a command for an important enterprise is made known, exclaims, 'I will do it!' " He thrust both hands upward toward the heavens as he finished and stood for a moment so. Then he sat down. Applause rolled around the park like thunder. Cheers rang out and cries, "Huzzah for Joseph Smith!"

Then, suddenly, the band broke into a lively tune and people were on their feet, their voices joining in song:

So, ye wise men who've nothing else to do,
Help save our land from woe,
And rise in your might, like freemen ever true,
And elect our Gen'ral Joe!

Something drew Roger's eyes toward William Law. The man's face was dim in the gathering dusk, but Roger knew he had taken no part in the song of praise to Smith. And now he was leaving his place and making his way through the crowd toward the shadowy outskirts of the park. There was something furtive in his movements. Something vaguely sinister.

As Law disappeared behind a clump of shrubbery, Roger turned swiftly to John. "Will you make my excuses to the girls? I must go. I'm on the trail of something—something important, I hope."

Before John could answer, Roger was off across the park.

10

1.

At Water Street Roger halted in the shelter of a building. Law had turned right and was walking west toward the river. Roger walked on slowly. He must not attract Law's attention. It had been more than the sneer on Law's face that impelled Roger to follow him. The moment John had told him Law's name, his interest and suspicion had been aroused. That afternoon in the *Neighbor* office . . . "Viper! Judas!" Uncle Taylor had raged. "He must never set foot in this office again." But when Roger had questioned him, he refused to go into the matter.

And there were other things. William Law had a brother, John said. That must be Wilson Law. Roger remembered those names, William and Wilson Law. They had appeared in an article published in the *Warsaw Signal,* a non-Mormon paper, linked with the name of John C. Bennett. Bennett, Roger knew, had once been a prominent Mormon—mayor of Nauvoo; but he had broken with the Church and was now contributing articles to the *Sangamon Journal*—articles which made vicious attacks on the character of Smith and the practices of the Church. Roger had read some of the articles. He knew that they were arousing enmity in the non-Mormons of Hancock County. Now they seemed to take on a deeper significance.

Law was crossing Main Street. The business district was almost deserted at this hour. Roger quickened his pace until he, too, had crossed. Law continued along Water Street, down the gently inclining hill toward the river front, with Roger trailing well behind; but Law seemed to have no suspicion that he was followed. He walked steadily on, his shoulders hunched, his hands thrust deep in his pockets. About a block from the river front he stopped before a low, frame building. Roger stepped back into a store entrance and watched. Law, after a quick look up and down the street, entered a black doorway and disappeared.

In another moment Roger stood before that door. To the left of the building was a vacant lot and on the river side a two-story warehouse. All was silence and blackness. Roger stole closer to the building Law had entered. There were two windows facing the street, but the shutters were tightly closed, not even a gleam of light showing. He turned his attention to the warehouse—used for storing cargo unloaded from Mississippi river boats. There was a narrow passage between the two buildings.

Roger entered the passage and felt his way along in the inky blackness. Either his eyes were adjusting themselves to it, or he could see a faint glimmer of light at the far end. His heart beat faster but he moved on with slow caution. There was a light. As he emerged from the passage, he could see the dim yellow square of a window in the building Law had entered. Roger crept closer. Five men were gathered around a table. They were blurred shapes in the light of the single candle, but Roger could plainly recognize William Law. Law sat facing the window. He was leaning forward, talking earnestly and with vehemence, gesturing with his hands, thumping the table with his clenched fist.

Roger stood motionless, his nerves tingling. He could not hear a word, but he knew that he was right. Whatever was hatching in that room, it was something important. Important and serious—even threatening. Again that intangible foreboding settled down upon him. He sighed and made his way silently back to the street.

2.

As he walked rapidly away from the river front, Roger realized with a shock that it was still early. So much seemed to have happened in the short time since he had left the square. His thoughts were in a whirl. His first instinct was to go to his uncle with the news. But was there any news? After all, boiled down to essentials, he had very little basis for his suspicions. And how would Uncle Taylor take it? *He'd probably think I was presumptuous,* Roger thought. It rankled a little that he had been trusted with nothing of importance. So far, the work he had been given to do was purely routine. *I might as well be the errand boy,* Roger told himself.

He slipped along back streets and gained the house and his room unnoticed. For a long time he sat at his window in the dark and when he finally undressed and lay down to sleep, he was still undecided about revealing to his uncle the chain of small, related things that seemed to link up so unmistakably.

But in the morning John Taylor did not come to the office. He was away for the day, Henry told Roger; if anything came up, they could handle it between them. *Henry is much more in his confidence than I am,* Roger thought wryly. Of course, Henry had been with his uncle for a long time, but after all. . . .

John Clark dropped in about noon and Roger greeted him with enthusiasm. John was exactly the person he wanted to see. He had supposed John would return to Montrose on the early morning ferry.

"Well, young man," John said in his slow drawl, "did you get your story?" He grinned broadly.

Roger laughed ruefully. "Not exactly, but I believe I'm on the trail of something big."

"Want to tell me about it?" John questioned.

"I've got to tell somebody," Roger said explosively, rumpling his hair with nervous fingers.

"I'm going home on the noon ferry. Why not walk down to the boat with me?"

"Just a moment," Roger said, "while I tell Henry." Already he had his hat in his hand and was dashing toward the pressroom.

"First," Roger said as they started toward Water Street, "tell me something about William and Wilson Law. Are they brothers?"

"Yes, but I know very little about them," John said. "They have been prominent in Church affairs and in business, too, because of their steam mill. I can tell you this much, though—there have been many rumors lately that all is not well between them and Smith. But I don't know what the trouble is."

"Do you think it is serious—this trouble?"

"I believe it is."

"Then that explains a lot of things," said Roger. He went on quickly, giving John a clear account of his experiences the night before and the deductions he had made about the Laws. They walked slowly, John listening without comment. When they reached the foot of the hill near the river front, Roger paused. "That's the building," he said, "directly across the street."

"Hmmm," John said, his eyes traveling over the frame structure beside the warehouse. There was nothing unusual about it except its tightly closed shutters. "Have you told your uncle about this, Roger?" he asked.

Roger flushed, partly from a sense of guilt, but mostly in pleased surprise. It was the first time John had called him "Roger." It seemed to draw him closer to this big, quiet man he liked and admired so much. He could tell John how he felt about Uncle Taylor. John would understand. "I don't know just what to do, Clark," he began. "I'm sure this is important, yet I hesitate to tell Uncle."

John listened thoughtfully while Roger explained. "I can see your position," he said, "but I still think you should tell Taylor."

"I suppose you're right. Whether he pays any attention to me or not, I ought to tell him."

They had reached the river front and stood for a moment watching the crew of the *Maid of Iowa* unload her varied cargo. Boxes of tea and sacks of sugar from New Orleans—dry goods from New York—barrels of pottery from Connecticut—shoes and military goods from Philadelphia.

The *Good Luck* was anchored at the ferry landing. A shrill whistle shattered the air. "That's the first warning," John said. "I must be getting aboard." They walked toward the landing. John smiled. "Speaking of warnings, look out for the girls. They were rather put out with you for leaving so suddenly last night."

"It was rude and ungracious of me—especially when I'd had such an enjoyable time. I'll apologize to Mary Ann."

"Only to Mary Ann?" John asked, his eyes twinkling.

"Oh, to all of them, of course," Roger's face flushed. "But I had planned to walk home with Mary Ann." He looked at John, his blue eyes clear and frank. "Paulina and Clarissa," he said, "I like them. They entertain me. But Mary Ann—" he hesitated. "Look here, Clark, do I have to explain?"

John laughed. "No," he said. "I think I understand."

There was another blast from the ferry whistle. John laid his hand on Roger's shoulder for a moment and withdrew it with a friendly slap on the back. "I wish I could stay and help you, Roger, but at least I can wish you good luck—and I mean good luck in *everything*."

Roger watched John go aboard the ferry, then he turned and began walking slowly up the hill. He could not explain to John how he felt about Mary Ann. He didn't know, himself. He only knew that she was never out of his mind. She was different. He'd known plenty of girls. They'd interested him—amused him—he'd even made love to some of them. But he had never felt toward any of them as he did toward Mary Ann. She gave him something to think about. She was . . .

He stopped abruptly. He had come to the warehouse and the small, secretive building beside it. John Clark was right. He would have to tell his uncle.

II

1.

But now that he had nerved himself for the ordeal, Roger had no opportunity to talk with his uncle. Taylor had not returned. He had gone on to the neighboring city of Carthage —on a business trip, Aunt Leonora said. *Mysterious business,* thought Roger, but he knew it was no use to ask questions, even if his aunt could have answered.

Henry probably knew. But Henry went on about his tasks, unruffled and uncommunicative; although now and then, it seemed to Roger, he detected a speculative gleam in Henry's eye—particularly at times when the front office of the *Neighbor* was filled with men heatedly engaged in political discussion. *Henry,* Roger thought, *disapproves.* He could well imagine the gist of Henry's report when John Taylor should return from his trip, but with stubborn perversity Roger encouraged visitors. After all, a newspaper office was the natural center of public opinion. Perhaps, by listening to these arguments, he might learn some of the things that were being withheld from him.

With the Whigs nominating Clay and the Democrats Polk, interest in national politics was intense. Smith's political ideas were compared with those of the other candidates. Bitter attacks were made on Clay. The Mormon attitude toward expansion—the big issue of the campaign—interested Roger. Clay straddled this issue; Polk favored it; and Joseph Smith had announced himself in favor of "federal jurisdiction to the west sea, when the red men gave their consent." Interest was also strong in the new Liberty Party, with James Birney, Abolitionist, as its candidate. Smith recommended not only the abolition of slavery by 1850, but compensation for the slave-owners as well. Roger took little part in these discussions, but listened intently and at no time was he able to detect anything but the greatest loyalty to Smith.

The latest issue of the *Warsaw Signal* was filled with anti-Mormon material, but nowhere was there any reference to the Law brothers—nothing to give Roger any clue to the local situation. The opposition on the outside was gaining momentum, but Roger could feel that this was not all—that there was unrest within. A queer tension was in the air. It showed in the faces of the men who came into the office to talk. Even the spirited political arguments could not conceal it. And the building on Water Street remained shuttered and darkened—a constant challenge to Roger's mounting curiosity.

2.

In spite of the general unrest and confusion, one thing remained strong and steadfast—Roger's deepening interest in Mary Ann. The day was not right unless he saw her; more than that—it was decidedly all wrong. It was the joy of being with her that he longed for. Beyond that, he did not attempt to think.

On the fourth afternoon of his uncle's absence Roger met Mary Ann at the Bonnet Shop. They turned their steps toward Temple Hill. The day had been very warm and the sunshine was still brilliant. Roger and Mary Ann were silent as they came up the hill, but as they neared the Temple, Mary

Ann stopped and stood for a moment looking up at the inscription engraved in gold letters on the slab of stone beneath the tower. *The House of the Lord, built by the Latter Day Saints. Commenced April 6, 1841. Holiness to the Lord.*

Roger's eyes were fixed on Mary Ann. There was a strange, exalted expression on her small flushed face. She turned impulsively to Roger.

"Every time I come up here I have to look a long time at the Temple to make sure it's real—that it isn't something I have dreamed." She laughed a little.

"I don't understand," Roger said with a puzzled look.

"Well, you see, when I was a little girl my father was called on a mission. He spent a number of months in Kirtland, Ohio. The Church headquarters were there at the time and the Mormons were building a Temple. When Father wasn't preaching the Gospel, he worked on the Temple." She paused and smiled, tilting her head a little to one side. "Father used to write to Mother about the Temple and she would tell Paulina and me about it. From the things she said I built a picture in my imagination. It's been with me all these years." She laughed again, a little embarrassed. "I suppose you think that's silly."

"Silly? Not at all. I understand," Roger assured her. "I'm a dreamer, too. Does this Temple live up to the one you pictured?"

"Oh, yes!" she exclaimed.

"But I thought the Mormons built a Temple in Missouri?"

"No." Mary Ann shook her head. "Land was consecrated in Independence as a site for a Temple. I can't remember that—I was just a little girl. But I do remember the day the cornerstone was laid for the Temple in Far West. It was on the Fourth of July—the summer before the Saints had their dreadful trouble there. Father took us to the ceremony. But the next spring we all had to go to Quincy. The Temple was never built."

"This Temple has been a long time under construction. Why is that?" Roger asked.

"Father says the Mormons had a lot of trouble in Kirtland because they got into debt building the Temple there. President Smith was determined," Mary Ann went on, "that this Temple should be paid for as it was built." She sighed. "It hasn't been easy, but everyone gives what he can. President Smith has kept his promise."

"You mean that the people donate money, of their own accord?"

"Oh, yes, and their labor, too. Many of the men who work here give their services. They work after hours and on holidays. Father does." She looked up at the Temple again. "We are all very proud that so much has been done. It will be finished within a year."

They were silent for a time, looking down from the hilltop. The city and the river spread out before them, serene and lovely in the calm clear air. The bright glare of the sun had mellowed to the deep yellow that comes before sunset. There was a hush over everything.

Roger was looking at Mary Ann. She turned to him suddenly and smiled. "I love this time of day. Mother always spoke of it as the peaceful hour."

The quiet held them in its spell. They stood looking out across the river. Their shoulders touched. Roger became achingly aware of Mary Ann—her warm softness—the tender curve of her lips—the sweet earnestness of her face. He wanted to touch her, to hold her in his arms. The sun caught the gold in her hair and it shone like a pale nimbus around her little head. Roger put out his hand, then drew it back. "Mary Ann," he said huskily. Mary Ann—dear. . ."

She turned to him quickly, looking up with wide eyes,

startled back to reality. Roger took both of her hands in his. Their eyes held for a moment. "Mary Ann, I—I—" His voice caught in his throat.

A slow crimson wave spread upward from Mary Ann's throat and flared in her cheeks. She dropped her eyes to their hands, then freed herself gently. "Gracious!" she said breathlessly. "I've forgotten the time. Whatever will Mrs. Rich think of me?"

She turned and started down the hill. Roger followed.

3.

Roger walked under the starlit sky for a long time that night. He knew now that he loved Mary Ann. He had never been so happy—so exhilarated—so finely attuned to beauty. The river, the stars, the fragrant summer night—all seemed a part of him, connected in some mysterious way with Mary Ann. He was glad, though, that he had not really spoken, up there on the hill. Mary Ann's eyes had betrayed that this was a new and strange experience to her. She was so young—much younger than most of the girls he had known. Her emotions had never been awakened. He must not startle her. He knew that she was fond of him. Love would come gradually. He wanted it that way.

He made his way homeward scarcely conscious of the streets he followed. Mary Ann and his new-found love had crowded all else from his mind. But he was jerked back sharply on entering the house. His uncle had returned. The sight of him, pale, distraught, moodily silent, brought Roger face to face with his own recent decision. *But I can't talk about it tonight,* Roger thought. *He looks miserable enough as it is.*

12

1.

Roger arose early. He had not been able to sleep. Thoughts of Mary Ann—fleeting pictures of her beside him there on the hilltop—circled through his mind, but the exaltation of his mood had been shattered. Other pictures forced themselves into his consciousness. His uncle's somber face—those five men grouped about a wavering candle flame—Again that intangible foreboding kept Roger turning restlessly on his pillow.

He dressed quickly and tiptoed down the broad stairway. He would go to the office for a while and return to the house in time for breakfast. He closed the door softly behind him. The morning air was fresh and cool. The streets were deserted. The river sparkling in the sunlight was the only thing astir.

A folded newspaper lay where it had been carelessly thrown in the entrance to the *Neighbor* office. For a moment it meant nothing; but even as he stooped for it Roger knew that something was wrong. A newspaper? But there was no local newspaper except the *Neighbor*. Roger unfolded the sheet quickly. His heart jumped as he read the words blazoned across the top:

THE NAUVOO EXPOSITOR
"THE TRUTH, THE WHOLE TRUTH AND NOTHING BUT THE TRUTH"

A low whistle escaped his lips. So the *Neighbor* had a rival.

He stood in the doorway, his eyes fixed on the boldly displayed names of the publishers. William and Wilson Law headed the list. This, then, was what had been going on in that building on Water Street! Rapidly he ran through the other names listed. The only one familiar to him was Francis Higbee. Higbee had recently sued Smith for libel, but the Nauvoo Municipal Court had cleared Smith of the charge.

Roger fitted his key in the lock and entered the office. He tossed his hat onto the peg near the door. He was burning with excitement—eager to learn what the *Expositor* had to expose.

2.

Almost an hour had passed. Breakfast forgotten, Roger leaned back in his chair staring through the window and rumpling his hair abstractedly. People were beginning to pass now. The city was awake. And what an awakening this would be!

Some of Roger's excitement had abated. He was calm enough now to analyze the contents of the *Expositor*. This was schism! It meant a break in the strong Church unity. It was interesting that the people behind this movement styled themselves "seceders from the Church at Nauvoo," and in the same breath affirmed their belief in the Book of Mormon and the Book of Doctrine and Covenants. It was a repudiation of practices then, not doctrines. What it really amounted to was an outright defiance of Joseph Smith.

Roger picked up the *Expositor* again and studied the "Prospectus" set up, boldly conspicuous, in the center of the page. The seceders favored "unconditional repeal of the Nauvoo Charter, to correct abuses of *unit* power. . .uncompromising hostility to any union of Church and State. . .unmitigated disobedience to *Political Revelations.*"

Roger put down the paper and rising, began to pace the room. He had always felt that the Nauvoo Charter invited attack. It was a constant challenge to outsiders by marking the Mormons for special privilege. It was the other point of attack that would precipitate trouble. This matter of plural marriage. The "direct cause," the seceders claimed, for their break with Smith. Roger's eyebrows drew together in a straight, black line. This was something he knew very little about. There were rumors, of course, but everything was beneath the surface—or had been, until now. He halted in the middle of a stride and sat down again to pore over the *Expositor,* his elbows on the desk, the fingers of both hands clutched in his disordered hair. The *Expositor* did not mince words. It certainly dragged things out in the open. Roger scowled at it thoughtfully. He had no facts to go on, but somehow he was beginning to feel that there was more to this than idle rumor. If it was true that the practice of plural marriage was sanctioned by the Church, what effect would it have on the Mormons' private lives? Mary Ann might even become involved! He turned cold at the thought. There must be someone he could ask about this. Someone who would tell him the truth. His mother! Of course. She was the logical one to turn to. He would ask his mother. He was on his feet, starting for the door; but he halted suddenly. His uncle was coming across the street.

Taylor was staring straight ahead, a copy of the *Expositor* jammed under his arm.

Roger stepped forward. "Good morning, Uncle Taylor."

But John Taylor gave no sign of having heard. His eyes glittered angrily and his lips were drawn in a tight line. His glance flicked Roger as he pushed roughly by, strode toward his private office, jerked open the door, and without even a backward glance, entered and slammed it behind him.

3.

For a moment, Roger stood staring at the closed door. He felt as though he had been slapped in the face. Then anger seized him. With quick, purposeful steps he walked to Taylor's door, but paused with his hand on the knob. There was a low murmur of voices inside. Uncle Taylor was consulting Henry. This was too much. He might as well get out. He wasn't needed here. He grabbed his hat from the rack, and stalked out into the street.

Roger's anger cooled a little as he walked along Bain to Water Street. Excitement pushed it into the background of his mind. More and more people were gathering, all hurrying toward the business section. Roger glanced at his watch. It was still early—about the time that stores and offices would be opening. Undoubtedly each business man had received his copy of the *Expositor*. He walked on toward Main Street, quickening his pace. Store doors stood open, but owners, clerks and early morning traders were knotted in small groups on the sidewalks, business temporarily forgotten. Arms waved in angry protest, and excited voices clamored and questioned, as newcomers paused on the fringes of groups that were rapidly fusing into an angry crowd.

Roger moved on toward Parley Street, weaving in and out, scanning faces, pausing here and there to catch snatches of conversation. Some of these people were grim-faced and stern—their comments brief and restrained. "The situation was without precedent." "Something for the Church officers to handle." Others talked volubly, eyes blazing with anger.

"A disgrace!" "Not to be tolerated." "The *Expositor* must be destroyed."

Near the corner of Parley, Roger stopped and peered in at the open door of the Bonnet Shop. Miss Ellis was nowhere about. Mary Ann, of course, never came down until afternoon. He walked on, thinking of her, of the things she had told him about her childhood—about her mother. Not much, but enough to give him a clear picture of Laura Phelps—of how close she had been to everything that concerned the Mormons, and how strongly her faith had impressed itself upon her daughter. Mary Ann must be dreadfully upset by all this. He wanted to talk with her now. It seemed a long time until five o'clock when he could meet her at the Bonnet Shop.

At the corner he paused before the eating-house window. Several men were seated at one of the tables, talking earnestly, their faces intent. The proprietor, a large, florid-faced man, was noticeably torn between his duty to his patrons and his desire to be out on the street. He set down plates of ham and eggs before the man, sidled to the door, peered up and down the street, and hurried back to the kitchen.

The odor of coffee reminded Roger that he had eaten no breakfast. *And besides,* he thought, eyeing the group of men as he entered, *this may prove interesting.* He chose a table near the window, as close to theirs as possible. The proprietor twisted the corner of his apron nervously as he took Roger's order. "This is the most excitement we've had since we left Missouri," he volunteered, waving a hand toward the street, then sighed and shook his head as he wheeled and started back toward the kitchen.

The men at the table behind Roger were talking in low tones. He leaned backward a little, straining his ears. The murmur ceased. He could feel their eyes upon him. He straightened casually, pulled a letter from his pocket and studied it with absorbed interest. The voices began again in fierce undertones. Suddenly a chair scraped back and a man spoke angrily aloud. "You fools! I tell you it was bound to come. Some people refuse to be led like sheep." A small, sharp-featured man, his face crimson with fury, brushed past Roger's table and walked swiftly to the door. Roger looked around quickly. The remaining men were grim. Black looks followed the small man as he went out into the street.

The proprietor eyed Roger curiously as he poured steaming coffee into a thick cup. "Say, ain't you that young man from the *Neighbor* office?"

Roger carefully measured sugar into his coffee. "Yes," he said, without looking up.

"Pretty stirred up over there, ain't they?"

"Not particularly," Roger said, concentrating on his eggs.

"Well, they ought to be. There's likely to be trouble. Sort of quieting down now, though."

Roger looked out of the window. The crowds were thinning out. People were going on about their business.

"That's the way it is," the man went on. "We'll just have to wait like we always do, and see what happens." He sighed heavily and turned to greet new customers who had entered.

Roger finished his breakfast, pondering. "Wait and see what happens." That's what he would have to do, too. But, Lord! how he wanted to get hold of this thing. He was no longer angry with his uncle. He was beginning to understand that the *Expositor* was much more than a rival newspaper to Taylor. It was a blow at the foundations of Mormonism, at everything he believed. Roger pushed his plate aside and rose. He'd go back to the office at once.

13

1.

The sweet, shy panic that had overwhelmed Mary Ann on Temple Hill kept her nervously chattering to Roger all the way home. Once there, she had taken leave of him hurriedly and escaped into the house, plunging into her evening's work with a concentrated energy that gave her no time for reflection. But in the secret darkness of her bedroom that night she had surrendered herself half fearfully to a tumult of strange emotions. There had been no mistaking Roger's feeling for her. Little as she knew of men and their ways, instinct told her that he loved her and had wanted to tell her so; and her cheeks burned as she admitted to herself that she wished she had not stopped him. Her own feelings she did not try to understand, but the exciting new sense of power made her heart throb faster as she lay wide-awake for hours.

But she awoke at the usual time. The sky was deep blue and birds were twittering in the elm outside her window. Happiness surged through her. For a moment she lay there dreamily wondering why—then, fully awake, she remembered. She dressed slowly, pausing to examine herself critically in the small mirror over the washstand. She didn't look any different—yet she felt different. It was a new feeling and it sent pleasant chills over her. She couldn't define it, but she knew that she liked it.

A ray of sunlight touched the sacred Mormon books on the table by the window. "A thought for each day," Mother always said. Surely, this was a day when she specially needed the guidance she always found in the holy books. She began thumbing through the Book of Doctrine and Covenants, but a sudden thought clouded the brightness of her face. Roger was not a Mormon. She stood quite still for a moment, then her fingers marked a place and she opened the book. Her eyes turned instinctively to an underlined passage: "For verily the voice of the Lord is unto all men." A soft breeze stirred the looped-back folds of the fresh muslin curtain. On the trellis over the garden gate bright purple morning glories lifted their faces to the sunshine. Mary Ann looked back at the book in her hands. "There is no eye that shall not see, neither ear that shall not hear, neither heart that shall not be penetrated," she read, murmuring the passage softly to herself. She lifted her head, her eyes shining. A message. A promise to her. Roger would become a Mormon!

2.

Mrs. Rich was spreading a bright yellow cloth over the table near the window. "Good morning, Mary Ann," she said. "This is *Neighbor* morning. Will you bring in the paper?"

Mary Ann stepped outside and drew a deep breath of the fresh, sweet air. There were two papers on the porch. She was faintly surprised, but she tucked them, still folded, under her arm, and stood for an instant looking at the garden. It was so lovely out of doors. Everything seemed to sparkle. She returned to the kitchen. Mrs. Rich was tying a bib around little Jane and settling her in her chair. "Two papers?" she questioned. Mary Ann nodded absently.

Mrs. Rich sat down and opened one of the sheets. Mary Ann busied herself at the stove. But a startled exclamation made her turn quickly. Mrs. Rich was staring at the paper, her face pale, her eyes wide and frightened.

"What is it, Mrs. Rich?" Mary Ann asked anxiously. "Bad news?"

"I—it's nothing. I'll talk to you about it later. Will you get the baby, please, Mary Ann?" Mrs. Rich quietly laid the paper aside. "This young lady seems to be hungry." She smiled, her lips still pale, as she sprinkled sugar over Sarah Jane's mush.

Before they had finished breakfast, a message came. Sister Evans was very ill. Would Mrs. Rich come at once? Sister Evans was a close friend. Mrs. Rich, worried but calm, made hasty preparations to depart. "You are a real comfort to me, Mary Ann," she said as she put on her bonnet. "With you here I feel perfectly safe in leaving the children and the house. I'll try to get back in time for you to go to the Bonnet Shop," she promised. "If I'm late, call Sister Childs from down the street. She'll be glad to come."

But Mary Ann scarcely heard the directions. Mrs. Rich had picked up that paper—the one that had upset her so. She was going to take it with her. Whatever could it be that had made Mrs. Rich look like that? Could anything have happened to General Rich? Oh, *no!* Mary Ann's own heart almost stopped. Her knees weakened, and she sank into a chair, her eyes wide with horror. But the shock passed after a moment. If it had been anything like that, Mrs. Rich would have told her. But what was it?

All during the morning the question nagged at Mary Ann's curiosity. But there was nothing she could do about it. She hoped fervently that Mrs. Rich would return before it was time to leave. But Mrs. Rich did not return. At one o'clock Mary

Ann dutifully called Sister Childs and went on her way to the Bonnet Shop.

3.

Miss Ellis, a distracted look on her face, met Mary Ann at the door. "I'm glad you're here, my dear. An important business matter has come up. I must go to Lawyer Emmons' office at once." She paused. "I may be gone all afternoon. Do you think you can manage?"

"Of course, I can." Mary Ann smiled confidently, thrilled at the prospect of being left in charge.

Miss Ellis hesitated on the threshold. "I hate to leave you today. A new paper called the *Expositor* came out this morning. It made some dreadful charges against President Smith. There was great excitement around here for a while, but everything is all right now, I think. Did Sister Rich tell you about the paper?"

"No." Mary Ann answered. "Mrs. Rich was called away early this morning."

"Well, I wouldn't discuss it with customers," Miss Ellis cautioned. The line between her eyebrows deepened. "If you should have any trouble"—she motioned toward the hardware store across the street—"ask Brother Allen to come over."

Mary Ann watched Miss Ellis leave. The *Expositor*. So that was the name of the paper. Her curiosity was thoroughly aroused, now. She wondered if Miss Ellis had a copy? But Miss Ellis did not—at least no copy was visible, and Mary Ann wouldn't have considered looking in the desk or Miss Ellis' private cupboard.

She walked about the shop restlessly. The street was quiet. No customers came in. After a while she went into the back room and began to unpack a shipment of bonnets from New York, carrying them one by one into the front room and arranging them in the cabinet. Twice, as she passed the front window she noticed a short, stocky man lounging against the hitching-post on the opposite corner. She had never seen him there before. She looked again. Yes, he had a bundle of papers under his arm! Even as she watched, he thrust one into the hand of a passer-by.

Mary Ann stood at the window, her back stiff and straight. Then, quite suddenly, she marched out of the door and across the street. She kept her eyes fixed ahead. She dared not look at the man yet for fear of losing her courage.

He looked up as she reached him, his eyes alert. "*Expositor,* ma'am?" he asked in a gruff voice.

Mary Ann nodded mutely taking the paper he held out, then turned quickly and went back across the street, her head high. She closed the door firmly behind her and went into the back room. Her cheeks were flaming, her heart beating wildly. *What* had she done? But she had to know. Her hands trembled as she opened the paper and began to read.

14

1.

Roger, on his way back to the *Neighbor* office, was in an uplifted mood. He had conquered his injured pride. He had forgiven Uncle Taylor freely. He was going to prove it—to show that he understood—to apologize for the angry impulse that had led him away from the paper just when he might be needed most. But to Roger's chagrin, John Taylor and Henry were still closeted. His departure, evidently, had been unnoticed. Probably they had not even missed him. His high resolves seemed a bit ridiculous now, but he refused to be angered further. Doggedly, he remained at his desk, trying to behave as usual—ignoring Taylor's gloomy silence and Henry's grim aloofness. But it was doubly hard to concentrate on routine work when every instinct was tormenting him to be out mixing with people, comparing opinions, digging out information—and this he dared not do. It was safer to avoid people. He must wait and learn Uncle Taylor's stand before taking part in any discussion.

It left him plenty of time to think.

It was well before five as Roger neared the Bonnet Shop, but he wanted to be there early. He knew just how Mary Ann would look, stepping demurely into the street, carrying herself with that quaint dignity she felt her position demanded. He smiled tenderly. What a child she was—and yet how womanly and sweet. All day, regardless of tension and confusion, she had been present in his thoughts. He had found himself considering everything from two viewpoints—his own and Mary Ann's. There was so much he wanted to say to her—

Suddenly, Roger halted in his tracks. Surely, it couldn't be! Yes, it was. That was Mary Ann, already a block beyond, hurrying along Main Street away from the Bonnet Shop. Roger lengthened his stride and gained on her. What could have happened? Why hadn't she waited? He called for her every afternoon. She knew that. And today above all days—after what had happened on Temple Hill—

"Mary Ann?" There was reproach and a question in his voice as he dropped into step beside her.

Bright color stained her cheek and she avoided his eyes. "I was—in a hurry," she said hesitantly.

Silence fell between them. Uneasy silence. Strain. Roger could not understand it. Yesterday they had been so close and now they were miles apart. The *Expositor*. That was it. She hadn't mentioned it, but he felt sure it was responsible for the barrier between them. No wonder she was not being natural. There was plenty in that paper to make a modest young girl self-conscious. He must find some way to break down her reserve ——to make her understand that she could turn to him with everything that troubled her. That she could depend on him always. To shield her and make her happy seemed the most important thing in the world. He had never thought of love as being like this, but now he knew he wouldn't have it otherwise.

As they neared the Rich home, Mary Ann broke the silence. "Roger," she demanded suddenly, "did you know anything last night about—about the *Expositor?*"

"Not a thing. But I had a feeling that some trouble—"

"Trouble!" She caught up the word. "Oh, Roger. No! I can't bear to think of trouble coming again. Our beautiful city—everything—"

"Mary Ann," Roger linked his arm through hers and drew her close to his side. "Don't worry so, dear. After all it's only a rival newspaper. Things like this happen every day in other cities. You are taking it too seriously."

"But it *is* serious. Those terrible lies they told about President Smith!" She pulled away from him, her eyes blazing.

Roger regarded her in silence. The flare of color in her cheeks—the fire in her eyes. She was lovely—lovelier than he'd ever seen her, and it was concern for Joseph Smith that had kindled this anger. *I didn't realize,* Roger thought. *She idolizes the man.* It jolted him sharply, leaving him with a baffled, curiously helpless feeling. She would believe anything—accept anything that Smith sanctioned. Perhaps even plural marriage. Sick revulsion seized him, but Mary Ann must not suspect it. This was not the time nor the place to broach that subject. It was an effort to speak. His voice sounded almost gruff. "There will be a way to deal with Smith's accusers," he said, "—if the charges they've made aren't true."

Mary Ann said nothing. There was a quiver about her lips. She kept her eyes averted for a moment, then turned them, wide and reproachful on Roger. "You don't understand," she said in a low tone.

"I'm trying to," he said.

They were at the Rich gate now. Mrs. Rich was in the garden. Roger lifted his hat and bowed, smiling, as she looked up. She acknowledged the greeting courteously. He wondered if it was his imagination that made her seem distant—a little cool.

"I must go in," Mary Ann said.

"Will I see you tomorrow?"

"I don't know," she answered slowly. She was inside the gate, facing him.

"Well," he smiled with an assurance he did not feel, "I'll see you sometime—some place. Goodbye—dear," he added softly.

2.

It was cool and restful on the Taylor porch. From the broad step at her feet, Roger regarded his mother, wondering how he could ask the question that burned in his mind. The sun was low, but the light was still good and Ruth Parker's dark head was bent over her needlepoint, her hands darting like small white birds, swift and strong for all their seeming fragility. She was like that, herself, Roger realized; softly feminine, smiling serene but with a new quality of inner reserve—a withdrawal into some secret place. *She looks the same,* he thought miserably, *but she's different, somehow.* In the old days he would have gone straight to the point, confident of her understanding, no matter how it might embarrass her to discuss such intimate matters with him; but now—He cleared his throat nervously and she looked up.

"Mother," he began abruptly, "how close are you to this Mormon situation?"

"Close?" she repeated. "What do you mean, Roger? I am as good a Mormon as I know how to be."

"Yes, I know that. It's the present situation I'm interested in."

"But surely, Roger, you know as much about that as I do."

"That's where you are mistaken, my dear mother. Uncle Taylor has not confided in me. Do you think I'd be sitting here idly twiddling my thumbs if he had?"

Ruth Parker sat up very straight and her eyes were level and unsmiling. "You must not blame your Uncle Taylor. After all, you *are* an outsider, and that is your own fault."

Roger laughed shortly. "I know, Mother. You needn't remind me. I understand how Uncle feels, but it doesn't make things easier." He moved a little and looked up into her face. "I want you to tell me something. Is it true that plural marriage is being practiced by Joseph Smith and some of the high church officials?" He was a little breathless as he finished. In the still air the fragrance from the garden was almost unbearably sweet.

Ruth Parker began gathering her work into a small silk bag; her fingers shook a little.

Roger stared at her fixedly. "I understand," he said heavily. It was all clear now. His uncle's attitude, Mary Ann's diffidence, Mrs. Rich's coolness. Even to his own mother he was an outsider.

"Mother," he began desperately, but she was standing now, straight and still, looking down at him with strange, remote eyes.

"Come, son," she said. "It's supper time. We musn't keep your Aunt Leonora waiting."

3.

Sarah Rich sat by the center table in the sitting room. Her knitting, with needles sharply protruding, lay untouched in her lap. Somehow she could not bring herself to take up her work tonight.

The candles in tall holders on the table made a warm pool of light around her. She sighed. She had not been surprised when Mary Ann confessed that she had read the *Expositor.* Mary Ann was a girl of spirit. She wanted to know things. *I should have told her,* Sarah reproached herself. *I should have explained the facts—not let them come to her twisted and distorted.* There had been hurt bewilderment in Mary Ann's eyes. This had been a rude shock to her. *And to me,* Sarah thought grimly. A shudder of disgust ran through her as she remembered, unwillingly, the crude vulgarity and viciousness of those printed words.

She leaned her aching head against the back of the chair and closed her eyes. They stung, and her face felt hot. Wearily, she tried to push all thoughts from her mind. After a moment she straightened and took up her knitting. The click of the needles made a pleasant sound in the quiet room.

Sarah looked up, smiling, as Mary Ann came in from the kitchen. "Sit over here, my dear." She nodded toward a low stool at her feet. "I want you to wind this yarn for me."

Mary Ann seated herself obediently and began separating the strands of newly spun yarn.

"Mary Ann," Sarah began, "I'm sorry that I was called away this morning. I wanted to talk with you before you read the *Expositor*."

Mary Ann's face crimsoned. "I'm sorry," she murmured. "I know I shouldn't have done what I did. Please don't be—"

"I'm not put out," Sarah reassured her quickly. "It's just that I would have liked to talk with you about some of the things the paper mentioned." She paused, carefully examining a row of knitting. Her voice was casual as she added, "Especially about the doctrine of plural marriage."

Mary Ann looked up, her eyes wide and troubled. "You mean," she said slowly, "about the Prophet—about other Mormon men having more than one wife?"

Sarah Rich did not answer at once. She sat for a moment thoughtful, her knitting needles poised. She was remembering the evening, only a few months ago, when Charles had first explained this to her. She commenced to knit again, slowly. "Mary Ann," she said, "you believe in the Book of Doctrine and Covenants—you know that from time to time new doctrines are revealed to our Prophet—that according to our belief, we should live according to these revelations?"

"Yes," Mary Ann said gravely. Her small face looked white and drawn in the candlelight.

"This new doctrine which teaches that a man may have more than one wife was revealed to the Prophet about a year ago." Sarah put down her knitting and leaned forward, talking earnestly. "The Prophet has taught it secretly to some of the Church leaders who are very close to him." She could see a question in Mary Ann's eyes, but she did not pause. "It is something so very personal—it reveals a new marriage relationship so different from the accepted custom, that the Prophet has hesitated to proclaim it generally You see, Mary Ann, it must be studied carefully. The Prophet taught it to Charles—and Charles has taught it to me."

"You don't mean that you—that General Rich—" Mary Ann stared, fumbling for words.

"No. No. We believe, of course, that the doctrine is right, but as yet it has not touched our lives."

"But—but," Mary Ann pushed back the hair from her forehead, in a confused gesture. "It seems so strange. I don't understand—"

"You will, my dear, as time goes on. I can't tell you any more now—not until Charles comes home. It is a secret we have shared. I know you will not discuss it with anyone. I wouldn't have told you this much if the *Expositor* hadn't come out."

Mary Ann shook her head. "Those awful things in the paper—" she began.

"There are two sides to every question, Mary Ann." Sarah Rich sighed. "The *Expositor* was published by men who no longer agree with our Prophet. They have shared the secret, but they refuse to accept the doctrine."

"Do you think that means trouble?"

"I'm afraid it does. But then," Sarah smiled and began to knit again, calmly, "we've had trouble before. We can face it."

4.

In the small sitting room of the Taylor home, Roger waited for his uncle's return. It was almost midnight. The measured tick of the tall clock in the hall echoed hollowly in the silence. Taylor had not come home to supper. It had been a dismal meal, with Roger silent and morose—his mother and aunt talking little and with effort. The two women retired early and he had been left alone with his thoughts—turbulent, angry thoughts, rebellious thoughts — and underneath, a fear that would not be quieted. Fear for Mary Ann. He closed his eyes, and her grave little face floated before him. The soft, golden hair. The deep blue eyes—with their childlike candor. It was monstrous to think of plural marriage for her. And the worst of it was that if she thought it was right, she would accept it without question. Roger gripped the arms of his chair fiercely. She shouldn't! He'd marry her and take her away. He'd— He groaned aloud and bent forward, elbows on his knees, his long fingers thrust into his thick black hair. What could he do? Mary Ann had withdrawn from him. He wasn't even sure when he would see her again.

A key scraped in the lock. Roger sprang to his feet and was out in the hall before the front door opened. John Taylor closed it behind him and stood looking at Roger. The light from the candelabra on the newel post fell across Taylor's face. It was white and drained of all vitality. "You still up?" he asked abruptly.

"I waited for you," Roger said. "I thought there might be something I could do for you." At the moment he felt intensely sorry for his uncle.

"It's good of you, Roger, but I'm afraid there is nothing you can do"; Taylor thought for a moment, "except to carry on the routine of the office." His eyes met Roger's, then turned away. "The City Council is going to handle everything," he said, with peculiar emphasis. "I'll have to attend the sessions."

Roger noticed how carefully his uncle had avoided any reference to the *Expositor*. But he made no comment.

Taylor was moving toward the staircase. "I'm going to bed, now. Have to be up early. The Council session begins at eight. See that things are fixed for the night, will you?"

He started upstairs, moving slowly — as though weights were dragging at his feet.

15

1.

For the next two days Roger scarcely saw his uncle. The Council was in session. Taylor was taking his meals at the Mansion House. His visits to the *Neighbor* office were brief and infrequent, and on each occasion one or another of the Church officers was with him. But this afternoon Taylor came in alone. One glance at his uncle's face told Roger the suspense was over. The tense lines were gone from around his mouth. He wore a look of relief—an expression almost of secret satisfaction, that was echoed in his voice and manner.

He greeted Roger briskly. "Well, young man, have you caught up all the back work?"

Roger smiled and shrugged. "Everything I could handle, sir. Frankly, there wasn't much to do."

"There'll be plenty from now on," Taylor said. "I'll want you here early in the morning."

Roger's interest awakened. His blue eyes searched his uncle's face, but it revealed nothing.

"You'd better go along now." Taylor paused in the doorway of his private office. "I expected to be home for supper, but I can't, after all. Tell your aunt not to wait for me. I have some business to attend to." The words trailed back over his shoulder. Already he was hurrying toward the pressroom.

Never a word about the Council session—about what vital decisions had been made in this crisis. *Errand boy,* Roger thought. He laughed, a short harsh laugh, grabbed his hat and went out of the door whistling defiantly.

He might as well face the truth. He could never have any real part in things unless he became a Mormon. The talk with his mother had made that clear. He'd done some serious thinking during those long, empty hours at the office, waiting for something to happen. He walked along Bain Avenue, head bent, frowning. As he understood it, the Mormon creed must be accepted wholeheartedly or not at all—and there was much, even in the little he knew of it that he could not accept. There was a new significance now in John's comment that "it had to come from within."

At Parley Street, Roger's feet took the familiar route to the Bonnet Shop. Miss Ellis greeted him pleasantly. Roger liked her. She seemed the only one who had not looked on him with suspicion, these past few days.

"Mary Ann isn't here, Mr. Parker," she told him. "She won't be down for several days. Mrs. Rich is ill—not seriously, but she needs Mary Ann more than I do. I'm sorry."

"I'm sorry, too," Roger said slowly. He could not conceal his disappointment.

"Why don't you call at the Riches?" Miss Ellis suggested.

"Oh, I wouldn't intrude there—not when Mrs. Rich is ill."

He thanked Miss Ellis, bade her goodbye and turned toward the Knoll section. It was torture not to see Mary Ann. The barrier that he had sensed at their last meeting was becoming more tangible every moment that he was away from her. If he had only told her of his love that night on Temple Hill. He had been certain then that she cared for him. He knew now that he wanted her more than ever before. But—Mary Ann was a Mormon. There it was again. Wherever he turned, it loomed up squarely in his path, a solid wall, barring him from all that he longed for. His work—after all, that didn't matter. Other places were open to him. Places where he would have real responsibility. He could leave here. But life without Mary Ann—The thought wrenched his heart with an almost physical pain. Surely there was some way to work this out—some middle course to follow. If Mary Ann loved him. *If Mary Ann loves me,* he repeated to himself. But she did. She must. Until he could see her again, he had to believe that.

2.

Roger prowled restlessly about Taylor's garden. Supper was over. There was no place he wanted to go, yet the thought of sitting quietly at home visiting with his mother and Aunt Leonora was unbearable.

The sun had set in a red glory, and long streamers of rose and violet stretched above the housetops. It was clear and very quiet. There was something almost ominous in the hush that enveloped the Knoll.

Roger stopped walking and stood looking across toward the other side of the city. Lights were beginning to twinkle in windows, but it was still fairly light outside. The spire of the Temple etched against the sky, pointed heavenward like a slender finger. Roger sighed. So much outward peace—So much inward strife.

In the clear, soft light the business section was plainly visible. From somewhere on Water Street a thin spiral of smoke drifted lazily upward. Roger's eyes followed it, but his thoughts were far away. Another spiral rose, thicker and heavier. Roger stiffened. The smoke was a lurid column now, shot through with orange streaks of flame.

Roger ran across the garden and through the gate, his feet flying toward the hill that led toward the heart of the city.

Even as he ran, Roger wondered at the deserted streets. It was not more than eight o'clock, but dark enough for the fire to attract a crowd. Yet there was no crowd. No excitement. No noise but the thud of his own running feet, and a distant sound of crashing, heavy blows. At Water Street he paused, breathless, and slowed to a walk. The air was acrid with smoke. Roger choked and his eyes smarted, but through the blur they beheld a strange scene. In the vacant lot next to the *Expositor* office a huge bonfire roared. A group of men, quiet, orderly, moving with almost mechanical precision, were feeding the flames with bundles of papers and books. Other men filed in and out of the building, carrying fresh supplies of the fuel. In the glare of the fire the uniform of the Nauvoo Legion was unmistakable. Legion officers formed a wide circle around the blaze.

"Halt!"

Roger started. A Legion officer was blocking his way. Intent upon the scene before him, Roger had not noticed the cordon drawn across the street.

"I'm Parker," he said, "of the *Neighbor*. I'd like to get through, please. Newspaper business."

"Sorry, sir." The man was respectful, but firm. "Orders are orders. You can't come any closer. But don't worry about your story." He grinned. "John Taylor's over there in the thick of it."

"Oh," Roger said. "Thanks." So this was the "business" that kept Uncle Taylor from his supper!

The splintering, crashing noises had begun again. In the blocked-off street before the *Expositor* office men with crowbars and sledge hammers swarmed around the dark bulk of a printing press, their brawny arms rising and falling in the crimson glare—their shapes distorted by inky shadows. It was fantastic, Roger thought. A scene from *The Inferno.*

He became conscious of excited voices near-by. One of them seemed vaguely familiar. Roger looked around. A knot of men were arguing. The familiar voice belonged to the sharp-faced man who had left the eating-house in such a rage.

"Pretty high-handed action for the Council," he said. "You mark my words. There'll be hell to pay when those non-Mormons over in Warsaw and Carthage hear about this. They've just been waiting for an excuse."

"But what else could we do?" another demanded. "We couldn't sit back and wait for the people to act. That would have meant violence and bloodshed."

"Well," said another, "at least there were some of us who held out for moderation."

"Those Law brothers must have been plenty guilty, the damned scoundrels!" a high pitched angry voice broke in. "You don't see 'em around, do you, tryin' to defend their property?"

"Well," challenged the first man, "what would you do if the Council got after you, with the Legion back of them? You wait. We'll be hearing from those fellows."

They moved away.

It's unbelievable, Roger thought. *They couldn't do a thing like this.* Yet in the back of his mind he knew it was true. "The Council," Uncle Taylor had said, "is going to handle everything." Roger wondered how they had kept the people off the streets. He shook his head. That would be a simple matter for the Council. The leaders had their flock well in hand.

The Legion officer was approaching again.

"You still here?" he demanded, suspicion in his tone. "It's about time you moved on."

Roger shrugged and walked away. The old story. Being pushed aside and kept out of things. But he no longer cared. One of his problems was settled. He would resign from the *Neighbor* tomorrow.

16

1.

John Taylor was absent from the breakfast table, but Roger asked no questions. He ate hurriedly and silently, with occasional glances at his mother and his aunt. They were pale but entirely composed. *Too composed,* he thought. That unnatural calm was the only indication that they were aware of last night's happenings.

Roger had slept well. His decision to leave the *Neighbor* had brought such a feeling of relief and freedom that he realized for the first time how great the strain had been. He was eager now to confront his uncle, to thresh things out. There need be no quarrel, no hard feelings. But he owed it to himself, Roger felt, to declare his principles; his complete lack of sympathy with a code that could sanction what he had witnessed last night.

He entered the office with a firm step, his body tense, his eyes unsmiling. At the sound of the door, John Taylor stepped from his room, a sheaf of papers in his hand. He strode toward Roger, relief in his haggard face.

"Roger, my boy! I need you." He waved the papers excitedly. "We're rushing through a special edition. Sit down here."

With his free hand, he pushed Roger into a chair and stood facing him, outlining the situation in swift, desperate words. News of the *Expositor's* destruction and the Law's flight to Carthage was spreading like wildfire. The special edition was to publish the minutes of the Council meeting. "We must hurry," Taylor said, his voice high and strained. "We must get it to the non-Mormon centers. We don't want those fellows to get the wrong ideas." He thrust the papers into Roger's hand. "Here, lad. Get this ready for the front page." He hurried away.

Roger sat motionless, staring at the scribbled notes.

From the doorway of his office Taylor spoke again. "I've sent Henry for extra help," he said. "Thank God you're here, Roger."

"I need you, boy." "Thank God you're here." Roger knew now what he must do. His personal affairs could wait. He peeled off his coat and went to work.

By late the following day the special edition had been distributed far and wide, but it did not stem the tide of anti-Mormon feeling. News filtered into the *Neighbor* office. The Laws had appealed to the County Court at Carthage. The Court there had issued a writ demanding the appearance of Joseph Smith and his counselors in Carthage. They were charged with riot in connection with the destruction of the *Expositor*. The Mormon answer came promptly. The Nauvoo Municipal Court set aside the Carthage action and released the accused. Feeling mounted higher against the Mormons.

It was ironic, Roger thought. Now that he was through here, he found himself at last in the center of things. There were no more reservations. John Taylor did more than turn to his nephew—he leaned on him. But Roger's attitude was curiously impersonal. He was needed and he was here. He worked feverishly, but without enthusiasm. His decision had not altered. One thing he was thankful for. He had no time to brood over Mary Ann.

At the last moment, the regular edition of the *Neighbor* was broken down. Space must be made for a proclamation by Joseph Smith. It began with details regarding the recent action of the Nauvoo Municipal Court, and finished with an impassioned burst of eloquence. "Our city," Smith said, "is infested with a set of blacklegs, counterfeiters and debauchees, and that the proprietors of this press were of that class, the minutes of the Municipal Court fully testify, and in ridding our young and flourishing city of such characters, we are abused by not only villainous demagogues, but by some who from their station and influence in society, ought rather to raise than to depress the standard of human excellence. We have no disturbance or excitement among us, save what is made by the thousand and one idle rumors afloat in the country. Every one is protected in his person and his property, and but few cities of a population of twenty thousand people, in the United States, hath less of dissipation or vice of any kind than the city of Nauvoo. Of the correctness of our conduct in this affair, we appeal to every high Court in the State, and to its ordeal we are willing to appear at any time that his Excellency, Governor Ford, shall please to call us before it. I, therefore, on behalf of the Municipal Court of Nauvoo, warn the lawless not to be precipitate in any interference in our affairs, for sure as there is a God in Israel we shall ride triumphant over all opposition."

In the first light of the June dawn Roger sank wearily into his chair and looked over the revised edition. Smith's proclamation was both an appeal and a challenge. Which way would it be taken?

2.

When the proclamation reached non-Mormon centers, fires,

long smoldering, burst into flame. Public meetings were held in Warsaw, Carthage, Rushville and Green Plains. The *Warsaw Signal* came out with a bitter blast against Smith. Anti-Mormon feeling in the community crystallized in a set of resolutions adopted by its citizens. "The time in our opinion, has arrived, when the Prophet and his miscreant adherents should be demanded, and, if not surrendered, a war of extermination should be waged, to the entire destruction if necessary for our protection, of his adherents."

Roger watched the Mormons wait—proud—defiant—with nerves stretched like brittle threads. On the surface he was casual—he worked—he carried out orders—he accepted responsibility. But under his calm Mary Ann's words were sharp in his memory. "Our beautiful city—everything—I can't bear it." He did not want her to be hurt, but the avalanche had been set in motion. Every day it was gaining momentum.

Governor Ford had come to Carthage. The non-Mormons had demanded definite action, and the Governor was to conduct a personal investigation. At his request Joseph Smith dispatched a committee to Carthage to relate the story of recent happenings in Nauvoo. John Taylor headed this committee. There was a brief lull.

3.

On a stifling hot afternoon, Roger, unable longer to restrain his longing, persuaded his mother to accompany him to the Rich home.

Mary Ann was stiffly polite as she invited them to sit on the porch. She was pale, and there were faint blue shadows under her eyes.

"You must be lonely, my dear, alone here, with Mrs. Rich ill." Ruth Parker's tone expressed gentle concern.

"Oh, no." Mary Ann objected quickly. "I am very busy

and the children are good company." She was seated on a rustic bench, her hands loosely folded in her lap. "We expect General Rich back soon," she added.

It seemed to Roger that she brightened visibly as she mentioned Rich. As if the mere voicing of his name had kindled a light within her. A cold hand seemed to clutch his heart. He remembered a scene in this very garden. Mary Ann's ardor. The warmth in her eyes. "It's General Rich!" she had said. And later, at the gate, "Isn't he a fine man?" *Yes,* Roger thought, *he is a fine man. He's a man any girl might admire.—And he's a damned good Mormon, besides.*

Mary Ann was speaking to his mother. "I think Mrs. Rich would like to see you," she said, carefully polite. "I'll take you to her."

Roger waited impatiently for Mary Ann's return. How she'd changed! Was it shyness, because of his mother? He knew in his heart it was more than that. She looked so tired. She was working too hard. She shouldn't be here at all. He got up and began to pace back and forth, rumpling his hair violently. How he longed to take her away from all this.

He moved toward her impulsively as she stepped outside. "Mary Ann," his voice was choked with emotion. "Mary Ann, I've missed you so."

He caught at her hands, but she drew back. "Don't," she said sharply; then stood looking up at him with unhappy eyes.

"What is it, Mary Ann? What's wrong, dear? Don't you know that I—"

"Mary Ann—Mary Ann," a forlorn little wail broke in.

She was down the steps and along the hollyhock-bordered path in a flash. Little Sarah Jane was sobbing, screwing her small fists into brimming eyes. Mary Ann dropped to her knees, her arms around the child. "Whatever happened?" she demanded tenderly.

Roger stood on the porch and cursed softly. His moment was gone. What foul luck!

On the way home his mother spoke abruptly, startling him out of a reverie. "You love her very much, don't you, Roger?"

"Yes, Mother." His blue eyes met hers squarely. "I want her for my wife."

Mrs. Parker sighed. "Nothing would make me happier, dear. But Mary Ann is a very good Mormon. Have you thought of that?"

"I've thought of it night and day." Roger made an angry gesture. "But if we love each other—why should that make any difference?"

"Perhaps it wouldn't," said Ruth Parker slowly, "if she loves you. Have you asked her, Roger?"

But Roger did not answer. His head was bent as they walked on side by side in the hot sunshine.

4.

John Taylor returned from Carthage late that evening. His face was gray with fatigue, but his eyes were like live coals as he gave an account of the trip. "We told our story," he concluded bitterly, "but we didn't make any impression on that man Ford. He's determined to make us come to Carthage for a hearing."

The following day, Ford's conclusions were made public. The Mormon committee by their own account, he said, had convinced him of the necessity for drastic action. Joseph Smith and the members of the City Council must be brought to justice. The Mormon people could rest assured, however, that this would be accomplished without putting them in danger of attack from a mob.

But Joseph Smith, seemingly, did not put much faith in Ford's promises. He lost no time in assembling the Legion and placing Nauvoo under martial law. John Taylor explained this to Roger. "We *must* be assured," he said earnestly, "that we are protected against a mob."

Legion officers patrolled the streets; and in obedience to Smith's command, Mormon people from outlying districts were pouring into Nauvoo. Everyone who entered or left the city was subjected to rigid questioning.

And in the midst of this tension, Ford's official mandate was delivered to Joseph Smith. The governor pledged protection to him and his associates if they would give themselves up in Carthage. If they failed to comply, their arrest would be brought about, "even if it took the whole state militia to do it."

17

1.

John Taylor took leave of Roger in the *Neighbor* office. It was a cloudy morning, gray and dismal. In a few moments Smith, with Taylor and the other Counselors, would start for Carthage.

Taylor laid his hand on Roger's shoulder. "Don't come to see me off, lad," he said. "I'd rather think of you here. I know that you and Henry will take care of things."

"I'll do my best, sir," Roger promised. "Do you suppose—" he hesitated. "Could there be some special reason why Governor Ford insists upon all of you coming to Carthage?"

Taylor's lips tightened. "We are complying against our better judgment," he said. And then, with a flash of his old fire, "But we'll be back! We are not licked yet."

Those few moments of farewell, it seemed to Roger, had drawn him closer to his uncle than he had ever been. His heart ached for Taylor. As he sat at his desk in the *Neighbor* office, he could picture the little group of Mormons, heavily guarded, riding out of Nauvoo to face they knew not what.

And they were scarcely on their way before the first blow fell. The Legion must surrender all arms to the State.

Governor Ford had issued the order, and Joseph Smith had commanded its execution. There was no choice but to obey.

Time stood still in Nauvoo. People went about with inscrutable faces, talking little, seeming, by common consent, to circle warily around what was uppermost in every mind. They were brave, these people, Roger thought. They realized their danger—knew that they faced destruction of all that they held dear. Whatever might happen, he felt, they would be prepared to meet it.

And at last news came from Carthage. The accused had submitted to arrest on charges of riot. They had appeared before a justice of the peace and given bond to present themselves at the next regular session of the Circuit Court.

Roger felt queer prickles of apprehension. It didn't make sense, somehow. Things couldn't be settled as simply as that. The trouble was too deep-seated. Too much violence simmered underneath. He was not surprised when the second message came. Joseph Smith and his brother, Hyrum, had been arrested, charged with treason in levying war against the State by placing Nauvoo under martial law. They had been committed to the county jail in Carthage.

"Everything," John Taylor's letter read, "is being done to prove this action illegal. The only satisfaction we've got is the promise of a military guard about the jail. But that isn't much help, as most of the guard are enemies of President Smith. It is a great comfort to me that you are there, Roger. Tell your aunt and your mother not to worry. I am staying on here in case there is something I can do."

Aunt Leonora received the message with a quiet smile. "Thank you, Roger," she said. "Ruth," she turned to Mrs. Parker. "We can clean house thoroughly while John is gone. You know how it annoys him to find the furniture out of place."

2.

John Clark came to the *Neighbor* office the following day.

Roger sprang to his feet. "What's kept you away, Clark?" he demanded. "I've looked for you every day."

John pushed back his hat and dropped into a chair. "My father has been sick," he explained. "It hasn't been easy to stay on the other side—with so much going on over here. I—"

"Have you seen Mary Ann?" Roger broke in quickly.

"I've just come from the Riches." There was a momentary shadow in John's eyes. "Mary Ann is fine," he said. "But tell me—how've things been with you?"

"I've been working hard, but, of course, I'm merely waiting for Uncle's return. Here's the latest news." He handed over Taylor's letter and sat down, his eyes fixed upon John's face.

John shook his head. "I don't like it, Roger. The people of Carthage are very bitter against the Mormons—the militia worst of all. I think Ford's inviting trouble by appointing Smith's guard from the Carthage Grey's."

Roger's face was troubled. "He claims they have pledged to refrain from violence. He insists he can depend absolutely on their loyalty and integrity."

John lifted one shoulder slightly. "I hope he's right. The Mormons are certainly doing their part toward keeping peace."

"I know they are, Clark. It's astonishing that things have gone on this far without something breaking loose. This tension can't go on indefinitely. It's bound to snap sometime."

"I feel that way, too. That's why I'm staying over for a few days."

"Are you? I'm glad. I'll feel a lot easier about Mary Ann if you are here." Roger's blue eyes held John's in a steady gaze. He flushed a little as he went on, but they did not waver. "You're the only member of her family that I know very well, Clark. I've met her father, but only casually. You seem closer to her than he is. And," he added, "you're not a Mormon. You'll understand how I feel." He paused for a moment, his face darkening. "I could never become a Mormon. But I love Mary Ann." He sighed deeply. "I believe she was beginning to care for me before all this trouble started, but I've only seen her once since then and she seemed changed." He leaned toward John, his voice shaking a little. "Have I any right to hope that she will become my wife? How would you feel about it, Clark?"

John stared thoughtfully into space for a long moment. "I would welcome it, Roger," he said slowly, "but I must be frank with you. If Mary Ann loves you enough, it might be all right. But her convictions are strong, and Mormonism is a vital part of her life. Remember that—but by all means tell her how you feel." He rose and extended his hand. "I must go now, but I'll drop in again after supper."

Their hands met in an understanding grip. John smiled. "Of course, I wouldn't attempt to influence Mary Ann, but I do wish you luck with all my heart."

Roger walked with John to the door and watched him move away, his long unhurried strides carrying him swiftly down the street. It was strange how a talk with Clark always straightened things out. It was simple enough, after all. He would see Mary Ann and ask her to be his wife. She would say "yes." She must. She—

"Roger! Roger!" It was Henry bursting in from the back room, his voice shrill and tremulous, his leathery face working with excitement. "Roger," he burst out again, "Ford's in town. He's over at the Mansion House. They say he's here to search for counterfeiters."

"Counterfeiters!" Roger stared. "That's queer. Why should he come to Nauvoo now, while the Smiths are in jail at Carthage?"

"I don't know," Henry quavered, "but it don't look right. Couldn't you sort of slip over there and see what you can find out?"

"Why don't you go?" Roger asked. "I'm not a Mormon, you know. I'm not supposed to know things." As soon as the words were spoken, he regretted them. Poor old Henry. This was no time to pay off personal scores. "All right," he said, "I'll try. But I don't think it will do much good." He took his hat from the peg and started out leaving Henry, worried and bewildered, in the doorway.

In the late afternoon Governor Ford issued a statement. Before starting for Nauvoo, he said, he had, as a guarantee of good faith, disbanded all State forces under arms with the exception of three companies. Two of these companies were now in Carthage guarding the jail. The other would join him in Nauvoo tomorrow, to assist in the search for counterfeiters. Any retaliatory measures by the Mormons, he warned, "would mean the destruction of their city—the extermination of their people."

3.

It was past midnight when Roger started home. He and John had spent an anxious evening in the office, but as the hours dragged by with no reports of trouble, they began to relax a little.

"We may as well go," John said. "Nothing's likely to happen now before morning. We'd better get some rest."

"I suppose you're right," Roger admitted. "Still, I feel very uneasy."

And the uneasy feeling persisted as he neared the Taylor home. The house looked stately and serene in the moonlight. *A gracious house,* thought Roger. *No wonder Uncle Taylor is proud of it. If he should be forced to abandon it—* Silver light etched the trees on the knoll with eerie loveliness. It was clear and still. Roger went up the steps slowly and paused with his hand on the knob. The long, mournful howl of a dog broke the stillness and trailed away into the night. Roger sighed heavily, held for a moment by a strange sad loneliness. Then he shrugged and went on into the house.

4.

Roger opened his eyes and sat up in bed. The sound of insistent knocking still echoed in his ears. He hadn't imagined it. But who could be knocking at daybreak? Then, suddenly he was out of bed, scrambling into his clothes as the mists of sleep cleared away. He raced down the wide stairway straining his eyes into the dim hall below. Fully dressed, Leonora Taylor was standing, her back braced against the newel post, her eyes enormous in a paper-white face.

"Aunt Leonora," Roger cried out. "What is it? Bad news?"

She nodded mutely. Roger's arm encircled her waist as he half supported, half led her out into the kitchen and helped her to a chair. She stared at the row of potted plants on the window sill, then lifted her eyes to his.

"The Prophet and his brother Hyrum are dead," she said tonelessly. "A mob attacked the Carthage jail last night."

Roger dropped to his knees beside her and gathered her cold hands in his. "Uncle!" he said. "Was Uncle—?"

"John was with them. He was wounded—trying to defend the Prophet." For a brief moment she clung to Roger, then almost imperceptibly, he could feel her draw away. She straightened. "Call your mother," she directed firmly. "We are going to Carthage at once."

But before they were ready to depart, another message came. John Taylor was not fatally wounded. He was being cared for by his friend Willard Richards. They would be home that afternoon.

Roger went to the Mansion House at once. Governor Ford, the clerk said, had left for Carthage before news of Smith's murder reached Nauvoo. Avoiding Roger's eyes, the man quoted Ford's words with careful exactness. "He said he was uneasy about affairs in Carthage. He had decided to go back at once without bothering about the counterfeiters." The clerk's face was a pale mask but his hands, fumbling with some letters, were shaking.

For a moment Roger stood, shocked into silence. This was incredible. Transparent. Why, a child could see the truth! Anger seized him, forcing the blood tumultuously through his veins. Anger and a kind of shame. The mere fact that he was not a Mormon seemed somehow to align him with their enemies. Ruthless, unscrupulous enemies who had not stopped at murder.

He thanked the clerk briefly and left the Mansion House. There was no use going to the *Neighbor* office. The community was paralyzed. Everywhere—on the streets—in the stores—along the river front—people were going through motions of living without seeming to be alive. What form would the reaction take? It was bound to come when the first shock of grief had abated. Already rumors were seeping in of panic in non-Mormon centers. The Mormons were sure to seek vengeance for the murder of their Prophet.

5.

Pale and hollow-eyed from loss of blood, John Taylor lay inert in his wide white bed and outlined in broken sentences the tragic happenings in Carthage. He had been visiting with Joseph Smith. An armed mob of masked men had attacked the jail. The Prophet and his brother had been shot down. Foully murdered before his eyes.

Taylor's voice rose hysterically and he began to tremble. His wife was beside him in an instant.

"You must leave him, Roger," she commanded. "He mustn't talk about it until he's stronger." She leaned over the bed, her hands gentle, her voice a soothing murmur.

Roger tiptoed from the room, unnoticed.

6.

The Mormons were assembled in the public square. From outlying farms and settlements, from stores and business houses, from luxurious Knoll section homes and from humble cottages the Saints had come forth at Willard Richards' call. Quietly they had come, by ones and twos and in larger groups, an ever-increasing throng with grief-stricken faces and anxious eyes. There was scarcely a murmur among them.

From the shelter of a clump of trees, Roger and John Clark looked on in silence. Roger's throat ached. This was the kind of thing you couldn't talk about.

The sun had set. In the warm light of the afterglow Willard Richards rose to speak. He was a small, mild man, with a round affable face, unnaturally pale now, and grave. There was dead silence as he stood for a moment facing the crowd.

"I am here," he began quietly but firmly, "to make an appeal to you. The Prophet Joseph and the Patriarch Hyrum are dead. Brother Sidney Rigdon is away on Church business. Brother Brigham Young, the ranking Apostle—President of the Twelve, is also away. Of the quorum of the Twelve only Brother John Taylor and I are here in Nauvoo and he, as you know, is sorely wounded." He paused briefly, then went on with simple dignity and directness. "Brother Taylor and I, as

Apostles of the Church, have already pledged ourselves that there will be no violence." His figure, in the deepening twilight, seemed to grow taller and more impressive. His voice took on a deeper note. "We feel," he said, "that the Mormons should depend upon the law to deal retribution for the deaths of the Prophet and his brother. We offer this to you as a resolution."

The words died away. There was not a breath nor a movement. Then, through the crowd, a subdued murmur ran. It gathered in volume. Small groups engaged in earnest discussion—heated discussion, here and there. But Roger could see heads nodding vigorously. A tall, raw-boned man in the center of the crowd raised his voice. "Brother Richards, I move that we accept this resolution." There was a quick second. The "Ayes" rang out. There was no dissenting vote.

This, Roger thought, *is true courage.* Pride surged through him. Pride in his uncle who had helped to bring this about. He turned to John, his blue eyes shining.

John nodded thoughtfully. "Pretty fine, aren't they? You know, Roger," he said as they walked away, "we have just witnessed a great moral victory. Whatever may happen to their Church, the Mormons have pledged peace. I can go home tonight. There'll be no more trouble now."

But as Roger took leave of John, a mounting excitement set his pulse to hammering. The Prophet was dead. The future of the Church was at stake. Now, surely, he might hope to win Mary Ann.

18

1.

It was a perfect June day. The sky was blue and cloudless. From the Mississippi, glittering in the sunshine, came a gentle breeze that touched the rose vine climbing around the open casement and wafted fragrance into that somber room in the Mansion House.

In at one door—out at another—since early morning an endless, sad procession had been passing. The Saints were taking their last farewell of the Prophet Joseph. Pouring into Nauvoo in a great stream, to trickle one by one through that door.

It was mid-afternoon when Mrs. Rich and Mary Ann, with the children clinging to their hands, took their places in the line that crept, inch by inch, nearer to that still form. A choked sob, a faint moan now and then—no other sound broke the slow, dreadful rhythm of those shuffling feet. Mary Ann's heart pounded thickly. She must get away somehow. She couldn't bear it. But, no. It was too late now. Mrs. Rich, the baby in her arms, was pausing beside the bier. Little Sarah Jane whimpered softly and hid her face in her mother's skirts. Another step—Mary Ann forced herself to look.

Why! she thought. *I'm not afraid.* How noble he looked. Like the waxen effigy of a great king—or a saint. But he *was* a Saint. He was the Prophet. The Lord's anointed. He couldn't be dead. He couldn't.

Once outside of that room, the single line was broken up and lost in the eddying crowds that choked the halls and grounds of the Mansion House and swarmed the streets of the city. Mrs. Rich and the children had disappeared. There was no use searching for them among all these people.

Mary Ann wove her way in and out along the evergreen-bordered path and started slowly along Main Street. She felt lost and alone. If Uncle John could only have stayed longer . . . but, of course, he couldn't; not with Grandfather ill and frightened. It was late afternoon now, but she didn't want to go home. The house seemed empty and full of sorrow. If General Rich had been here, perhaps these terrible things wouldn't have happened. But suppose he had been here? He might have been with the Prophet in Carthage. *Oh, thank God he wasn't here,* she thought. *Thank God he is safe!* Would she ever be able to forget those two wagons lumbering into Nauvoo—the rude covering of green twigs and boughs only half concealing their ghastly loads? She shuddered. Violence, bloodshed, murder. What would become of the Saints, now that the Prophet was gone?

"Mary Ann!" She started at the touch on her arm. For a bewildered moment she looked at Roger without recognition.

"Mary Ann," he repeated urgently, "I've been following you all the way from the Mansion House, but the crowds got in my way. Where are you going?"

"Does it matter?" She tried to smile.

"Of course, it matters. You're in no state to be wandering about. Let's find a quiet spot."

She scarcely noticed the warm pressure of his hand on her arm. It was comfortable, somehow, to be dominated, not to be forced to think. Unquestioning and docile she allowed herself to be led toward that familiar bench overlooking the river.

2.

It was cool and restful under the trees. Mary Ann gave Roger a grateful smile. Its pathos wrung his heart. He leaned toward her and gathered her hands in his. "I'm sorry, dear. Believe me, I'm sorry. I know how you must be feeling."

She shook her head sadly. "No, Roger. You can't know. You are not one of us."

" 'One of us.' " He repeated the phrase impatiently. "I wish you wouldn't talk that way. You don't belong with these people, Mary Ann. You are sweet, and young and—normal." He drew a deep breath and gripped her hands more firmly, although she made no move to withdraw them. "I'm going away, Mary Ann, and I want you to come with me."

"Away?" Her eyes were wide and puzzled.

"Yes. Far away. East. Anywhere you want to go." The words were coming in a torrent now. His voice shook a little as he hurried on. "I have a fine offer from a New York newspaper, but we needn't stay there unless you like it. All I want is to make you happy, darling. Marry me, and let me take you away from here."

Her hands still lay limply in his, but he could feel her becoming remote and on guard. "You never talked this way before, Roger," she said steadily.

"No, but I've felt this way. I've honestly tried to understand—your people. For a while I thought I could, but I've given up. I've told my mother and Uncle Taylor. This plural marriage question has opened my eyes. It's abominable! How any decent man could subject a woman to such dishonor—"

"How dare you!" Mary Ann freed her hands with a jerk. Her eyes were blazing. "How dare you condemn a doctrine you don't understand? It's beautiful and—and it's holy. Mrs. Rich has explained it to me. The Prophet taught it to General Rich, and—"

"So it *is* Rich! You love him." Roger was on his feet, facing her, half beside himself with jealousy and pain. Mary Ann's white startled face—the incredulous look in her eyes, told him how gravely he had blundered, but he plunged on, unable to curb the words. "I've seen the way you look at him. If he should ask you to marry him, I suppose you'd think it was right, even if he has a wife!"

Mary Ann looked up at him with strange, unfathomable eyes, an odd spark of excitement in their depths. When she spoke, her voice was low and controlled. "You have no right to say such things. The General and Mrs. Rich have been very kind to me. I admire and respect them both."

Roger groaned. "Forgive me," he begged. He dropped down beside her again and reached for her hands, but she put them behind her hastily, bracing herself against the back of the bench. Roger sighed heavily. "Please, dear," he said, "try to understand. Plural marriage isn't good enough for you. I want you for my wife. You, only. All my love and devotion for you."

She did not move or speak.

"So it's no use," he said at last. With a despairing gesture he buried his face in his hands. "It's driving me crazy," he muttered, "the thought of leaving you here in all this. I—"

"Don't, Roger," Mary Ann said softly. There was no anger in her voice now, only compassion. " 'All this,' as you call it, is part of my life. You can't understand that. You don't know all that has gone into building this life for me." She touched his crisp dark hair with gentle fingers. He lifted his head and their eyes met. She smiled. "Dear Roger," she said, "don't grieve. We could never be happy together. We couldn't be true to ourselves." She cupped his face between her palms and kissed him on the lips. Their first kiss. Yet Roger knew that it meant farewell. He got to his feet, turning his head away, fighting for control.

Mary Ann, too, arose and stood beside the bench. Across the river the sun's luminous disk was slipping into a froth of rose and violet. The Mississippi was a ribbon of shimmering gold. In the deep silence a bird twittered sleepily from the treetop overhead.

Mary Ann's face was lifted toward the sky. A tender smile curved her lips. "The peaceful hour," she murmured. "What a beautiful sunset. It must be a good omen."

Roger turned and started down the hill. He looked back once. Mary Ann's hands were clasped upon her breast, her face uplifted, her bright head shining in the rays of the setting sun.

BOOK THREE

PROMISE OF BEAUTY

Such duty as the subject owes the prince,
Even such, a woman oweth to her husband.

—SHAKESPEARE.

I

1.

It was mid-February of 1846. At Sugar Creek, Iowa, nine miles west of Nauvoo, a thousand Saints had gathered to await marching orders from Brigham Young.

The Mormon Church was still without a president—but not without a leader. Brigham Young, the ranking Apostle, had become a dominant figure in the Church. At the time of the Prophet's death, no definite provision had been made for his successor. The Twelve Apostles constituted the high authority, and during the troubled months that followed, it was Young's skillful management and forceful personality that had held the main body of the Church loyal to the Twelve. Now, he had designated Sugar Creek as the starting point for the Mormons' westward trek.

The sky was gray and lowering. Mary Ann stood on a knoll overlooking the creek and scanned the trail below anxiously. John would soon be coming along that trail. She had given up hope of seeing him before she started her westward journey. He had been in St. Louis since December. But yesterday, Aunt Rhoda and her husband had come from Montrose bringing news. John was in Nauvoo. He would reach Sugar Creek today.

Mary Ann shivered. Her fingers, stiff with cold inside her knitted mittens, fumbled awkwardly with the woolen scarf that covered her bright hair. Perhaps after all it would have been better to go on without seeing Uncle John. . . . There was a smell of snow in the air. She hugged her heavy shawl closer to her body. Her eyes wandered over the rows of tents scattered over the flat to the north. A month ago there had been only a few families here. Now it was a small tent city. "The Camp of Israel"—so named because Brigham Young and the other Apostles were living there.

Smoke rose and drifted upward from the open fires. The wagons that stood by the tents were packed and ready, with only the barest necessities kept out. Orders to go forward would come any moment now. Another group would gather here; then another. And the routine would be repeated until every Mormon was on his way to the new home. Mary Ann was proud to be going west in the first party—to be a part of the Rich group.

A chill wind caught her skirts and wrapped them around her knees, then whipped on down the knoll. She stamped her feet and began to walk back and forth, swinging her arms in a circular motion.

She looked backward toward Nauvoo. The city was shrouded in a gray haze, but in imagination she could see the Temple, its golden spire uplifted to the sky. A feeling of exaltation swept over her. In spite of everything the Temple had been completed. Outsiders could not understand this desire to finish a structure so soon to be abandoned. Mary Ann could. "Let this house be built unto my name, that I may reveal mine ordinances therein, unto my people; . . . that you may prove yourselves unto me that ye are faithful in all things whatsoever I command you, that I may bless you, and crown you with honor, immortality and eternal life." How often she had read those words in the Book of Doctrine and Covenants! But she had never realized their full significance until now—now that she had become one of the inner circle. In the newly completed House of the Lord she had received her blessing. There, a month ago, she had gone through the ceremony of endowment—had proved herself "faithful in all things." Accepting this ordinance, she knew, was the most important step of her life.

The heavy clouds were darkening. Snow was beginning to fall in large, scattered flakes. A long shiver ran through Mary Ann and left her shaking—her teeth chattering; for down on the trail she could see a lone horseman approaching. Uncle John. He always rode in that slow, deliberate way. Cattle huddled together near-by lowed mournfully. Mary Ann's heart was like lead. In a few moments Uncle John would be with her. How could she tell him what she had done?

2.

John Clark was not surprised that the Mormons had decided to move on. Smith's death had not destroyed the roots of the trouble. It had cropped up anew when the Nauvoo charter was repealed a year ago. Through the spring and summer months John had watched the breach widen. The Illinoians had not openly demanded that the Mormons leave, but had made it plain that they were expected to do so. The Church leaders knew that the Mormons "must go"—but to uproot twenty thousand people—to move them to a new home—it seemed impossible.

Yet, late in September, just when John was laying his plans for the St. Louis trip, Brigham Young issued a proclamation. In the spring the Mormons were to leave, "for some point so remote there will not need to be a difficulty with the people and ourselves." Somewhere west of the Rocky Mountains was the destination Young had in mind. And the Saints voted to support the proclamation. Wherever the new home might be, they would move to it en masse.

Nauvoo bustled with activity as Young's plan began to take practical shape. Wagonmakers, blacksmiths and carpenters worked at top speed. Every family was sorting its possessions —deciding what might be taken, what must be left behind. John was filled with misgivings. Perhaps he ought not to go. But the trip concerned arrangements for his long hoped-for journey to Oregon and, after all, Mary Ann was happy with the Riches. She would stay with them until he returned, and he'd be home before the new year. If things worked out as he hoped, he would take her to Oregon with him.

But John's business in St. Louis took longer than he had expected. In late January a disturbing letter had come from Rhoda. Brigham Young had ordered that the first party should leave in mid-February—and Mary Ann was planning to leave with the Riches in this party. John wound up his affairs and started back at once. Every slow mile of the way the urgency of Rhoda's "please come home" had troubled him.

Rhoda had behaved oddly when he arrived. "I've not tried to persuade Mary Ann to give up her trip west," she said. "I'm leaving that to you. You've always known how to handle her. But don't lose any time. Get over to camp at once."

As John rode into the Sugar Creek Camp, he was still puzzling over her words.

3.

Pale light filtering through the unfastened tent-flap revealed the determined angle of Mary Ann's small jaw, and the half-scared look in her eyes.

Seated beside her on a crude pine bench, John stared, shocked and incredulous. "You can't mean this, Mary Ann.

I won't believe it. You—the plural wife of Charles Rich?"

"Yes," she said defiantly.

She means it, John thought. *It's true, then.* His stunned bewilderment was passing. Anger burned within him like a slow flame. Always before he'd been patient with her, but this was too much. "You little fool!" he burst out. "I won't let you do this thing. Get your things together. You're going back to Montrose with me." He gripped her arms with his big hands and shook her fiercely.

For a moment she looked at him, lips quivering, the hurt, unbelieving look of a child who has been struck. Then her mouth set in the familiar stubborn line and she pulled away from him sharply. "You are forgetting, Uncle John," she said, "I am not free to go with you. I am married now." Her voice had a thin edge.

"Married!" John echoed. "This isn't marriage." His voice was angry.

"It is for me," Mary Ann retorted. Her breath was coming in quick, hard gasps. Then suddenly she looked at him pleadingly. "It's because you aren't a Mormon that you say these things. You just don't understand. I have taken my vows in the Temple. I am Charles' wife for time and eternity."

John shook his head. "I know you believe all that, Mary Ann. I shouldn't have lost my temper. But I can't stand by and see you ruin your life." He clenched his hands and his voice roughened with emotion. "You just don't realize what you are doing, dear. Your Church may sanction this marriage, but the world won't. You can never be recognized as Rich's wife."

"Not here, Uncle John. I know that." For a moment she paused, then went on, an eager note in her voice. "But when we reach our new home, I'll be the same as Sarah. We are going to find a place where we can live our religion."

"You've been persuaded into this."

"No, you're mistaken." She was completely mistress of herself now. "I've known about plural marriage for a long time. It was Sarah who explained it to me; but I never considered it for myself until two months ago."

John looked at her with miserable eyes. That was about the time he'd gone to St. Louis. Stupid fool! He was responsible for this.

"Sarah told me," Mary Ann was saying, "that she and Charles had agreed he should practice plural marriage. He wanted me for one of his wives." For a moment she paused, lost in thought, then went on hurriedly. "Of course, I talked to Father about it. He was willing—but that did not influence me. I thought it all through and decided. I wasn't hasty."

"But if I had been here—?" John questioned.

"No, Uncle John. Even you couldn't have stopped me. I made up my own mind." She leaned forward and laid her hand on his arm. For an instant she was a little girl again, appealing to him as she had done so often. Then she withdrew her hand and straightened her young back proudly. There was a new dignity about her. "Charles is a fine man," she said. "He's been wonderful to me and he'll give me a good home." She paused. "A home," she said. "Children. To be with the Saints—to be doing my share. That's what I want." Her eyes were blue and brilliant. "You *do* understand, don't you, Uncle John?"

"No." John said. He got to his feet and stood looking down at her unhappily. He sighed. "If that's the way you want it, Mary Ann, there's nothing more I can do." A gust of wind jerked the tent-flap wide and rustled the straw on the hard earth floor. It was almost dark. "Well," John muttered, "I might as well be moving on."

"Oh, Uncle John!" Mary Ann was on her feet, clinging to him, her face buried on his breast.

John put his arms around her and held her close. For the

moment he could comfort her, but this moment would pass. She had chosen her road and there was no turning back. He could never really reach her again.

Silently he stood with his arms about her, staring out over her head at the snow swirling furiously against a leaden sky.

4.

Charles Rich was troubled as he saw John leave Mary Ann's tent and start down the trail toward the center of camp. He had been uneasy all day about the outcome of this visit. He could not forget the queer catch in Mary Ann's voice when she said, "Uncle John's coming today to tell me goodbye."

Rich watched John now, walking slowly, heavily, his head bent against the driving snow. He opened his lips to call out, then closed them again. There was nothing he could say to John. They were too far apart. John had been with the Saints for many years, yet he had not accepted the Faith. He would not be able to understand what Mary Ann had done. Charles Rich stood, his brows contracted, watching John's figure blur and disappear in the gray distance. He sighed heavily. He was genuinely sorry that things must be this way—yet the break had to come sometime. And Mary Ann would be needing him now. He turned and walked swiftly toward her tent.

She was a small, pathetic figure, huddled there on the pine bench. She lifted wretched eyes to Charles as he entered, but did not speak. He dropped down beside her and took her hands. "My dear—you should be with Sarah and the others. Over near the fire where they are preparing supper." Gently he pulled off the clumsy mittens and began chafing her icy fingers with quick, firm strokes.

"Please—" she said. "Not for a little while. I can't go over there right now." Her soft young mouth was trembling.

Charles got up and with calm, matter-of-fact motions

lighted the lantern and hung it on its peg above Mary Ann's head. For a moment it swung, and the light danced crazily about the tent, painting grotesque shadows on Mary Ann's white face. She was shaking with cold. "You'll freeze sitting there," Charles said. "You must move about. Come." He helped her to her feet and tucked her arm through his.

For a while they were silent as they paced the narrow confines of the tent—back and forth, back and forth—Mary Ann, stiff and tense, taking two steps to Charles' one. Then Charles began to talk. It was casual news of the camp he gave her. Another party had come in from Nauvoo today. Emeline Grover was with them. "You'll be glad of that," he said. "I'm glad, too. I want my wives with me. I wish all five of you were safely here, but Eliza isn't well enough to travel now."

Mary Ann said nothing, but she had stopped shaking; she was beginning to relax. The straw crackled under their feet. "Thomas Ricks and George Stailey are here," Charles went on. "They're the boys I've hired to help with my teams. We'll be needing them now. The Apostles met this afternoon, and we are starting west day after tomorrow."

Mary Ann drew in her breath sharply. Her arm grew rigid under Charles' fingers, and he pressed it gently. "Aren't you glad?" he asked. "It will be fine, don't you think, to be in a place where we can really live in peace?"

She did not answer. Charles halted abruptly and stood facing her. The lantern blinked, and the tent shivered in the wind. He put his hands on her shoulders. "There is something I've been wanting to say to you, my dear. You—you are very young. It's hard to put it into words. Some day—you'll want children. But on this journey you'll want to be free—to adjust yourself to your new life." His fingers tightened a little on her shoulders. "I want you to understand. I shall not ask you really to become my wife until we are settled in our new home."

She lifted her head and looked up at him for a long, still moment. "Thank you, Charles," she said, very low. In the wavering light of the lantern he watched the brief inward struggle reflected in her face. Then she drew a deep quivering breath. "I'm ready, now, Charles. Let us join the others."

A smile softened the firm lines of Charles' mouth. "I'm proud of you, Mary Ann," he said, and his hand on her arm was warm and reassuring as they faced the snowy night together.

5.

The morning of departure dawned cold and clear. The sky was vividly blue and the fresh snow sparkled in the sunshine.

Mary Ann stood looking over the Rich outfit. Three covered wagons, two yoke of oxen and a team of horses, Charles' saddle horse, two milk cows, three sheep, two beef cattle. She checked the items over in her mind. Charles hadn't planned to go west with the first party. It was an honor to be included in this group, but it had been a struggle to assemble this much equipment on such short notice. All that Charles had to start with was his horse and a very little money. But his friends had been a wonderful help.

Emeline scrambled down from one of the wagon-boxes and came to stand beside Mary Ann. "Those wagons won't hold another thing," she declared loudly. "I guess I was lucky, coming late. I didn't have to help with the packing."

Mary Ann smiled absently. A picture of the hodgepodge under those canvas covers flashed through her mind. Garden tools, seeds, bedding, foodstuffs, furniture—all crowded together in confusion. That was how it had to be.

Emeline was regarding her with curious gray eyes. "Dreaming again?" she demanded. "From the looks of things," she sniffed, "we could have used another wagon."

"We're lucky to have three." Mary Ann frowned. "I

do hope that five hundred pounds of flour will be safe." Her eyes were troubled. As it was they had less than the minimum for a family of five grown people, and there were eight in their group—not counting Sarah's children.

Emeline twisted her shoulders impatiently. "If Brother Young is going to speak, I wish he'd hurry up about it. Now that we're ready, I'd like to start." She stared at the wagons speculatively and changed the subject with characteristic abruptness. "What did Sarah do with all her furniture?"

"She left most of it in the house. I suppose it will be sold later. She was heartbroken about leaving her grandfather clock." Mary Ann sighed. "I'm glad I didn't have anything of my own. It hurt enough to leave Sarah's things."

"Well, I didn't have anything worth worrying over." Emeline stamped her feet. "Let's walk. I'm freezing."

They linked arms and began walking back and forth between the wagons. There was activity all about them, but the tents were gone. Only patches of straw on the snow-covered ground marked where they had stood. Mary Ann felt a pang of loneliness. Crude as it was, this had been home for a little while.

Thomas Ricks and George Stailey, lanky youths of eighteen, were busy yoking the oxen to the Rich wagons. They called out a greeting to the girls.

"Which one of them is going to drive our team?" Emeline asked.

"Thomas, I believe."

"I'm so glad Charles arranged for us to ride together. You know," Emeline's voice dropped to a confidential pitch, "I feel nervous with Charles' other wives. I suppose it's because they are older."

"I feel that way, too. That is, except with Sarah. I know her so well." Mary Ann was thoughtfully regarding Charles' saddle horse, tethered to the back of a wagon. His coat that had been so black and glossy was matted and dull. Charles had little time for grooming him these days. The horse whinnied wistfully as they passed. Mary Ann broke away from Emeline and started toward him, but just then the clear notes of the bugle sounded.

"It's about time! Brother Young is going to speak at last. Come on!" Emeline seized Mary Ann's hand and began to run, half dragging her toward the spot where the crowd was assembling.

6.

Charles Rich, standing a little apart, was watching Brigham Young. The man's personality fascinated him. There was something about Young—the easy grace of his fine, vigorous body, the rugged strength of his features, the piercing intensity of his gaze, that conveyed an impression of abounding energy and controlled force. Charles Rich admired him. Young had always been loyal to Joseph Smith and after the Prophet's death had worked quietly but determinedly to disperse the rival claimants for Smith's position. Sidney Rigdon, James Strang and Lyman Wight—one by one he had eliminated them. The Smith family had gone their separate way. Brigham Young had been content to remain President of the Twelve Apostles. He had not asked to be proclaimed "Prophet, Seer and Revelator." The confidence of his people had rewarded him.

Young was mounting a wagon-box. Quietly he stood there waiting for the stragglers to come down from the knolls. A vital man in the prime of life. His head was tilted backward and a mane of thick hair swept below the muffler wound about his neck. Charles moved in closer to the wagon. He wondered what Young would say. The man had little education, but he did know people. *That more than makes up for the lack,* Charles thought.

"At-tention! the whole Camp of Israel!" Young's deep, resonant voice rang out. A hush fell over the crowd. Charles listened intently. Forcefully and clearly Young was explaining—giving the carefully thought-out details that showed plainly how well he understood the necessity of advance planning. It held a special interest for Charles. As early as 1843 items had begun to appear in the Church papers—information about the almost unknown Rocky Mountain area—reports seeping through from Fremont and the fur traders. It was evident to Charles that Brigham Young, too, had kept closely in touch with these matters. The Mormon party was to move westward across Iowa. Council Bluffs, on the Missouri, was their first objective point. The Governor of the Territory of Iowa had been informed of their intention. He had assured the Mormons that they would receive the same protection afforded to any law-abiding citizens who passed through the domain.

For the time being, Young said, the company would be directly responsible to the Twelve Apostles. He ceased talking for a moment and leaned forward slightly, his eyes narrowed. "It is our business," he said, "to find a new home for the Saints. We must not fail." His mouth was grim. "We will have no law in this camp we cannot keep, but we *will* have order in the Camp." He drew himself to his full height, eyes flashing, as his voice rose in a final command. "If any want to live in peace when they leave this place, they must toe the mark!"

For a moment there was dead silence. Then a wild burst of applause.

Practical—hardheaded, Charles thought. *The will to rule with an iron hand. He is a born leader. This must be the will of God.*

7.

Thomas Ricks turned the wagon westward. Mary Ann

and Emeline leaned out of the back to catch a last glimpse of Nauvoo.

The spire of the Temple was clearly visible today—a slender golden shaft glittering against the sky's deep blue. Far below, the ice-bound Mississippi lay like a sheet of glass.

"Well, we are on our way." Emeline waved a sweeping farewell toward the scene.

"We'll never see Nauvoo again," Mary Ann said softly. "But we are going forward—to something new—and beautiful."

2

1.

The trek became Mary Ann's world. Long, shivering hours beside Emeline on the wagon-seat—with George urging the ox team over snow and ice rutted roads. Bitter cold nights when snow must be scraped away before tents could be stretched and beds made down. Mornings—with breakfasts hurriedly prepared over a wan camp fire. Always moving, moving, moving. Sometimes Mary Ann wondered if she had really ever known any other life.

On the second day out she had watched the tiny settlement of Farmington slip behind. There would be a long stretch of practically uninhabited country to cover before they reached the Des Moines River. It would be months before she would see her family again. What were they doing now—the girls, Joseph, Father—Uncle John? Mary Ann had been so happy when Paulina married Apostle Lyman. Paulina would be going west with her! But Apostle Lyman had changed his plans. His family was to come on later. There was a sharp ache in Mary Ann's heart. She'd never been completely separated from all of her family before. The party moved steadily onward.

"And I thought I'd known hardships!" Emeline's voice was a muffled wail through the shawl wrapped about her mouth. It was late afternoon. They were making camp for the night. Emeline gave her broom a vigorous thrust and new-fallen snow whirled about her feet.

Mary Ann made no answer. She was kneeling beside a bed roll, her head bent low, her fingers numb and clumsy with cold tugging at the rope that bound blankets inside of a rag carpet.

"I do declare, Mary Ann," Emeline pushed the shawl down from her chin. "You always seem to be in a study of late. Whatever ails you?" She leaned on her broom and gave Mary Ann a penetrating look. "Are you sick?"

"No, I'm not sick." Mary Ann said briefly, her tone a little sharp.

Emeline shrugged and went back to her sweeping.

Mary Ann began to unwind the bed roll. Her hands were cracked and bleeding. So Emeline had noticed her long silences. It was difficult to talk when her thoughts were so far away. The ache in her heart had dulled but it was still there. In spite of the cold her face began to burn hotly. She wasn't the only one. Others had left their families behind. Besides, she reminded herself, Charles was her family now. But it seemed sometimes that with every mile her girlhood was slipping away, and sadness settled more and more upon her.

At Bonaparte Mills on the Des Moines River the Rich family stopped for three days. Charles and some of the brethren had contracted to clear a plot of ground for a farmer living near the settlement. "I must work every time I get a chance," Charles said. The Iowans were willing to hire the Mormons as long as they showed no disposition to become permanent settlers. The added store of hay, grain and provisions they earned was well worth the delay, Charles felt.

They caught up with the main caravan at Richardson's Point, fifty-five miles west of Nauvoo. Brigham Young had designated this as the first temporary settlement. Mary Ann's spirits lifted a little. It was good to mingle with friends, to exchange greetings and bits of news, to absorb some of the cheer around her.

On the evening before they were to take up their journey again, Mary Ann and Emeline, arms linked, were standing near the camp fire. Through the still night air the sound of band instruments being tuned came softly to their ears. Captain Pitt's Nauvoo Legion Band had returned triumphant from a near-by settlement. They had given a concert and earned twenty-five dollars for the company. Everyone was jubilant. Brigham Young had ordered a celebration. A band concert around the fire—a dance in a sheltered spot that had been cleared of snow. Mary Ann's heart leaped as the lively music began. She gave Emeline's arm a little squeeze. To-night she was happy, too.

But once back on the road again her sadness returned. A heavy thaw had set in. Mary Ann sat silent—huddled close to Emeline while they jolted and splashed over roads that were little more than trails through the soft mud.

On a night in mid-March when the temperature had dropped to freezing, Mary Ann and Emeline were preparing for bed in their tent. Cold rain had turned to hail that battered viciously at their canvas roof.

"Mary Ann," Emeline demanded suddenly, "why didn't you marry Roger?"

Mary Ann was taking off her shoes. For a moment she was rigid. Then she straightened up and looked at Emeline. "Roger wasn't a Mormon," she said quietly.

Emeline went on plaiting her luxuriant red brown hair into a long braid. "Aren't you sorry now?"

"Of course, I'm not sorry." Mary Ann regarded Emeline steadily. "Why should I be?"

Emeline shrugged. "Oh, I don't know. I just wondered."

But after they were in bed, Mary Ann lay staring into the darkness. She hadn't wanted to marry Roger. But life with him would have been different. A home—comforts—perhaps even luxuries. And love. Roger had loved her, she knew that.

The hailstorm was over, but the wind whistled about the tent. Emeline was breathing heavily. Carefully, Mary Ann turned over in bed. She must not wake Emeline. If she could only get to sleep. "This isn't marriage." John's scornful words echoed in her ears. What was wrong with her? She had been so sure of herself that day—yet nothing had changed. Her belief was the same . . . .

It was nearly morning when she closed her eyes.

2.

At Chariton Creek, late in March, the caravan was divided into companies; fifty wagons in each company, with a captain in charge. Charles Rich was made captain of the "fifth fifty."

That evening at supper he explained the details to his family. They, of course, would travel with his fifty. As captain, he would be directly responsible to the Twelve Apostles. "Brother Brigham," Charles said, "has again urged order and cooperation on the line of march." This would be the caravan's farewell to the settlements. From now on they would be journeying into the wilderness, with a scouting party going on ahead to select campsites and open roads.

"There will be danger," Charles said, "and hardships; but we shall be prepared to face them. I have called a meeting for tomorrow morning. The men and their wives." He paused, his glance resting briefly upon each of the women gathered around his table. Sarah, his first wife, calm and poised in her gentle dignity; Mary Ann, her bright head bent, her small tightly clasped hands resting on the table before her; Sarah Peck, tall, large framed—her red head inches higher than any of the others; Emeline—elbows on the table, chin propped upon her hands—regarding him with frank, interested eyes. Charles' voice deepened. "You are fine, courageous women. You make it possible for me to do my share." He hesitated for a moment and went on, a shade of anxiety in his tone. "If all of us try—if we keep the right spirit, we shall find our reward in our new home."

Mary Ann could feel his gaze pulling her like a magnet. She looked up. A worried frown shadowed his dark eyes. She had not imagined it, then. He *had* been speaking directly to her. She looked away quickly, her cheeks hot. She was conscious of Charles' voice going on with details of the journey, but she was not listening. *What has happened to me?* she wondered dully. All the high resolve, the eagerness, the joy she had felt at Sugar Creek were gone. The days stretched before her bleak and drab. *What shall I do?* she thought. *Oh, what shall I do?*

3.

Charles Rich and Brigham Young stood on a hill overlooking a bend in the Grand River. There was a lush, earthy smell in the soft air of this late April morning. The river was a glistening stripe across acres of untilled soil.

"I believe our scouts were led to this place." A slow smile curved Brigham Young's firm mouth. "You can see why they called it 'Garden Grove.' "

Charles Rich nodded. The fifth fifty had arrived only the night before. Brigham Young had been here two days. Charles' dark eyes shone as they swept the river and the grassy hills bright with wildflowers. He dug the toe of his boot into the soil. It was rich loam. "Yes," he said. "It is well named."

"It is, indeed," Young declared. "And I think you will agree with me that this is an ideal spot to establish the first way station for oncoming parties. The right distance—a hundred and fifty miles from Nauvoo—and the right time of the year for planting. There's plenty of water—good soil—fine timber for building cabins and storehouses." He waved his hand toward the timberland bordering the hills.

"It seems to have everything," Charles said.

"But we can't waste any time." Young frowned. "We begin plowing and planting in the morning." He turned abruptly and stood facing Charles, feet wide apart, hands rammed deep in his trouser pockets. "Brother Rich," he said, "I want you to take charge of the rail cutting. And let there be no shirking!" His gray eyes were cold and hard. "Everyone's got to work."

For the Rich family, the pause was all too short. Brigham Young had dispatched Parley Pratt with a scouting party to locate the next site, and early in May a messenger returned with news. An excellent place had been found on another branch of the Grand River several miles west of Garden Grove. They had named the place Mount Pisgah.

In mid-May, Brigham Young departed for Mount Pisgah. Ten days later Charles Rich followed with his fifty.

4.

It was the last day of the journey to Mount Pisgah. Mary Ann, busily stowing things in the wagon-box, looked up to see Charles beside her. "Never mind that, my dear—Emeline will finish." He smiled. "You are riding with me today."

Panic gripped Mary Ann. Her hands shook, and there

was a gone feeling in the pit of her stomach. She hadn't been alone with Charles since that night at Sugar Creek. She wasn't at all sure that she wanted to be alone with him. She was self-conscious and stiff as he helped her up to the wagon-seat, but once settled she relaxed a little. It was exciting to be riding beside him in the lead wagon—the only horse-drawn wagon in the company.

Charles, occupied with the team, was silent for a while. The horses jogged along, but their pace seemed rapid after the oxen. In stolen glances Mary Ann studied Charles' face. She found herself wishing that she could read his thoughts. She started to speak—then changed her mind and turned her head resolutely away. The air was soft and sweet. The green velvet prairie seemed to ripple away before them. This was a morning to be happy. A prairie lark called near-by, and her heart leaped. Again the birdcall sounded, this time almost in her ear. Mary Ann turned to Charles, her eyes wide and puzzled. He pursed his lips and the prairie lark called again.

"Why—why it was you!" Mary Ann exclaimed.

Charles broke into a hearty laugh. "Don't look so startled," he said. "Didn't you like it?"

"Oh, yes! But," she hesitated, "it surprised me. You're always so—so serious and—" she broke off, at a loss for words.

"Responsibilities make a man serious." Charles gazed out over the prairie, and shook his head. "It's been a good many years since I've tried to do that. I learned to imitate bird-calls when I was a young fellow teaching school in Illinois."

"I didn't know you had been a school teacher."

"There are a lot of things you don't know about me," Charles said. His eyes were warm and smiling. Mary Ann looked into them and felt a sudden throb of joy. How kind he was, and how easy to talk to after all. Before she realized it she was telling him things about her childhood. Little happy intimate things. Mother had taught school when Father was away on his mission. Mother had loved birds, too—and spring. She had always said that anything begun in the spring was bound to come out right.

"Spring makes me feel that way, too," Charles said. "Days like this."

Mary Ann was suddenly aware of his nearness. The horses were climbing a gentle rise—The wagon rocked and Charles steadied her with a firm brown hand on her arm. The touch of his fingers sent the blood racing to her cheeks. "Where—where do you suppose we are now?" she asked hastily.

"I think we are nearing camp," Charles said. "Brother Pratt's scout said when we reached the hills we would almost be there." He motioned toward the timbered hills that dotted the prairie like round mounds.

"Charles, do we have any idea where we are going? I mean any more than we had when we left Nauvoo?"

"Not much more," he admitted. "Of course, the Missouri is our first goal—we should be about half way there now. Brother Young says that the Rockies will be next. He has information about places beyond them, but he hasn't set any destination." He sighed. "I imagine it will be some time before any of us push beyond the Missouri—once we get there."

"Oh." Mary Ann's tone was flat.

"Mary Ann," Charles spoke her name softly. She looked up at him. His dark eyes held hers. "Our new home—you are anxious to get there, aren't you? It does mean something to you?" There was urgency in his voice. A muscle twitched in his cheek.

An unaccountable tremor swept over her. She couldn't answer. All of the doubts she had been fighting closed in upon her again, a black pall, smothering her happy mood. Charles' eyes were still fixed upon her, a long, penetrating look. His mouth tightened. "Well," he said, "we'll have to hurry if we expect to reach Pisgah by noontime." He flicked the whiplash across the horses' backs and the wagon plunged forward. Mary Ann gripped the seat with both hands, but Charles made no move to steady her.

5.

The Rich family was to remain in Mt. Pisgah. Brigham Young had placed William Huntington in charge of the way station, with Charles Rich and Ezra Benson to act as his counselors.

Mary Ann received the news with a mixture of emotions. Being settled would be a relief—but there would be so much time to think! Still—if they had gone on, each day would have brought her nearer to the time when she must tell Charles of her doubts. At least, this was a respite. By early June when Brigham Young and his party left to continue their westward march, she knew that she was glad to be staying behind.

Charles plunged into his new duties with enthusiasm, and for Mary Ann the first few weeks were almost happy. She loved the location of Mt. Pisgah—on the wide fork of the river with the green prairie stretching westward to timber-skirted hills. Time passed quickly, with the family making temporary camp in a secluded spot on the knoll above the river. Mary Ann threw herself wholeheartedly into the work. Physical activity pushed the turmoil from her mind. Wagon-boxes were unpacked and converted into bedrooms. A tent was put up to serve as a dining room. Clothes were washed and repaired.

"This certainly is comfort." Emeline crawled into the wagon-box and stretched herself out luxuriously. "When I think of sleeping on the ground all those weeks—under that clammy bedding—Um-m-m!

Mary Ann settled herself beside Emeline. "It's wonderful," she said. "Almost as wonderful as the feel of clean, dry clothes."

By mid-June hundreds of acres had been plowed and planted and protected against cattle by stake and rider fences.

"Now that the planting is finished," Charles said, "we'll have to start work on living quarters. We are going to build cabins down by the river."

"Why not here?" Sarah asked. "It's so pleasant up here on the knoll."

"But not in winter," Charles said. "We would get the full sweep of the wind. And besides," he added, "there may be heavy snows. It will be better to have wood and water close by."

6.

The United States was at war with Mexico. A regiment, the *Mormon Battalion,* was formed at Council Bluffs. In July William Clayton made a quick visit to Mt. Pisgah to arrange final details for the departure of the regiment to California. Clayton was a small, energetic fellow with a genius for organization. As Young's chief of the commissary, Clayton had at all times a fairly clear picture of the trek as a whole. He brought news of the advance party to Huntington and his counselors. Brigham Young had established camp on the east side of the Missouri at Council Bluffs, on land owned by the Potawattomie Indians. The Indians had been quite willing for the Mormons to make use of their lands, and Young was now negotiating with the Omahas for permission to establish a settlement on the west side of the river.

Over the Rich supper table, in the tent at the top of the hill, Clayton chuckled. "It was the Legion band that won over the Potawattomies." His bright eyes twinkled. "Brother Young had the band give a concert in the Indian agent's home, and then held a council with LeClerc, the Potawattomie chief. He was so spellbound he was willing to agree to anything."

"The band's been helpful in more ways than one," Charles said. "We could do with some lively music here," he added soberly.

Clayton looked up quickly. "Aren't things going well?"

Rich sighed. "As well as can be expected, I suppose. The planting was late, but we've had warm nights and the corn is coming along fine. I think we'll be able to harvest most of it. Of course, losing so many of our young men to the *Battalion* makes things hard, but all of the brethren who can be spared are in Missouri, working. That will be some help." His brow creased in a worried frown. "Staples are low, and I dread to think of the winter months. Parties from the east are always ready to share their supplies—but many of them are destitute when they get here."

Clayton shook his head. "Brother Young's got a bad job on his hands. There's a thousand with him now, but with upwards of twelve thousand on their way from the Mississippi, there'll be three times that many before snow flies. We will have shelter ready for them, but God help us if they don't bring supplies." He sighed. "Keep as many of them here as you can."

But the Mormons who came pouring into Mt. Pisgah were impatient of delay. The arguments of Huntington, Benson and Rich were of no avail. Most of them pushed on toward the Missouri.

Charles' second wife, Eliza Graves, arrived with one of the groups and brought letters from Nauvoo. There was one for Mary Ann, from her father. Things were pretty bad, he said, for the Mormons left in Nauvoo. The Illinoians seemed to doubt their intention to leave. There might be open war before long. The family was all well—planning to start within the month. Mary Ann sat for a long time with the letter in her hands. It had been written early in May. They must be somewhere along the way now.

7.

Brigham Young had succeeded with the Omaha Indians. The Mormons were establishing a settlement on the west bank of the Missouri River. They called it "Winter Quarters."

Charles, at work in his log cabin office on an August afternoon, felt a surge of pride in his leader when the news arrived, but it made him even more sharply aware of his own responsibility. He was now in sole charge of the Pisgah settlement. Ezra Benson, who was to be made an Apostle, had already left to join Brigham Young; and William Huntington—Charles sighed heavily. Only this morning he had read the burial service over his good friend and superior. Three thousand people in Pisgah—more coming every day—and he alone was responsible for their welfare. It appalled him to think of it.

He wiped the perspiration from his forehead and got wearily to his feet. If only this dreadful, humid heat would break. There wasn't a breath of air stirring. He went to the open door and stood looking out at the rows of new log cabins dotting the river's edge. Tomorrow his family—other families, would be moving into these cabins. Perhaps it would have been wiser to build on the high ground. Those swamps further downstream were infested with mosquitoes. The heat was bad enough, without them.

He turned and went back to his desk, but he could not keep his mind on the reports he was preparing for Brigham Young. Poor Huntington. What he had died of was surely intermittent fever, but Charles had never seen the disease in so severe a form. Of course, Huntington had been an old man. . . . But there were other cases in camp—young men—women— After months of privation, vitality was low, and with this heat . . . . He must not think about it. Resolutely, he set to work on the reports.

8.

Mary Ann and Emeline, grimly silent, were settling their few possessions in the new cabin near the river. The tiny box-like room swam with heat. Droning mosquitoes swarmed about their heads. Through the open door came a sickish odor of stagnant water from the swamplands.

Emeline muttered angrily as she straightened up from making the low cot bed. She dug savagely at the red welts on her arms.

"Why don't you try rubbing some oil on those bites?" Mary Ann looked up from a roll of clothing she was unpacking.

Emeline's eyes flashed. "You make me tired—you and your advice. What do you know about it? Mosquitoes don't bother you."

"I'm sorry." Mary Ann's face flamed. "I only wanted to help you," she said stiffly.

Emeline plopped down on a corner of the bed and sat staring morosely at the peeled oak bark floor.

Little angry prickles were running through Mary Ann as she hung her faded calico dresses on pegs in the wall. It was best to keep silent. This had been a bad day for both of them. She was dripping wet, and the sticky folds of her dress clung unpleasantly to her body. Emeline rose suddenly and walked to the door. *I wish she'd go out for a while,* Mary Ann thought. She turned her back deliberately, but the bang of the door made her whirl about.

Emeline was braced against the closed door. Her eyes

were defiant. "I know what you're thinking," she accused shrilly. You're thinking we'll stifle in here. Well, I don't care if we do. Land o' Goshen! Heat's better than those infernal mosquitoes."

They stood motionless, glaring at each other. The air was charged. A mosquito settled on Emeline's arm. She slapped at it viciously, and missed. Her eyes flew to Mary Ann and suddenly they both began to laugh. It seemed to Mary Ann that she could never stop. Their eyes were brimming when they finally quieted.

"Oh, what's the use!" Emeline threw the door wide and Mary Ann came to stand beside her. They linked arms and stood gazing out into the blazing sunlight. "Well," Emeline said, "this is home." She half turned and motioned toward the interior of the cabin.

"Yes," Mary Ann said. "At least for a while," she added tonelessly.

9.

Mary Ann closed the door of the Judson's cabin carefully behind her, and sank down for a moment on the step. Her head swam. The September evening was still and sultry. No freshness was in the air, but she drew it into her lungs greedily. She could not have endured the foul, fever-laden closeness of that room for another moment. Yet if Sarah hadn't come to relieve her, she would have stayed on—she knew that. Some power of endurance had been given to her these past few weeks since the dreadful sickness had spread through camp.

She pushed herself to her feet and started slowly toward the trail that led to the river. Even this far from the cabin she could hear Timothy Judson's pitiful little voice. Her eyes filled with tears. She could not shut out the picture of the little lad, burning with fever, tossing and turning on his pillow, calling for his mother. She wondered if he would live to know—Her eyes turned toward the hill. Just a week ago she and Sarah had stood up there while Charles had said a prayer over a new grave. Timothy's mother, father and sister were buried in that grave. There had been no time to dig three. No time for a service. No one to fix proper burial clothes. Every well person was needed to nurse the sick. And there were other graves—many others. Mary Ann shuddered. Things were a little better now, praise the Lord. There had been no new cases these past two days.

She moved slowly down the trail. How wonderful Charles had been through all this. Everyone turned to him—everyone depended upon him. He scarcely took time to eat or sleep. She wondered how he stood it. Even his own wives had been down with the fever—all except Sarah and her. Poor Emeline. How she had fretted because she couldn't be up helping. "Here I am," she moaned, "flat on my back. Not able to do the thing I can do best." Emeline was a born nurse.

Mary Ann had reached her own cabin. She stood for a moment looking at it. So much had happened since the day she and Emeline had moved into that house. So much that she had had no time to think—not really. But all through these weeks she had been conscious of a sense of awe; a conviction that she had been spared—singled out—chosen by the Lord to be of some real use. She understood now what Charles had meant by "the right spirit."

"They *do* need me." She spoke the words aloud and the heavy feeling of weariness left her. The very fact that people depended on you made you strong. She lifted her head proudly and walked into the cabin.

Now that Mary Ann knew she was needed, it was surprising how many things she found to do. A small shop had been set up where household articles were made to be sold in the neighboring Missouri towns. She helped there making baskets. She found a new zest in working at the loom. She helped Charles with his records. And no matter what she did, it had a special meaning.

It came to her one day at the loom, how selfish she had been in allowing doubts about her marriage to hold her back from becoming a part of things. This piece of cloth. Everyone had helped with it—the men who sheared the wool—the women who spun it into yarn and dyed it. Now, under her fingers, it had become cloth. And all this had been done since the march started. How insignificant her personal problems seemed in comparison with this great undertaking. She would stop worrying about the future. Things would work out.

10.

It was in those first October days when the epidemic had about spent itself that Charles Rich succumbed to the fever. Mary Ann and Sarah took turns at nursing him. The other wives were still too weak to be in the sick room.

Mary Ann slipped noislessly into the cabin and laid her hand on Sarah's arm. It was nearing midnight. The room was dim, and hushed except for Charles' rapid uneven breathing.

"He's about the same," Sarah whispered. "Keep bathing his face and moisten his tongue often with the consecrated oil. Brother Snow will look in on you every few minutes. Be sure to call me if there is the slightest change." She stood beside the bed, her face still and white, looking down at Charles for a long moment, then turned and left the cabin, closing the door softly.

Charles muttered and stirred. Mary Ann wrung out a cloth from the basin of clear cool water and bathed his forehead with tender hands. She forced a few drops of oil between his fever parched lips and smoothed the coverlet. He was quiet again, now. She sat down near the bed, her eyes fixed on his face. How changed he was. She remembered the first time she had seen him—that day on the reviewing field at Nauvoo. He had looked so strong that day. So handsome. Her heart ached as she looked at him now, ill—helpless. He *must* get well. He was needed. He was a leader. So important to everyone—so important—Her breath caught sharply. He was important to her because she loved him. For a moment she closed her eyes and let the feeling flow through her, warm and tingling in every nerve. She had always loved him. Ever since that first day. But she hadn't known it until now.

She rose and approached the bed. She must be close to him—touch him. Half timidly she took his hand, but at the touch she stiffened, her heart sick with foreboding. His hand was cold and clammy. She leaned forward. Great beads of moisture stood out on his forehead. She knew what that meant. This was the crisis. She must call Sarah.

11.

"We must keep faith," Sarah said.

Mary Ann nodded mutely. The phrase had a familiar ring. . . . Mother! How often she had heard Mother say those very words. *Oh, Mother,* she thought. *I need you so. Faith—faith,* she kept repeating to herself. *"The substance of things hoped for, the evidence of things not seen."*

The night dragged on—endless—anguished. So little she could do, when she longed with all the fierce, protective instinct of her new-found love, to hold him, to keep him safe, to bring him back—to her.

The sun was rising. Through the uncurtained window a soft glow of rosy light slanted across the bed. It touched

Charles' face and the yellowed skin took on an almost natural look. He was breathing easily, too; deep, regular breaths.

"He's asleep," Sarah said. "He'll be all right now." Her mouth worked and her eyes were wet.

"You two go and get some rest," Lorenzo Snow said. "I'll stay on with him for a while."

But Mary Ann did not go at once to her cabin; she climbed the hill. She must be near the sky—out in the sun. Charles was going to get well. She loved him. That was all that mattered just now.

3

The new year brought to Charles an important letter from Brigham Young. The Council of the Twelve was sending a pioneer party westward. Details for organizing this important expedition had been given to Brigham Young "by the word and will of the Lord." Charles Rich was to come to Winter Quarters. "Your name is up," Young's letter read. "Gird up your loins, Brother Rich, put on your armor, cheer up your heart and being filled with almighty faith, prepare for the battle as fast as possible. If you are sick be made well, if you are weak be made strong. Shake yourself like a mighty man."

"Put on your armor. Shake yourself like a mighty man." Charles' eyes were thoughtful. Whatever Brother Young had in mind for him must be very difficult. And he must face the task of getting his family to Winter Quarters. It would be no small task. His family had increased. New babies—Eliza coming on from Nauvoo—and Harriet Sargent. Sarah had been wise in urging Harriet to join the Rich household. Harriet was alone after her father left Pisgah with the *Battalion*. She was a young and lovely woman who needed the protection of family life. Of course, Harriet would expect to go with them—he wanted her to go. But he would need more wagons and there were none to spare in Mount Pisgah. "Gird up your loins." Charles smiled. Preparing for the trip meant just that. Yet for the first time in weeks he felt completely alive—pulsating with energy. He wanted to get started.

Mary Ann was delighted when Charles told her. The last few months had been serenely happy. She was occupied with her work, living all the while in a secret world of her own, absorbed in the knowledge of her love for Charles—rejoicing to see him grow well and strong—proud as she realized more than ever how much he meant to the settlement. But with the coming of the new year, she had begun to feel uneasy. Charles must not discover that she loved him. She was sure of her love, but she still had doubts about her marriage. In Pisgah it was hard to conceal her feelings. She was with Charles so much. When they were traveling, things would be different.

Mary Ann plunged energetically into the preparations for departure. In early February word came from Brigham Young. He was sending wagons from Council Bluffs to bring them on. "This," Charles told Mary Ann, "solves our greatest problem."

In mid-February the thaw set in. Almost overnight, the sparkling white landscape changed to a dirty gray. Mary Ann trudged about the settlement, her feet weighted down with mud; but her heart was light. The wagons had arrived from Council Bluffs. It was almost a year since the Rich party had left Sugar Creek. It seemed a good omen that they would be moving on before that year had passed.

On the last day of February the Rich family left Mount Pisgah. Charles bid a sober goodbye to the friends he had come to know so well. But Mary Ann felt no regrets as she watched the settlement fade into the distance. She would never forget Pisgah. She had learned so much there. Yet she was impatient to go on.

Council Bluffs, in 1847, was a city of tents overlooking the Missouri River. It was humming with activity; yet the three days the Rich family delayed there dragged interminably for Mary Ann. With so many parties waiting to cross the river, Charles was not able to arrange for a flatboat any sooner.

On the morning the family was to go across, Mary Ann came down to the river early. She had slipped away from the others as soon as the wagons were packed. It seemed important, somehow, to have a few moments alone.

The river bottoms teemed with vehicles and cattle. Women were busily washing along the banks, their chatter and an occasional laugh floating up to Mary Ann where she stood. Traders in fur caps and rawhide coats hurried in and out of of the American Fur Company Post. Mary Ann watched the busy scene. She understood what Charles meant when he said that "being in Council Bluffs made him feel he was part of the world again."

The flatboat, ready for the Rich wagons, was moored alongside the landing. Mary Ann forgot the activity around her as she looked out across the slow moving waters of the Missouri. Another river to be crossed. So many things had begun for her with the crossing of a river.

"Mary Ann." Her heart leaped at the sound of Charles' deep voice. A long stride brought him to where she stood. He patted her shoulder gently and his hand slid down to grasp her arm. She could feel the blood tingling in her veins. "Why are you here alone?" he asked. "Where's the rest of the family?"

"Oh," Mary Ann hesitated, "doing some last minute visiting, I suppose." She was a little confused. She couldn't tell Charles that she had wanted to get away from the family.

"Well, I'm glad I found you. I've been wanting to talk to you." Her eyes fell before his direct, dark gaze.

She sought desperately for something to say—something safe. "Charles," her voice was breathless, "why do the Indians run the ferry?" She gestured toward the flatboat with its red-skinned crew.

"The Potawattomies cut the approach to the river and established the ferry before many white settlers came," Charles explained. "They are entitled to the business they get now."

"How long do you think we'll be in Winter Quarters?" She looked across to the settlement on the west side of the river.

"That's hard to say." He paused, his eyes searching her face, then went on abruptly. "I haven't spoken about this to anyone but Sarah, but I may have to make a trip to Nauvoo after I get you all settled."

"Oh, Charles, no," Mary Ann protested quickly. A little sick feeling rushed over her. That would mean weeks in Winter Quarters without him.

"I don't see how it can be avoided," he said. "I've never disposed of my property there." There was mild reproof in his voice.

Mary Ann turned away hastily. Her eyes stung. She hated herself for showing her feelings so plainly.

"Here comes Harriet," Charles said. "I think she's looking for me." He was gone before Mary Ann had found her voice.

4

1.

Charles Rich and Brigham Young stood in front of the Council House. It was the principal building of Winter Quarters—a long, low structure of logs, located in the center of the settlement. The Rich family had arrived the night before.

"What do you think of our miniature city, Brother Rich?" Brigham Young motioned to the hundreds of log and sod dwellings scattered about in every direction.

"Miniature city," Charles repeated. "I hadn't thought of it just that way."

"We've made it do," Young said. His eyes narrowed. "But we must get on—find the spot where we can build a real city." He threw back his head and took a deep breath. "Spring's here, I believe."

"Have you set the date for the departure of the Pioneer Party?"

"About mid-April—near as I can tell. There are only a few details left to arrange."

"How many will there be in your company?"

"One hundred and forty-three men, more or less, but very

few women. Trail blazing is not women's business. We'll bring our families on later." He paused. "It's a hand picked company. I'm sorry you are not going. But I want you to be one of the leaders of the first company to follow—so don't tarry in Nauvoo."

"You can depend on it that I'll be in that company unless the Lord wills otherwise," Rich answered.

"I've just heard from Brother Taylor and Brother Pratt," Young said. "They got back from England right after the first of the year. They'll be here any day, now. They are bringing us some valuable astronomical instruments and more money. Both will be welcome."

"Won't Brother Taylor and Brother Pratt be wanting to go with the Pioneer Party?"

"No." Young shook his head. "It will be too late for them to get ready. They can look after things here and take charge of organizing the company to follow this summer. When you return from Nauvoo, you can work with them."

Charles looked at the man. *How strong he is,* he thought. *How sure of himself and his decisions.* "What locality are you aiming for, Brother Young?" he asked.

"Somewhere in the Great Interior Basin. As to the exact site, I feel that the Lord will direct us to it. I'll know the spot when I see it. I've been gathering information about the country west of the Rockies. The government reports of John Fremont's expedition to the Great Basin should be reliable. I had Brother Stratton bring maps from St. Louis—Mitchell's maps of Texas, Oregon and California, and the latest maps of the Indian countries. Come into my office and have a look at them."

"Thank you," Charles said. "I will. But first, may I consult you about a personal matter? I want to take another wife."

Brigham Young regarded him thoughtfully. "Who is the woman?" he questioned.

"Harriet Sargent. She has been in our household ever since her father joined the *Mormon Battalion.* Now we feel that we want her to become one of our family."

"Then it's all right, Brother Rich," Young said heartily. "I like to know the circumstances. I am not generally advising the brethren to assume more responsibilities right now—unless the circumstances warrant; but men like you should have large families."

"Thank you, Brother Young. Will you marry us before you leave?"

Young smiled. "Bring her to see me tomorrow and we'll arrange for the ceremony."

2.

The cabin door burst open. Mary Ann, startled, looked up from her sewing. "Why, Emeline," she exclaimed. "Whatever is the matter?"

"Matter!" Emeline flung her sunbonnet into a corner and flounced down on the bench beside Mary Ann. "Charles has married Harriet."

Mary Ann sat very still, looking stupidly at her finger. It was trickling blood, but she had felt nothing. She still felt nothing. She was numb—frozen.

Emeline's indignant tirade went on. "I think he might have told us," she spluttered. "I wouldn't have known it if I hadn't gone over to Sarah's. There was Harriet, and they were both all dressed up. I suppose I looked surprised, because Sarah began explaining that they'd just come from Brother Young's, and that Harriet and Charles were married." She paused for a breath. "They're planning to tell all of us at supper tonight. Well," she demanded, "why don't you say something?"

"You haven't given me a chance." Mary Ann avoided Emeline's eyes. If she could only get out of this cabin—be alone.

"Land o' Goshen!" Emeline fumed. "I don't see why Charles wants another wife."

"It's not for us to say what he should do." Mary Ann put down her sewing and rose abruptly. She *must* get away from Emeline. She looked down at her shoes. "I just remembered. I must see Cobbler Stone before supper time." Her voice sounded high and queer. She snatched her sunbonnet from its peg and hurried to the door. "I'll see you at supper," she mumbled.

Once away from the cabin she followed the trail blindly. Her face burned and her eyes were blurred with tears. She walked on with no thought of her surroundings, but the sight of the Council House roused her. She must get away from the settlement. She couldn't bear to see people. She turned into a secluded path that led toward the river. "Oh, Charles," she whispered. "Charles." Why should she be feeling this way—so hurt—so crushed? She was selfish. She was wicked. Charles had two wives when he married her and had taken two more. She hadn't minded then—But then she hadn't known that she loved him . . . .

She threw herself prone upon the bank and lay there motionless, listening to the mocking gurgle of the river.

3.

Mary Ann was late for supper. It was a warm spring evening, and the family was gathered outside Sarah's tent. She could hear them laughing and talking as she came up the trail. She knew that they were waiting for her, but she could not force herself to hurry. There was a cruel wrench at her heart as she came closer. Harriet was standing close to

Charles, smiling up into his face. *She's beautiful,* Mary Ann thought. Her throat tightened. Would it always be this way? Would he go on taking other wives?

"Here's Mary Ann, now." It was Emeline's voice. Heads turned in her direction. She steeled herself for the ordeal.

"Mary Ann," Charles said, "I've been looking for you. I've some special news for you."

Special news, she thought. *Why should he consider his marriage special news to me?*

But Charles had turned back to Harriet. His hand was on her arm. "Harriet is one of the family now," he said. "We were married today."

"Yes, I know." Mary Ann's mouth was dry. She must say something to Harriet. She swallowed painfully and forced a smile to her lips. "I am very glad, Harriet." Her voice was hollow in her own ears.

"Come, Charles," Sarah urged. "We must sit down. Everything's getting cold."

The group began moving toward the table, set outside tonight, and festive with its bowl of wild flowers. "Come and sit with us, Mary Ann." Charles linked one arm through Harriet's, the other through Mary Ann's. She walked beside him woodenly. "And now for your news," Charles said. "Clarissa Allen and her family arrived late today. They brought you a message. Your father is in Council Bluffs. He'll be coming across any day now—he and his family."

For a moment the words had no meaning; then a great wave of relief almost swept her from her feet. Clarissa was here. Father was coming. She would have someone to talk to—something else to think about. As she sat down at the table, she felt that she could almost smile.

5

1.

Often, during the weeks that followed, Mary Ann wondered how she could ever have been estranged from her father. Those rebellious years on the farm—the defiant spirit that had taken her to Nauvoo, seemed remote and unreal, like the experiences of a stranger. Father was so kind. So understanding. From the moment she had gone running to meet him and his long arms had closed about her, she had felt strengthened and comforted. Just to know that he was here—loving her, believing in her, wanting her to be happy, eased the pain in her heart. It was good, too, to see the children again. She was even glad to see Sera.

With Charles away, Mary Ann found plenty of time on her hands and most of it she spent with her father. The reunion with Clarissa was pleasant but disturbing. Clarissa was shrewd. Mary Ann dared not subject herself long to the scrutiny of those bright dark eyes. With her father she could be natural. If she was silent, he did not question her. How she wished that he would! A word from him would have unlocked her lips, but somehow she could not force herself to confess her doubts—to ask for the guidance she needed so desperately.

They explored the countryside in long, leisurely walks, talking of this and that. Paulina was somewhere along the way with the Lyman family. John Clark, Morris said, had been in St. Louis when last he heard, expecting to set out with an Oregon Party. No, that was all he could tell her about John. Rhoda was still in Montrose—she might have later news. Mary Ann could feel herself crimsoning under her father's level gaze. She might as well give up hope of reaching Uncle John. She couldn't turn to him anyway—not after the way she had talked at Sugar Creek. Hastily she changed the subject. And the weeks slipped by, with no mention of the thing that lay heavy on her heart.

Then Charles returned. He was full of enthusiasm, already laying plans for the family's immediate departure. The sale of his Nauvoo property, he told them, had not brought much, but funds were forthcoming from an unexpected source. On the return trip he had met two friends eager to join the first party going west—men of means, who would gladly help Charles in return for his efforts on their behalf. "We are going to be fitted out comfortably, thanks to them," he exulted.

Mary Ann slipped away into the shadows. She was a coward. She should have faced things long ago. Now it was too late. She couldn't bear to upset Charles now.

2.

In the soft light of an early June evening Mary Ann waited for her father near the Council House. This would be their last walk together. Early in the morning the Rich family was leaving for the Elkhorn River, where the first westbound party was assembling. Mary Ann sighed unhappily, then tried to smile. Her father was coming along the trail.

"I'm sorry to be late," Morris said. He put his arm around her shoulders and drew her to him for a moment.

"Shall we walk beside the river or under the cottonwoods up on the hill?'

"The hill," Mary Ann answered quickly. She did not like the river. Like her thoughts, it was never clear.

"I am going to miss you, my dear," Morris said. They were seated on the grass under a cottonwood. "These have been precious weeks to me."

"And to me, Father."

"Is everything ready? You're really getting away in the morning?"

"At sunrise. We'll go as far as the Elkhorn River. Brother Pratt and Brother Taylor are waiting there for Charles."

"And the others will join you there?"

"Yes, there will be five groups—about two thousand all together, Charles says. Brother Pratt and Brother Taylor are in charge. They'll have the traveling plans all worked out by the time we arrive."

Morris sighed. "I wish I could go on now, but it will be a long time before I can get an outfit together." He sighed again. "You should be very happy, daughter."

"But I'm not. I'm miserable." The instant she had spoken Mary Ann was sorry. She turned her head away. Her lips were trembling.

"Yes, dear," Morris said. "I know."

"You mean—But you couldn't, Father. You've never said anything." Mary Ann was facing him now, her blue eyes incredulous.

"You are like your mother," Morris said slowly. "When she had heartaches, she wouldn't discuss them—always kept her feelings to herself. That's why I haven't urged you to confide in me. But I wish you would," he added.

Mary Ann hesitated. This had been pent up within her for so long. She took a deep breath. "I'm in love with Charles."

"Well, that's nothing to be unhappy about."

"Oh, it is, Father. It is! You don't understand." Now that she had started, talking was a relief. She plunged in, going back to those unawakened days in Nauvoo, pouring out her innermost thoughts and feelings. "I was so sure," she said bitterly. "I wanted to be a plural wife."

Morris listened attentively, his face grave. She told of the first months of the trek—her homesickness—her doubts—her inner struggle. Vividly she outlined the harrowing weeks at Pisgah, with Charles stricken down at last. Her voice dropped to a lower pitch, warm and tender, as she told of Charles' illness—of how she had helped to nurse him. "And on the night of the crisis," she said, " I realized that I loved him."

For the moment, Morris knew that she had forgotten him, that she was living over again the details of that night. He did not move or speak. "Afterward," she said, "when Charles was well, I was happy. Sure that everything would be all right." She stopped abruptly. "Then Charles married Harriet." Her tone was flat—all the warmth gone.

"But—what do you mean?" Morris was bewildered. "Do you dislike Harriet?"

She shook her head. "It isn't Harriet. It's Charles' taking another wife that has made me face things squarely. I can't feel that it's right to *go on.* I—" She dropped her eyes. "I forgot you didn't know, Father. I've never lived with Charles—that way. We were waiting until we reached our new home. This must all seem very strange to you," she finished miserably.

"No, my dear, it doesn't." Morris prodded at the turf with a small stick. "But I do want to ask you one question. Is it only your marriage that troubles you, or do your doubts touch your Faith?"

"Oh, not my Faith," she protested.

Morris made a neat row of holes with the stick. "Then," he said, "it's just that you're confused about living this new principle. I can understand that. When I accepted Mormonism, I was as sure of myself as you were when you married Charles." He tossed the stick away and leaned toward her. "But I had doubts, too. Many times I wondered if I'd made a mistake. But things always worked out right. I know now that it was because I was firm in my Faith."

"Things were different then," Mary Ann said. "There wasn't any plural marriage. You and Mother had each other alone."

"We had other problems. And your mother did have to share me—in a different way, of course, but it must have caused her plenty of heartaches. You can remember what she went through in Far West and during those months I was in prison."

"I know, Father, but somehow I can't feel that she would think plural marriage is right."

"And I feel certain that she would," Morris said. He reached for Mary Ann's hands and held them between his palms. "Your mother gave the best years of her life to our religion," he said earnestly. "Her one desire was that the Church she helped establish should go on. If she were alive today, she would accept plural marriage because it is a part of our Faith."

"How can you be so sure, Father? How do you know what she might feel?"

"I knew your mother, Mary Ann." Morris released her hands and sat up a little straighter. "There may have been times when she was confused—when she doubted. I don't know. But I do know how strong she was—how courageous. You have her spirit, my dear. You can go on where she left off."

Mary Ann sat very still. The sun had set. A slender new moon was faintly outlined in the darkening sky. A cricket chirped loudly in the silence. Morris' anxious eyes were fixed on her face.

At last she spoke. "Very well, Father. I'll go on." Her voice was low, the words carefully distinct. "But I am still not sure about my marriage." She got to her feet quickly. "It's almost dark. We must hurry back."

There's nothing more I can say, Morris thought as they went down the trail. She would go on. She had made that bargain with him. But her marriage—she would have to settle that for herself.

3.

It was sunrise. On the outskirts of Winter Quarters the wagons of the Rich caravan were drawn up in a long line. People stood waiting in restless groups, or wandered aimlessly from wagon to wagon. All were anxious for Charles Rich, their captain, to give the signal for departure.

Mary Ann and Emeline stood with Morris Phelps, a little apart from the others.

"I wonder what's keeping Charles?" Emeline fretted. "He went to look for those boys who are to help with our teams."

Mary Ann said nothing but she, too, wished that Charles would come. She did not want to prolong the moment of farewell. She moved closer to her father. She could feel him watching her. She was glad he did not talk. Her heart ached and there was a great lump in her throat.

"Do you suppose one of the new boys will drive our—" Emeline caught Mary Ann's arm. "Here comes Charles now. He seems upset about something."

Charles came swiftly toward the little group, his face dark with worry. "We are going to be delayed," he said.

"Why?" Emeline demanded.

"I am short of drivers. Two of the boys I'd hired won't

be able to go. We'll have to wait until I can find others. It's very—"

"Charles," Mary Ann broke in, "let me drive one of the teams."

"And I'll drive the other," Emeline volunteered quickly.

Charles shook his head. "It's fine of you to offer, but I couldn't let you do it."

"But you must," Mary Ann insisted. Two red spots flamed in her cheeks. Her eyes were brilliant with excitement.

"We know something about oxen," Emeline said. "Thomas let us help him sometimes."

"But that was different," Charles said. He turned to Morris. "What do you think?"

"It isn't for me to say, Brother Rich, but perhaps you might give them a trial?"

"We're supposed to reach Elkhorn tomorrow." Charles rubbed his chin thoughtfully. "Brother Pratt and Brother Taylor are expecting me." He stood looking at the girls, his dark eyes clouded. "All right," he said suddenly. "You may try it as far as Elkhorn—that's about thirty miles. If things don't go well, I'll make other arrangements there." He turned away. "Come with me, Emeline. Your team is over here."

"I'm proud of you, Mary Ann," Morris said when they were alone. "This won't be easy, but you'll be happy doing it. And you'll get along all right." He paused. "Don't you see? Things are working out. Already you are needed."

Mary Ann's eyes were shining. "I am so glad I can help Charles," she said softly.

"Here is something for you." Morris took a small, square package from his pocket. "It's your mother's copy of *The Doctrine and Covenants*. I know she would want you to have it now." He laid the book in her hands, clasped them in his own and drew her close to him until her wrists rested against his broad chest. "Keep your Faith, dear—and your love for Charles. Some day you'll know."

A flurry of goodbyes was running along the wagon train. Morris stooped and kissed his daughter's forehead. "I see Charles coming. Goodbye, dear, and God bless you."

"Goodbye, Father—and thank you for everything," Mary Ann said. She watched Morris as he walked away, then turned to Charles, her head held high. "Where is my team?" she asked. "I must not delay the caravan."

6

1.

Four great circles of wagons were already drawn up near the bank of the Elkhorn River when the Rich caravan reached camp on the second afternoon.

The moment they halted, Emeline threw herself on the grass beside her wagon. "Come over here in the shade," she called to Mary Ann, who had pulled in just behind.

The oxen were placid and content. Mary Ann left them and dropped down on the grass at Emeline's side.

"I'm dead," Emeline groaned. "O-o-h—but it feels good to stretch." She threw her arms over her head and sighed gustily.

Mary Ann fanned her dirt-streaked face with her sunbonnet. Perspiration trickled into her eyes. "My feet feel like balls of fire," she said. "But Emeline—we've made it." There was triumph in her voice. "I'm sure Charles will let us keep on with the teams."

"I'm afraid he will." Emeline groaned again.

Mary Ann regarded her. Nothing, she was sure, would keep Emeline from going on with the team, yet perversely she goaded with a question. "Are you going to quit?"

"No." Emeline sat bolt upright. "I'm not going to quit." She looked at Mary Ann through narrowed lids. "We made a bargain, didn't we? Here comes Charles," she added hastily.

The girls scrambled to their feet as Charles approached. His face was stern. "Why are you loitering here?" he demanded sharply.

"Why—why—" Mary Ann faltered, "we were waiting for Thomas and George to take our teams. Last night—"

"Last night they helped you," Rich said. "I know that. But from now on you'll have to take care of your own teams. That's part of your job. Make haste, now. Get your wagons in the circle." He motioned toward the fifth circle already forming beside the river. Then, before either of them could answer, he turned and walked away.

"Well!" Emeline exploded. "I've never seen him like that before."

"He needn't think he can talk to me that way!" Mary Ann's eyes blazed. With a violent gesture she dashed her sunbonnet to the ground. "He might at least give us credit for getting here."

"Oh, well—" Emeline shrugged. "Losing your temper won't help. Come on—let's put the teams away before he comes back."

2.

Charles held himself stiffly erect as he stalked away from the girls. He would not look back—it might spoil the effect. They had managed their teams remarkably well, but he must discourage them. The caravan was heading into wild country. There would be constant danger from Indians and wild animals. The girls had courage and pretty fair judgment, yet they were young—and they were women. It would be a great risk.

He sighed and quickened his pace. It was hard to find

boys for this work. There were so many more women than men in the party. Mary Ann and Emeline had no family responsibilities—they could be relieved of camp work. . . . He frowned thoughtfully as he hurried toward John Taylor's tent. He was anxious to talk with Taylor; there were still many organization details to be threshed out. This business of the teams could wait until morning. Perhaps the girls would have changed their minds by then. He smiled, remembering the look on their faces when he had ordered them to get their own teams into the circle. Of course, they wouldn't get into real trouble. Thomas and George would see to that.

3.

It was almost noon the day following before Rich saw Mary Ann and Emeline. Sarah had given him a late supper and an early breakfast. Conferences with John Taylor and Parley Pratt had occupied every moment. But now that Brother Taylor and Brother Pratt had departed with their caravans, Charles knew that he must get this matter of drivers settled.

He found Mary Ann and Emeline coming up from the river where they had washed their clothes. He swung alongside and dropped into step. Emeline's greeting was brusque—Mary Ann's remote and cool. Charles concealed his amusement, yet he felt guilty, too. He had heard of the difficulty they'd had getting their teams placed. They had a right to be angry.

"You managed very well coming over from Winter Quarters," he said.

Neither of them spoke. They kept their eyes straight ahead.

"The hard part of the journey is to come," Charles went on. "You are sure you don't care to change your minds?"

"No," they chorused emphatically.

Charles watched them for a moment. Heads high, eyes snapping, their skirts swishing angrily over the grass. Even after their experience last night, they were more determined than ever. They had courage, and they were waiting for his decision.

"Then I'll depend on you," he said in a matter-of-fact tone. "I'll explain how the march is organized." He went on then with the details. Parley Pratt and John Taylor had gone on, with Pratt in the lead. The Rich company would be third and the other two companies would follow. "It seemed wiser for the groups to travel separately," Charles said.

The girls listened intently, their pique forgotten. They were eager to learn every detail.

"Will we travel two abreast as we did from Winter Quarters?" Emeline asked.

"Whenever we can. It's safer that way. I'll keep you two together and near the lead wagons. I hope we can leave day after tomorrow."

They halted at the edge of the wagon circle. "Our company will have charge of the artillery that's being taken west," Charles said. "That reminds me—Do either of you know how to handle a rifle?"

"I don't," Emeline admitted.

"Neither do I, but you can teach us, can't you?" Mary Ann's eyes were wide.

"Yes," Charles answered. "Be ready for your first lesson this afternoon, about three. That's all for now." They paused beside Mary Ann's wagon. "I forgot to tell you," Charles smiled. "Clarissa Allen and her family are enrolled in my company, but I don't suppose you'll see much of her. You two will be doing men's work. I'm proud of you." He turned and walked away.

4.

Just before the Rich caravan left Elkhorn, Charles had a written message from Brigham Young. It was delivered by Charles Beaumont, leader of a party of French trappers on their way from Fort Laramie to Council Bluffs. The message was addressed to the Church at Winter Quarters. It had been early in May when they met Young in the Grand Island country, Beaumont explained. They had expected to deliver the letter to Winter Quarters, but illness and slow trade with the Indians had delayed the trappers. They had met Pratt and Taylor two days ago and after reading the letter, Taylor had sent it on to Rich at Elkhorn.

"We are about two hundred and fifty miles from Winter Quarters according to our reckoning," Young wrote. "The brethren are all well, and never was a company more united in the best of feelings." The letter ended with a bit of characteristic advice. "Organize and keep strict discipline; bring all the cannon and take care of yourselves."

Beaumont gave Charles another important detail. Young had debated regarding the route west from Grand Island. He had decided to continue along the north side of the Platte rather than cross the river and head into the Oregon Trail.

That was like Brigham Young, Charles thought—wanting to blaze a new trail. And probably it was wise. After all, the Mormons wanted to be independent.

7

1.

It was the first week of July before the Rich caravan overtook John Taylor's party at Grand Island.

The clear waters of the creek flowing to the Platte River danced and sparkled in the afternoon sun. Mary Ann was relieved that her team was disposed of for the night. She stood quietly watching the caravan form its circle along the creek bank. Emeline was just bringing in her team, her face intent, her lips drawn in a firm line as she expertly guided her oxen—careful to see that the front wheel of her wagon just touched the hind wheel of the one ahead. That was important. Mary Ann smiled. She and Emeline had found that out at Elkhorn. She could laugh now, looking back at that night. The whole circle had been in commotion before they got their teams settled. She had been close to tears. She'd always be grateful to George for coming to their rescue. That seemed a long time ago.

Now another stage of the journey lay behind them. There were parts of it she would never forget. Those first long days, learning to manage her team—so determined not to fail. The way her hand had trembled when Charles gave her the first lesson in handling a gun. She was no longer afraid of the gun—not since she had killed the wolf that leaped out of a thicket in the path of her team. She sighed. Long days. Breakfast and prayers at five—on the road at seven. Heat. Dirt. Endless rivers and creeks. And the nights. Too tired to think—numbly grateful for safety and a chance to sleep.

There was a rustle in the grass and Emeline stood beside her. "There's one thing I like about managing a team," she said jauntily. "It relieves me of kitchen duty." She wiped her dirty face with the hem of her wide gingham skirt. "My shoes are full of sand. Come on, let's go over to the creek."

"Mary Ann—Emeline—wait for me!" From the row of tents outside the wagon circle a girl came running along the trail.

"It's Clarissa," Emeline said waving a greeting. "She's up to something, I'll be bound."

Clarissa was breathless when she reached them.

"Where on earth are you going with those clothes?" Emeline asked, pointing to the dress and petticoats draped over Clarissa's arm.

"News!" Clarissa exclaimed, ignoring the question. "There is to be a big bonfire tonight with singing—and Brother Pidcock is going to play his fiddle for dancing." She finished gasping.

"You'd better get your breath," Emeline advised.

"Oh, a dance. That will be fun." Mary Ann was surprised at her own enthusiasm. She wasn't tired tonight. She wanted to take part in everything. Maybe Charles would have time to dance . . . .

Clarissa tossed her black curls. "I'm going to have a bath in the creek," she announced.

"Clarissa!" Mary Ann reproved. She looked up and down the creek. There were people everywhere.

"Well, at least my feet," Clarissa giggled, her eyes sparkling. "And don't you worry, I've found a secluded spot up yonder." She waved her arm. "Aren't you going to change?" She looked at their bedraggled dresses. "You'll have to hurry if you're coming with me."

But Mary Ann was already running toward her wagon, with Emeline close behind.

2.

The dusky light of evening hung over camp. Mary Ann, Clarissa and Emeline strolled along the river bank, waiting for the fire to be lighted.

"I feel like a new person," Mary Ann said. She smoothed the folds of her blue calico dress. It was the only one of her three remaining dresses that wasn't faded and patched. Soon she would have to start wearing it every day.

"Oh, there's Cobbler Stone," Clarissa exclaimed. She pointed to the small rotund man sitting on a near-by stump. "I almost forgot I'm supposed to find out about Mother's shoes. Come along with me."

"This is the first time I've ever seen him idle," Emeline said as they climbed the grassy bank. "I wonder how we'd ever get along without him?"

"Well, well, well!" Cobbler Stone greeted them. "All fixed up for the dance." His brown eyes twinkled under heavy white brows. "You look mighty pretty." He nodded his head approvingly. "Make merry tonight—work tomorrow—that's the right spirit." He crinkled his eyes at Clarissa. "Your mother's shoes are ready. You can get them if you'll stop at my wagon.—How are you girls getting on with your teams?" he demanded, transferring his gaze to Mary Ann and Emeline.

"Fine," Mary Ann answered.

"And how do you keep busy, miss?" He turned again to Clarissa.

She tossed her head. "I find plenty to do helping Mother and Father."

"You ought to be married—like these girls." He nodded toward Mary Ann and Emeline.

"Like that?" Clarissa's tone was disdainful. "I'll never be married that way."

Mary Ann felt a quick flash of anger. She could see Emeline's mouth tighten. They had had this out with Clarissa before. Now, when the subject came up, they ignored her.

"You might do worse," Cobbler Stone retorted. "And don't wait too long to find the right man. You may go through the woods and in the end pick up the crooked stick."

Clarissa's eyes snapped. "That may be. But at least," she added crisply, "the stick will be mine alone."

The cheerful scrape of a violin sounded in the distance. "Come on," Clarissa said, and walked away, her nose in the air.

Emeline and Mary Ann bade Cobbler Stone good night and followed Clarissa in silence. "Mine alone"—"mine alone"—the words echoed in Mary Ann's mind. Somehow all the zest had gone out of the evening.

3.

The leaping flames of the camp fire painted the trees with a rosy glow. Snatches of talk and laughter drifted down to the creek where Charles Rich and John Taylor were walking.

"Brother Pratt left here two days ago, following the north bank of the Platte, of course." Taylor paused. "I want to leave in the morning, but you'd better wait here until Brother Grant and Brother Hunter come in. They aren't far behind."

"Not more than a couple of days," Charles said.

"That's good. You can tell them that our route is on the

north side of the Platte. I may wait for you at Fort Laramie but don't count on it. I may go straight ahead."

The crackle of the fire mingled with the strains of a merry jig. Hands clapped and there were shouts of laughter. Charles Rich and John Taylor stood silent for a moment. Stars burned brightly overhead. The long, narrow island was a dark, timbered mass in the river. Shadowy forms slipped in and out among the wagons—the ever vigilant guards, patrolling the circle.

"Charles." John Taylor's voice had a rough edge. "These people—listen to them. They are facing danger and uncertainty, yet tonight how happy they are." His voice broke.

"They are not thinking of danger, John—and for them there is no uncertainty. They have faith," Charles said. "That's it. Faith."

5.

Mary Ann sat for a long time, staring out of the end of her wagon-box. "Mine alone." She could not forget Clarissa's words. She couldn't go on this way. She must get things straight in her mind. In two days, now, they would be moving on. Fort Laramie, in Wyoming, was the next goal. Before she reached there, this thing must be settled. She must know what she wanted to do.

8

1.

Through her threadbare calico, the hot July sun beat down on Mary Ann's shoulders. The morning was not far advanced, but they had been hours on the march. The soft shuffling tread of oxen and the creak and groan of rolling wagons wove a familiar measured background. *The music of the trek,* she thought.

Creak, squeak, plod—creak, squeak, plod. Mary Ann moved with the rhythm, her gait timed perfectly to the pace of her slow-moving beasts. Today her team was fifth from the lead wagon. She was glad to be up near the front, ahead of the choking dust.

She turned to look back at the caravan—a long unbroken line—hugged close to the river bank. Her eyes lingered on the saffron waters of the North Platte. She hadn't given much thought to the river until after they had passed the junction of the north and south forks; nor had she been conscious of the great prairie's sweeping beauty—not until the excitement of the buffalo country was over. Those days in the buffalo country were still a confused blur. Great herds, one moment peacefully grazing, then, startled, stampeding madly across the prairie. It was wonderful and terrifying. She had hated the long stops, but the men reveled in the excitement of the hunt, and all of them craved fresh meat. The smell of it, roasting over open fires made of buffalo chips still clung to her nostrils. She was thankful that there was plenty of it jerked and sacked for future use.

"Land!" Emeline complained as they moved steadily westward over Nebraska. "Nothing but land and prairie dogs." But for Mary Ann there was something peaceful about it; something calm and reassuring. The river drifting lazily eastward, the vast flat stretches of country, the even course they were following day after day. It was a peace that lay outside of her at first but today, somehow, it had become a part of her.

She thrust back the brim of her sunbonnet and strained her eyes ahead. The country was beginning to change in appearance. There were low rolling hills, and in the far distance the purple outline of mountain peaks. They must be nearing Fort Laramie. She half closed her eyes against the glare. Those two black specks far ahead must be Charles and Brother Spencer. They always rode in advance of the train, on horseback.

There was a sudden commotion just ahead. Emeline—cracking her whip and berating her oxen.

"What's the matter?" Mary Ann called.

"Nothing." Emeline turned, a broad grin on her face. "I just have to do something to break the monotony."

Mary Ann's eyes went back to her own team, lumbering along, their great horns swinging slowly back and forth. Stupid dumb beasts. Once the pace was set, there was nothing to do but crack the whip occasionally. Stupid. No! not stupid—Wonderful dumb beasts! They were carrying her forward . . . forward. . . . Of course. That was it! And there was no road back. The rhythm flowed through her. Forward . . . forward . . . and suddenly words were fitting themselves to it. "Some day you'll know." "Some day you'll know." Father's words. She laughed aloud—a joyous, carefree laugh. Father was right. She did know. She was sure of herself again. It was like groping in a black, narrow passage and all at once touching a door—a door that swung wide open into light and joy. She knew now what she wanted to do. She would never doubt again.

2.

Charles Rich was weary, but a sense of well-being filled him. His caravan was in Fort Laramie, safely across the Platte River. Captain Bordeaux, commander of the Fort, had given him heartening news of Brigham Young. Young and his company had been at Fort Laramie in June and had passed forward without delay, following the Oregon Trail. "The Oregon Trail is best," Captain Bordeaux said. "I convinced your leader of that. Breaking a new trail would have meant unnecessary danger and delay." It was now early August. Brother Young's company should be established in the new home by now. And all was well with Parley Pratt and John Taylor. They had left Fort Laramie the previous week.

The Lord is good, Charles thought. Everyone in the company well and in good spirits—and within two days they, too, would be moving west along the Oregon Trail. They would no longer be isolated. With good luck, they should reach South Pass in the Rockies by early September.

On the morning of departure Mary Ann stood beside Charles near the lead wagon. "It seems no time at all," she said, "since we were at Chimney Rock on the prairie. Time has passed so quickly these last few weeks."

Charles, expertly scanning the long line of wagons, turned quickly and met her eyes smiling up at him. The morning sunlight touched her bright hair. There was a radiance, a sparkle about her that made his heart quicken. She'd been different lately. Now that he thought about it, he'd noticed the change about the time they had left Chimney Rock.

Under his gaze, a deep flush glowed through Mary Ann's rich tan. She turned her head, looking away toward the high adobe walls that surrounded the Fort, but Charles continued to study her. He'd been alone with her very little, yet all along he had sensed her doubts. Once or twice, even, he had felt sure that she regretted her step. He'd known that she was unhappy, yet somehow he couldn't question her. Yes, she was different this morning. The strained look was gone. There was a new poise and self-assurance . . . a new maturity. His heart beat faster. He put out his hand, but she turned before he touched her.

"Charles," she said, "I'd hoped there might be some Oregon bound parties here."

"Why?" His dark eyes searched her face.

"Uncle John is with an Oregon party. He left Independence, Missouri, about the time we left Winter Quarters." She hesitated. "I suppose it's foolish of me—yet I did hope I might meet him here. I want to see him—so much. I suppose there's no use hoping, now."

For a moment Charles did not answer. So this was what had changed her. The hope of seeing John Clark. What did it mean—this anxiety to see John? He was remembering her small white face, that night at Sugar Creek. He'd been mistaken. She wasn't sure of herself. He was glad that he hadn't spoken the words that welled from his heart a moment ago. He sighed heavily. "I wouldn't give up hope, Mary Ann. Captain Bordeaux says that there are many Oregon parties ahead on the trail. We may overtake your Uncle John's party—or he may overtake us. I'll ask Bordeaux to keep on the lookout for him."

"Oh, Charles! Could you do that?" Her small brown hands were tightly clasped. "You don't know what it means to me."

"I think I do, my dear. I think I do," he said softly as he walked away.

3.

One hundred and twenty-four miles west of Fort Laramie the Oregon Trail crossed the North Platte River and here the Rich caravan had a pleasant surprise. Mormons, all members of the Pioneer Party, were operating the ferry. Charles Rich was delighted to find an old friend in charge—Francis Pomeroy, whom he had known well in Nauvoo.

"You don't know how good it seems to find our own people here." Charles gripped Pomeroy's hand. They were standing near the river's edge on an afternoon in mid-August. The Rich party had just arrived. "How did you happen to stay here?" Charles questioned.

Pomeroy laughed. "When we reached here in June, the river was too high to ford and a number of Oregon parties were stranded." He chuckled again. "But we solved their problem with Brother Young's sole leather boat. The Oregon parties (Missourians, by the way) were willing to pay us any price to get across. So we went into the ferry business. It was very profitable."

"But that boat was only a skiff," Charles exclaimed. "How about the wagons?"

"They unloaded them and floated them over. When all the parties, including our own, were safely across, Brother Young decided it would be wise to leave a group of us here to take care of our oncoming parties. So we built the flatboat." He indicated the boat, now half-way across the stream with its load of wagons. "Lucky we stayed, too, because the water hasn't gone down much."

"When did Brother Pratt and Brother Taylor leave here?"

"About ten days ago."

"In those Oregon parties—" Charles hesitated, "you didn't happen upon anyone you knew?"

"No—Why do you ask?"

"My wife Mary Ann's uncle, John Clark, is in a party bound for Oregon. She is anxious to see him."

"I remember Clark, but he hasn't been with any of the parties that have gone through so far."

Later that afternoon Charles told Mary Ann what he had learned. "It would be well," he said, "for you to see Brother Pomeroy. I know he will be glad to give John a message for you."

"Oh, thank you, Charles," she said. "I do want—"

But Charles was walking away. He had purposely avoided her ever since they left Fort Laramie. He would continue to do so. If she came to him, it must be of her own free will.

4.

Mary Ann was puzzled. Whatever had possessed Charles to walk away like that? While she was still talking to him, too. It wasn't like him. He was always so courteous, so kind. He was more than kind. He was wonderful. Making inquiries of every emigrant party, going to all that trouble just now with Brother Pomeroy. It must have been her fault. She must have said or done something to disturb him. Perhaps she shouldn't have mentioned Uncle John, in the first place. She was sorry now that she'd made such a point of wanting to see him. Ever since that day Charles had been so distant, so aloof. There had been a time when she dreaded being alone with him, but now that was all over. She wanted to be with him now, and he seemed always to shun her. Yet he hadn't seemed angry a moment ago—only thoughtful and grave. She didn't understand. It was all very strange.

5.

Just before the Rich caravan departed, Mary Ann gave Francis Pomeroy her carefully worded message for John. "Please tell him," she said, "that everything is all right—and that I am very happy."

9

1.

After they left the Platte, Mary Ann's spirits flagged. The river had been their guide for so long she was strangely lonely without it. And Charles was avoiding her. She was sure of that now. *Charles!* her heart cried out. *Charles, will things never be clear between us?*

Barren sand. Not a living, growing thing but scattered clumps of wild sage. Alkaline marshes. The foul odor of swamps. No water fit to drink. Fear gripped the caravan. Mary Ann thought with longing of the creeks and rivers they had crossed. Another day. Nightfall. Camp. No water—no wood—no grass. How casually they had always accepted these precious things. Now the night brought no rest. It meant only lying stiff and tense, with parched lips and aching throat—tired nerves flinching from the plaintive bawl of thirsty cattle.

Again Charles studied his copy of Fremont's Journal. They must be nearing the Sweetwater River. Unless they were off the trail. . . . At daybreak he and Brother Spencer set off to reconnoiter. The caravan dragged wearily behind.

Through the merciless glare of mid-afternoon Mary Ann

drove her oxen, her red-rimmed eyes fixed on their drooping heads. On—on—on—they must keep going. If once they paused, she might not be able to start them again. If Charles and Brother Spencer would only return. Everything else seemed unimportant now. She shaded her eyes and peered into the distance. Were those two dark spots horses? Probably not. With dull indifference she shrugged and looked away. She had been disappointed so often—deceived by shimmering heat that distorted the sagebrush, seeming to give it motion. A sudden shout rang out and echoed along the wagons. "It's the Captain!" men were yelling. "The Captain and Brother Spencer!"

Mary Ann could see them now, clearly recognizable, bending low in their saddles, urging their weary horses on. She did not join the throng pressing forward toward the riders. Stiff and white she stood beside her wagon, her body shaking with the frantic pound of her heart. But her first look at Charles' face broke the tension. Knees trembling, she sank down on the dusty trail. Tired, haggard, caked with sweat and dust, Charles' face was radiant. They had found a guidepost. The Sweetwater was not far ahead.

2.

"I'd like to be a sponge," Emeline said. "I don't think I'll ever get enough of this." She knelt on the bank of the Sweetwater and bent forward, filling her cupped hands, drinking thirstily again and again of the clear, cool water.

It was early evening. Mary Ann sat, her arms hugged about her knees, dreamily watching Emeline. "It will be good to follow a river again," she murmured.

"I'm anxious to get to the mountains. Real mountains." Emeline climbed up the bank and seated herself beside Mary Ann. Both heads turned toward the southwest, where the towering peaks of the Rockies reared themselves against the darkening sky. The day had been warm but now, after sunset, fall was in the air. The river whispered and swished over its pebbles. A child's cry floated down from camp. A woman's laugh.

The peace was shattered by a sudden clamor. The girls' eyes met in a questioning look.

"What do you suppose—" Emeline's words were cut off by a long blast from the bugle. Then two short blasts.

"General camp meeting!" Mary Ann exclaimed. "Something's happened." They jumped up and started running.

People were hurrying from every direction, gathering around a team and wagon that stood outside the circle. Mary Ann and Emeline pushed through, standing on tiptoe in an effort to see over the heads of the jostling crowd. Snatches of conversation enlightened them. "Brother Benson and Brother Rockwell." "Word from the Pioneer Party."

"Did you hear that?" Emeline gripped Mary Ann's arm and with one accord they braced themselves, forcing a pathway. More blasts from the bugle. Charles Rich was mounting a wagon-box. Quiet fell over the crowd.

"Brethren and sisters." For a moment Charles paused, his dark eyes alight as they swept the faces before him.

"Oh, Emeline!" Mary Ann whispered.

"I have news," Charles was going on, "the most important news in the world." His voice shook a little. "Brother Young has found our new home—in the valley of the Great Salt Lake." There was complete silence for a moment, then a great burst of cheers.

The next few minutes were a blur to Mary Ann. She was hugging Emeline—shaking hands with someone—jostled about—buffeted—whirled this way and that. The bugle blared again, bringing them back to sanity. After the hubbub, the quiet seemed profound. Men and women alike, with tear-filled eyes and happy faces listened intently, drinking in Charles' words. Brother Young had already started on the return trip to Winter Quarters. They should be meeting him any day, now. He had sent Brother Benson and Brother Rockwell ahead, to bring the news to parties still on the trail.

"I have here a letter from Brother Young," Charles said. "Listen to his own words:

> 'Let all the brethren and sisters cheer up their hearts, and know assuredly that God has heard and answered their prayers and ours, and led us to a goodly land, and our Souls are satisfied therewith. God bless all the Saints.' "

Charles' voice echoed in a throbbing silence. Straight and tall he stood, his motionless figure silhouetted against the purple dusk. "God has heard." Slowly and impressively he repeated the words. His head went up. "All of you know how this day began," he said. "God has indeed heard. Our journey has been blessed, our troubles have been few, and soon, now, we shall be in our new home. Let us give thanks to the Lord."

Mary Ann stood with the others, her head bowed, her heart overflowing. For a moment, a flash of inner vision pictured the vast movement in all of its majesty. How small, how insignificant she felt in contrast. Yet how proud she was to be a part of it.

10

1.

There was not a moment to lose. Brigham Young impressed that upon the Rich company when he met them two days later at South Pass. Charles Rich, he said, was sorely needed in the Salt Lake Valley. They must not underestimate what lay before them. In the new home their faith would be put to its greatest test. Jim Bridger, "Peg Leg" Smith, Major Harris—every explorer and trapper he'd met on the trail had advised against going to the Salt Lake Valley; but that had not deterred him, Young said. "The Lord guided us to the spot—it is the place," were his words as he took leave of the caravan.

"Not a moment to lose." Mary Ann awakened to the watchword—went to sleep with it on her lips. Those seven days from South Pass to Fort Bridger! She thought she had known rigid routine, but there never had been anything like this. Yet in spite of the grueling demands, she had never felt so alive—so strong.

"We are making even better time than I had hoped," Charles said, his face glowing, when they made camp at the head of Echo Canyon.

The September days slipped by as they followed the trail through Echo Canyon. The narrow shadowy passage hemmed in by mountain walls filled Mary Ann with vague uneasiness. Weighed down—she felt. Suffocated. Not until they began the ascent of the mountain range beyond, did she feel that she could breathe again.

But the mountains made new demands. Mary Ann marveled at her own endurance. Narrow, rough trails along dizzying heights with chasms yawning below. Long uphill pulls—the weary oxen faltering in their tracks. Sharp dangerous descents, with the back wheels locked and sliding. Only the certainty of their destination not far ahead carried her on. Yet, she reminded herself, they were fortunate. Suppose they had been forced to blaze this trail?

And there were pleasant interludes. Indian summer days with skies of vivid blue. A mountain ravine, thickly wooded, ablaze with flaming scarlet and bright yellow leaves. The sunset hour, when mellow light touched the mountain peaks and deepened the blue of shadows in the deep canyons. Each evening she watched the sun go down—the gray mists gathering in the canyon. And every sunset hour found her more sure of herself. Of her love for Charles and for the life she had chosen.

"Only a few more miles," Charles told his family one sparkling late September morning. "This canyon will lead us into the Salt Lake Valley."

Mary Ann, looking back over the long months, wondered if it could be true. A ripple of happiness ran through her, leaving her body buoyant and her heart singing. She knew now exactly what she would say to Charles when they reached their destination.

2.

It was the last afternoon of the journey. The caravan had

emerged from the canyon. The valley of the Great Salt Lake lay spread before them.

Triumphal shouts had died to an echo in the clear October air. The first great surge of joy had spent itself. Sobered, quiet now in realization of the deeper meaning of this hour, the company gathered around their Captain in a prayer of thanksgiving. Then, one by one, each went about his task in the routine business of settling camp. The last camp. Tomorrow they would go down into the valley.

Charles Rich lingered on the grassy knoll, still gazing across the wide-flung valley. His throat was tight, his heart full. "God guided us to the spot—it is the place." Rich understood. A valley walled in between a great mountain range and a long lake. "A point so remote" that there need be no difficulties with other people. Brigham Young had kept his word.

"Charles?"

Rich turned quickly, his face lighting up. "Mary Ann! I didn't see you—didn't know you were here."

"I wanted to be with you," she said, very low. "Charles—" she looked up at him, unable to go on. She could feel the warm blood staining her throat, flaming in her cheeks, but her eyes held his bravely.

Charles placed his hands on her shoulders and stood looking down at her. "You want to tell me," he said, "that there are no more doubts."

She drew in her breath sharply. "You—you knew?"

"All along," he answered.

His eyes looking deep into hers burned with a strange fire but it did not frighten her. It seemed to be enveloping her with warmth and joy. His arms encircled her and drew her close in their first embrace. She closed her eyes and rested her bright head against him. This was peace. This was joy.—

This was home. *Home,* she repeated to herself. *A home that will be my very own—and children.* She withdrew a little from his arms, tilting her head to look up into his face. "My new life is just beginning," she said simply.

"*Our* new life," Charles said. He smoothed back the soft hair, bent his tall head and kissed her gravely, full upon the lips. "Look," he said after a moment, clasping her hand and turning again to the panorama unrolled before them—towering snow-capped peaks—the lake glistening in the sunshine. "This is all ours, Mary Ann. Fresh—unspoiled, as God made it. We can build here—something beautiful and lasting."

"Our home, Charles," Mary Ann said.

BOOK FOUR

FULFILLMENT

God fulfills Himself in many ways.

—TENNYSON.

I

1.

Her thirty-fifth birthday! Mary Ann Rich was again reminded of it as she wound the clock. The sudden stillness of the big kitchen had startled her until she realized that the clock had stopped its measured ticking. *But time is passing just the same,* she thought. *Nothing can stop time.*

She stepped to the west window and drew the calico curtains against the hot August sun. For a moment she stood there in the warm darkened room yielding herself to a flood of half-forgotten memories and emotions. She was glad to be alone. Her four children were at Emeline's cottage at the opposite end of the lane. If only none of Charles' other wives would run in this afternoon. On her thirty-fifth birthday a woman should have time to take stock of herself. She gathered up her sewing from the table. She must finish that shirt for Charles. It would be pleasanter outside under the big cottonwood.

Mary Ann paused on the doorstep of her rock and adobe cottage. A puff of wind sent little swirls of dust along the willow-bordered lane that followed the creek into Centerville. Centerville. The village of the farming community. Less than fifteen miles from Salt Lake City—*but it might as well have been a hundred,* Mary Ann thought. During the six years they had lived here, she had felt cut off from everything.

The years had darkened her corn-yellow hair. It was light brown now, and her skin, too, was brown, weathered by sun and wind. The tender curve of her mouth had straightened a little and there were lines about her eyes, but she had lost none of her slender lithesomeness as she walked lightly toward the cottonwood, her eyes on the fields of ripening wheat. Charles was proud of his land—of the rich crops and the herds of fine cattle grazing in the pastures beyond the new log barn. Mary Ann sighed. Now that Charles, an Apostle, and away so much on Church business, had little time to enjoy the farm, *it was fortunate,* she thought, settling herself on a bench under the tree, *that some of his sons were old enough to assume responsibilities.*

Old enough. Yet how young all of them were compared with her. Half of her life was over. She had awakened with that thought. All morning it had been on her mind, causing her to pause at her work and stare into space. Mary had noticed. Mary was fifteen, and inclined to seriousness. "Mother," she had questioned anxiously, "don't you feel well?" And ten-year-old Nanie had chimed in, "Oh, Mother, you can't get sick today! Not on your birthday—with the party at Aunt Emeline's." No, she had assured them, she wasn't ill. But it had been hard to enter into their enthusiasm about the party in her honor.

When her boys came in for their noonday meal, it had swept over her afresh. William was twelve—his boyhood slipping behind. And little Amasa, her baby. It didn't seem possible that he was seven.

Overhead, the leaves rustled softly. Mary Ann frowned at her own neat stitches. The children's future was so important. There was so much to do in the years that were left. She must make plans. Plans! How could she make plans? She wasn't even certain of what this next year might bring. She jabbed her needle into the finely tucked shirt-front. Right now, Charles was away exploring a new region. The Bear Lake Valley, at the far northern end of Utah. She shook her head. She wouldn't let herself think of that. . . .

Her hands lay idle in her lap. Sixteen years since she'd first seen the Salt Lake Valley, yet the memory was still vivid. How transported with joy she had been that day. All of life before her—all of her dreams to be fulfilled. And most of them had been. The years had given her love, children, more enduring faith—everything but permanence.

Three short years in Salt Lake, a home established, ties formed—then another long trek begun; this time to the San Bernardino Valley in far-off California. "We'll form a chain of settlements to the sea!" President Young had declared. He had selected Charles as one of the leaders of the expedition, and because they were young and strong, she and Emeline and Harriet had gone with him. The new community would have need of youth and strength. A wry smile played about Mary Ann's lips as she remembered how she had fought with herself about going. It was an appalling prospect with Mary just a babe in arms. . . . But Charles had needed her, so she had gone.

Those seven years in California seemed like a dream now. There had been joy and sadness. New friends had come—old friends had dropped out. It was there that she heard of Uncle John's death in Oregon. He had reached the end of the Trail only to begin a stranger journey. Even after all the years, the thought of John wrenched Mary Ann's heart. *But,* she thought, *California meant happiness more than grief.* It had meant comfort, beauty—contentment. It had been too good to last. Charles was recalled to Utah. A European mission awaited him. Again wagons were packed, ties severed, her fine home left to be sold. Another trek, this time with Amasa in her arms. And no home to return to in Salt Lake. That had been sold while she lived in California.

But coming here to Centerville had been the bitterest disappointment. Six years here. Six years of day by day living, with Charles away more than he was home. Her hands clenched themselves into small, brown fists. She might as well be honest with herself. She had always hated this place. Even though most of Charles' interests were here—even though all of them (except Sarah) were living here on the farm, she could never feel that Centerville was the spot for a permanent home—a deep-rooted home for the children.

There was longing in Mary Ann's eyes as she gazed toward the south. If they could only live in Salt Lake, like Sarah—live where the children could have advantages; where she, herself, could keep in touch with things—mentally alert—stimulated. Six years was enough. She had earned a change. A change. . . . She shivered suddenly. Even Centerville was better than pioneering a new region. She would feel easier when Charles came home.

A joyous whoop sounded from the lane. Mary Ann left her bench and walked to the gate. Amasa was pursuing a puppy, a roly-poly mite that growled ferociously as he made playful swoops at the boy's feet, then darted away from his eager grasp. Mary, her small, well-poised head tilted quizzically, looked on with sisterly amusement, while Nanie ("Minerva" simply didn't fit the child) her nut-brown curls flying, jumped up and down shrieking suggestions and encouragement.

How she loved them! No sacrifice was too great. It was all for them. Everything that had gone into the years past was preparation for the years to come; Mary Ann knew that now. Her heart lifted. Life half over? Life was just beginning! But things must be different. There must be a permanent home, no more day to day living. She *would* make plans. Not because of herself, but because of the children. She would talk to Charles—he would understand.

She stood there, with the sun slanting through the willows, the soft breeze stirring her hair. The children would have their dreams as she had hers, but she had something more. The years had given her experience, strength, faith. She could make all of their dreams come true. She lifted her head and smiled as the children came trooping toward her.

2.

The sun hung low over the lake when Mary Ann and her family started to Emeline's for the party. Mary walked sedately beside her mother, while Nanie, William and Amasa ran on ahead. It was pleasantly cool now. A rosy glow spread over the valley.

"Mother," Mary hesitated. There was something disturbing in her tone as she went on. "Mother, do you think we'll always live in Centerville?"

Mary Ann was silent for a moment. The question did not surprise her. Mary had reached the age when she was beginning to reach out—to express desires. "I don't know, dear," she answered at last. "Why?"

"I—" Mary broke off and made a fresh start. "Perhaps it isn't important—perhaps you won't understand; but I want to be a school teacher, and you know I've finished all the work I can get here in the public school."

Mary Ann felt as if she had been plunged into icy water. It most certainly was time she was making plans! She turned to her daughter squarely and looked into her face. "Mary," she questioned, "what makes you think I won't understand? It makes me proud and happy—to think that you want to go on, that you want to be a teacher. Today—this very afternoon, I've been thinking about your future. I am going to talk to your father. I believe I can promise you that we'll be living in Salt Lake this winter."

"Oh, Mother!" Mary's larkspur eyes were shining. "That would be wonderful." She paused for a moment, unable to go on. Mary had difficulty in expressing her emotions. "I'll promise to work very hard," she said. "I won't waste a minute, Mother."

Mary Ann smiled into the ardent young face. Outwardly she was calm, but inwardly she was a little aghast at what she had done. She shouldn't have been so definite. She should have talked to Charles before she said anything to Mary. *But I have said it,* she thought exultantly as they turned in at Emeline's gate. *I've made a beginning. Nothing can stop me now.*

2

1.

Mary Ann's fingers gripped the handle of the big wooden spoon. Her back to Charles, she carefully stirred the bubbling preserves and pulled the heavy iron kettle to the back of the stove before trusting herself to speak. She drew a deep breath and turned to Charles, seated at the table near the window.

"Are you trying to tell me," she asked, "that we must start all over again?" Her lips felt stiff as she spoke.

Charles regarded her steadily. "I am trying to tell you, Mary Ann, that this is a *call.* A service to be performed for our Church. As an Apostle I couldn't refuse to go—even if I were unwilling," he added, half to himself.

It was mid-morning. In spite of the fire, the large airy kitchen was comfortably cool. And they were alone. Mary Ann had seen to that. William and Amasa were busy at the barn, and she had sent the girls on an errand. She had known that something momentous was at hand. She had felt it pulsing through the darkness last night, when Charles had come in so quietly. She had gained a reprieve then by feigning sleep, but for long hours afterward she had lain wide-eyed, listening to Charles' deep, even breathing, dreading what the morning might bring.

Bright red juice, dripping from the spoon in her hand, was spattering the snowy pine floor. Mary Ann moved slowly across the room and placed the spoon in a tin saucer on the table. She sank into a chair and fixed Charles with somber, accusing eyes. "It's too much to ask," she said bitterly. "At our time of life—to go to an isolated, unsettled country—no advantages—no schools—It's bad enough for the children to be growing up here."

"Don't you suppose I've thought of all that?" Charles frowned and his lips set in a stern line. "It was uppermost in my mind when President Young sent me to explore the region. I knew even then that I'd had my call, and I almost hoped the place would be unfit for settlement. But when I saw it—" He broke off abruptly, his mouth relaxing, a glow kindling in his dark eyes. "It's a wonderful country, Mary Ann. I can't describe it. When you see it, you'll know what I mean."

Mary Ann's lips twisted. "California was wonderful, too," she said, "but we were taken away from it after seven years. Oh, Charles. Why must you always be the one to go?" Her heart was thumping and her hands shook, but she plunged on defiantly. "You'll go into this raw country and work and struggle to build it up—and then have to leave it, as you did San Bernardino."

"You forgot, my dear," Charles said. "San Bernardino is no longer a Mormon city. My work there was not lasting. Oh, I know—" He silenced her protest with an upraised palm. "It was not my fault that we abandoned the settlement. The Saints were thriving there when I was recalled. But to me, San Bernardino means failure." He sighed. "Even though I helped to found it—watched it grow and prosper—I failed. My work there had no permanence."

"Permanence?" Mary Ann repeated wonderingly. She leaned forward a little, her lips parted, her eyes searching Charles' face. "Do you mean—Is that what you want, too?"

"Didn't you know?" The clock ticked loudly and the sweet, pungent odor of the fruit filled the room. "I've always wanted it." Charles spoke slowly, the words seeming to force themselves from his lips. For the first time he told her of his heartaches, his disappointment, as one cherished plan after another had been relinquished. "Of course," he said, "my duty to our Church came first. I was needed and I did not question. But all this change—this leaving things unfinished—it hasn't been easy. That's why I'm determined to pioneer that new country." He struck the table with his fist and the spoon on the saucer clattered.

Mary Ann looked at him. *I have never seen him more alive,* she thought. His eager face, his dark strong hair, scarcely touched with gray, his eyes, so brilliant and compelling—Against her will she was being fired with his enthusiasm.

"When will you begin?" she asked.

"I've already begun," he said. "I couldn't leave that place without making sure. I found thirty families in the Cache Valley who were willing to go to the Bear Lake district at once. Before I left we laid out a town. Named it Paris, after the man who surveyed it for us. More settlers are coming across from the Cache Valley. President Young was delighted when I told him. My work is started, Mary Ann—and now I need my family."

He reached for her hand and held it in his strong, firm clasp. Mary Ann could almost feel the throb of blood in his fingertips.

"But the farm—" she began uncertainly.

He released her hand and made a sweeping gesture. "I'll

dispose of the farm. This has been only a temporary stopping-place." He eyed her keenly. "You've felt that, I know."

"Yes," she admitted.

Charles pushed back his chair and stood there for a moment. "That country," he said. "I have a feeling about it—It's isolated and it's virgin, Mary Ann. It will be our very own. Our last move. We'll be there at the beginning, and we'll watch it develop. It will be important to the Church, but to us—" he paused, "to us, it will be what we've longed for all these years."

"Yes, Charles," Mary Ann said. She looked up at him with shining eyes. She understood him completely. His words were a pledge and a challenge. She had never felt so close to him before.

He smiled down upon her, came around the table and stood beside her, his hand resting on her shoulder. "I must go now," he said. "Sarah is expecting me in Salt Lake tonight. Goodbye, my dear, and don't worry." He patted her shoulder and was gone.

2.

Mary Ann set the jars of preserves on the shelf in neat rows. The array of small crocks, with their carefully lettered labels, filled her with satisfaction. Something well done. Something completed. That was what Charles wanted. He could see beyond the first years of heartbreak and sacrifice. He had a dream to fulfill. More than a dream—a beautiful reality. He wanted the same things she wanted. A real home for the children—a different life—a fuller life. . . . But her face was troubled as she set the last jar in its place. It was going to be hard to tell Mary. She had raised the child's hopes, and at fifteen, disappointment is close to tragedy.

3.

Mary Ann had framed her explanation with care. Mary listened quietly. Too quietly—her blue eyes veiled, her face inscrutable. "But why do we have to go?" she questioned when her mother had finished. "Anyway, I thought Father was needed in Salt Lake."

"Your father is needed more in this new country, dear, and he needs us. He can't ask other families to go if he leaves us here. You must have faith, Mary," she went on after a moment, her heart wrung by the still whiteness of that small face. "This doesn't mean giving up your plans—only that you will have to wait a little while. You're young, and your father understands. He will see that you go to Salt Lake to school the moment things are going well in our new home."

"Our new home!" Mary echoed. "Very well, Mother." But her voice was brittle, and there was a hurt, rebellious look in her eyes that frightened Mary Ann.

But there was no rebellion from William. The Bear Lake region, his father had told him, was made for cattle. Already, William was laying plans for the time when he would have his own cattle ranch. And Nanie and Amasa were wild with excitement. It was something different. They wanted to start at once.

If we only could! Mary Ann thought. The months of waiting were a real challenge to her. But snow was flying before Charles was able to wind up his affairs in Centerville and Salt Lake. And early in December Mary Ann found that another child was coming. She wondered then if she had courage to go on. But there was always the memory of her talk with Charles that August morning.

Charles had decided to keep his Salt Lake property, and although he sold the farm in late fall, he arranged for the family to stay on until spring. During the long winter months he talked often with Mary Ann, telling of his hopes and plans for the new country. It was almost, she thought, like a mother's feeling for her child—his absorption in the new venture, his personal, almost possessive interest in it.

In the spring Charles made a hurried trip to the Bear Lake Valley. It was early May when he returned. The family must be ready to leave within the month. "Sarah," he explained to Mary Ann, "is staying in Salt Lake. She will look after our orchard and see that the fruit is harvested. Also, I think it wise to keep our home there. It will be convenient for all of us." He took Mary Ann's hands in his and looked at her anxiously. "I'm worried about you, my dear. Don't you think it would be wiser to stay with Sarah until your baby is born?"

For a moment she did not answer. "I would love staying with Sarah," she said at last, "but I am not afraid, Charles. I have faith that everything will be all right, and besides I can depend on Emeline." She looked up at him, smiling. "I *must* go, don't you see? I must be there at the beginning."

3

1.

William was taking his responsibilities seriously. His father was allowing him to drive the family wagon. Each of the Rich family groups had its own wagon and there were three more, loaded with household goods and supplies. Charles Rich, on horseback, guided the party. Mary Ann's eyes crinkled as she looked at William, but she was careful not to smile. William's back was very straight as they drove from the farm. His face was solemn—his eyes alert. Even Amasa, beside her on the wagon-seat, seemed impressed and a little awed by "big brother's" importance. Mary Ann hoped it would last. Amasa was difficult at times. She glanced back over her shoulder. Mary and Nanie, their arms entwined, were kneeling on the floor of the wagon, looking their last at Centerville. They had chosen to ride in the back where they could look out of the flap.

It was good to relax after the exertion of last-minute packing. Mary Ann leaned back in her corner, not trying to think, just letting her thoughts drift, dreamily conscious of the beauty all around her as they traveled through the fertile Weber Valley. Late spring was the loveliest season, with the fruit trees in full bloom and the crops still tender green. Something, she did not know what, took hold of Mary Ann. The soft air on her cheek, perhaps—or the haunting fragrance of blossoms. But suddenly it was another spring morning, long ago. Paulina, Harriet and Joseph were with her in the wagon and Mother—Mother was singing, "Wait for the wagon. Oh, wait for the wagon . . . ."

How they'd loved that song! It had made the whole journey a happy memory. With a sudden smile, Mary Ann sat erect and began to sing.

"Early in the morning with Amasa by my side,
Jump in the wagon and we'll take a ride."

Amasa, startled, looked up at her with wide gray eyes. Mary Ann pulled him close and dropped a kiss on top of his head. William looked bewildered, and behind her, in the wagon, the two girls were very quiet. "Come up here," Mary Ann called to them. "I'm going to teach you all a song. But first I want to tell you about another journey like this."

She wondered if it were putting it into words that made everything so clear. Never before had she fully realized the courage that prompted that song. "Your grandmother was a wonderful woman," she said. "Her husband was in prison. She had been driven from her home. She had undertaken a long and hazardous journey with four young children to look after. Yet she sang to keep us happy." Briefly, her eyes sought Mary's. "How fortunate we are," she said, "to be with your father, going of our own free will—because we want to go." Mary's eyelids fell, but although she made no comment, she did join in the song.

Songs, stories, new places, new things to see—the miles slipping behind. Of course, jouncing about in a wagon wasn't easy for Mary Ann just now. She hated her heavy, cumbersome feeling. Yet most of the time she forgot her physical discomfort in watching the children. Nanie—her brown eyes dancing, her cheeks like the wild roses bordering the creeks—loved everything. For her this was pure adventure, just as it was for Amasa. William was a bit aloof and dignified. He knew that he was doing a man's work. Amasa asked endless questions and was supremely happy when William allowed him to hold the reins. It was Mary who worried her mother. She wasn't sulking—she entered into everything dutifully. But there was no enthusiasm—no sparkle, and there were times when she was so very quiet that Mary Ann wondered fearfully what was going on in that proud little head.

In Ogden, principal town of the Weber Valley, the party stayed over for a day and night. Charles had business there and Mary Ann proudly took her children to see Clarissa, who lived in Ogden. The reunion of the two friends was joyful; more so than ever when they discovered that both were to have babies in the same month. Clarissa's black hair was streaked with gray, but her eyes still danced. Four-year-old Moses was spending the day with his grandfather, but Clarissa presented her husband with a flourish. "And don't you dare to call him a 'crooked stick,' " she warned with a chuckle. *The same Clarissa,* Mary Ann thought fondly. But afterward, she couldn't help gloating a little. She had four children, two of them fine sons. Clarissa had only the one. Of course, the new baby might be a boy—*but mine may be, too,* Mary Ann thought.

Ogden, of itself, was interesting and so were the other settlements of northern Utah—Brigham City—Logan in the heart of the Cache Valley. All of them, it seemed to Mary Ann, had a look of stability, of promise for the future.

In Franklin, a small settlement at the extreme north end of the Cache Valley, the party rested for two days before starting across the mountains.

"Are you sure you're all right?" Charles questioned anxiously. "We haven't much farther to go, but it's a long, hard pull over the mountains."

"Don't worry, Charles," Mary Ann said. "I am fine. Just anxious to get on, that's all."

"The next few miles won't be easy for you." Charles frowned thoughtfully. "I'll drive for you," he decided suddenly. "William can help with one of the other teams until we are out of the mountains."

2.

Out of the mountains! Mary Ann's first feeling on that June afternoon when their wagon emerged from the last canyon was sheer relief to be on level ground again. Those two horrible days were over—with the team crawling over the twisting, turning trail along Mink Creek to the summit, while she lurched and pitched in the wagon, fighting nausea, her head whirling, her battered body cold with sweat. It was all over now. The road to Paris lay straight ahead.

Charles pulled over to the edge of the road and stopped the team in the shade of an aspen grove. "We'll wait here for the others," he said. Mary and Nanie scrambled out and threw themselves down on the grass, stretching their legs in ecstasy. Amasa was fast asleep in the wagon-box.

Mary Ann sat very still. She was acutely conscious of Charles beside her—the tired droop of his shoulders, the drawn lines around his mouth. He, too, had been through an ordeal. She put out her hand and touched him. "Charles," she said, "I'm sorry. I should have stayed in Salt Lake. I've been such a burden to you."

"A burden!" Charles' voice was almost rough. He turned and drew her to him with fierce sudden tenderness, then released her gently. "You are so brave, Mary Ann," he said. "So valiant. I dread having you face your time in this isolated country. It was selfish of me to let you come. But I do need you, my dear."

From behind them came a familiar creak and rumble. The other wagons had arrived. Charles took both Mary Ann's hands in his, held them tightly for a moment, and laid them gently in her lap. "I must get back now," he said, "and see how the rest of my family is getting along." He vaulted lightly from the wagon.

Mary Ann watched him walk away, her heart overflowing with love for him. Moments like this were worth everything. Her eyes were shining as they followed him—seeing him pause to talk with Emeline, then with Sarah Peck and Eliza, and finally, for a long moment, with Harriet. He loved them all, she knew that—each in a special way. It had been a hard lesson for her—learning to share him. Once she had thought she couldn't face it. But some way, sharing him made their moments together more precious, more important than if she'd had him alone. *Yes,* she thought. *I've gained far more than I have given up.*

Amasa had awakened and was clambering over the seat. He rubbed his eyes with his small fists and snuggled drowsily against his mother. Mary and Nanie were chattering with Carolyn and Nancy—Emeline's girls. But Mary Ann made no effort to join the family. Smiling and content she sat, with Amasa's warm little body hugged to her side, waiting to go on to Paris.

4

1.

Paris, Mary Ann found, was not unlike other Mormon settlements. The streets, defined by drainage ditches, were wide and crossed at right angles. In the center, to the left of the main street, a block of ground had been set aside for a public square. Log cabins—some mere weatherbeaten huts, others new and more commodious—were scattered about. The Stake House, Church headquarters of the valley, fronted the main street and to its right was the common supply and storehouse. And there was the familiar "Bowery"! Four posts set in a quadrangle and bound together by poles at the top—the whole covered by aspen boughs, occupying a corner of the public square. Mary Ann smiled. No Mormon community was complete without its Bowery. This one would serve as the chief public meeting place until other places could be provided. And always it would be the scene of happy gatherings—dances, socials—the many occasions when the Saints would make merry together.

Yes, Mary Ann thought, all this was familiar. But there was something about this place that set it apart from anything she had known before. The settlement nestled at the foot of low hills that rolled gently westward to the rugged mountains. Bluebells and purple larkspur carpeted the hills, with here and there a flaming patch of Indian paint brush. There were wild roses in profusion along the wide creek that meandered through the south end of the town. Beyond Paris the valley widened and spread fanlike to the north and west, with meadows sloping southeastward to the snow-crested mountains.

"When you see it," Charles had said, "you'll know what I mean." Mary Ann did know. This was where she belonged.

2.

Six one-room log cabins were to house the Rich family. These cabins, each with its own lot, occupied a block of ground.

On the morning they were to move from their wagon-boxes, Mary Ann took stock of her cabin. *By this time,* she thought with a rueful smile, *I should know all the tricks of making a place livable.* But the prospect was not so bad. The cabin was new, and although it had a sod roof and a dirt floor, it was large. She began mentally to arrange the furniture, debating the best place for the beds, the stove, the table—the big chest that held their clothes. She frowned at the stove-hole in the wide west wall. That would have been exactly the right place for the big bed. The windows—(or, rather, those holes in the walls that served for windows) they would be a problem. She might stretch muslin across them . . . .

"Mother, I've been looking everywhere for you." Mary Ann came back suddenly from her contemplation of the windows. Mary had burst into the room with all of her old-time enthusiasm.

"May William and I start unpacking the wagon?" she asked a little breathlessly, not giving her mother a chance to speak. "You see," she rushed on, "we have everything planned about getting settled. You're not to do any of the work—just oversee."

Mary Ann looked up quickly. There was peace in Mary's blue eyes. Whatever battle she had been having with herself was over. She was one of them again, and this was her way of saying, "I'm sorry, Mother."

Mary Ann put her arm around Mary and gave her a quick squeeze. "Come along then, and let's get started. We'll all work together."

Magically, the big bare cabin began to look like home. The spinning wheel was in its niche by the fireplace, and everyone was doing his share. William set up the beds. Mary stuffed the ticks with straw, and unpacked trunks and boxes. Nanie carried small objects into the house, placing them experimentally, now here, now there. Amasa helped by being a good boy and keeping out of the way.

Charles spent almost a whole day with them, doing the heavier work. All of his older sons worked together clearing the lots, spading the soil for gardens; and the Rich women were in and out of one another's cabins, comparing progress, exchanging ideas and advice. Emeline's home was next to Mary Ann's, Harriet's around the corner, Sarah Peck's and Eliza's around the block. The sixth cabin, fronting the main street, would be used for storage purposes.

Mary Ann pondered the wisdom of laying the big rag carpet on the earthen floor. She decided against it. Men were hard at work in the saw pit—Charles said they must have wood floors by fall, and the small braided rugs did very well for now.

Busy about her work, Mary Ann thought of those other homes she had settled. The first home, in a valley between the great lake and the towering mountains. That other home, also in a valley. A luxuriant valley sheltered by low hills that were brown many months in the year. And now this home. But this home was different.

And at last it was finished. The boys were to sleep outside in the wagon-box, but the two big beds were freshly made, covered with bright patchwork quilts and screened about with curtains. And there were gay red and yellow curtains hanging at the windows. Emeline stared openmouthed when she saw them, then burst into laughter. "Land o' Goshen, Mary Ann, your dress pattern! What will Charles say?"

Mary Ann smiled demurely. "I don't think he'll remember it. Anyway, it wasn't suitable for me but it does brighten up the room." She had always felt guilty about not making up that dress. She had brought it back from California. Charles had purchased the bolt of calico in San Francisco—dress patterns for all of them. The other wives had made theirs and worn them out long since. *But it's much more useful here,* Mary Ann thought. *It makes things more cheerful.* She looked around the room approvingly, her eyes lingering on her most treasured possession, her mother's maple rocker. Her father had given her the little chair when she left Centerville. It was one of the few things he had brought with him to Salt Lake.

Mary was humming to herself as she set the supper table. "Mother," she said, "this is a special occasion. Our first supper in the new house. I think I'll get some wild flowers."

Mary Ann turned the fish in the iron skillet. Freshly caught brook trout, golden brown and savory. "That will be lovely," she said, "but don't be long, dear. And call Amasa and Nanie. William should be here any minute."

But in a moment Mary was back again. "Mother!" she protested. "Wouldn't you just know it? Amasa's found a stray dog."

Mary Ann stepped to the door. Amasa, a beatific smile

on his face, was coaxing up the pathway a sad-eyed cringing beast, its ribs showing through its gaunt sides, its tail quivering between knobby legs. There had been times when she had been forced to curb Amasa's inclination to pick up strays, but never had he produced a specimen like this. Still, the little fellow had been heartbroken over leaving his puppy behind. Mary Ann stooped and snapped her fingers. "Come here," she cried. "There's a good dog!"

"Are you going to let him *keep* it?" Mary demanded.

"Of course, we'll let him keep it." There was a joyful lilt in Mary Ann's voice. "Don't you see, dear? Amasa's at home now." And to herself she added, *so are we all.*

5

1.

The community turned out to welcome Apostle Rich's wives. Sister Atkins and Sister Sleight, whose husbands had been in the first company Charles Rich brought from Cache Valley, arranged a picnic supper in the Bowery. Everyone came—husbands, wives, children—all bent upon being neighborly, getting acquainted, making the newcomers feel at home and by the warmth of their welcome to his wives, showing Apostle Rich how sincerely he was trusted and admired.

It was stimulating and satisfying, Mary Ann thought. To feel really at home, to know that, even though she couldn't go out much just now, there would be new friends to chat with after church or at an occasional public meeting.

And there were old friends, too. Almost every week wagon trains were arriving from the southern settlements. There were many familiar faces. Friends of the California days, others from Salt Lake and Centerville, even a few who had made the long trek from Illinois with the Rich party. "It seems like a gathering of folks we'd known here and there," was the way Emeline expressed it.

But there was not much time for visiting. It must be a

summer of hard work for everyone. The season was short—there was much to be done. Crops must be cultivated and harvested, lumber sawed and floors laid, new cabins built—others made secure against the weather. Logs must be hauled from the canyons. Work began for the men even before the sun rose over the rim of low mountains to the southeast and lasted until the last glimmer of the long twilight faded. And the women did their share, too; settling homes, preparing meals, caring for children, planting and tending gardens.

Charles was everywhere. In the fields with the men, overseeing his own farm, conducting church services, settling disputes, presiding over public meetings.

"We see less of him than ever before," Harriet complained.

"We must expect that," Mary Ann told her. "Others need him more than we do. We will always have to share him." For a moment the memory of how she had learned that lesson was vivid in her mind. Harriet had never endured that. Harriet was the last wife . . . . And after all, Charles was careful to show no partiality. A day and a night he spent in each of his homes. He was just and he was kind. He was a great man.

By the end of July there were a thousand people in the valley. Five new settlements had been established. Liberty and Montpelier to the north, Fish Haven, Bloomington and St. Charles to the south end of the valley, along the lake; and in all Charles was equally important. The district had been organized as "Richland" County of the Territory of Utah and although county officers had been elected, everyone still looked to Charles, who had been elected to represent the County in the Legislature.

"Brother Wixom and Brother Bowman are going to Salt Lake this week," Charles told Mary Ann one late July day. "I am sending word for your father and his family to come to the valley. I can use him in Montpelier."

For a moment Mary Ann could not speak. She knew that Charles was expecting her to say something, but apprehension filled her and little fears began darting through her mind. Father was an old man now. His health was good, yet a change would be hard on him, and she knew that he would not refuse his call. "But, Charles," she started to protest and then broke off. It wasn't for her to question Charles' judgment.

"But, what?" Charles questioned. His eyes, dark and penetrating, were fixed on her face.

"Nothing, really," she answered, a little confused. Then suddenly an idea came to her. "Why not have James and Harriet come along with Father? They're eager to make a change." She looked at Charles hopefully. Harriet had always been close to their father. It would be a relief to know that she and her husband were coming with him.

"That's a splendid suggestion," Charles answered quickly. "Brother Holmes is just the kind of man I need."

There was a twinkle in his eyes. Mary Ann found herself wondering if by any chance he had read her thoughts—or if, perhaps, this had been part of his original plan. She smiled suddenly and so did he. "Thank you, Charles," she said.

2.

Sister Poulson and Mary Ann had something in common. They were both expecting babies. Whichever child was born first—if the child were a boy—would go down in history. The first white male child born in the Bear Lake Valley. It was a little joke they shared. Secretly, Mary Ann hoped that her child would be a boy; not because of the honor—but because she felt that life was easier for men. She knew that her time was near at hand and the early August days dragged. Sometimes in the night she awakened with fear in her heart. The nearest doctor was one hundred miles away. But she had known that before she came. And the morning sunshine always restored her faith. *Still,* she thought, *it's comforting to know that Emeline is here.*

But when the day came, Emeline was not there. It was early morning. Caroline had developed a high fever and was dangerously ill. "Emeline's beside herself," Charles told Mary Ann, "but, of course, she can't leave the child."

"Of course not." Mary Ann muttered through lips white with pain. She made the round of the room again. "Walking about makes it easier," she explained to Charles, with a pitiful attempt to smile.

He watched her for a moment, his brow furrowed, his hands clenching and unclenching spasmodically, *almost,* Mary Ann's blurred thoughts ran, *in time with my pains.* He stood up suddenly, with a muffled exclamation. "Don't worry. There are plenty of women here who know what to do. I'll go for help." He turned and seized both of her hands. "Have faith, Mary Ann. The Lord will not fail you."

Mary Ann was scarcely conscious that he had gone. A great wave of pain enveloped her. She gripped the back of a chair and stood there, trembling. She was very sorry for herself. Gray light filtered through the windows. The pain ceased. There was peace—blissful peace. Of course, Emeline's place was with Caroline. *I understand,* Mary Ann thought. *We must always think of the children.* She hoped Amasa was being a good boy. It was good of Eliza to look after the children. Now the pain was coming again. There was no one like Emeline at a time like this. She sank into the chair—great wet drops beading her forehead—her whole body tormented.

It seemed a long time that she sat there, but she knew it wasn't. The sun marked a thin line across the floor when Harriet came. "Oh, Mary Ann," she wailed. "I wish I knew something about babies. Charles is bringing the elders to pray over you. He told me to stay with you until he can bring another woman."

After the Church elders had left, Mary Ann let Harriet prepare her for bed. She was calm and self-possessed. What had she to fear? The elders had anointed her head with holy consecrated oil. They had promised her a safe delivery. "Don't be frightened, Harriet," she said. "Everything will be all right."

Harriet's lips trembled. "I wish Charles would hurry," she said. "I'll do the best I can, Mary Ann, but you'll have to tell me what to do."

Afterward, when she was able to think again, Mary Ann smiled even in her weakness. Poor Harriet. So willing, yet so terrified. Mary Ann's last memory, before tearing agony blotted out consciousness, was Harriet running out of the door screaming for Charles.

So Mary Ann Rich brought forth her son alone. She named him "Ezra Clark."

"You were a little late." Charles chuckled as he looked into the tiny wrinkled face. "Brother Poulson's boy won the honors." But Mary Ann smiled as she closed her eyes. She had her son and she was happy.

6

1.

The Rich cabins had become cottages, or so it seemed to Mary Ann, with floors laid, glass panes fitted into window frames, and two rooms added to each cabin.

Because of the baby, Mary Ann's home was the last to be remodeled, and September was a month of confusion for her. But she did not mind. She was happy to be well—up and around again. And the baby, bless him, was so good. During the worst of the upheaval Emeline kept him at her house with Mary Ann running over at intervals, to nurse him.

School had started, and with Nanie and Amasa out of the way Mary Ann and Mary set systematically to work arranging the remodeled house. The big beds had been moved into the new east room. "It's wonderful," Mary said, "to have a bedroom again." But Mary Ann was more relieved when the aspen-pole cots had been set up in the small north room. The few Indians who straggled into the settlement were friendly—still she always felt uneasy with the boys outside in the wagon-box. And the nights were much colder now. Yes, everything would be much more comfortable and convenient. The new lean-to was a fine place to keep the loom and the dye-pot. That made so much more room. *Now,* Mary Ann told herself, *I can begin to make this a real home.*

When the cabin was practically settled, Charles left for Salt Lake on business. He carried with him a long list of items that his wives hoped he might bring back. "I shan't be long away," he told them. "The wheat isn't ripening as it should. I'm afraid I'll have to send over to Cache Valley for flour and supplies. We needn't worry about blankets and clothing—there was plenty of wool at the spring shearing—but we are very low on staples."

After he had gone, Mary Ann and Mary laid the rag carpet over the straw padding on the floor of the big west room. "There," Mary Ann said, "that's done. I'm going to let you finish, dear. I must get at the mending, its piled up so."

But her eyes kept straying from her work, following Mary about the room. She seemed interested in what she was doing—putting dishes away in the new cupboards, arranging their few books on a corner shelf, frowning in deep concentration over the decision to use Grandmother Phelps' Paisley shawl as a cover for the big trunk . . . . Mary Ann wondered. Mary had been happy this summer. Her resentment once conquered, she had entered wholeheartedly into the business of living. She had been a real help, too, revealing unsuspected good judgment and depths of womanly understanding. Quietly but firmly, she had taken over many of her mother's duties. "Let me do that, Mother. You sit here and rest." *Yes,* Mary Ann thought, *she's been happy this summer.* But winter was almost upon them. The months would be long. Time would drag. If there were only some interest for Mary. Something to keep her occupied—to take the place of school. School! Mary Ann sat bolt upright. Amasa's woolen stocking, the knee still yawning raggedly, slipped unheeded to the floor. The one-room schoolhouse housed all ages and sizes of children.

Brother Sleight and Brother Ricks must find them a handful to manage. Perhaps . . . .

Mary Ann regarded her daughter thoughtfully. It was too late now to consult Charles; he might be gone several weeks. *Besides,* she thought, *it is my responsibility, really. I'm the one who knows how she feels.* And it would be easy to talk with Brother Sleight. She knew him well enough to speak freely. She nodded her head vigorously. Now was the time to act, with the school term just beginning.

2.

The new schoolhouse at the north end of the public square was a sturdy building of aspen logs, covered with dirt and brush. Six good-sized windows provided ample light at the split timber desks—empty now—for Mary Ann had waited until school was dismissed.

She was not sorry she had come. Thomas Sleight's mild blue eyes were very kind behind the steel-rimmed spectacles. He listened attentively as Mary Ann explained the reason for her visit. "Mary is not the only one, Brother Sleight," she said earnestly. "Many of our young people are restless and in need of new interests. But Mary's heart is set on teaching. If there is anything she could do to help you—I don't want to ask special favors for her, but—"

Thomas Sleight removed his spectacles and carefully polished them with his handkerchief. "I'm very glad you've come to me, Sister Rich," he said. "Brother Ricks and I have our hands full here. If your daughter is willing and in earnest, I believe she could be a great help to us. I'll talk it over with him tonight and let you know."

"Oh, thank you!" Mary Ann said. "You don't know what it will mean to me—to Mary." She rose and started toward the door with Thomas Sleight at her side. "If there is any way I can show my appreciation—" she hesitated.

"I think there is, Sister Rich. This matter of our young people." Sleight sighed. "Brother Ricks and I are troubled about it. We can't offer much here beyond the 'three R's,' but we must find some way to keep them occupied. I'm going to call on you to help us," he said as they shook hands.

The last rays of the afternoon sun slanted across the hills kindling the foliage into a blaze of yellow. There had been a heavy frost the night before and the crisp, cold air gave promise of another. But it was not the cold alone that made Mary Ann's blood tingle as she hurried across the square. If she could only tell Mary now! *But that would never do,* she thought. *Suppose Brother Ricks said, "No"?*

On the main street she slowed her pace, tempted to stop in for a moment at the new store. Joseph Rich, Sarah's oldest son, was the owner. *Little Joey.* Mary Ann smiled and hurried on. She was very fond of Joseph. Always, she thought of him as the toddler she'd looked after so long ago in Nauvoo. And now they all turned to him as head of the family, when Charles was away.

It was almost dusk when Mary Ann turned into her own pathway. She lingered briefly on the doorstep, her eyes wandering toward the creek, its banks brilliant with scarlet sumac. Fall was a lovely season. Lovely, but very sad. A strange loneliness swept over her. Her exhilaration was gone, quenched by dull foreboding. Even the hills she loved were suddenly remote—threatening. She shivered. How she dreaded the winter.

7

1.

No one was prepared for the winter that gripped the Valley that year of 1864. "Of course," they all said, "in the high altitudes we must expect early frosts and plenty of snow. It won't be as mild as last year. That's too much to hope for." But no one expected nature to go to the other extreme.

Charles' first act upon returning from Salt Lake was to dispatch teams to the Cache Valley for supplies. He had made a quick trip. The Phelps family, with Harriet and her husband James Holmes, was with him. Mary Ann's heart was full as she welcomed them. It had been so long. And the moment she saw her father, she knew that this move had been right for him. Morris Phelps' hair was white, now—his shoulders bent; but his eyes shone and his voice was strong and vigorous. "It's wonderful, Mary Ann," he said, "wonderful to be starting all over again in this new country." *Charles knew best,* Mary Ann thought, *and our Heavenly Father is kind.*

And later that day another weight was lifted from her mind. Thomas Sleight sent for Mary. She was to take her place in the school, to help with the younger children. Mary Ann sought out Charles and tried hurriedly to explain, but although he listened courteously, she was not at all sure that he grasped the import of her words. He was thoughtful, abstracted, noticeably worried. But she did not question him. The failure of the wheat—the scarcity of food—his feeling of responsibility for the settlers . . . . Mary Ann longed to comfort him, but she gave no outward sign. Time enough to offer him comfort when he asked for it.

Snow began falling within the week—not in flurries, but steadily, purposefully, in white feathery flakes soft as down, that piled up and up relentlessly, closing in the little community with barriers like steel. Charles wasted no time in indecision. "We don't know these winters," he said. "It may not be necessary, but we'll take no chances. Another party must leave at once to meet our supply teams."

Another party. More men to worry over. Women went about silently, their faces grim, their lips set, not daring to think, as the October days dragged on with the smothering snow still falling and no word from the absent ones.

"Sometimes I think I can't bear it!" Sarah Peck burst out one day. She had come to sit at Mary Ann's fireside, seeking refuge from her own fears. "I know I shouldn't complain," she went on, "but when I think of my Hyrum out there in those mountains—frozen, maybe, or torn to bits by wolves—" Her voice broke. For a moment she sat staring into the fire, then straightened up and began knitting again, furiously.

Mary Ann's heart ached for her, but there was nothing she could say. Suppose it were William instead of Hyrum. How would she feel? Swiftly she got up from the spinning wheel and moved to Sarah Peck's side. She put her arm around the angular shoulders and squeezed them gently.

"There, now," she said. "Cry if it will make you feel better; but don't go imagining things. We *must* keep our faith."

At least, she thought, *we have been spared the War.* In their far outpost of Salt Lake the Saints had been little affected, even less here in the Valley. Reports of fierce battles fought, of thousands killed and wounded, of cities burned, of homeless women and children starving—all of this seemed unreal and fantastic in this far removed spot. Yet Charles had heard in Salt Lake that the South was in a bad way—that it was unlikely the Confederacy could hold out much longer.

It was late October when the men returned. They were gaunt—haggard—weary. But no one was missing, and everyone was far too happy to worry over frostbitten ears and feet. "But the teams are in bad shape," Charles told Mary Ann, "and the supplies are all too scant." He shook his head dubiously. "I'm afraid food will have to be rationed. I can tell better when Joseph has finished unpacking at the store."

William was grieved about the stock. Bundled against the cold in homemade buckskin britches, hickory shirt, and beaver-lined vest, he was up and away at daybreak to join with the men in their constant search for stray cattle and the shivering, frightened sheep huddled in pitiful groups to freeze. Mary Ann watched him night after night, worn out with labor and anxiety, his young face drawn and lined. *He'll be an old man before his time,* she thought with an inner wrench. But William had no thought for himself. "Oh, Mother," he would say, twisting his red, chapped hands, "it's terrible to see our fine stock freezing to death. If only we had the right kind of sheds for them . . . "

"If only." Those words, it seemed to Mary Ann were on everyone's lips these days, with snow covering the fences and towering outside the cabin windows in white walls that shut off the light. "If only we had built better cellars for our potatoes." "If only we had got in more supplies." "If only" this. "If only" that . . . .

"Hindsight," remarked Emeline bitingly, "always was better than foresight." And at that moment, perversely, Mary Ann thought longingly of California where there had been no snow.

In late December Charles would be leaving for Salt Lake. As the Valley's representative he must attend the regular session of the legislature. Mary Ann dreaded his departure. "*Must* you go, Charles?" she questioned.

"You know I must, my dear. The people have chosen me to represent them. I must go and see that they are fairly dealt with."

"But how will you get out?"

"On snowshoes—over the mountains to Franklin."

"Not alone?" Mary Ann cried out.

"Yes, alone. Unless someone else happens to be going to Franklin."

And the next week a miracle happened. It was almost frightening, Mary Ann thought, to have prayer answered so promptly and so definitely; for it was an answer—there could be no mistake about that. The first mail came to the Valley—brought from Franklin by a mail-carrier on snowshoes! He would be going back. Charles would not have to make the trip alone. In the face of that fact, the arrival of the mail seemed almost unimportant.

Charles left the Valley on the last day of the year. It would be weeks, Mary Ann knew, before they could hear from him.

2.

School during January was impossible. It was bitterly cold. Huge snowdrifts blocked the roads. Children, thin and undernourished, were kept close to their own firesides.

"Mother," Mary said one morning, "I can teach Nanie and Amasa at home. That is, if they are willing," she added. "They'll be willing," Mary Ann announced with a stern eye on the children. "I'll see to that."

Constantly, she marveled at Mary's patience and ingenuity. She had so little to work with. One or two books Brother Sleight had loaned her, a few copies of *The Deseret News* that Charles had brought back from Salt Lake, a biography of George Washington, a McGuffey reader—Mary made use of everything. She cut out letters from the *News* and pasted them on squares of cloth for Amasa. She read to Nanie from the life of Washington. She went over the multiplication tables countless times and worked out new and fascinating games for spelling drills. *Perhaps,* Mary Ann thought, *this is what she needed. This may do more for her than a year in Salt Lake.*

3.

Mary Ann had an uneasy feeling every time she glimpsed Jerusha Trigg's sharp profile just beyond Hannah Clifton. Sister Trigg had attached herself, uninvited, to Mary Ann and Hannah as they came out from Church. It was a Sunday morning in mid-February, with a blustering raw wind. But it was not the wind, Mary Ann knew, that made her shiver. It was Sister Trigg. *Why is it,* she wondered, *that she makes me feel this wdy?* It was so different with Hannah Clifton. She had loved Hannah from the moment they first met. But not Jerusha. And this morning it was worse than ever.

"Have you heard anything from Apostle Rich?" Hannah asked. She linked her arm companionably through Mary Ann's as they walked, three abreast, along the snow-banked street.

"We've had one letter—it came in the last mail. He won't be home until about April first."

"Is it necessary for him to be gone so long?" Jerusha Trigg's tone was skeptical, her thin lips primly set.

"Why, yes. Yes, of course," Mary Ann replied, a little confused. "This time last year," Hannah interposed hastily, "the snow was almost gone."

"Well, I don't know about *last* year," said Jerusha acidly, "but next year *I* shan't be here."

Mary Ann turned to stare at her and after a moment Hannah spoke. "Just what do you mean by that, Jerusha?" Snow crunched under their feet. A small, black dog darted across the path.

"I mean," Jerusha said, carefully deliberate, "that our family is planning to leave the moment we can get out of here." They had reached her street and she halted abruptly, facing Mary Ann. "In case you're interested," she said, her pale eyes mocking, "we'll have plenty of company."

Mary Ann and Hannah stood for a moment as she turned and stalked away; then they walked on in silence. Mary Ann dared not trust herself to speak. She was angry and she was afraid.

Hannah Clifton's gentle fingers pressed her arm comfortingly. "Don't mind her, Sister Rich," she said. "I've known her for a long time. She doesn't mean half what she says."

But she did mean it. Mary Ann found that out a week later. The Relief Society was meeting in the schoolhouse and Mary Ann arrived a little late. As she paused in the entry to remove her shawl, Jerusha Trigg's voice was clearly audible. "A lot Apostle Rich cares what happens to us." Mary Ann stood motionless, listening shamelessly. *"He's* in Salt Lake," Jerusha went on. "We're starving, but *he* is well fed and warm."

"For shame, Sister Trigg!" Hannah Clifton protested angrily. "You don't know what you're talking about. Aren't Apostle Rich's own wives and children here? They are suffering just as we are. And besides, it's because of us that he is in Salt Lake. He risked his life for us—to get there and look after our interests."

There was an excited buzz of voices. Mary Ann's first impulse was to slip away, but it was only a fleeting impulse. Her chin went up and her eyes were snapping as she stepped outside and re-entered the schoolhouse—this time announcing herself by banging the door. But though the group welcomed her warmly, she could feel tension in the air. Their practiced fingers were busily carding wool, but there were furtive looks, forced bursts of gaiety, sudden, uneasy silences. *They're trying to be kind,* Mary Ann thought. *They don't want me to know how they feel.* But her heart sickened within her.

And as the weeks of March lagged by, things became steadily worse. "The supplies in the store are gone," Joseph said one day. Mary Ann looked at him wordlessly. She knew the state of her own cupboard. Others had little or less than she. Frozen potatoes—wheat ground in the coffee mill and boiled . . . . She shuddered—the revolting stench of boiling wheat suddenly strong in her nostrils. A diet like that might undermine anyone's loyalty. "No. No!" she whispered to herself. "This must not happen. Heavenly Father, don't let it happen." But scarcely a day passed now, without word of some other family beginning to pack. Sister Trigg had been right. She would, indeed, have plenty of company . . . .

4.

The Rich family was holding council. All but the younger children were assembled in Mary Ann's cottage. Even William was there—tall, lanky, his thin face intent, seated among Charles' older sons. But William had earned his right to be there, Mary Ann reflected; he was a man now, with the others.

Charles Rich faced them from his big chair near the hearth. It was a late April evening but still cold after sundown. The firelight, flickering upon Charles' face, revealed new lines and furrows. His eyes were sunken, his cheeks hollow. *He looks,* Mary Ann thought, *as starved as we are.*

But it was not that, she knew. There was a tired, beaten look about him that wrung her heart. For the first time in all the years she had known him, Charles was visibly discouraged. It had been a crushing blow to him—what he had found awaiting him in the Valley. He had returned in early April. A thaw had set in and teams were already on their way to Cache Valley for supplies, but many families doggedly continued packing. Some had already left . . . .

A log fell and sparks sprayed up the chimney. "There is nothing more I can do," Charles said heavily. His eyes traveled the circle of anxious faces. "If the people wish to leave, that is their privilege. I can't stop them. I can only tell them that my own faith in this country is unshaken." He paused for a moment and took a deep breath. "I've called a public meeting for Friday," he said. "I shall tell them then that they are free to go. But," his voice deepened and the muscles bunched at his jaws, "no matter what they do, I'm staying on here. Is that asking too much of you?"

There was a profound hush in the room, then a sudden stir. Joseph had risen and was crossing the room in rapid strides. He halted behind his father's chair and laid his hand on Charles' shoulder with a gesture that brought tears to Mary Ann's eyes. In a moment all of the boys were crowding around their father, their broad shoulders and tall young bodies concealing him from view. Not a word was spoken, but although Mary Ann could not see Charles' face, she knew that he understood.

5.

Mary Ann stayed away from the meeting. Emeline was shocked and disapproving. "I do declare, Mary Ann, I'll never understand you. How will Charles feel?" she scolded.

"If his own wives can't stand by him at a time like this—" She was gone, still sputtering.

"*How will Charles feel?*" *That's just it,* Mary Ann told herself. *That's the reason I can't make myself go.* She couldn't explain to Emeline—to anyone. *I could bear it for myself,* she thought. But to sit there quietly watching and listening, giving no sign, with Charles being pilloried before her eyes, his defenses crumbled, his dream shattered . . . . Hastily she got to her feet and hurried into the big bedroom. "I can pray for him here," she said aloud. A small, worn, leather-covered book lay on the table. Her mother's *Doctrine and Covenants.* Mary Ann picked it up and, holding it tightly with both hands, pressed it to her breast. She sat down in the little maple rocker and closed her eyes. *Oh, Mother,* she pleaded silently, *Mother. Help me to pray.*

6.

May brought clear days, brilliant with sunshine. The last of the snow had disappeared. Teams were at work in the fields marking the rich earth with long, brown furrows. Planting had begun. New seed that had been brought from Cache Valley. New seed. A new season. A new start. Mary Ann exulted. Charles' faith had won. No more settlers had left. Once more there was unity in the Valley. And unity in the nation. Word had come that the Rebellion was at an end. Another cause for rejoicing.

The scream of the saw and the steady rap-tap of the hammer were music to Mary Ann's ears. Never again would winter find them unprepared. They were building now—storehouses, shelters for the stock. Strong, substantial structures that would endure. Lasting. Permanent. Mary Ann turned her eyes to the hills already misted with tender green. *My hills,* she thought. *My home. Now I can plan for the future.*

8

1.

On an early September morning in the year 1874, Charles and Mary Ann Rich were driving at a leisurely pace along the main street of Montpelier. Everyone knew the Rich rig—a fine surrey drawn by a span of spirited horses, one pure white, the other glossy black. It was the talk of the Valley. Always it gave Mary Ann a little secret feeling of elation to travel with Charles in this rig. Her head, the neat black bonnet set squarely on top, was proudly erect as they drove toward the highway that led out of town.

It was the last day of Charles' annual tour of the Bear Lake Valley. He had begun the practice at the close of his second year's residence and had not abandoned it, even after the survey of 1872 had disclosed that the northern half of the Valley lay not in Utah, but in the Territory of Idaho. Although there were now two counties, each politically responsible to a different Territory, the people of the Valley remained one in spirit — one unit, still looking to Charles Rich for guidance.

Stores and business houses were beginning to open for the day. There were warm smiles and pleasant "good morning's" all along the way. Charles' face beamed as he spoke to this one and that—his beard startlingly white in contrast with the still dark hair, brushing his immaculate linen shirt front as he bowed. *They are all his friends,* Mary Ann thought. *They know what he has done for them and they love him for it.* A feeling of warmth and well-being glowed within her. She shared Charles' joy. These last eleven years had been the happiest time of his life. He had told her so, more than once. And he had reason to be proud—with well-established settlements scattered the length of the Valley, population increasing, industries thriving. . . . Mary Ann sighed happily. These years had been generous to her, too. Ezra and Edward had come to her here. The older children had grown up here, developing—fitting naturally into their places in the community. And most precious of all, the Valley had given her permanance. Well ordered living.

They had left the main street now, and were turning into the highway. Mary Ann pulled the light lap-robe closer about her knees. Last night's shower had left a chill in the air. They rode on in comfortable silence. It was foolish, Charles often said, to make talk for the sake of talking. She felt that way, too. They could jog along for miles enjoying real companionship without uttering a word. Mary Ann settled herself more comfortably in the surrey seat. Charles still had a number of calls to make. It would be nearly evening before they reached Paris. She found herself wishing that they were going directly home, but, of course, they must stop at both of Charles' ranches and at the cheese factory in Bern. It had been thoughtful of Charles to take her on this trip. It had given her a week with her father and Harriet. Yet she still felt a little guilty about going—being away for a whole week just now, with school about to begin and Mary deep in preparations for her year's teaching. But Nanie had been so insistent. . . . *If I hadn't gone,* Mary Ann reflected, *she might have thought that I didn't depend on her*. She smiled to herself. Nanie was a natural-born housekeeper, and after all, she was twenty now —old enough to look after things. Still . . . Mary Ann's smile faded. She couldn't explain it, but this morning she had a strange conviction that she was needed at home. She stirred in her seat.

"Comfortable?" Charles turned his head to look at her.

"Oh, yes," she said. "But I'm anxious to get home. I've enjoyed every minute, but I'm afraid the girls have had their hands full with the house and the cooking, and four boys to manage."

Charles smiled. "You forget, my dear. At Mary's age you had your own home and three children of your own to manage." He tightened his grip on the reins, and the horses arched their necks, straining at their bits. "The girls are capable and responsible," he added.

"Of course, they are," Mary Ann answered quickly. "And so are the older boys—but Amasa has his own ideas. Sometimes he and Mary clash. And Ezra's so active and so strong-willed." She hesitated, gazing out over the fields of yellow stubble.

"And I suppose you are worrying about Edward?" There was a note of gentle raillery in Charles' voice. "Are you always going to think of him as a baby. Remember, he's six years old."

Mary Ann smiled. "He's the only baby I have," she said softly. Dear little Edward. He *always* needed her. She felt so close to him—so tender. Much as she loved the others, her feeling for him was different. Perhaps it was because he was so like her mother. She had noticed that from the time he had begun to prattle and try to walk. She leaned forward and looked up into Charles' face. "Please," she said earnestly, "don't think that I want to keep them dependent upon me. It isn't that. It's just that I feel I am needed as—as a balance wheel." She stopped abruptly. She could not tell him of her strange anxiety to get home. A man would think that foolish.

Charles reined the horses to a walk. "I know what you mean," he said gravely. "The mothers must provide balance in a family like ours. You mothers have borne the real responsibility of bringing up our children—and you've done well." He sighed. "I've been so occupied—the Church—public affairs. Yet it had to be that way."

Mary Ann was almost indignant. "Don't you suppose we realize that?" she demanded. "And the children are so proud of you, Charles. Having you for their father gives them something to live up to."

Charles shook his head. "You are very loyal, my dear, but a father should be more than a good example. Still, I have a feeling that my turn is coming. Sometimes I think that children need more guidance as they grow older. But we have no cause for worry," he added. "Ours have been trained to live and think right. They are all strong in the Faith. All we can do is point the way," he added after a moment, his voice low. "We must remember that we can't be with them always." He turned away and silence fell between them.

Mary Ann was glad. That remark he'd made about all of the children being strong in the Faith . . . She wondered. She had worried so much about Mary. Ever since Mary had gone to school in Salt Lake, she had taken a different attitude toward her religion. Of course, there had been no open defiance. It was an indefinable something—a skeptical look—a remark dropped now and then—but Mary Ann's heart would stumble, and sick little fears would grip her.

She had never told Charles. There was nothing tangible—she did not want to worry him. And Mary, she thought, would surely get over this phase. She would be busy and happy in her teaching. It was unfortunate that she had been in Salt Lake when the Godbeite movement was organized. A group of

Mormon reformers had openly rebelled against the policies of President Young.

But Mary had not forgotten. For the first years, she had thrown herself completely into her teaching, and Mary Ann's fears were lulled to false security. Mary had seemed so happy. But lately she had been noticeably restless. There was not the same zest in her work. Her school, the Mutual Improvement Society where she had accomplished so much with the young people—nothing held her interest. Her remarks were becoming more pointed. "Mother, why should the Church always come first?" and again, irritably, "Mother! What possible harm could come from our having some copies of the *Salt Lake Tribune?*"

"None—perhaps," Mary Ann had replied. But, she explained patiently, the *Tribune* was the organ of the Liberal Party, and its editorials were unfriendly to the Church. "Your father would not like it," she said. "Besides, the *Deseret News* is a very good paper." Yes, these outbursts were a danger signal. Someday there would be an explosion. Someday she would have to discuss this with Charles. . . . She stole a glance at him, guiltily. It seemed impossible that he could sit there so close to her, so calm—oblivious to the turmoil within her. How good he was—how strong. If Mary would only make up her mind about Harley Morey. Poor Harley. He had been so faithful, so patient—waiting all these years. He'd make Mary a good husband. With his steadying influence and a home and children, Mary would surely be happy. But—would she? Mary Ann pushed the question away.

One thing she could be thankful for. Nanie's future was settled. Nanie had no troublesome doubts. She was strong in the Faith. She loved keeping house. A home and children were what she wanted, and when she met Hyrum Woolley, it had been love at first sight for both of them. But Mary was different. *Perhaps, after all,* Mary Ann thought, *I should tell*

Charles. She opened her lips, but closed them again with a sense of reprieve as Charles spoke.

"Remind me to have a talk with Amasa and Ezra the next time I'm at your house," he said. "We don't want them getting out of hand."

"Yes, Charles," Mary Ann murmured.

2.

The sun was sinking behind the mountains. Charles kept a tight rein on the team. They had made many stops, but the horses were still fresh, and Mary Ann knew that Charles was purposely holding them in until they reached the straight three-quarter mile stretch outside of Paris. He turned his head now and smiled at her. "Yes," he said, "I'm satisfied with the way things have gone, but there is still much more to be done in the Valley. And besides," his voice warmed with enthusiasm, "I want to begin colonizing the Star Valley—northeast of here, in Wyoming."

Mary Ann sat up very straight, her eyes fearful. "You don't mean—" her voice died away.

"No, my dear," Charles spoke quickly. "There will be no more moves for us. I can promise you that."

She sighed and sank back in her seat, an immense relief sweeping through her as the tension left her body.

"That reminds me," Charles said, "I hope to start building new homes for all of you next spring."

"Oh, Charles!" Mary Ann exclaimed. "That will be wonderful." She leaned forward a little and looked up at him, her eyes shining. "Will they be—will you build brick houses?" Always she'd longed for a red brick house.

"Why, yes," Charles said, "I'd thought of brick. The older boys can help with the building."

Mary Ann sighed deeply in utter content. She'd been envious, she had to admit, when one after another of her friends had built new homes. She knew how it was, of course—Charles always so busy with Church and public duties. *"Church before private"* was his motto. But he had managed to keep them comfortable—adding a room now and then as the children grew older, keeping the house in repair—although there had been times. . . . She smiled suddenly, remembering that spring when she'd hung the rag carpet overhead to keep the rain out. Oh, it would be good to have a fine new home. It seemed absurd, but she was as excited as a child. And the girls would be so happy. The girls? That thought sobered her. With Nanie engaged to Hyrum, and Mary on the verge of accepting Harley, they'd soon be married and gone. Well, that was as it should be. She wanted them settled in homes of their own—William and Amasa, too. *But at least,* she thought, *Ezra and Edward will be with me for a long time.* And home would always be a pleasant gathering-place for them all. That was important.

"Now I'm going to show you what these horses will do!"

Mary Ann started. She hadn't realized that they had reached the three-quarter mile stretch. The horses broke into a rapid trot. They needed no urging. Mary Ann looked at Charles. He was leaning forward, his face alight and eager. The wheels of the surrey whirled over the hard dirt road, the horses' hoofs clattering, their gait perfectly matched. The swift motion, skimming through the darkening shadows, filled Mary Ann with joy that was almost ecstasy. She closed her eyes and lifted her face to the strong, cool wind, yielding herself up to the moment. But later, when Charles turned the team into her street, there was that queer feeling again, that tightening about her heart. She was relieved that Charles was going straight to Emeline's. Whatever might await her here, she wanted to face it alone.

9

1.

Mary Ann opened the door and swept the big room with an anxious glance. Everything seemed all right . . . Mary and Nanie were lingering at the supper table, and Edward was at play before the fire blazing cheerily on the hearth. There was a chorus of greetings. But Mary Ann was still uneasy. Where was Ezra? Where were the older boys? Edward was clamoring for her attention, and Nanie was urging her to take off her bonnet. She sat down near the fire and stretched out her hands toward the heat. She must not let the girls see that she was worried. "This is very comfortable," she said. "The nights are getting chilly."

"Yes," Mary said. "William thinks we may have early snow. He and Amasa went out to the Bern ranch yesterday to fix the barns. They took Ezra along. I hope you don't mind, Mother."

"Of course, I don't mind." Mary Ann smiled. The boys were all right then. William often took Ezra to the ranch—and then, Charles would be going out in the morning. She must stop imagining things. "How have you all been?" she demanded. Then quickly—"Has anything happened while I was away?"

"We've all been fine," Nanie answered. "And nothing exciting has happened. Has it, Mary?"

Mary Ann, her eyes on Mary busy at the stove, saw the sudden start, the betraying flush, and wondered; but within the instant Mary was on guard. "No," she answered composedly. "Now, Mother, do come to the table while we fix your supper. We thought you weren't coming—that's why we didn't wait," she added.

Settled in her chair at the table Mary Ann dismissed her fears and gave herself up to the joy of being home. Of *course* everything was all right. She worried too much, just as Charles said.

"Mother," Edward, pressed close to her knee, looked up at her. "Mother, I want to eat with you."

Mary Ann smiled and leaned down to kiss his small, solemn face. "Now, now," she chided, "you've had your supper, dear." But she slipped her arm around him and hugged him to her.

Candlelight from the shelf above the stove fell across Mary's face and brought out golden gleams in the thick braids of light brown hair that bound her shapely head. *She looks almost beautiful,* Mary Ann thought. Nanie was the family beauty, but there was something about Mary tonight—an inner glow, a radiance . . . A little bemused smile curved her lips. An excited little smile. She was stirring the scrambled eggs, but she was miles away. Something had happened to Mary. She never showed her feeling this way . . . .

"I hate to run away the first night you are home, Mother," Nanie said, "but it's Mutual night, and I promised Hyrum I'd go."

"Of course." Mary Ann nodded. "I'd almost forgotten. You go right along." She liked the girls to be regular in their attendance. The Mutual Improvement Society did so much for the young people.

"Here you are, Mother." Mary placed a well-filled plate before her. The savory odor of the food made Mary Ann realize that she was hungry. Edward had climbed into a chair beside her, his round eyes hopefully expectant.

Mary Ann smiled up at Mary. "Get me a small plate, dear; I want to give Edward some of my supper."

"There you go again, spoiling Edward." Mary laughed, but she brought the plate and sat down across the table from her mother.

Mary Ann looked up in surprise. "You'd better run along, dear, and get dressed for Mutual. I'll clear up."

"I'm not going to Mutual," Mary said. "I want to stay here with you."

Mary Ann's protest died on her lips. There was that same strange look—that hint of suppressed excitement. *She wants to tell me something,* Mary Ann thought. *That's why she's staying at home.* But later, when Nanie had gone and Edward was tucked in bed, Mary talked only of casual things. How were Grandfather Phelps and Aunt Harriet? Had the trip been pleasant? It was lucky they had returned today instead of tomorrow. Tomorrow was the day that the county teachers were meeting in general session. "And, of course," Mary said, "you know the new school is being dedicated tomorrow?"

"Yes," Mary Ann answered, "I know." She regarded her daughter, seated there on the little low stool, outwardly so controlled. Inwardly . . . "Mary," she said, "I feel guilty. I believe you stayed at home because you thought I'd be lonely. I wish you had gone, dear. I like having you with the young people." She leaned forward a little, looking into Mary's face. "Wasn't Harley expecting you?"

The moment she had spoken, Mary Ann regretted it. Mary was on her feet, rigid and defiant. "I may as well tell you now, Mother," she said crisply, "I'm not going to Mutual this winter. Those meetings mean so little to me, really. I don't care to go." She turned swiftly, picked up the poker and began to jab at the burning logs. "As for Harley—" She laid down the poker and faced her mother, her blue eyes stormy. "I suppose he *was* expecting me but I don't care. It's time he learned that I don't belong to him."

Mary Ann did not answer. Her heart was heavy. She had seen Mary flare up before, but never this way. What was back of this?

The candles flickered and a log crackled loudly in the stillness.

"I'm sorry, Mother," Mary said miserably. "I know you'd like me to feel differently about Harley but I can't. He's too—too—We just don't think alike."

"Don't be upset, dear." Mary Ann reached for Mary's hand and squeezed it gently. "I am sorry that you feel as you do, but that doesn't change matters. This is something you'll have to work out for yourself."

"But, Mother." Mary freed her hand and stood there, small and desperate. "You don't understand. I don't feel guilty about Harley. He's known from the beginning that we could never be anything but good friends." She paused for breath and hurried on, a shrill little hysterical note in her voice. "It's his own fault if he's hurt. It isn't my fault if people take things for granted."

"I suppose you're right. We have all taken for granted that you and Harley would marry some day. But you will have to tell your father soon." Mary Ann rose from her chair and stood for a moment looking straight into Mary's eyes. She sighed. "We won't talk any more about it now, dear. You're tired, and tomorrow will be a hard day. Run along to bed now."

"Well—" Mary hesitated, but relief was plain in her face. "Perhaps I'd better," she said. "Aren't you coming, too?"

"Not just yet. I must get the oatmeal in the kettle first. Good night, dear." *That was best,* Mary Ann thought. *She is in no mood to reason, now.* She pulled the stool closer to the fire and sat down, sighing heavily. Mary would never marry Harley. She had made that clear. *I've known this was coming,* Mary Ann realized, *but I wouldn't admit it.* The strange thing was Mary's violence. Something had stirred her deeply. But what? "If I only knew!" Mary Ann said aloud. And suddenly she was remembering Charles' words this very morning. "Sometimes," he had said, "I think they need more guidance as they grow older—but we can only point the way." *How true that is,* she thought wistfully. Yet there might be something she could do. Her place was here. She was needed. At least she hoped she was.

2.

Mary undressed quickly. She was ashamed. She had behaved badly just now, out there by the fire. She should go back and talk things out with her mother. *But I just can't,* she thought unhappily. She extinguished the candle and slipped into bed. She never had been good at talking things out, even with her mother whom she loved so dearly.

She lay rigid and tense. What was it that made her draw within herself just when she most wanted not to? This evening was to have been so different. Alone—just the two of them there. She had planned to tell about meeting Ashbel Pomeroy. She knew how interested her mother would be. Ashbel Pomeroy—the son of her old friend Francis Pomeroy. She would remember Ashbel. He had been a young boy the summer his parents came to the Valley—the same summer that the Rich family had come. The Pomeroys had moved to Bloomington, later. So much had happened to Ashbel since then. She had wanted to pass on to her mother all the things he had told her. After his mother's death, he had lived in Salt Lake with his grandmother. He had finished school, and then found a post as Assistant Superintendent of a mine at Bingham. But the mine was temporarily closed now, so Ashbel was here for a long visit with his father.

Mary sighed a long quivering sigh, and two big tears slid down her cheeks. She was dreadfully disappointed. It had seemed so important somehow—telling Mother about Ashbel. She had only seen him a few times but she liked him immensely. "He wanted to meet you, Mother. He called while you were away but he's coming again soon." That's what she had planned to say. And then that hateful business of Harley had spoiled it all. She hadn't meant to lash out that way—to hurt Mother, or worry her. Yet she'd meant what she said about Harley. She was sick and tired of people behaving as if they were practically married.

She sat up in bed and pounded her pillow. Moonlight streamed in the window and picked out the pattern of the patchwork quilt. Mary sat there wide-eyed, hugging her knees. She ought to be asleep. Tomorrow was an important day for the school. Brother Sleight would be depending on her. She should be looking forward to the teachers' meeting, too; but—she might as well face it—even her teaching had become a burden. She wanted to get out of the Valley. It was dreadful, this feeling of being shut in by something that smothered you; of being held down by ties you hadn't the strength to break. She'd been born and reared a Mormon. She knew how the Mormon people felt and thought—what they had put into the building of the Church. She admired and respected them, but . . . . It was frightening, this something inside of her—this desire to reach out, to question, to determine for herself. *I've tried. I've honestly tried,* she thought, *but I haven't been the same since Salt Lake.* Outwardly, she had taken an active part in things. It was easier that way—living from day to day—not allowing yourself to look ahead. But this last year had been unbearable. She couldn't go on this way. Somewhere, something was waiting for her. Outside of this valley. Away from the Mormon people.

Ashbel Pomeroy. She felt a warm rush of excitement. Perhaps he was the answer. But that was foolish. Her imagination was running away with her. Yet she kept thinking of the things she had liked about him that very first evening, at the dance in the Bowery. The straight firm line of his chin—his compelling gray-blue eyes—the slow, deliberate way he talked. And how he could talk! That evening he had called, with Nanie and the older boys away and the children in bed, she had felt self-conscious until he began to talk. He had told her of his ambition to study medicine—(the mine was only temporary); of books that he liked; of places he wanted to see. She had felt that she could listen to him forever. He was different from anyone she had ever known. He spoke of the things she dreamed of.

And she would be seeing him tomorrow. Seeing him was much more important than dedications and teachers' meetings. Her heart raced and her cheeks burned in the darkness. She mustn't let herself feel this way. She must get to sleep. She buried her head in the pillow and pulled the covers about her. But it was long after Nanie had come in and undressed quietly in the dark, before Mary slept.

3.

At breakfast Mary seemed her cheerful, normal self. She was full of animation, talking enthusiastically about the program for the day. Yet Mary Ann, watching her closely, saw faint shadows under her eyes and a strained look about her mouth. And she was talking much too fast—determined, it seemed, to keep the conversation in safe channels, avoiding anything that might recall last night.

"The dedication is at ten o'clock," she said, turning to her mother, "and I want you and Nanie to be sure to come." She paused. "Perhaps I shouldn't tell you ahead of time, Mother, but Brother Sleight is going to mention you in his speech."

"Mention me?" Mary Ann echoed. "But why in the world should he?"

"He wants to express his gratitude," Mary said; "to tell everyone how much you helped him that first winter in the Valley. He says you insisted that we young people must be kept happy. He's going to show how important we have become in the community and he says we have you to thank."

"Oh, that." Mary Ann flushed a little. "I don't deserve any special credit for that." *I wonder,* she thought guiltily, *if Mary suspects that what I did that winter was mostly for her.* "Really," she said earnestly, "everybody helped. Sister Clifton, Sister Atkins, Aunt Harriet, Aunt Emeline—everybody. When we got things started, you young folks took hold and we weren't needed any more."

"Don't be so modest, Mother." Mary smiled. "And don't look so alarmed. The others will get credit, too."

Nanie beamed. "I think it's a grand idea. We'll be there, Mary. Never fear."

"I'll depend on you, then." Mary smiled and smoothed the lace collar on her blue cashmere dress. "I like this dress so much better since you fixed it, Nanie. I don't know what I'd do without you to take care of my clothes."

"Oh, that was nothing," Nanie said, flushing with pleasure.

How lovely she is, Mary Ann thought. In her simple pink gingham, dark eyes shining, brown curls piled high on her head, Nanie was a picture. Mary Ann was so glad Mary had mentioned the dress. Nanie had a way with clothes.

Mary Ann watched her girls. *They are so different,* she mused, *yet so devoted.* They shared everything. "If you are going to do my part of the housework, you should have part of my salary," Mary had said when she started teaching. Nanie had protested, but each month, as soon as Mary received her meager pay, Nanie had a share of it. Mary would have her way. There was a quiet forcefulness about her as marked as Nanie's joyousness. For Nanie life was happy, life was good. She accepted it. Mary questioned it. Even now, as she sat listening to Nanie, there was something on her mind . . .

Mary Ann sighed. What a responsibility children were. But how much people missed who didn't have them.

4.

Mary Ann always saw her children off in the morning. She had formed the habit when they were little tots going to school. The excursion to the doorstep gave her a chance to see if small hands were clean, if there were fresh handkerchiefs in pockets, if coats were snugly buttoned. As the children grew up the custom became a tradition—something never to be omitted unless Mary Ann were ill or away. And there was still much to attend to in those parting moments. A word of cheer to be spoken—a confidence to be shared. On one of those rare occasions when Mary expressed her feeling, she had said, "It makes the day seem right, Mother—this little chat on the doorstep with you."

But this morning Mary did not linger to chat. Brother Sleight was waiting, she explained. He wanted Caroline and her to be there early. With a hurried goodbye, she started down the path, her back held very straight, her blue skirt swirling about her small ankles. Mary Ann turned to re-enter the house, but changed her mind. She felt impelled, somehow, to wait until Mary was outside the gate. And afterwards she was glad, for at the gate Mary turned. She stood there for a moment very still, not moving, not smiling. Just looking. Mary Ann smiled and lifted her hand to wave. In a flash Mary was back up the path, standing before her, looking up into her face. Mary Ann's heart was in her throat. She knew now that Mary had something to tell her, but she must be careful. She must not force a confidence.

"Did you forget something, dear?" she questioned, making her tone casual.

"No, Mother." Mary's voice was breathless. "I only wanted to know if you will be home today after four o'clock? I—I want to bring a friend to meet you. The son of an old friend of yours."

"Why, of course, I'll be here and very glad to meet your new friend. Whose son did you say—"

"Ooh-whoo! Mary!" A hail cut short Mary Ann's question. A small dark-haired girl was cutting across the lot from Emeline's cottage. Caroline. "I thought you'd gone, Mary," she said. "How are you, Aunt Mary? Did you have a pleasant trip?"

"I'm fine and I enjoyed the trip. Is your mother all right?" Mary Ann questioned.

"Oh, yes. She's fine, too." Caroline linked her arm through Mary's. "We're late," she said. "We'd better hurry."

Mary Ann's eyes followed the two girls. She was sorry that Caroline had interrupted, but perhaps it was just as well. The son of an old friend. *Who could he be?* she wondered. Whoever he was, he was very important to Mary.

5.

Later that morning Nanie innocently supplied the missing details.

"There was a lovely party in the Bowery while you were away, Mother," she said, taking a pan of ginger cookies from the oven.

Mary Ann, busily scraping carrots, was only half listening. Of course, she was interested in what had been happening, but she couldn't get Mary out of her mind. And this young man . . . .

"Everyone turned out," Nanie was going on. "Even some people from Bloomington and St. Charles. And speaking of Bloomington reminds me, Mother. Mary and I met the son of an old friend of yours."

Mary Ann was suddenly alert—waiting.

"Ashbel Pomeroy is his name," Nanie said. She finished taking cookies out of the pan. "Francis Pomeroy, I think he said, is his father. But Mary can tell you all the details—she danced with him several times." And before Mary Ann could speak—"Mother! Will you look at that clock! We've just time to dress."

Francis Pomeroy. Relief poured through Mary Ann. Brother Pomeroy was a fine man, firm in the Faith. His son would be the right kind of a young man for Mary to know. She dressed carefully, but her thoughts were far away. She was remembering that day at the ferry crossing, long ago. How kind Brother Pomeroy had been to her then. She'd seen very little of him here in the Valley, but Charles often spoke of him—of how conscientious he was as Justice of the Peace, of his loyalty to the Church—his splendid pioneer work in Bloomington. Thankfulness glowed within her. Now that she knew what to expect she could scarcely wait until four o'clock. She was eager to meet Ashbel.

6.

Everything was ready—the big west room neat and shining—Mary Ann immaculate in a fresh cambric print dress. It was cheerful, she thought, with the afternoon sun pouring through the windows and the bowl of bright goldenrod on the shelf above the fireplace. Nanie had promised to spend the afternoon with Nancy, and Edward was at Sarah Peck's, playing with her boys. Mary Ann was glad. It would be easier for Mary, with none of the family around.

From the south window she watched Mary and Ashbel coming up the path. There was something familiar about the big, broad-shouldered man swinging alongside Mary. He reminded Mary Ann of his father. She had been years younger that day at the Platte River than Mary was today, yet she must have been older in many ways. Girls grew old younger, those days.

I've never seen her look so happy, Mary Ann thought as Mary presented Ashbel. "It is indeed a pleasure to meet you again, Mrs. Rich," he said. "Father speaks so often of you and Apostle Rich." His voice was warm and his handclasp firm. Mary Ann liked the clear-eyed directness of his look.

When they were all three comfortably seated, Mary Ann found herself talking easily to Ashbel—relating experiences of the days when she had known his father. And Ashbel, in turn, told her of his family. Mary Ann watched him closely—"sizing him up," as Charles would say, while he talked.

"I know what you are thinking," Ashbel said suddenly, a twinkle in his eye. "You are trying to remember me as a sixteen-year-old, ten years ago."

"But I do remember," Mary Ann was a little confused. *Better let it pass that way,* she thought. She had really been thinking how likable he was. He had plenty of self-assurance but there was no arrogance about him. There was deference in his manner, but he had his own ideas and was ready to defend them. Yes, she liked him. Decidedly she liked him. She could understand that shining look in Mary's eyes.

Later, when she had excused herself to prepare some refreshments, she purposely dawdled over the tray of ginger cookies and apple cider. Mary and Ashbel were discussing (of all things) national conditions. It was stimulating to listen to them. Yes, Ashbel was very sure of himself—too sure, perhaps. But Mary was holding her own. Mary was smart. She kept up with things.

And Ashbel was no longer a stranger. It was amazing, Mary Ann thought, how natural it seemed to have him there. Over the cider and cookies they talked of many things. "I am sorry Apostle Rich isn't here," Ashbel said. "I am anxious to know him again." He laughed. "When I was a little chap, I was wild about horses and some way or other I learned that Apostle Rich was, too. After that he couldn't get rid of me. I was always around when he came to see Father. But he was never too busy to talk horses with me." Ashbel paused. "He was very kind," he said. "I've never forgotten him."

Mary, passing the cookies, smiled. "Father still loves horses," she said, "and he's still kind. You'll enjoy him even more, now, than you did then."

Mary Ann felt a surge of happiness. Coming from Mary, those words meant a great deal. Mary was proud of her father. She loved him dearly. Impulsively, Mary Ann turned to Ashbel. "Apostle Rich will be here Tuesday evening," she said. "Can't you have supper with us then?" But when he promptly accepted, she felt some misgivings. Had she been too hasty? No. She dismissed her doubts. Ashbel was one of their own. Charles would want to see him. *And the sooner the better,* she thought, watching Mary's radiant face.

10

1.

Mary Ann was in the midst of her Saturday bread-making. Her fingers worked with practiced skill as she kneaded the loaves and placed them side by side in their pans; but her eyes and her thoughts were on Mary. Seated at the big table, her smooth brown head bent over a book, Mary was deep in preparation for her first day of school. Mary Ann sighed. Last night, with Nanie and Edward coming in, and supper to prepare, there had been no time for confidences. And afterward the girls had hurried off to the Dramatic Society. But this morning she and Mary were alone, yet the minutes were passing in silence.

It's no use, Mary Ann thought, absently scraping dough off her fingers. *Mary is not going to let me under the surface. She won't tell me her real feelings. It's too soon.* One by one she placed the pans of bread on the back of the stove to rise, and covered them with a clean soft cloth. *Too soon,* she thought again. Then it was too soon to say anything to Charles—anything that might direct his attention to Mary's interest in Ashbel. Better let Charles and Ashbel get acquainted first. *After all,* she thought, *I mustn't take things for granted.* She smiled ruefully, remembering Mary's indignation about that.

"Mother."

Mary Ann looked up quickly. Mary had pushed her books aside and was standing by the table. "Don't you think," she began without preamble, "that it would be nice to have some of the young people drop in Tuesday after supper—to get acquainted with Ashbel Pomeroy? Mostly family, of course. There's Caroline and Nancy and Caddy," she went on, "and some of the others around our age—" She paused, her blue eyes thoughtful. "We could ask the Poulson boys and Mable Clifton and the Sleight girls. And, of course, Nanie will want Hyrum. Would it be too much work, Mother? Do—do you think Father would mind?"

"Of course, it isn't too much work, and I'm quite sure your father won't object. He'll be here tomorrow and I'll ask him. Better not count on it, though, until we see what he says."

"Then we'll talk about it later." Mary picked up her books. "I'm going over to school for a while. Goodbye, Mother."

Dear child, Mary Ann thought. *She has told me more than she knows.* There was no doubt, now, about her interest in Ashbel. But she was showing her good sense. This party—it would introduce Ashbel to the family without centering any attention on Mary. Mary's head might be in the clouds just now, but she was keeping her feet on the ground.

And Charles was pleased. When he came in from the ranch on Monday, Mary Ann told him about Ashbel—casually, she hoped, without placing too much or too little emphasis on Mary's attitude.

"I'm glad you invited him," Charles said. "Brother Pomeroy told me young Ashbel was coming. I'll be glad to see him again." He chuckled reminiscently. "How that boy did love horses."

"Then having the young folks in will be all right?"

"By all means," Charles answered heartily. "It will be good for Ashbel. His father says he's been something of a hermit these last few years."

As simple as that! Mary Ann thought. *I needn't have worried.* But she was still uneasy.

At the supper party, watching Charles and Ashbel enthusiastically renewing their friendship, the feeling persisted. Charles must be told about Mary and Harley. He would be disappointed—hurt. He'd counted on their marriage just as she had. But that expression on Mary's face! She was off guard for the moment, looking at Ashbel. Mary Ann caught her breath. *I must talk to Charles,* she thought. *I must prepare him for what to expect.* But she turned a little sick at the prospect. Why must things tangle themselves up so?

2.

A week had passed and the Rich family had settled into the routine which came with the opening of school. Always before Mary Ann had welcomed it. Summers were pleasant, but she liked to get back to normal, to take up again the orderly pattern of living. But this year something was wrong. She couldn't put her finger on it. It was an intangible something—a shadowy dread of things to come. Her face was troubled as she sugared the batch of golden-brown doughnuts, but Ezra's shrill whistle brought a smile to her lips.

"Fried cakes—fried cakes!" Ezra whooped joyously. He slammed the door behind him, sent his cap spinning toward a chair and made a beeline for the table.

"Wait a minute, young man," Mary Ann said. "Wash your hands first—and hang up your cap."

"Aw, Mother!" Ezra complained good-naturedly; but he hung up the cap and began to dabble his hands in the tin basin on the washstand. Mary Ann watched him fondly. He was such a happy, lovable little rascal, yet he did keep her guessing. He was utterly unpredictable.

"Golly, Mother, but these are good," he exclaimed, reaching for his third doughnut. Mary Ann smiled. It was worth all her efforts just to hear him say that. Ezra had a way with him. It wasn't so much what he said as the way he said it. *He could make the least thing seem important,* Mary Ann thought.

"Did Mary say when she'd be home?" she questioned.

"Oh." Ezra stopped to swallow. "I forgot. She won't be home till supper. She went for a ride in the country." He grinned wisely. "Not with Ashbel Pomeroy, this time. With Father."

"*Brother* Pomeroy," Mary Ann reproved automatically; but inwardly she was reproaching herself. She had waited too long to talk with Charles. Mary would keep her promise—she would tell him about Harley. Well, it had to come. Perhaps it was better this way. "Change your clothes, Ezra, and get at your chores," she directed. But her anxious thoughts were with Mary and Charles as she set about getting supper.

The moment they came in Mary Ann's heart sank. Charles was stern and preoccupied, short with the boys, ominously silent. And Mary—it was there again, that rebellious defiant look. Supper was an uncomfortable meal. Nanie's efforts at conversation met no response. Even the boys seemed to sense something wrong; they were unusually quiet.

Always, Mary Ann looked forward to the hour when, with the supper things cleared away, the family gathered together for prayers. But tonight as Charles' deep, still vibrant voice asked the Lord for guidance, it seemed to carry an undertone of warning. Mary Ann's own fervent prayers were for Mary to find the way.

After prayers Mary and Nanie hurried away to a rehearsal.

When the boys were in bed, Mary Ann joined Charles beside the fire. He sat there frowning, staring into the flames. How tired he looked. It hurt her to see the lines deepening in his face, the once erect shoulders beginning to sag.

He stirred in his chair. "I had quite a talk with Mary this afternoon," he said slowly. "I suppose she has told you how she feels about Harley?"

"Yes."

"I am greatly disappointed." Charles spoke heavily. "Mary should be married—have children. Harley is suitable for her in every way." He was silent then, but to Mary Ann there was a look on his face of things unsaid. She must not let him utter them. She must say something before he went on.

"I'm disappointed, too," she began hastily. "Nothing would have made me happier than Mary's marriage to Harley." She paused on a sudden thought. Was it their wishes or Mary's happiness that was most important? She looked at Charles, an appeal in her eyes. "There are other young men," she said. "Mary will find someone suitable—someone who will make her happy."

"Can we be sure of that?" he demanded. "All this delay—Mary is getting on. She is wasting the best years of her life." He straightened up in his chair and his voice took on a sharp note. "These young people of today—they think too much of love. They have lost sight of the real values of marriage. They don't understand that love grows out of respect; that mutual understanding of our gospel is the real basis for a happy marriage."

"You feel that Mary is like that?" Mary Ann questioned. She must find out. She had to know what had happened between Mary and her father.

"No," Charles said. "She's not that bad. But she is making too much of the point that she doesn't love Harley."

"Did you tell her that?"

"Yes, but—" It seemed difficult for him to go on. "I couldn't reach her," he said. "It was strange. She didn't disagree—yet she didn't agree. The more I talked, the more she seemed to withdraw."

"She's like that sometimes," Mary Ann said. "You haven't been with her enough to know." She had a mental picture of Mary withdrawing, building a wall around herself. But, oh, how thankful she was that Mary hadn't flared up. "She'll think this through, Charles," she said. "She always does, and generally sees the right way. That is why I feel sure that time will work this out."

"I hope you are right." Charles sighed wearily.

Mary Ann's heart ached for him, but there was nothing more she could say now. She was immeasurably relieved that it was love Mary had made a point of. Suppose she had told her father that she and Harley didn't think alike. What might that have led to? A little chill ran over Mary Ann. She could understand Mary's feeling about love, but her doubts about the gospel . . . *If only,* she thought fearfully, *her doubts have not gone deep enough to touch her Faith!* If Mary's Faith held, everything would work out. *It did for me,* she thought.

There was a sharp knock at the door. Mary Ann jumped.

"Oh, my dear, I'm sorry," Charles was on his feet. "That must be Joseph. I'm expecting him in from Cache Valley tonight. I left word for him to come here."

Joseph entered with a breezy greeting. Mary Ann was glad for the interruption.

"Come in, Joseph," she said. "Take off your coat and sit down."

"No, thanks, Aunt Mary," he said. "I can only stay a moment. I've news for you, Father. President Young is in Logan. He and his party came up by train yesterday, and they're coming on to Paris. They will travel by way of

Blacksmith's Canyon and work through the southern settlements. He asked me to have you make arrangements for his stay here."

"I'm pleased to hear this news," Charles said. "How many in the group?" he asked, "and when may we expect them?"

"Ten altogether. Four in President Young's personal party. They should be here Friday."

"Friday," Charles repeated. He turned to Mary Ann. "My dear, I shall want you to take care of President Young and his own party."

3.

Mary Ann awoke very early. She lay quiet, not moving, not daring to sigh for fear of disturbing Charles. Last night's news had changed everything. She wouldn't have time to worry now. She had always looked forward to President Young's visits. It was an honor to act as hostess to him—an honor that Charles had often conferred upon her; yet this time she could almost wish that one of Charles' other wives had been chosen. Right now with all that was on her mind it was going to be difficult. She hoped Brother Young wouldn't notice the strain between Mary and her father . . . He was not likely to. Still, Charles might mention the break between Mary and Harley. The thought threw her into a panic. That would antagonize Mary more than ever. If only President Young could have come at some other time.

She crept out of bed and dressed quietly, but once outside the bedroom she began resolutely to plan. The time was so short—there was so much to do, she thought, as she put the kettle on. The bedrooms must be thoroughly cleaned and freshly made up. Charles, of course, would be staying here. She and Charles could move to the north room and the boys to the loom room. Nanie and Mary could stay with Caroline and Nancy. It was fortunate that William and Amasa were at the ranch. She stepped to the window and examined the curtains critically. Perhaps a good pressing . . . No. President Young was bringing Amelia. The curtains must be washed.

As she fixed breakfast, her thoughts turned to food. Charles wanted a supper party Friday evening. She would have stewed chicken and dumplings—and apple pie. Brother Young was fond of apple pie. And she must bake extra bread . . . She sighed. She and Nanie certainly had plenty of work ahead.

Yet late the next afternoon all was in readiness. The cottage was spotless. Tantalizing odors filled the air. Mary Ann stood back and surveyed the crisp white curtains. It was wonderful what clean curtains did for a room. She sighed. She was very tired—but everything was ready. She turned her head. That was Mary's step. She'd been delayed at school working on the program in President Young's honor. "Come in, dear, and tell me how things look," Mary Ann called out. "Is everything all right, do you think?"

Mary's mouth was grim. "Why wouldn't it be, with you working your fingers to the bone these last two days? It makes me boil. It's an imposition to ask you to do this—and I don't like it."

A wave of anger swept over Mary Ann. "This isn't a matter of what you like, Mary," she said sharply. "It's what I want to do. It is an honor to entertain President Young. I am proud and happy to do this for your father. You should be proud, too."

The cheerful humming of the tea kettle was suddenly loud in the stillness. Then Mary sighed. "I'm sorry, Mother," she said, and turning abruptly, left the room.

II

1.

For the next three days the Rich household revolved around Brigham Young. Mary Ann, during his previous visits, had become familiar with his wishes. His shaving water must be just so—not too hot, not too cold. His fine linen shirts, freshly laundered, the pleats ironed with knife-like precision, must be ready for him each morning. And this time Amelia's presence in the house brought a new sense of strain. Nothing, Mary Ann felt sure, escaped those brilliant, inscrutable eyes; and nothing, she was determined, should be found wanting.

But even as she worked and planned for the comfort of her distinguished guests, Mary Ann's thoughts were never far from Mary. Mary, after her outburst, was making a special effort to be agreeable. Surely no one could tell from Mary's manner that she resented these visitors. She was modest and retiring and sweetly deferential. And it was not pretense—she was really trying. *That's like her,* Mary Ann thought. Always, after Mary's rebellion had spent itself in a spurt of temper, the lovable side of her nature was uppermost. But Mary Ann's forehead puckered in a worried frown. This change was not permanent. Deep down, Mary was still in an inner turmoil. *How can I help her?* Mary Ann wondered, as she pressed the rustling silk of one of Amelia's dresses. *How can I make her understand that I want to help? Certainly not by losing my temper,* she reproached herself, thinking of that angry scene. She pushed the hair back from her forehead with a weary gesture. There was plenty to do without worrying over Mary. That would keep.

Yet when the guests had gone at last she was too tired to think. Even after a night's rest she was still languid—still sunk in apathy. She had been a credit to Charles. He was pleased. That was all that really mattered. *I'll rest today,* she thought. *Tomorrow I'll face things again.* The house seemed blissfully quiet after all the activity. Charles had gone to Montpelier with President Young. It might be a week before he could get back.

But late that afternoon Charles returned. She heard his step on the doorstep and half started from her chair. "Charles!" she exclaimed, "is anything wrong? I thought you were staying in Montpelier until President Young left for Salt Lake?"

"I came home," Charles said, "because I have news. Important news." There was a queer breathlessness in his voice. He pulled up a chair and sat down opposite her. "Hyrum's been called on a mission," he said. "To the Sandwich Islands."

"Oh, poor Nanie!" Mary Ann's face was full of concern. "So far away—she will be heartbroken."

"But, my dear," Charles said, "Nanie is going with him. President Young has arranged it. He feels that she should go along." He paused. "They'll have to be married within the next two weeks. They sail from San Francisco in early October."

Mary Ann heard the explanation, but it made no sense.

"Nanie is going with him." "Nanie is going with him." Those words were echoing in her mind, gathering in volume, roaring in her ears. She sprang to her feet and stood close to Charles, facing him, her eyes wide and stricken, her hands gripped together. "Oh, no," she whispered. "No, Charles. You can't mean this." She caught her breath sharply and spoke again, a hint of hysteria in her voice. "Nanie isn't going with him—not out there across the ocean. Anywhere—anywhere in this country—but not out there." She buried her face in her hands and sobbed. She could not keep back the tears.

"Why, Mary Ann," Charles said. "Why, my dear!" He was on his feet, his arms around her, holding her close. She pressed her face against his shoulder and abandoned herself to her grief. When her sobs had subsided a little, he spoke again, gently. "You're tired out," he said. "I didn't realize. This week has been too much of a strain."

Mary Ann dried her tears and looked up at him, mute and miserable.

"Come," he said, "sit down and let's talk this over." The pressure of his hands on her shoulders was firm and kind. She sank into her chair and he sat down again facing her, leaning forward to grasp her hands. The room was shadowy now, and dim. "I am sorry the news has upset you so," Charles said, "but I know you'll see it as I do when you are rested a little." He released her hands and sat erect, his head thrown back, his voice vibrant and full of fire. "Think," he said. "Think of those two young people going out—carrying our Gospel to the people of those Islands." He drew a deep breath. "It's a real challenge to Hyrum. The beginning of life for both of them."

He went on then, without pause, telling her of the Islands, the people, of why Brother Young had chosen Hyrum to carry the Mormon faith to them. Mary Ann sat listening, yet scarcely hearing. She was wrapped in her own thoughts. In the relief of tears she had found herself again. She could not stop Nanie. She had no right to try. An underscored passage in her mother's *Doctrine and Covenants* pictured itself before her eyes. "And behold it shall come to pass that my servants shall be sent forth to the east and to the west, to the north and to the south." *Mother would want Nanie to go,* she thought. And Nanie loved Hyrum. Her place was by his side. That was the answer.

2.

Ashbel Pomeroy held the little roan mare to a walk as the rig turned into Mary's street. It would postpone the moment of parting. These afternoon rides with Mary had become oddly important to him. No matter what he was doing, as four o'clock approached he would become uneasy, impatient—holding himself rigidly in check until the sight of her waiting in the schoolhouse doorway released the tension and sent the warm blood sweeping through him in a strong, even flow.

He looked at her now seated beside him, a little smile touching her lips, her small hands relaxed, lying loosely clasped in her lap. They had reached the Rich cottage. *I can't let her go,* Ashbel thought—and then, *but I must let her go.*

Mary laid her hand on his arm and leaned forward suddenly, her face anxious. "There's Father's rig in the lane," she exclaimed. "We weren't expecting him for several days. Can anything have happened?"

Ashbel jumped out of the buggy and helped her to alight. "Would you like me to go in with you, Mary?" he asked. "Or I can wait here until you see if everything is all right."

"No," she said. "No, thank you, Ashbel. I'm sure nothing is wrong. It's just my silly imagination." She smiled up at him. Her eyes were very blue—the mellow light of the setting sun burnished her smooth brown head. "It's been a wonderful afternoon," she said softly. "Goodbye, Ashbel."

He stood for a moment, watching the small, graceful figure hurrying up the path, then climbed into the buggy and slapped the reins across the mare's rump. She leaped forward, and he guided her with frowning concentration, not turning to look back.

But once out on the road to Bloomington he gave the mare her head and allowed himself to think. He was in love with Mary Rich. There was no use trying to deceive himself. He was in love with a Mormon girl. An Apostle's daughter. He—who did not believe in the doctrines of the Mormon Church! The irony of it struck him with full force. The mare, headed for home, trotted briskly over the familiar road. Ashbel gazed moodily into the shadows settling upon the hills, gathering at the roadside. He should never have let this happen. He should have stopped seeing Mary when he realized that seeing her meant so much to him. It wasn't her fault. She was always the same—gay, natural, friendly. There was no sentimental nonsense about Mary. That was one of the things that had attracted him from the first. That pleasant companionship—laughing a lot, arguing a little, discussing politics, books, everything except religion. She had never mentioned that. But why should she? She, of course, took it for granted that he was a good Mormon.

Ashbel shifted his position uneasily. He was face to face with the same old problem but this time his carefully worked out philosophy would not help. He had stayed in the middle of the road. Because of his father, he had made no open break with the Church. During his last years at school he had leaned strongly toward the Liberal Party, but he had kept his own counsel. After all, he was not a reformer. And keeping his own counsel had become his rule of living. It had worked well. Because of it he'd felt free to accept Matthew Walker's offer of work at the mines. His father had been disturbed. "How," he demanded, "can you, a Mormon, work for a man who openly opposes President Young?" But Ashbel had reassured him. "Walker is interested in my ability," he said, "not in my religious convictions."

Yes, he had managed well—until now. Coming to the Valley for a long visit, he had intended to tell his father—to confess his real feeling about the Church, that at heart he was not a Mormon—never would be. Instead he had drifted. Accepted the hospitality of these good people. Accepted Mary's unsuspecting friendship. Mary. The thought of her flooded through him in a rush of tenderness. How sweet she was, how fine, how honest. And how she would despise him when she knew. He was awake at last. Shame and bitterness struggled within him. Because he loved Mary, he must not tell her so. He must not stay and try to win her. Even if that were possible, he couldn't ask her to give up her Church—the thing that was so much a part of her life. And he couldn't remain a Mormon. There *was* no middle road.

He aroused himself with a start. The little mare had stopped and was standing quietly before the Pomeroy house with its lighted windows beaming hospitably through the darkness. How solid and peaceful it looked. Ashbel sighed heavily. He dreaded what was before him, but he would be honest with himself at last. He would tell his father tonight. Then he would get out.

12

1.

Nanie and Hyrum were to be married in the Endowment House in Salt Lake City. Charles and Hyrum had gone ahead to make the arrangements. Mary Ann and Nanie were to follow in a week.

One week. Mary Ann's panic-stricken thoughts whirled. *One week to get Nanie ready. I can't do it.* But she was reckoning without the family.

"Whatever ails you, Mary Ann?" Emeline scolded. "Fluttering about like a silly hen!" Her tone was exasperated but her eyes were soft with understanding. "You stick to your loom," she commanded. "Those blankets have to be finished. We'll manage the rest."

Mary Ann swallowed hard. "Thank you, Emeline," she said meekly, then smiled in spite of her sorrow. Emeline loved an emergency. She was in her element now, marshaling her forces, outlining work and seeing that it was done. Harriet was to complete several quilts in the making. Sarah Peck and Eliza would assemble the linens and look after the packing.

"And I," Emeline announced grandly, "will help Nanie get her clothes in order."

How good they all are, Mary Ann thought. *What would I do without them?* Working furiously at the loom she felt oddly detached—an onlooker only—watching as one task after another was completed. Nanie moved about starry-eyed, in a rosy dream. But Nanie was the bride. That was her privilege. *It would break my heart,* Mary Ann thought. *if she wasn't happy, her last week at home.*

After school hours Mary helped out with odds and ends, but mostly she was staying close to Nanie. Mary Ann, folding the new linsey-woolsey blankets for packing, watched them one afternoon. *My girls,* she thought. *My brave girls.* Outwardly they were gay, but their hearts, she knew, were aching like her own. Except for Mary's year in Salt Lake they had never been separated. It was going to be harder for Mary. Nanie was embarking upon her great adventure. Mary was being left behind. Fervently, Mary Ann wished that Ashbel Pomeroy would call. If there was ever a time Mary needed diversion it was now. It had been several days since Mary had mentioned Ashbel. Could anything be wrong?

But there was no time to think of that. Already it was Wednesday. Three precious days of the week gone. Things were in that state of disorder from which, Mary Ann knew, order was about to emerge; but Nanie was sure they could never be ready to leave on Saturday. *I wish we couldn't,* Mary Ann thought guiltily. *I wish that Saturday need never come.*

By Friday evening the big trunk was packed and strapped, ready for Joseph to pick up in the morning. He would drive Mary Ann and Nanie to Logan. They would go on from there Sunday, by train. All the small details had been attended to and the family was relaxing. William and Amasa had come in from the ranch to tell Nanie goodbye. For supper, Mary

Ann had prepared all of Nanie's favorite dishes, but looking at her family gathered around the table she could not force herself to swallow; and Mary and Nanie, she noticed, were scarcely touching their food. Poor Mary. What a relief it was that Father and Harriet were coming tomorrow. It would be unthinkable to leave Mary here alone.

When the "good night's" had been said, Mary Ann lingered in the big west room. They were to leave early. Everything must be made ready for breakfast. The girls had offered to help, but she had sent them to their room. She wanted them to have the time alone together. She was laying the table when she heard a door close softly.

"Mother." Nanie was standing there, her young face tragic. With a little desperate gesture she took a swift step forward and threw her arms around Mary Ann. "Mother," she said again. "I can't go. I can't leave you." She buried her face on her mother's shoulder, her slender body shaken with sobs.

Mary Ann held her close, not trying to speak. She had been expecting this—had nerved herself to meet it. Tenderly she stroked the soft brown curls. "There, there, dear," she soothed. "You feel that way now, but in the morning everything will be different."

Nanie lifted her head, her dark eyes swimming. "Oh, Mother—" her voice broke again.

Mary Ann put her hands on Nanie's shoulders and stood quietly looking at her. Always she wanted to remember Nanie as she looked tonight. That sweet girl face . . . "You believe in what you're doing, don't you, my darling?" she questioned.

"Oh, *yes,* Mother. I do. I do. It's the thought of all those miles between us—"

"If you believe in it, it's right, Nanie. And the miles—"

Mary Ann paused. "Our Faith will bridge the miles. A bond between us. You must go, dear."

Nanie's head was high, now. Her lashes were still wet, but her eyes were seeing visions. "Our Faith." she repeated softly. "And Hyrum needs me. That's why I must go."

Familiar words. *My whole life has revolved around those words,* Mary Ann thought. Yes, Nanie, too, was working out the pattern.

2.

The post was due on Saturday. Joseph brought the mail when he came for the trunk. "Here's one for you, Aunt Mary," he said, "and several for Father that you'll want to take along."

Mary Ann stood looking at the envelope in her hand. It was postmarked Salt Lake City, but she didn't recognize that firm, distinctive handwriting. Curiously, she tore open the flap of the envelope, unfolded the single sheet and read the signature. Ashbel Pomeroy! Ashbel in Salt Lake. Gone. *But why on earth should he be writing to me?* she wondered.

> *"It was with deep regret,"* Ashbel wrote, *"that I left the Valley. My visit there was so pleasant. I am sorry that I was unable to see you and Apostle Rich before my departure, but I wish to express my gratitude for your kindness and gracious hospitality. Please give my regards to Miss Mary and thank her for the happy times we had together. My best wishes to you and Apostle Rich."*

Mary Ann stood perfectly still, the letter in her hand. Through the half-open door a wedge of sunlight streamed across the floor. A chorus of gay voices floated in from outside. Nanie's friends had gathered to say goodbye. *And I'm going with her,* Mary Ann thought. *I must go with Nanie and leave Mary to face this alone.* What could have happened?

There was something behind this—something she did not understand. And Mary did not know, she was certain of that. Mary would have mentioned Ashbel's leaving or in her very concealment of it would have betrayed herself. Mary Ann cringed. What a blow this would be to Mary. And coming just at this time . . . *But I can't keep it from her,* she thought. *I must give her the letter before I leave.* Slowly she folded the sheet and slipped it into the envelope. *It is the Lord's will,* she told herself. *A test for Mary. She is strong—she will face this. And she must work it out alone.*

3.

Mary sat at the table with Ashbel's letter spread out before her. It was late. The house was still. Grandfather and Aunt Harriet must be asleep by now. She had got through the day somehow. Her lips twisted. Teachers couldn't have heartbreaks; and with Grandfather and Aunt Harriet here and the boys to look after—Well, she was alone now. She could think things through.

Ashbel was gone. He had not bothered to tell her goodbye. He had written to her mother—not to her. Her first quick reading of the letter had told her that much, and now, though she had read it over many times, it was still the same. There was nothing between the lines. "Give Miss Mary my regards." Polite, impersonal words. "Thank her for the happy times we had together." He had made it very clear. Their friendship, their rides, their talks, had meant nothing to him. Not even enough to warrant his writing to her.

Mary's face burned. How could she have been so foolish! Ashbel had never said or done a thing to indicate that he cared for her—that his interest in her was more than casual. True, he had always seemed eager to see her. He had enjoyed their companionship, she was sure of that. They had been really happy together. "Happy times." Exactly what he had said. Happy times, but nothing more. She scoffed at herself. Anything more had been in her imagination.

She snatched up the letter and crushed it convulsively in her hands. One thing she could be thankful for. She might have let her emotions run away with her, but only in her own feelings. Neither Ashbel nor anyone else suspected. But, no, that wasn't true. Mother had guessed. The look on Mother's face when she held out the letter . . . Mary got up and walked to the hearth. Embers still glowed under a gray film of ash. She stood for a moment looking down at the crumpled letter in her hand then, with a sudden violent gesture, flung it into the fire. Her eyes were somber as she watched the paper smoulder, its edges curl and blacken, the bold, upright letters stand out for an instant in the burst of yellow flame. *So that is finished,* she thought dully. How brief an interlude it had been. Perhaps Father was right. Perhaps love wasn't important.

She blew out the candles and in the faint glimmer of the dying fire, made her way slowly to bed.

4.

On the evening of Mary Ann's return from Salt Lake Harley Morey had supper with the family. Mary Ann greeted him with surprise that was difficult to conceal, but Mary seemed casual and matter-of-fact enough. "I hope you don't mind, Mother," she said. "Grandfather and Aunt Harriet had to leave today, and I thought company might help us not to miss Nanie."

"And a very good idea," Mary Ann agreed; but she wondered. Something seemed strange—but she wouldn't start worrying about that. Her relief at finding Mary so composed, so much her old self, made her realize how she had been dreading this homecoming. Buoyed up by the excitement of the wedding and the necessity of keeping cheerful for Nanie's sake, she had not dared let her thoughts dwell upon Mary; but the sick consciousness of Mary's unhappiness was always there, waiting, and every mile of the homeward journey had deepened her forebodings. And apparently they were groundless. *I've been upset—all worked up over nothing,* she thought. She felt bewildered and a little ridiculous but she was too tired to care.

It was good to be at home. It seemed as if she had been away for months. William and Amasa were at the Bern ranch, but supper was a cheerful meal with Edward's chair crowded close to her own and Ezra plying her with questions about the train ride. She told them of the wedding, of family and friends who had been there, of Nanie and Hyrum's departure, of the amazing growth and changes in Salt Lake. And all the time—watching Mary and Harley—she was aware of that inner something . . . *I don't understand it,* she told herself, *but I must not meddle.*

Later, in her mother's low rocker beside the fire, Mary Ann gave herself up to languor. She was utterly spent. These last few weeks had been hard on her. How thankful she was that Mary had come through safely. Whatever had happened between her and Ashbel, she was all right now, Mary Ann assured herself. The boys were in bed and Mary had gone to the door with Harley. *I should go to bed myself,* Mary Ann thought, *but it's so comfortable here.*

She heard the door close but did not turn her head or speak. Mary, too, was silent. She dragged a low stool to her mother's side and sat down facing the fire, her small capable hands clasped about her knees. "Mother," she said, her voice very low, "I have something to tell you. I've promised to marry Harley."

Coming without warning, the words struck Mary Ann like

a blow. For one blank moment, thought itself was suspended. "I asked him not to mention it," Mary was going on. "I wanted to tell you, myself."

"But, what—" Mary Ann caught herself sharply. This was no time to mention Ashbel. This feeling of shocked dismay would pass. Surely Mary knew what she was doing. And after all, wasn't this the thing they had hoped for—she and Charles? "What happened, dear?" she altered her question. "What made you change your mind?"

The soft young shoulder resting against her knee tensed for a moment, then relaxed again. "I've had time to think while you were gone, Mother. Perhaps Nanie's marriage has opened my eyes."

Mary Ann laid a caressing hand on the brown head. "Your father will be much pleased," she said slowly.

With a sudden twist of her body, Mary flung out her arms and buried her head upon them in her mother's lap. The fire crackled merrily, but there was no other sound. Mary was trembling. Mary Ann could feel the quivering shudder of her body. "Don't cry, dear," she said gently.

"I'm not crying." Mary lifted her head. Her eyes were dry and bright. Feverishly bright. "Mother," she said, "I've been a dreadful worry to you. I know I have. But it's all straight now." For a long, still moment, her eyes held Mary Ann's, a strange, driven look in their blue depths. Then Mary turned back to the fire. "I'll marry Harley," she said quietly, "and I'll be a good wife to him."

"Of course, you will," Mary Ann agreed. "You were confused. You didn't know your own mind. I understand." *But I don't,* she confessed to herself. *I don't understand at all.*

13

1.

When Ashbel Pomeroy left the Bear Lake Valley, he was determined to put Mary Rich out of his life. At Bingham, Matthew Walker welcomed him with enthusiasm. He was badly needed at the Emma mine. The company was being reorganized. There was much to be done. For the time being, at least, Ashbel felt this was where he belonged.

Yet, absorbed though he was in work, he could not keep Mary out of his mind. Her face had a way of forming before his eyes—blotting out a neat column of figures—shining at the end of a dark tunnel, encircled by the halo of a miner's lamp. Lying in his bunk during the long winter nights he would remember her smooth brown braids, the deep blue of her eyes, the way she had of coming out of a thoughtful silence with a quick, clear question—a pertinent observation. She seemed closer to him now than when they had been together. He loved her. He could not forget her. But at least he kept faith with himself. He had not written to Mary; he had made no attempt to keep track of her. Cut off as he was, at the mine, no news of the Valley reached him, not even from his father who had been sent to Arizona on Church business shortly after Ashbel had left the Valley.

So the months slowly passed until spring.

Sometimes the longing to see Mary was almost more than Ashbel could bear. It would be so easy. A quick trip to the Valley—the familiar walk to the schoolhouse—and there she would be, standing in the doorway, her blue eyes alight with welcome . . . But would she welcome him? Leaving as he had done without a word to her—how would that look to her? She did not know his reasons. She thought him a good Mormon and there had never been a word of love between them. All he was sure of was that there was no one else, with her. He had wondered about Harley Morey at first, but she had cleared that up. "We are good friends," she said, "nothing more." And added with a little smile, "No matter what other people want."

No, he dared not risk seeing her. The situation had not changed. What he must do was to put miles between them. Things were straight again at the mine. Matthew Walker could replace him. He would go East as he had planned—take up the study of medicine—make a new life for himself. A life without Mary.

When Matthew Walker found a man, Ashbel was impatient to be gone, but he stayed on long enough to train his successor. That was no more than fair to Walker, he thought; Walker had been good to him. But at last he was free. In the deep blue twilight of a late May evening he walked the streets of Salt Lake, restless and undecided. Now that the time had come he was reluctant to go East. As he moved aimlessly toward First South Street, the dome of the Tabernacle, mysteriously veiled in shadow, lifted its pure arc to the sky, but Ashbel was not conscious of its beauty. Over and over again he was asking himself two questions. Could he shut Mary out of his life? Did he want to shut her out? He did not know the answers.

2.

In an upstairs bedroom of Sarah's home Mary was slowly unpacking. From below, where the women of the family were preparing supper, came a clatter of dishes, a hum of voices, an occasional laugh. Mary was glad of an excuse to be alone. From the valise spread wide upon the bed she lifted a dress of creamy white mull. Her wedding dress. She held it at arm's length, shook out the soft folds and hung it carefully in the tall mahogany wardrobe. For a moment she stood there, fingering the material. If she could only feel some response—some quickening emotion. Excitement. Fear, even. Anything but this wooden acceptance of things as they were—and as they were to be. She moved back to the bed and began methodically to remove the neatly folded garments from the valise and sort them into orderly piles upon the bed. *Carefully arranged,* she thought. *Just like my life.* Just the way these past months had been. Decorous, proper, monotonous. A daughter of the Church betrothed to a steady young Mormon; taking part in community affairs, saying and doing the things that were expected of her. And knowing every minute of every day that she could never, never love Harley.

Abruptly, she turned and walked to the window. There was a golden glow over the garden, a delicate fragrance of apple blossoms in the air. Mary drew a sharp breath. That brief taste of love—if she hadn't experienced that, all of this wouldn't seem so drab. But pride forbade thinking of that. Ashbel hadn't loved her, but Harley did, in his way. And she was truly fond of Harley. He was dependable and he was kind. Love wasn't important. She must remember that . . . .

The golden glow had faded and long blue shadows were gathering in the garden. "Mary!" someone called. "Mary, stop mooning about up there and come to supper." She turned slowly away from the window and started toward the stairway.

3.

Sarah hadn't changed much, Mary Ann mused. Her hair was white, but her face still had a fresh, alive look as she beamed at the group around her table. She must be lonely here sometimes, with her sons and daughters married and in homes of their own. No wonder she loved having company; especially when there was the excitement of a wedding in prospect.

"We mustn't dawdle here at the table," Sarah warned. "We are all invited to spend the evening with the Taylors."

"You'll have to make my excuses, Mother." Joseph looked at his watch. "I have an appointment to keep at the Clift Hotel."

"Do you suppose I might be excused, too?" Mary asked. "I have so much to do."

Sarah smiled. "I think they'll understand," she said, "with only two days till the wedding—" she smiled again, indulgently.

"I'll stay with you, dear," Mary Ann offered quickly.

"Oh, no, Mother," Mary protested. "I wouldn't think of letting you."

"John and Leonora will be expecting you, Mary Ann." There was a hint of reproof in Charles' voice.

But later, on their way to the Taylors', Mary Ann was full of misgivings. She hadn't liked the way Mary looked and acted at supper. She sighed. Would she ever really understand Mary? *A year ago,* she thought, *I would have been overjoyed about this marriage; but now . . .*

4.

It seemed to Ashbel that he had walked for miles. He was thoroughly weary as he neared the Clift Hotel. *Perhaps,* he thought, *I shall be able to sleep tonight;* but in the back of his mind he knew that he could not rest, not while his thoughts were chained to this hopeless treadmill. Still preoccupied, he entered the hotel and walked toward the desk.

"Ashbel Pomeroy!" A hand fell on his shoulder with a resounding thump and he whirled to face Joseph Rich. "Ashbel!" Joseph exclaimed again, "it's good to see you after all these months. We were just getting to know you up our way when you left us."

"I was sorry I had to leave," Ashbel said without further explanation. "Are you down for long?"

"About a week, I expect."

"And your family—I trust they are all well?" The question was deliberate. Ashbel waited for the answer, concealing his inward anxiety by an impassive face. There was a chance, a bare chance, that Joseph might mention Mary.

"They are all fine," Joseph chuckled, "unless, maybe, Father. They're keeping him busy getting the girls married. Nanie started it and now it's Mary. You remember Harley Morey, don't you? She's marrying him on Friday."

The proprietor was lighting the lamps—placing them in their brackets on the wall. Ashbel watched him intently, following every movement. It seemed important, somehow. He heard himself speaking. "Yes. Yes, indeed. I remember Harley. I hope they'll be very happy."

"Why don't you drop in on the family?" Joseph suggested. "They are all staying at Mother's."

"Thank you," Ashbel said. "Perhaps I shall."

The proprietor had advanced and was speaking to Joseph, a deferential hand on his arm. "There's a fellow waiting to see me," Joseph explained. "Don't forget, Ashbel. We'll be expecting you at the house." He walked away with a genial wave of parting.

Ashbel stood without moving, unconscious of jostling elbows and curious stares. *She's going to be married,* he thought numbly. *She's going to be married Friday. What am I going to do?* Then suddenly, he wheeled and bolted out into the street.

5.

When the family had gone, Mary wandered aimlessly into the sitting room and sank into the wing chair near the window. How thankful she was that no one had insisted on her going. She was fond of the Taylors, but she didn't want to talk to anyone, tonight. The long May twilight had faded. She couldn't just sit here indefinitely, in the dark. She rose slowly, went to the center table and lighted the lamp. The flame flickered uncertainly as she adjusted the wick. She was replacing the chimney when she heard a knock. Dismay filled her. *Some neighbor,* she thought. *I shouldn't have made a light.* The knock came again, more insistent this time; more demanding. Mary sighed and opened the door.

"Ashbel!" she whispered. "Oh, Ashbel!"

In one swift motion he was in the room, his arms around her, crushing her to him. "I had to come," he said thickly. "Joseph just told me. I had to come, Mary."

He tilted back her head and looked into her eyes. Then he kissed her.

Mary felt her lips clinging to his, her arms around his neck, holding him close. She could not think, she could only feel. Something had seized upon her. Something powerful and strong that was sweeping her up—up—up to unexplored heights of ecstasy.

"Why, Mary!" Ashbel gripped her by the shoulders and

held her so, a little away from him, his eyes searching her face. "You love me," he said, wonder and exultation in his voice. "You love me, Mary. You can't marry Harley or anyone but me. You're mine."

Mary closed her eyes. After her self-betrayal she could not look at him. She was trembling and abashed. How could she have let herself go like that? And so much remained unexplained—She found her voice at last. "You went away," she said. "You didn't even say goodbye to me."

"I was a fool." Ashbel drew a deep breath and swept the room with a quick glance. "Let's get out of here where we can talk. Get your wraps, sweetheart. I have a rig outside."

Driving slowly under the stars Ashbel told her everything, not mincing words nor sparing himself. "I loved you from the first, Mary, but I didn't know it until that last afternoon. As I saw it then, going away was the only solution. I couldn't ask you to give up the Church. I hadn't the right—any more than I have now, I suppose. Only now I know you love me."

"Oh, why didn't you tell me, Ashbel? It would have saved so many heartaches." Swiftly, Mary plunged into the story of her own doubts and inner longings. "You see," she finished, "I've known for years that I wanted a different life, but I didn't have the courage to break away. And then, after you left—" she stopped abruptly. "Poor Harley. This is a dreadful thing I'm doing to him."

"It would be worse to marry him, now."

"Oh, I couldn't! Not now. I belong to you now, Ashbel."

Ashbel dropped the reins and gathered her close. "Oh, Mary," he choked. "Oh, my dearest!"

The horse stirred, ambled forward a few paces and stopped, dropping its head in lazy contentment.

"Do you mean," Ashbel asked soberly, "are you really willing to leave them all—everything—and go out into a strange world with me?"

Mary withdrew herself gently from his arms. "Yes," she said, "and whatever happens I'm going to be honest at last. If only," she added slowly, "it didn't mean hurting so many people . . . "

Ashbel seized the reins and turned the horse around. "There must be no more evasion," he said. "I'll see your father and mother tonight and tell them we're going to be married at once. We love each other. We'll face this together."

"No, Ashbel. No," Mary said. "I must see them alone first. Tomorrow you can talk to them, but tonight I must tell them the truth about everything."

6.

"I'm not going to marry Harley." Mary's words shattered the peaceful quiet of the sitting room. She sat on the edge of her chair, stiffly erect, looking at her father.

Mary Ann clenched her hands into fists and waited for Charles to answer, but he sat without saying a word, staring at Mary in stunned amazement. From the moment they had entered the house, Mary Ann had known that Mary was in one of her dangerous moods. She had braced herself for a shock when Mary asked them to stay downstairs after the family had said good night. "It's too important to wait," she had said briefly when her father protested that the hour was late.

Charles was frowning now, his face stern and forbidding. "Mary," he said, "you must be out of your mind. Your wedding two days off—all the plans made—But, of course, you don't mean it." With a quick gesture he brushed the whole matter from him. "You are tired and overwrought. A good night's sleep will make you feel better."

"You are wrong, Father." Mary spoke quietly, her voice low and clear. "I am not tired or overwrought. I know exactly what I am saying. I was wrong in consenting to marry Harley. I didn't know how wrong until tonight."

Mary Ann's fingers ached, but she dared not unclench her fists. She must hold herself tightly. She must not break in on this . . .

"You see," Mary glanced at her mother, "I love someone else and he loves me." Her head lifted proudly and her eyes shone. "I want to marry him at once," she said.

"And who is this other man?" Charles asked. He was breathing hard and his eyes burned dangerously.

"Ashbel Pomeroy. He was here tonight."

"Ashbel Pomeroy!" Charles' voice was a strangled shout. He gripped the arms of his chair and leaned forward, his face contorted with anger. "He's broken with the Church—did you know that? President Young told me so today."

"Yes, I know. Ashbel has told me everything."

"And you mean to say—"

"I mean that it doesn't matter. It makes no difference to me."

A curtain stirred in the breeze. Charles' chair creaked. *In all my life,* Mary Ann thought, *I have never faced a thing like this.* Mary's eyes were blazing, challenging her father. And Charles—Charles who could cope with any crisis, sat speechless, his shocked white face incredulous. *It's my fault,* Mary Ann accused herself. *I've seen this coming. I should have guided her. I should have told Charles. I might have spared him this.* These two whom she loved so much, measuring each other warily, ready to lash out—to wound . . . *I must stop them!* she cried inwardly. *I must keep them from saying things that can't be forgiven or forgotten.* "Charles," she began, but he silenced her with an upraised palm.

His color had come back now and when he spoke his voice was gentle. "You have been swept away by love, Mary," he said. He was plainly holding himself in check, trying to be patient, trying to reason. "Think what this means," he pleaded. "Surely you wouldn't choose to contract a marriage for time? You wouldn't sacrifice your right to wear a celestial crown?"

Mary Ann held her breath.

"I've thought of all that." Mary's eyes, blue and unwavering, met her father's squarely. "It doesn't change a thing. I still want to marry Ashbel."

Charles rose from his chair and strode to Mary's side. "I won't have it, do you hear?" he shouted. "I refuse my consent."

Mary, too, was on her feet, her face set and cold. "I'm sorry, Father," she said. "Ashbel and I wanted your consent, but we can be married without it."

"Mary! Wait! Oh, Charles, don't let her go like that!" But Mary Ann's anguished protest went unheeded. Mary had left the room without a backward glance.

I must go to her, Mary Ann thought. *I must persuade her to think this through.* She hesitated for a moment, her eyes on Charles. He had moved to the window and stood there, perfectly still, gazing out into the darkness, unyielding anger in every line of his rigid back.

Mary Ann left the room quietly. *I must hurry,* she thought as she climbed the stairs. Tomorrow might be too late. Outside Mary's door she paused. Her heart was beating a wild tattoo, and she waited until it slowed a little; then she knocked lightly. "It's Mother," she said.

"Come in." Mary's voice sounded harsh and unnatural, but Mary Ann turned the knob and entered. On the threshold she halted, transfixed by what she saw. Mary was standing beside the bed, a half-packed valise spread open before her. Mary Ann tried to speak but no sound came, and in another moment she was glad, for Mary was explaining. "I haven't finished unpacking," she said. "I had planned to do it this evening but—Ashbel came."

"Let me help you," Mary Ann said. With stiff fingers she picked up a white frilled petticoat. "Here," she said, "better lay this full length in the drawer so it won't be mussed." They worked on side by side in silence. *It's like a nightmare,* Mary Ann thought. *This dreadful thing inside of us, and we can't let it out.* But at last she forced herself to speak, calmly, she hoped—naturally—without looking up. "How did Ashbel find you, dear?"

"He happened to meet Joseph at the hotel."

Mary Ann buckled the straps of the empty valise. "There," she said. "Push this under the bed, Mary. Everything is nicely put away." She sat down on the edge of the bed. "You love Ashbel very much, don't you?" she asked gently.

"Oh, Mother, you *do* understand!" Mary dropped down upon the bed and seized her mother's hands. She bent forward, her eyes desperate in their appeal, and began to talk swiftly, pouring out her heart. Now that release had come, she seemed fearful of omitting something, grimly determined to withhold no detail. Mary Ann yearned over her. Poor child! So strong. So stubborn. So self-contained. *If she had only confided in me,* she thought regretfully. She longed to put her arms around Mary, to hold her close until the tension relaxed—until she softened and yielded. But she knew better than to interrupt. At last Mary paused. "You do see, don't you, Mother?" she pleaded. "I can't marry Harley now."

"No. No, of course not. That is out of the question." Mary Ann stared into space, fondling Mary's hands absently. "Why," she demanded suddenly, "didn't you talk to your father as you have to me?"

"I couldn't. I wanted to, but I froze up somehow, inside. I did want to be honest with Father. We wouldn't be in this tangle if I had been before—about the Church, I mean."

"The Church," Mary Ann echoed. "Yes, that would have been far better, but what's done is done. We must think of the present, now. And the future," she added, half under her breath. "Don't you see, Mary, even though you were striking at the things dearest to your father's heart, he tried to be patient with you. He is a just man, but he is kind and he loves you. You wanted to be honest, but you needn't have defied him. Such things hurt most coming from those we love."

"I know, Mother." Mary's head was bent; her lashes were a dark smudge against the pallor of her cheek. "I'm sorry and ashamed," she said slowly. "I love you and Father so much I can't bear to hurt you. I've tried and tried to make myself feel as you do about the Church, but I can't. It just isn't in me."

The wick in the lamp burned low and there were queer shadows on the walls. "It has to come from within." Mary Ann spoke the words aloud. *That's what Mother believed,* she thought. *It must be right.* She sighed deeply. "I'm sorry, Mary. More sorry than you will ever know."

"But, Mother, what am I going to do? My love for Ashbel —I can't help that. It comes from within, too."

"Your love—" Mary Ann paused. "I wonder if it's strong enough? You understand what this means, don't you, dear? You will be cutting yourself off from the things you have always known, from your family—from the Mormon people. You will have to make a new pattern for your life. Is your love strong enough for that?"

"Yes." Mary lifted her chin and drew a long breath. "It's strong enough for anything. I know it is."

This was the moment. *Heavenly Father*, Mary Ann implored silently, *let the right words come!* She leaned forward. "Then, dear," she said, "it should be strong enough to bear the test of time and separation."

"Separation? You mean—"

"I mean that I want you to think this over and talk with Ashbel before you see your father again."

Mary was frowning thoughtfully. "You think we should wait—not be married now?"

"I want you to think of your father. This is a frightful blow to him. He is a leader. You know what he stands for—how the people of the Valley look up to him and believe in him. He cannot break faith with those people even for his own daughter." Mary Ann sighed. "He can never approve of what you're doing, Mary, but I believe in time he may become reconciled. That would mean something to you, wouldn't it, dear? Surely, you and Ashbel can be patient for a little while, to hold the family together. Think of the ties that bind us. The love—" Mary Ann's voice broke. She buried her face in her hands.

"Oh, Mother!" Mary cried out. "I didn't think of it like that. Truly, I didn't. I've been selfish and cruel. I'll tell Ashbel tomorrow. He'll understand. Please, Mother, look at me. Don't be unhappy."

But Mary Ann waited a moment before she uncovered her face. The great wave of relief left her weak and shaken. Mary would keep her word. There would be no break now. "Heavenly Father," she whispered, "I thank Thee."

7.

Mary Ann was in the kitchen early. She felt a strange embarrassment at the thought of seeing Mary after what had happened last night. She, herself, seldom allowed her emotions to get the better of her, and as for Mary, with her pride and reserve. . . . *I must behave naturally,* Mary Ann warned herself. *I must treat her exactly as usual.* And it was easier than she had hoped. The day went on with no outward sign of disturbance.

It was Mary Ann who met Ashbel at the door and led him to the garden where Mary was waiting. It was difficult to smile and leave them. If only she might stay and help! She sighed. No. They must work this out alone.

It was late afternoon. Sarah and Joseph were spending the day in Centerville but would be back in time for supper. It had been thoughtful of Sarah to arrange that—to leave them the house to themselves during this time of stress. From the kitchen window Mary Ann could see Mary and Ashbel, side by side on the bench under the apple tree. Mary was leaning toward him looking up into his face. The strained posture of her body, the quick, appealing motions of her hands were mutely eloquent. Mary Ann, painfully intent, found herself fitting words to Mary's gestures. This would never do. On the table, a pan of green peas, fresh from Sarah's garden, reminded her of supper. She glanced at the clock, took up the pan and seated herself near the window. But as the crisp pods snapped in her fingers, her eyes kept straying toward the garden. Ashbel was talking now, shaking his head slowly. . . .Mary Ann crushed a tender pod in her hand and hitched her chair around, its back to the window. After what seemed a long time the front door opened and closed. She turned hastily back to the garden. The bench was empty. Mary and Ashbel would be with Charles now. He had been waiting for them in the sitting room. Mechanically, she went on with her preparations for supper.

She was laying the table when she heard Charles' heavy tread in the hall. Her eyes flew to his face as he entered the room and her hands, neatly arranging the knives and forks, trembled.

"Everything is settled," Charles said. His face was grave but calm and his eyes, it seemed to Mary Ann, held a new light of hope. "They are going to wait," he went on. "Mary will return to the Valley with us, and Ashbel is going East. They have promised me not to communicate for a year; then, if Mary still feels the same, Ashbel will come for her."

"A year," Mary Ann said thoughtfully. "No letters— That's a long time."

"Not too long," Charles said, "for a real test."

"No, not too long," she echoed. *Many things,* she thought, *can happen in a year.*

14

1.

Looking back on that year it was quite uneventful, Mary Ann mused. Of course, at the time they happened, things had seemed important. Their return to the Valley. Explanations. "No, Mary's marriage had not been postponed. There will be no marriage." Curious glances. Well-meant sympathy from friends and family—both equally hard to bear. And those autumn months, with Mary withdrawn in loneliness and Charles away. Months best forgotten. But the winter. Those were months to remember. Charles at home again, spending hours with them—with Mary. "My turn will come," he had said. Often those words came back to Mary Ann as she watched and listened during those long winter evenings before the fire. The three of them. An intimate group at ease together, the barrier between them gone. Charles talking to Mary, drawing her out, asking her opinions, holding her enthralled by vivid tales of his early life. Discussing his own problems—revealing bits of his philosophy. He was making Mary see his background as something real and priceless. Yet Mary Ann marveled at his skill in avoiding personal things. Ashbel was never mentioned. Nothing was mentioned that might cause resentment or revive Mary's unhappiness. Mary Ann wondered if Mary really understood what her father had given her that winter. And what, if anything, had been its effect.

And now the winter was gone and it was spring. Mid-May. The year had passed and Mary Ann held Ashbel's letter to Mary in her hands. Slowly, she walked into Mary's room and placed the letter on the bureau. *We've known this was coming,* she thought. *Are we ready for it, I wonder?*

2.

The evening was almost gone when Mary joined her parents in the sitting room. Her cheeks were softly flushed and her eyes brilliantly blue.

"Ashbel is coming for me next month," she said simply. "I haven't changed, Father. We want to be married then."

It seemed a long time to Mary Ann before Charles spoke. "This year—it hasn't meant anything, then?"

"It's meant everything. It's been a wonderful year—one I will never forget. But—" Mary paused for a moment, "my life is with Ashbel."

"And you'll marry him and go away?"

"Yes, Father." Mary crossed the room swiftly and stood before Charles' big chair. "Please," she said, "I want to be married here—at home. It means so much more to me now. I—I want that to take with me."

He MUST *say "yes,"* Mary Ann willed. She sat motionless in the little rocker, her eyes fixed on Charles' face, as if her desperate longing could shape his answer.

He rose from his chair and stood, straight and tall, looking down into Mary's upturned face. "Very well," he said. "We'll arrange it. But you understand I can have no part in it. I can't even be present."

"Yes," Mary said, "I know. I know it must be that way."

3.

Alone on her doorstep in the soft gray of a June dawn, Mary Ann watched Mary and Ashbel drive away. They had been married the night before. By this nightfall they would be in Logan; two days from now on a train leaving Salt Lake—carrying them Eastward to their new life. The rig moved slowly down the street. Mary Ann's heart tightened. If only Charles could be here with her. She missed him now even more than she had last night. Yet it was comforting to know that he would see them off in Salt Lake.

They had reached the corner now and were turning into the main street. Mary Ann turned hastily away. She would not watch them out of sight.

Inside the cottage she stood quiet for a moment. A faint odor of lilacs still hung in the room. It had been a reality, then, that strange, stiff wedding last night. Only herself and the boys and Ashbel's family gathered here in this room as Francis Pomeroy read the civil ceremony. Watching. Listening. The words had seemed cold and meaningless. She was remembering her own ceremony in the House of the Lord; its beauty, its deep significance and promise. *Oh, Mary,* she thought sadly, *how much you are missing.*

She seated herself in the maple rocker. The cottage seemed still—almost an eerie stillness in the gray light. She was glad the boys had not awakened. They had said goodbye to Mary last night. Mary Ann pleated her cambric apron into careful folds, stared for a moment at the folds, then smoothed them out carefully. Her thoughts, confused for so long, began falling into order. Mary was gone because she wanted to go. She had known from the first what she was going to do. Not once, during this year, had she wavered. Mary Ann knew that, now. Mary had to work out a life for herself. She had always been like that—always reaching out for something, she didn't know what. Her flare-ups, her rebellious moods—they didn't mean she was bitter against the Church or had lost faith in the Lord. She was striking out at things that restrained her. Because she was unsure of herself. Now, for the first time in her life, she was sure of something. Her love for Ashbel was real and deep. *As his is for her,* Mary Ann thought. Ashbel was a good man. Even though he had broken away from the Church, his faith, like Mary's, was strong. They were going out alone, apart from family and tradition, determined in the face of opposition. *Just as Mother did,* it came to her. *Just as I did, myself.* The years rolled back and she was again in that bleak tent with the wind whipping the snow outside, as she said farewell to John Clark. Cold, wretched, miserably unhappy at the blow she was dealing him, but determined to begin her new life with Charles. That strong inner impulse—the longing for something new—Mary and Ashbel were yielding to that. *But they can't go far astray,* she thought—*not with their background behind them like a solid rock.*

A sudden glow of sunlight brightened the room. Like a good omen. Mary Ann got up from the little rocker and started toward the door to the kitchen. A new life was beginning for Mary and Ashbel, but life here at home must go on as usual. She found herself smiling. She would make hot biscuits. The boys liked a hearty breakfast.

Epilogue

EPILOGUE

Mary Ann Rich was celebrating her seventieth birthday. From far and near her family had assembled to do her honor. In the Rich family a seventieth birthday was a special occasion. Charles Rich, gone now, fifteen years, had established the tradition. On his own seventieth birthday, with the entire family gathered around him he had said, "Throughout the years we'll make this milestone mean a reunion."

In the red brick house, built on the site of the old log cabin and mellowed by the sunshine and snows of twenty years, there was laughter and a bustle of activity. Outside under the trees, shaded from the glare of the early August sun, a long table was spread. At the rear of the house the grandchildren played; thirty-two of them in all—some running and shrieking gleefully, some toddling on unsteady legs, even the wide-eyed babies crowing their delight. Under a clump of aspens to the south a group of tall broad-shouldered men were deep in conversation. A surrey, with a young man driving and two elderly women busily talking, moved through the lane at a leisurely pace.

From far and near they had come. Mary and Ashbel

from Cheney, Washington. Doctor Ezra and Doctor Edward, taking two precious days from their newly established practice in Ogden. Paulina Lyman, by stage and train from Parowan, in southern Utah. Harriet Holmes from Montpelier, and from Salt Lake Joseph, "the baby," his sandy hair only slightly grayed—his spirits as exuberant as ever. Nanie, William, and Amasa, of course, were already here. They made their homes in Paris.

All for me, Mary Ann thought, alone for a moment in the sitting room. She moved about absently, running a forefinger over the dustless arm of the walnut settee, straightening a crocheted tidy on a chair back. She enjoyed the brief solitude. The excitement of visiting with Paulina and Harriet with so many running in and out had left her a trifle breathless. The reunion with them was priceless—the first birthday they had been together since Nauvoo days—but it had been a relief when Edward came to carry them off for a drive.

From the window Mary Ann could see the group under the aspens. *My fine sons,* she thought with a glow of pride. She lifted her head and sniffed, the appetizing odor of roasting chicken in her nostrils. She'd wanted to help with dinner, but she had been banished from the kitchen and forbidden the yard. The table was to be a surprise. "We don't need you, Mother," Nanie insisted, "not with Aunt Emeline and Aunt Harriet to help. You go into the sitting room, dear, and hold court." *Hold court!* Mary Ann smiled. *I do feel like a queen. And why not—for this one day?* She tiptoed to the kitchen door and hesitated with her hand on the knob.

"Land o' Goshen!" Emeline was saying. "Just think of the years to come, and all the seventieth birthdays this crowd will celebrate."

Mary Ann moved away from the door and sat down quietly. Birthdays to come. It was of birthdays past that she wanted to think. Of the look on Charles' face when he said,

"Let's make this milestone an occasion." Eighteen years ago that had been, yet it now seemed like yesterday. If only he could be here! But she wouldn't have wished him back. He had escaped so much. Those years of strife between the government and the Church over plural marriage—they would have been hard for Charles. Yet he would be satisfied, she felt quite sure, with the outcome—glad the Church had renounced the practice. Once he had said somberly, "It is too pure an ideal for this changing world." He had not wanted plural marriage for his children.

"Alone, Mother?" It was Ezra coming in from the outdoors. His big, tall body seemed to fill the room. "I thought I'd never get a chance to be alone with you." He drew a chair close to her. "You're looking mighty pretty today," he said, smiling. "The years haven't changed you at all."

"Now, Ezra," she protested. Yet her softly crinkled cheeks flushed with pleasure. "If I look nice it's because of this lovely dress you and Edward sent. I feel very gay in a color." She fingered the folds of the blue silk lovingly. "Nanie dressed my hair." She touched the thin gray locks thoughtfully. "The years do change us on the outside, Ezra—and sometimes on the inside."

"What are you two so solemn about?" Mary questioned coming in, her arms full of packages.

"Oh, Mary," Mary Ann said. "I thought you were helping in the kitchen."

"I was, but Nanie sent me to the store." She paused. "Here, Ezra." She thrust the packages into his arms. "Take these to Nanie, will you? She will be frantic wondering what's become of me. I've been loitering in the public square thinking of old times."

"What do you think of the new tabernacle?" Mary Ann asked.

"It's lovely, Mother." Mary paused. "Ashbel and I said

so last night when we first saw it. This morning it is even lovelier. It's new, yet somehow it seems old—mellowed; like the pictures of the Old World churches Ezra sent us when he was on his mission abroad. It has done something for Paris, somehow. Set it apart from the other towns."

"It was one of your father's dreams," Mary Ann said softly. "He planned it all—even arranged for the building material before he—went."

For a little while they sat in silence. Mary Ann gazed at Mary, her heart warm and tender. Mary was calm and poised; her hair was touched with gray, her eyes were wiser. She was—

There was a step on the porch and Edward came through the doorway.

"Where are Paulina and Harriet?" Mary Ann demanded.

"I left them outside talking with Amasa," Edward said. "And Mary, Ashbel is looking for you. He wants your advice about something."

Mary was on her feet at once. "Will you excuse me, Mother?"

"Of course," Mary Ann said. That light in Mary's eyes. *Even after all these years,* she thought, *Mary is eager to answer Ashbel's call.*

"It's good to be home this way, Mother," Edward said, his thin sensitive face serious, "but I do worry about you living here by yourself. It is lonely for you."

Mary Ann smiled up at him. "I like being here alone, I have so much to think about. And I'm never lonely—not with Nanie, William and Amasa so close." Her eyes twinkled. "And twenty-six grandchildren to keep me company."

"Everything's ready!" Now it was Nanie, putting her head in from the kitchen. Her face was flushed and her hair in little damp curls on her forehead. Being a wife and a mother, Mary Ann mused, had made her even more beautiful. "Edward, you are to come out with me," Nanie directed. "William is coming for Mother."

William was already in the room, offering his arm with a flourish. Mary Ann looked up at him. Tall, broad-shouldered, a little portly, now. *But how like Charles he is,* she thought as she took his arm.

* * *

The afterglow of sunset lay upon the hills. On the porch of her home Mary Ann sat alone in the small maple rocker. Her day of days was over. The family had scattered. Ezra and Edward had started back to Ogden. Paulina had left for Montpelier with Harriet. Mary and Ashbel had gone with Nanie and Hyrum to see their new home. How quiet after all the confusion. But she wanted to be quiet. She wanted to go back over this day. To go back beyond this day, to the beginnings that made it possible.

Seventy years! she marveled. A long time. Yet not too long for all that had happened. A newborn religion grown strong and powerful. Long journeys to far places. Communities founded and developed. Cities built. Territories made states. *Outside things,* she thought, *yet all interwoven with my life.* Crickets chirped. A cowbell clanked musically in the distance. At thirty-five she had taken stock of herself. So much to be done. Now she could look backward. Heartaches, triumphs, sorrows and mistakes, yet her dreams had been fulfilled. Her thoughts touched the children, dwelt upon them fondly, one by one. William, successful in his business—President of the Stake. Amasa, Mayor of Paris and known as a public benefactor throughout the Valley. Nanie, rich in her contentment with her husband and children. Ezra and Edward, well established in their profession. *The only doctors among all your sons, Charles,* she thought proudly. And Mary—her thoughts halted, then went on confidently. Mary working shoulder to shoulder with Ashbel, pioneering the field of medicine in a new community. Still seeking—but with a purpose. Fine children, all of them. Each working out a different design, bringing beauty to the pattern in his or her own way. "You would be proud of them, Charles," she said aloud.

Her eyes sought the hills where he lay. The afterglow had faded and the deep golden summer twilight enveloped them in unearthly beauty. It seemed to surround her, too, filling her with peace deeper than she had ever known. *My work is done,* she thought serenely; and with a surge of joy, *I can go any time, now.* Quietly she sat there, her eyes on the darkening hills. Not until their outlines had blurred and mingled with the night did she move from her chair.

In the doorway she turned for a moment. "Good night, Charles," she whispered, and smiling happily she entered the silent house.

THE END

ISBN 978-0-8425-2602-9